The critics on Liz Evans

Liz Evans has worked in all sorts of companies from plastic moulding manufacturers to Japanese banks through to film production and BBC Radio. She was born in Highgate, went to school in Barnet and now lives in Hertfordshire. Visit her website at www.geocities.com/tartrouge.

By Liz Evans

Who Killed Marilyn Monroe?
JFK is Missing!
Don't Mess With Mrs In-Between
Barking!

BARKING!

Liz Evans

ORION

An Orion paperback

First published in Great Britain in 2001
by Orion
This paperback edition published in 2002
by Orion Books Ltd,
Orion House, 5 Upper St Martin's Lane,
London WC2H 9EA

Second impression 2002

Copyright © Liz Evans 2001

A CIP catalogue record for this book is available
from the British Library.

ISBN 0 75284 793 7

Typeset at The Spartan Press Ltd,
Lymington, Hants

Printed and bound in Great Britain by
Clays Ltd, St Ives plc

To Dad – with thanks for the support
during the writing of this book.

I should also like to send my
thanks to Rob Davis for providing
historical background information.

I

My contact with the paranormal started the day I knocked someone out with half a cow.

Can I make it quite clear that I don't believe in the supernatural? Personally I've always thought all that *X-Files* stuff and things that go bump, rattle and woooo! in the night are down to wishful thinking by people with monotonous lives trying to inject a bit of excitement into the old routine.

Having said that, I've always been careful not to mock too loudly just in case something that isn't there taps me on the shoulder one dark night.

In this case it snuck up on me on a warm October afternoon in the midst of an unexpected spell of Indian summer weather that had hit the south coast two days before, after a week of icy winds and lashing rain. Not that it had done much for Seatoun's tourist industry – we still looked like the Kosovo of the bucket-and-spade trade. Driving up to North Bay, I only passed one other person walking slowly up the pavement-less road on the way. She'd prepared for the changeable weather by wearing a large sun-hat with a fur coat. She was teetering slowly on unsuitable high heels as she slogged up the steep gradient. I wondered why the hell she didn't take the coat off, it must be sweltering inside. I was also curious about her destination. The nearest buildings were over the crest of this hill and a fair way down towards the next bay and definitely rated a taxi-ride in those shoes. On the other hand, if her only plan was to take a casual walk, it was an odd sort of outfit for a sightseeing stroll.

As I got a little nearer, I thought I'd cracked the mystery.

She was wearing black stockings, the sheer variety with the back seams that often featured in lingerie adverts attached to a sexy lace and satin basque but rarely rated as everyday wear. There was a small car park ahead, provided by the local council for motorists to enjoy the view over North Bay. At this time of year it was probably empty. Perhaps she and whoever were into a bit of fantasy role-playing – mysterious stranger slips into back seat of car, shrugs off fur coat and reveals all, sort of thing?

I drove past, then got an attack of conscience. I pulled up against the scrub grass, watching her in the side mirror. She'd stopped too. I waited. She didn't move. The heavy shadows cast by the broad hat brim prevented me from making out her expression. Leaning out of the window, I yelled, 'Want a lift?'

The intention was to let her see me and reassure her that I wasn't a mad axe-murderer cruising to pick up lone females. Either she wasn't convinced or she was shy about being seen in that get-up. Meeting someone she shouldn't, maybe? Whatever – I'd done my bit for the good-deed bank. Time to move on.

Her date hadn't arrived yet. The small parking area was empty. That suited me just fine. I didn't need witnesses for what I was about to do.

Lugging my holdall from my boot, I scrunched over the crumbling concrete and used the board annotated DANGEROUS DROP – DO NOT GO BEYOND THIS POINT as a foothold to clamber over the metal fencing. There were still several hundred yards to the cliff edge and the land swept up at the very rim like a tilted nose to give an added illusion of safety. However, the ground had been known to crumble away without warning, and the Council had yet to appreciate the advantages of rope-free bungee-jumping as a tourist attraction – hence the barriers. I hesitated, weighing up which way to go. There was a fifty-fifty chance of finding my quarry in either direction. But if I went left there was a slight chance that Ms Fur Coat might catch a glimpse of me through the protective fencing and this was not a spectator event.

Decision taken, I turned right, making my way between the stunted grasses and bushes to an area of cliff where the rim had already broken away and crashed down to form piles of boulders like giant's building bricks on the beach below, leaving the remaining land up here with a sheer incline seawards. Dropping to my knees behind a clump of bushes, I opened the holdall.

I was on a case. And I was the only one who could crack it. My client had said as much when she'd rung me this morning. 'It's down to you, babes. You're the only one who can pin the bugger down. Bring him back and I'll make it worth yer while.'

'I'm a bit busy at the moment, Arlene.'

'Don' give me that moody stuff. You go get my boy home. Otherwise I can make life tough. You know I can do it.'

I did. And she could. Arlene owned and managed my favourite spot for stocking up on household furniture and essentials – the local waste disposal site.

I wasted several hours scouring the pubs, cafés and amusement arcades to check he wasn't bumming a free meal somewhere before I finally admitted that he'd headed for his favourite spot, viz. the only patch of headland along this section of coast high enough to give anyone going over serious grief if they bounced on the rocks below before splashing into the rollers dashing in from the North Sea.

Tipping out the contents of my holdall, I sorted out the equipment I needed to bring Arlene's baby back alive: one battery-driven cassette recorder; a length of green nylon washing line, and a long greasy parcel that I'd just talked a local butcher into – illegally – providing out of the back door. Unwrapping the paper sheets, I twisted the rope several times around the bone's shaft and knotted it as tightly as shiny rope and fat-covered fingers permitted. Taking a final look to check I had the place to myself, I pushed down the 'play' button on the cassette. Rising to my feet, I whirled the bone around my head.

'Waterloo . . . hey Waterloo . . .' I bawled, jigging my bottom to the music and paying out the line.

I'm not much of a singer, but with no audience I was really belting it out and enjoying myself whilst I kept alert for any movements in the scrub. On my third chorus I caught a shiver of leaf out of the corner of my left eye. I started to turn, letting each revolution of the bone pull me round a fraction. Halfway round I realised I hadn't attracted the right target. And judging by the startled expression on the bloke's face, he hadn't expected to flush out a tall skinny blonde twirling a large beef shank and doing Abba impressions.

At that moment my knots gave up their battle with the bone's greasy coating and the thing slid out of the lasso and continued under its own momentum. It caught him in the centre of the forehead with a crack they must have heard in downtown Seatoun. After that he didn't look startled any more. He looked sort of . . . unconscious.

'Oh, hell!' Killing the music, I dashed over to check I hadn't achieved the same trick on my audience. A quick once-over confirmed his breathing and pulse were steady and he didn't appear to have snapped anything as he fell. The skin on his forehead hadn't broken under the impact but it had reddened up and pretty soon it would turn an interesting purply shade and start swelling until he looked like he was growing a third eye.

There wasn't much else I could do for the moment except keep an eye on him to make sure he didn't start vomiting and choke himself whilst he was out cold. If he didn't come round in the next ten minutes I'd have to start deciding whether I should leave him and go get help.

It wasn't a good option because if he regained consciousness whilst I was away, he might be disorientated enough to wander over the cliff edge. I could use the clothes-line to tie him up, but the ground sloped fairly sharply downwards as it got nearer the drop and if he tried to free himself and started to roll . . . ? That was apart from the tricky scenario of trying to explain to the local police – who mostly didn't like me anyway – how I'd clobbered someone unconscious and then trussed them up on the edge of a lethal drop. It was another situation where I found myself realising I was going to have to get a mobile phone. Perhaps my new acquaintance had one? Most mobiles, even those that have been password-locked, will connect to the emergency services.

Cautiously I started feeling his pockets. The fawn trousers held nothing more interesting than a clean handkerchief; the breast pocket of his shirt contained a money clip of folded notes; but I struck gold inside the beige jacket – car keys, house keys, wallet and mobile phone.

Unfortunately the display was flashing BATTERY EXHAUSTED. I tried it. And it was. I took a quick look in the wallet to see who I'd just committed ABH on, and found an impressive row of plastic squares – bank cards, credit cards and store cards. Assuming they were his, I'd just brained Mr S. Roberts. Was this Ms Fur Coat's date? If so they must have been planning an open-air performance.

I checked his breathing again and thought I detected a flutter of movement under the eyelids. Pushing his property back into his pockets, I slapped his cheek lightly. 'Hello? Can you hear me? Can you open your eyes for me?'

The lashes shivered again before coming to rest in the open position. I was relieved to see both his pupils were evenly sized and at a reasonable dilation, given that he was staring up at a bright blue sky.

He continued to look blankly skyward for another ten seconds before the hazel eyes swivelled in my direction and focused. 'Why?'

'I was looking for Waterloo.'

'The station or the battlefield?'

'The dog.'

He pushed himself up on his elbows. Reassured that it didn't seem likely he was going to take a retaliatory swing at me, I got an arm behind his back and helped him into a sitting position.

'How's that feel?'

'All r-right, I think.' Incautiously, he touched the impact site and drew in a sharp breath between clenched teeth. 'What did you hit me with?'

'The leg-bone of a cow. I was waving it around to disperse the scent in the wind. So Waterloo would pick it up quicker.'

'It was enormous. What is he? A pedigree w-werewolf?'

'His mum was an Old English bulldog and his dad seems to have been a large mongrel with ambition. Luckily he's a greedy mutt. Give him a nice juicy bone and there's no way he's going to let go. If it was small enough for him to carry easily he'd just grab it and maybe dash into oblivion over the cliff edge. I have to beg something from the butcher that slows him down enough for me to get the rope on him.'

'You do this a lot, do you?'

'It's my job.'

'Dog c-catcher?'

'Private investigator. This is a kind of sideline.'

Arlene had hired me a couple of years before when Waterloo had first started going walkabout – and I'd made the mistake of finding him. Since then I'd been appointed mutt-finder-in-chief. Every few months she called the agency's offices and demanded I drop everything and go find her baby.

'Why the concert?' S. Roberts enquired.

I'd have liked to know what that 'S' stood for. But it was tricky asking without admitting I'd been going through his wallet. 'His mum . . . I mean his owner . . . she sings it to him. Familiar sounds, that sort of thing. I don't suppose you've come across him?'

'Is he a similar beige shade to my jacket? With chocolate brown ears and paws?'

'That's him. Where was he?'

S. Roberts nodded behind me . . . and winced at the

6

movement. I looked round. The cunning little mutt had crept up on me with a belly crawl straight from the SAS manual and was now slithering back into the bushes with one end of the bone clamped in his massive teeth.

I dived for the other end and grabbed it. Waterloo growled, braced his heavy shoulder muscles and wriggled his rump. He pulled one way and I tried to heave him back the other. Flat on my stomach I was at a disadvantage. Craning my head round, I said, 'Could you just anchor this end while I go get the rope?'

Standing cautiously, S. Roberts tested his co-ordination. We were both relieved to see everything seemed to be moving as it should. He came towards me, but rather than take the bone, he went past and moved towards the dog, uttering encouraging here-boy-type sounds.

'Careful. He can get nasty if he doesn't know you.'

Waterloo tensed. His pudgy nostrils twitched and his jaws shifted. His eyes rolled at the slowly approaching figure. He uttered a low rumble from somewhere inside his chest.

I was just getting ready to hurl myself at his collar, before another area of S. Roberts's anatomy needed medical treatment, when Waterloo lay down and appeared to rotate his body whilst leaving his jaws clamped to his dinner. S. crouched down and scratched the proffered stomach. Waterloo squealed and wriggled in ecstasy. By the time I'd returned with the rope to thread through his collar, they seemed to be ready to pick out the bridesmaids' frocks.

I informed Waterloo he was a tart and offered a hand to the new love of his life. 'Grace Smith.'

'Stuart R-Roberts.'

'Pleased to meet you. Sorry I clouted you.'

'That's all right.'

It wasn't, of course. But I had already begun to form the impression that Stuart was probably one of those people who apologise when someone bumps into them. Now brain damage was a lessening possibility I was able to look him over for rating on the Smith Fanciability Scale.

Mid-thirties maybe, average height, brown hair, round face, clean-shaven, slightly overweight with the soft muscle tone that said not-enough-exercise rather than one-too-many-pig-outs. Mr Ordinary. Since I owed him one for that near braining, I rated him a generous four on the scale of one to ten. I apologised for messing up his plans.

'What plans?'

'I thought perhaps you were meeting someone up here.'

'M-meeting? No. I just wanted . . . I had some things to think out.'

And he needed to perch on the edge of a crumbling cliff edge to do it? I thought his denial that he'd expected to meet up with anyone sounded genuine, which made his situation even odder.

I couldn't get Waterloo out the way I'd climbed in. The fence at the viewing point was too high. It meant I had to make my way back down towards Seatoun for half a mile until the road barrier bent at right angles and ran down to the cliff edge, at which point it had been twisted down to waist height and I could heave the mutt over it.

'How does he get in?' Stuart asked when I explained the scenario to him.

'I don't know. I've never seen him jump anything that height so I figure there must be a gap in the fence some-where, but I'm blowed if I can find it.'

'I'll walk down with you.'

Since Waterloo seemed content to romp along with his new best friend and his new best bone, I left them to it. Stuart, I sensed, had something on his mind. Several times I caught him half looking at me and once he almost started to speak, but as soon as I made eye contact, he flushed and turned away. I gave up trying to start a conversation when all I managed to draw out were answers of the 'yes' and 'no' variety. I half wondered whether that slight stammer had made holding his tongue a habit – or if there was something else behind it.

When we reached the fence, he scooped Waterloo up

without being asked and dropped him over, hanging on to the rope until I'd scrambled across to take it, then clambering across himself.

'I have to double back to the car park,' I said. 'Can I give you a lift somewhere?'

'No. Thank you.'

'Don't you think you should go to the hospital? Have that lump checked out?'

'I'm f-fine.' He touched the bruised area and gasped. It was swelling up nicely and a demented punk-rock drummer was probably thundering away inside his skull by now. But he was adamant he didn't need a lift.

I found Waterloo's makeshift lead round my fist and started heaving summit-wards. 'Okay. Bye, then. And sorry about . . . you know . . .'

'C-concussion by cow.' For the first time he gave me a smile. 'Don't worry. It's the least of my problems really. Goodbye.'

'Bye.'

He still wanted to say something. But he waited until I'd put several yards between us before calling after me. 'Grace! Are you really a private investigator?'

'Unlikely as it seems,' I shouted back, trying to control a frisky Waterloo, 'yes, I really am.'

'Do you ever investigate deaths?'

'Sometimes. It depends on the death. What was it? Accident? Suicide?'

'Murder. I think I may have killed someone,' he yelled.

In which case I definitely didn't want him in my life, thanks a bunch! In fact, what I most wanted at that moment was to get back to my car and lock the doors. I was suddenly very glad I was hanging on to a bolshie dog with a jaw full of large sharp teeth (even one that appeared to like my self-confessed murderer more than he did me). Backing away at an ever-increasing rate, I hollered, 'Not my field. Go to the police.'

'I c-can't do that.'

9

'You can. Honestly. Get yourself a good solicitor and take them with you.'

'No. You don't understand. I can't tell the police. They'd just think I was crazy.'

'Why?'

Stuart's answer drifted back to me over the screams of the gulls.

'I think she might have been a ghost.'

2

It took fifteen minutes to lug Waterloo back to the car and get him inside – which I finally achieved by throwing the remains of a Kit Kat on the back seat and then getting my shoulder under his smelly bottom and heaving him arse over nose when he dived for it. There was no sign of Ms Fur Coat or her date. Either I'd scared them off or the fantasy had been a 'sexy hitchhiker' rather than 'passion in the parking lot' and they'd gone on somewhere else for the next scene. By the time I'd got under way again Stuart had twenty minutes' head start on me. I found myself scanning the roadside verges and then the pavements for him as I cruised to the sounds of Waterloo slobbering love and devotion over his bone and my upholstery.

A couple of minutes into the trip, I was forced to open the front window. Despite Arlene's denials, I always suspected she fed the mutt on baked beans and Brussels sprouts. The wind whipped strands of fringe into my eyes reminding me I was due for a session of stylish hacking with the nail scissors. And the root-retoucher, I decided, pushing layers back with one hand and squinting at the result in the rear-view mirror.

Aside from the shopping area – which was largely strung along the main high street – North Bay was divided into three distinct areas. The first few streets stretching back from the seafront were filled with the ubiquitous B & Bs (small boarding houses) and 'private hotels' (larger boarding houses with window-boxes). Next came the council estate, which hadn't been cutting-edge architecture when it was built in the sixties, and was now aiming more for blunt-edge slumitecture. And on the outskirts were the private detached houses, set around the edge of the golf course and pushing fingers into the farm fields. Guess where the Local Household Refuse Tip was situated?

Wrong.

Driving through the council estate, I navigated along several roads filled with gravel drives, double garages and don't-mess-with-me security systems before swinging left along a narrow lane bounded by high hedges and coasting a further few hundred yards to tag on to the end of a queue of vehicles waiting to obey the green and white signs and 'turn left only'.

Arlene had the place laid out so that incoming dumpers could take a circular scenic tour of her empire whilst being bullied in the lore of waste recycling. Straight ahead an enormous skip labelled ALL METAL HERE. Follow the white lines folks for the recycling bin for cardboard. Further along the green compost compactor with its constant aroma of warm rotting vegetation. And then continuing the tour, containers for used oil, glass, cans, newspapers and magazines, and shoes and textiles. I pulled in beside the crew cabin, closed my front windows as a precaution in case Waterloo made a break for it and went in search of his mum.

She was in her favourite corner – an area formed by the side wall of the cabin and the end of the metals skip – from where she could ensure the three blokes she employed to work the business didn't recycle anything worth real money into their own pockets, and the customers didn't dump anything they shouldn't into the compactors.

An old workbench had been set up out here and half a dozen twisted and unrecognisable pieces of metal were scattered across it. Arlene had the coppery end of one grasped in a large pair of pinchers whilst she pounded on the other end with a hammer. I let her beat them into sub-mission and sling the two separated sections into baskets behind her before whistling a hello.

She peeled the protective goggles over her head, leaving strands of coarse fair hair standing up. ''Ello, babes. You get him?'

'Don't I always?'

'Let's be having him, then. Where was he?'

'On the cliffs again.'

'I dunno. What's he want to keep doing a bunk for? Don't I give him everything his little choochy-face could want?' She rapped on the car window and mouthed kisses at Waterloo. The mutt ignored her. I unlocked the rear door. Waterloo wriggled back until his rump was pressed against the far door. Cradling the bone between his front paws, he pointedly slurped his indifference.

'Come on, baby. Don't be like that. Come to Mummy.' Arlene crawled in, grabbed both sides of his collar and heaved. After further token resistance, Waterloo sighed, picked up one end of the bone and bumped it along the ground into the cabin.

It was just one room with a corner partitioned off for a loo and washbasin and the rest taken up with battered filing cabinets, an old table with four mismatched chairs, a cupboard with a kettle and tea-mugs on top and a large wicker dog basket. The floor was scuffed laminate and the walls were an ever-changing barometer of what shades of half-used paint had been dumped recently. This month's selection was assorted mauves. Waterloo slouched off to sulk in his basket. His mistress took out a cash box and peeled out three tenners. 'Here you go, babes.'

'Cheers, Arlene. Mind if I use the loo?'

'Help yourself. Got time for a cuppa? I might have another job for yer.'

By the time I'd wriggled around in her elbow-cracking loo cubicle, she'd brewed up and put the biscuit tin on the table.

'Help yourself.' She lobbed a digestive at Waterloo who fielded it with a snap. 'Look at him, ain't he a bootiful boy? Doesn't his mumsy-wumsy love him?'

I tried to keep a straight face. Looking at her you'd never guess Arlene suffered from verbal senility. She was mid-forties as far as I could tell, shortish and plumpish, with a round, even-featured face. Despite the mini-heatwave, she was dressed in her usual working outfit of baggy denim jeans, heavy lace-up boots, black donkey jacket and fingerless knitted gloves. Her only concession to the temperature had been to remove the woollen helmet she wore in the winter. Her voice had the raw, consonant-impoverished rasp of South London rather than the local accent.

'I ever tell you how I got him?'

She had. Every time I came up here. But that didn't stop her. I helped myself to a handful of biscuits and sat through the story – yet again – of the bloke with the pedigree bulldog bitch who'd turned up just as the site was closing and left her barking frantically in the back seat whilst he dumped a black plastic sack into the compactor.

'I dunno what made me look. I shouted at Paddy to hit the stop button and jumped right in there. It don't bear thinking what would have happened if the teeth had got him.'

She'd left the door open so she could keep an eye on the site. We both went through the silent ritual of staring at the compactor that was currently in use – its teeth crushing and clawing the jumble of household rubbish back into its maw – and imagining a warm bundle being mashed to a pulp of blood and bone.

Then we moved to the next lines in Arlene's script. 'I wish I'd taken the b's number. His life wouldn't have been worth . . .' She snapped finger and thumb. But she hadn't and he'd never been back to the dump. Instead Arlene had found herself with the ugliest little runt in existence.

'Eighteenth of June it was. Battle of Waterloo, it said on

13

me calendar. So I called him that. Vet reckoned they'd knocked him on the head before they bagged him up. Tough little bugger. Thought I'd lost him a dozen times, but he just kept on fighting. And now mumsy-wumsy's got to leave her baby and go away. Will he miss her?'

'You going on holiday, Arlene?' I asked, dunking a Rich Tea in my mug.

'No, babes,' she said, returning to her normal voice. 'But I got to go into hospital. Eye op. That's why I need you. I need someone to look after my baby.'

She had to be joking! A couple of hours maybe. But days! 'I'm not really a pet sort of person, Arlene.'

'Course you are. He loves ya.'

He could have fooled me. I locked eyes with the mutt; his lips curled. There was no way I wanted to share my flat with a bum that could burp for England.

Apparently Arlene didn't want me to. 'You'd have to stop up my place. He's happiest in his own homesie-womesie.'

That suited me. And I'd stop in my homesie-womesie too – two miles upwind of his digestive system. 'Couldn't you leave him here? With Paddy or one of them?'

'Them' were the two teenagers who comprised the rest of the workforce around here. They were currently helping a couple unload the sawn-up remains of a tree from a trailer and stagger up the metal staircase to pitch them into the compactor's maw.

'Wouldn't trust them to notice if he hopped off. Me neighbour did offer to have him, but she's not too good on her legs these days and I don't want him pulling her over. Please, babes. It'd only be for a few days. And I'll pay you. Thirty quid a day? And there's plenty of booze and food in?'

I hesitated. It was free board and lodging, plus cash, in return for opening a few cans of dog food. And I could always leave the windows open. 'When do you want me?'

'Tomorrow afternoon. I'm first for the chop Wednesday

morning, so I'm gonna stay overnight Tuesday. They've got this hostel place attached to the hospital. You all right to run me to the station?'

'Sure. But where are you having this op?' Presumably not the local hospital as I'd been assuming.

'Moorfields. In London. Been under them for years.'

Moorfields: *the* specialist centre for eye diseases in the country. I'd have liked to ask Arlene just how bad her eyes were, but the way she collected up the tea-mugs and turned away from me to rinse them in the loo sink said, Don't probe. So I didn't. Instead I took down her home address and promised to be there by six tomorrow.

'Cheers. Come outside before yer go. Got something you might fancy for that flat of yours.'

She led me outside and round the back of the metals skip where thick sheets of plastic had been suspended over wooden slats to give a rudimentary greenhouse effect. This was where anything re-saleable was stored prior to its appearance in the 'For Sale' columns of the local papers or the windows of some more distant antique shops. At present it was home to a dozen almost new kids' bicycles, half a dozen baby buggies, assorted statues, candelabra, garden ornaments, clocks and small pieces of furniture.

Arlene climbed over and lifted something from the back. 'Here you go. Look smashing on yer wall, that would.'

It was an oval mirror, framed in a gold-coloured riot of carved roses, ivy and ribbons. 'It's a bit dirty, Arlene.'

She rubbed an elbow of the donkey jacket over the glass. 'Sheet of newspaper will get that up. And I'll tell you what you do with the gilt – mix up some egg white with a drop of bleach, slosh it over, let it dry and then brush it out with a toothbrush. Bring that gilt up like new. Go on . . .' She extended the mirror. 'My treat.'

I can't refuse a freebie. I stowed it in the car boot and waved my goodbyes. Waterloo had wandered to the cabin door, towing the bone like an anchor chain. On being instructed to say goodbye to 'Gracie-Wacie', he eyeballed me, inserted the bone's knuckle end in the side of his fangs and broke off a lump with a stomach-churning crack.

I drove back via the main promenade in Seatoun. The large semi-circular swathe of sand on my right was virtually deserted, apart from the odd dog walker on the wet strand that was being left by the retreating tide and a few souls stretched out on towels since the tarpaulined deckchair stacks were roped down and unmanned. If the weather held we'd get day trippers at the weekend and the Council would enforce the 'no dogs before 7 p.m.' rule and root out some temporary staff to man the deckchair concession and kids' play area.

I parked in front of the office, in the spot normally used by our esteemed leader, Vetch-the-Letch. Since his car wasn't there, presumably he wasn't either. I experienced that glad feeling that comes when you've overslept and arrived at work half an hour late – only to find the boss won't be coming in that day.

Technically speaking, Vetch *wasn't* my boss. All the investigators at Vetch (International) Investigations Inc. were self-employed and paid a monthly fee to Vetch to cover rent and office facilities (a fax machine and a bolshie receptionist-typist who was just killing time insulting us until she was famous). However, since he owned the building and had bagged the downstairs offices, most clients tended to cross his path first and the rest of us ended up with whichever he chose to assign to us. Which – if he suspected you weren't going to be able to meet your rent that month – meant pretty much any rotten job he felt like unloading.

At least that was the routine until a few weeks ago when my friend Annie was threatening to leave and decamp to London. Annie was the best investigator Vetch's had – and the little Letch knew it. Which was why she was now a junior partner in this business. And presumably why she was being allowed to use Vetch's leather-clad, executive-style office when he was out, rather than her own premises on the top floor.

'I've had an idea,' she said when I stuck my head in the door to say 'hi'.

'Another one?'

'Must you sound so negative?'

'Sorry, but I think I'm suffering from ideas overload. You do seem to be having a hell of a lot recently.' (And most of them were connected to the theme of turning Vetch's into a hot-shot business empire that would make Securicor look like a kindergarten protection racket. It was becoming exhausting for those of us who were content to muddle from cock-up to near disaster each month.)

I flopped down in the visitors' chair and looked at her across the vast expanse of Vetch's desktop. She was wearing her navy, long-line trouser suit that was supposed to make her look businesslike (it did) and slimmer (not a chance), a cream silk blouse and a new pair of large, gold-rimmed spectacles that said 'designer price tag'.

'You going out. Or is someone coming in?'

'I have a meeting. Jan said you'd gone out on a job?'

'Waterloo went walkabout again.'

'Ah.'

Annie could put a whole bucket of comment behind one syllable. As in 'Ah – you're stuck with the grunt work again, then' and 'Ah – you'll be pleading poverty when it comes to paying the rent *again*', or occasionally 'Ah – you don't think it's time you started thinking about a new career? One that might leave you slightly solvent?'

I changed the subject and told her about Stuart Roberts instead. 'I thought at first he was the Fur Coat's date, but I really don't think that was it. I didn't get the impression he was looking to meet anyone.'

'You think he was planning to . . . ?' Annie mimed a dive.

'I'm not sure. He had car keys but there was no sign of a motor, so he must have left it somewhere else and walked up there. Which is fair enough if he just wanted to stretch his legs and admire the view. On the other hand, he must have climbed past all those "Dangerous Drop" notices to go wandering on a crumbling cliff.'

'So did you.'

'But I don't think Stuart was looking for a straying dog. Unless it was the Hound of the Baskervilles.'

'Come again?'

'He's into the supernatural. He thinks he murdered a ghost.'

'Is he nuts?'

'No. At least – I don't think so. He seemed quite rational.'

'From your viewpoint.'

'Since I know you're about to get bitchy on me, I shan't answer that. Tell me about this idea to save Vetchy's empire.'

'No time. I have to get off to my meeting. Come over this evening? I'll get a pizza. And before you ask – yes, I'm paying.'

'You make it sound irresistible.' I opened the door for her and we stepped into the hall together. Just as Janice – the receptionist from hell – came in the front door.

'Where have you been?' Annie demanded. 'This reception desk is supposed to be manned all the time. Anyone could have wandered in.'

'You were here.' Jan removed a carton from her shoulder bag. 'We were out of milk. You said we had to have a choice to offer the clients.'

'Then get it delivered. Don't go wandering off like that again. If anyone calls for me, I'll be back tomorrow morning. You can ring urgent messages through to my flat this evening.'

She surged out on a wave of up-your-nose efficiency. Jan and I exchanged looks. For once we were in agreement.

'Something's got to be done,' Jan said, crossing her legs on her desk and giving me the chance to admire black lace-up knee boots. Ebony was her favourite shade and she'd indulged herself with it from head to foot today, right down to the nail shade and gooey lip-gloss that was currently sliding over the chocolate bar she'd also bought from the corner grocer's. 'She can't expect me to work properly.'

'Given your usual efforts, that would be a triumph of expectation over experience.'

Jan masticated a mouthful of milk choc and hazelnuts. 'I can understand long words, you know. Anyhow, if I had a proper job, I'd have a proper wage and everything, wouldn't I? I'm only doing this crappy number until I get a break in television or something. I'm going to be famous.'

'You said. Often.' Just how Janice intended to achieve fame neither we – nor she – were clear. She had no real talent for anything as far as we could discover. But she had unshakeable faith in her destiny – viz. to be stalked by paparazzi, featured in gossip columns and regularly splashed over six page spreads in *Hello!* and *OK!* magazines.

'Anyhow, you're her mate,' Jan said. 'Can't you do something? Find her a bloke?'

'Why should a bloke slow her down?'

'Bound to. Give her something else to tire her out.'

'That's a bloody patronising thing to say.'

Jan shrugged. 'True though. There was this bit in me mag last month. About women submitting their nurturing instincts in work.'

'Sublimating?' I suggested.

'Could have been. Anyhow, it said they get really uptight because they see their projects as their kids. And they got to make them do better than all the other kids in class. If Annie had a real bloke and kid she might give us a break. Course, I know she's getting on a bit . . .'

'She's thirty-three. Three years older than me.'

'Well, you haven't got a bloke either, have you? Unless that dorky one was after a date?'

'Any particular dorky one, Jan?'

'Didn't I say? He came in before I went to get me chocolate. Hang on.'

Heaving the rubbish bin from under the desk, she rummaged. Knowing her filing system, I waited. Eventually she unearthed a sealed envelope. 'Here y'are.'

It was addressed in block letters to Ms Grace Smith. 'Cheers, Jan.'

Turning my back to block her view, I ripped it open and unfolded a single sheet of paper.

8 Sailmakers' Row
Winstanton
Tel: 25188

Dear Grace,

I have been thinking about our conversation on the cliff and wonder whether I could explain further? I was serious about wanting to engage your services.

If you are free tonight would you consider coming to my place and I'll cook you dinner? Say around 8 p.m.?

Yours sincerely,
Stuart Roberts

P.S. I realise that our previous encounter might have raised some doubts in your mind regarding my sanity, so please feel free to bring your friend if you are worried about being trapped in a room with the local lunatic.

There was a heavy draught of breath in my right ear. I turned round to find Jan had knelt up on the desk to read over my shoulder. 'You going, then?' she asked.

'Probably. If I'm not back tomorrow, ring someone.'

'The police?'

'Ghostbusters.'

3

'Don't take my door paint off!'

'Well, how do you expect me to get out of here?' She'd parked three inches from the wall. I retrieved the leg I'd managed to ease out of the passenger door and stared up at the rough stones.

Winstanton was the next town around the coast from Seatoun. Once they'd both been small fishing villages, but Seatoun had grown and expanded in a multicolour, neon-lit arcade-fest of tackiness as holidaymakers had discovered it at the beginning of the twentieth century and then abandoned it again in the sixties once the Costa-del-Chips scene had become cheaper than a fortnight in Britain. Winstanton, however, had remained a working port, largely famous for its oyster beds. The small influx of tourists had had to be content with a pebble beach, local shops, unpretentious cafés and the cutting-edge sports facilities of tenpin bowling. Then, a few years ago, Winstanton had been 'discovered'.

It was being slowly colonised by double-income families who wanted a second home by the sea and high-fliers who could work partly from home. As a consequence, the local shops were being tartified back into ye-oldee-white-washed-fishermen's-cottages which mostly flogged cream teas and antiques, the cafés were reinventing themselves into pretentious eateries, and at least part of the quay area had been recovered in cobblestones and looks-like gas lamps.

The result of this transmogrification had been a rise in house prices and a distinct lack of parking spaces in lanes that had been laid out in an era when a pack pony was considered pretty flash transport around here.

I'd managed to persuade Annie to chauffeur me on the grounds that she had to eat dinner anyway and this way she was saving the price of a pizza.

'And you can knock back any free booze on offer. What makes you think I'll be welcome?'

'He said to bring a mate. In case he runs berserk and starts vomiting green slime or rotating his head through three hundred and sixty degrees.'

'It sounds almost irresistible,' Annie had said. 'But I think I'd rather curl up with a giant pepperoni and tuna.'

Fortunately, in the end, the idea of meeting a ghost-killer had proved intriguing enough to lure her along. Now all I had to do was get out of this damn front seat. After a second try resulted in an arm and shoulder escaping whilst a wavering foot threatened to chin Annie, I suggested she parked in one of the outer car parks.

'I'd rather not. There's been a spate of car crime around here recently according to Zeb. I'd like to keep it where I can at least hear the alarm.' She pulled away far enough for me to open the door. 'Hop out. I'll see you there in a tick. Number eight, wasn't it?'

It was. Access was down a narrow lane bordered on one side by the back yards of the main-street shops and on the other by the ten properties that comprised Sailmakers' Row. In the good old days it would have been a slum that stank of fish and worse. Nowadays it just stank of money.

The lapboarded upper storeys of the converted sailmakers' stores overhung the stone-built ground floors, rather like those old medieval timbered merchants' houses. It meant that the pedestrian lane was even darker than the street I'd just left and doors underneath the jutting upper section were in shadows so solid they were almost like physical barriers. To add to the sense of isolation that entering the gap induced, the row curved slightly, which meant that I couldn't even see the oblong of street lighting at the far entrance.

My eyes hadn't adjusted yet. I groped forward cautiously, getting my nose within a few inches of each door in order to read off the house number. The passageway was claustrophobic; if I stretched my hands out sideways I could practically brush my fingertips against the opposing walls. I was concentrating on where I put my feet. There was a slight dip scoring the centre of the lane which had probably been a drain once and was now a potential ankle-turner. I glanced ahead just once. And for a second I thought I saw something move in the shadows ahead.

Thinking that Annie might have entered the passage from the other end, I called out. 'Hello?'

There was no answer and the movement had stilled. I held my breath. Nothing.

'Get a grip,' I said out loud. 'There is no such thing as a ghost.'

'How about mad axe-wielding psychos lurking in dark passages?' enquired my personal demon.

'Shut up,' I ordered it. 'If I go – you go too.'

Fortunately number eight proved to be the next house, which curtailed my subconscious's habit of starting arguments with me. Stuart answered the door so quickly after my initial rap on the brass knocker that I suspected he must have been hanging around in the hall waiting for me. The purple egg in the centre of his forehead was swelling up a treat.

'I'm so glad you c-came. I wasn't sure you would. I didn't start the cooking until you arrived, but everything's prepared. We're upstairs.'

He stepped back to let me into the narrow passage with its open-back staircase leading to the upper floor. In the days of their original tenants, these solidly built downstairs rooms would have housed the sailmaker's nearest and dearest, whilst the sails were cut, sewn, stretched and mended in large wooden lofts that formed the whole of the upper storey. I started for the stairs and then paused, thinking I might have misunderstood, when I realised Stuart was still hanging on to the open front door. I also became aware of an odd smell. It was like decay – and rotting flesh.

'Everything okay?' I asked.

'Are you on your own?'

I'd been in far scarier situations than having a slightly overweight thirty-something between me and the exit. Nonetheless, I suddenly found myself glad to be able to say, 'No. My friend's right behind me.'

'Oh, good. I got him a special treat.' Taking a carrier from the hook behind the door, he unfolded the layers of newspaper inside – and proudly displayed the reason for that pungent smell. That was the moment Annie appeared in the doorway.

'Hi. You're just in time. Stuart's got your dinner.'

Annie stared at the greasy bone with lumps of flesh still adhering and murmured deprecatingly, 'Oh, really, you shouldn't have gone to all that trouble for me.'

Rosiness flooded Stuart's face. 'I thought, I mean . . . you'd bring . . .'

'He was expecting the dog, you idiot,' Annie said across him.

'Sorry. You said a friend.'

'No, no. My stupid mistake.' Stuart seemed to become aware he was still holding the bone and its stained wrappings under Annie's nose. 'I . . . I'll get r-r-r-rid of this.'

'Don't waste it.' I took it from him. 'I'm babysitting the mutt tomorrow.'

'Now don't be coy,' Annie said. 'You know that will keep you in broth for weeks. I'll get off again, leave you two to it.'

'Oh, no. Don't. I mean, unless you'd r-rather, of course. I c-can easily cook for three. It's just pan-fried fish. With warm chocolate t-tart to follow. Nothing fancy.'

Annie smiled. 'It sounds lovely. If you're sure . . . ?'

Stuart was. He was, in fact, almost embarrassingly eager to make amends for what was my mistake. He ushered us to the upper floor which had been left with the original open-plan design of the loft. The floorboards where the sail patterns would once have been chalked had been polished to a warm chestnut colour, and kitchen units and a preparation bar in the same shade had been tucked in one corner encircling the cooker, hobs and fridge. The rest of the place was taken up with sofas, rugs, a circular dining table, entertainment units and a small home office area in the opposite corner to the kitchen. The far wall, which would have had the shutters where the sails were lowered in and out, now contained a large picture window over-looking the sea.

'This is wonderful. Did you do it yourself?' Annie asked.

'Mostly. I rather enjoy DIY when I have the time. I find it relaxing. Makes a change from my work, where I have to be very precise. I like being able to just go for it, see my ideas c-coming to life.'

'Gardening does it for me. Since Grace plainly has no plans to introduce us, I'm Anchoret Smith.' She nodded at me. 'No relation to the dog-catcher.'

'Stuart Roberts. I am very glad to meet you. Anchoret? That's Welsh, isn't it?'

'It is. I'm not. My parents decided to lumber all seven of us with unusual Christian names. To offset the ordinariness of Smith. But call me Annie.'

'Can I get you a drink? Or take your coats?'

'Both.' I handed him my jacket and asked for a glass of wine. 'White, red, rosé. I'm not fussy.'

'This is true,' Annie agreed. 'Chateau meths will do her if you've nothing else.'

She took off her own jacket. We were both wearing loose trousers and flat shoes, the better for whacking or running should our sheep turn into the big, bad wolf. I'd tucked a purple silk shirt into mine which I'd found crumpled at the bottom of the charity shop bin. It was a snip at thirty pence – which was about the size it had been designed to fit. I stuffed several yards of material back into my waistband and re-rolled sleeves cut to please the fashion-conscious orang-utan. Annie soothed the simple grey number she'd chosen. Our fussing gave our host time to uncork a bottle of white and pour two glasses.

'I'll just nip your c-coats down to the bedroom.'

We waited until we heard the sound of a door opening below before we switched into cruise mode and checked out the room, trying to find clues to our host's tastes. Annie got the books and CDs (middle-of-the-road stuff) whilst I examined the art on display. That was pretty ordinary too – mostly smudgy abstract-type prints and a couple of watercolours of local views. The only oddly out of place item was a framed picture on the kitchen wall. A George Clooney look-alike was lounging in dishevelled gorgeousness against a sports car, with his dinner jacket hooked over his right shoulder, his bow-tie untied and his eyes promising bliss-on-a-stick. There were a couple of big-haired females in the shot, a blonde and a brunette, obviously hoping to take him up on this promise. It looked like it had been cut from a glossy magazine ad.

'What do you make of this?'

Annie scanned the shot. 'That looks like the casino in Monte Carlo in the background. Car's a Ferrari. The 288 GTO, I think. Clothes are out of date. What . . . ten, fifteen years? Assuming they haven't retouched it, the shadows suggest it was probably taken early morning. Plants look fairly perky still – must be early summer before the really hot weather starts.'

I was impressed, but I wasn't going to admit it. 'That's not fair. I'm supposed to be Sherlock, you're Watson.'

'I'm bored with Watson.'

'Maybe we should switch to Cagney and Lacey.'

'No thanks. You always make me be Lacey.'

'Lacey got fat first.'

'Watch it, Sherlock. Remember mini-cabs charge double in the evenings.'

'Cabs?' Stuart caught the end of this conversation. 'You're not going, are you?'

'Not at all.' Annie moved away from the incongruous picture. 'Can we do anything to help with dinner?'

'No thanks. Why don't you relax while I c-cook? I

haven't done a starter, I'm afraid. Unless you like oysters? There are some fresh ones in the fridge.'

'I love them.' Annie beamed.

'Really? So do I. I'll open a few, then.'

I passed on that one. Something the texture of raw egg white wasn't my stomach's idea of a good time.

They both moved away. And I noticed something that Ms Clever-clogs hadn't on the picture. Sliding two fingers under the bottom, I tilted it slightly so the light fell at a different angle. Someone had scored a large pencilled X across the brunette's head and then rubbed it out again. The indentations were just visible over her cheeks and mouth. Quietly setting the frame back, I rejoined Annie on the couch.

Stuart turned down the main lights and busied himself behind the preparation bar, fussing with herbs, oils and hot plates whilst we admired the view. It was pretty spectacular. The row had an uninterrupted view over the beach. A waxing moon and brilliant stars were shining from a near cloudless sky and reflecting off the fluorescent gleams in the oil-black ocean. Just away to our left we could make out the lights of the latest chic – i.e. over-priced – seafood restaurant whilst to the right was the shallow shingle beach that had housed one of the town's original boat-builders. The whole scene was only slightly marred by the lights of the container ships running on the horizon. Annie asked how long he'd lived here.

'Nearly t-two years. But my . . . problem . . . didn't start manifesting itself until about six months ago.'

'Manifesting' sounded uncomfortably solid somehow. I found myself glancing nervously into the shadowy far corners – just in case anything undead in a long white sheet and ankle chains was making a fourth for dinner. I was pleased to catch out Annie doing the same.

She rallied immediately. 'So tell us about it. Do you really have a ghost?'

'Yes. No. At least I'm not sure if she was a ghost or not. Look, let's eat first, shall we?'

He laid up three places, opened the oysters and set the fish to sizzle whilst he and Annie ate the oysters.

Even though I'd forgone this treat, I joined them at the table with my glass. Despite his self-confidence being knocked off-centre so easily by the bone episode, he'd cooked competently. He was plainly a dab hand at DIY and if he could afford one of these properties he had a seriously desirable income. And so far I'd seen no evidence of a Mrs Roberts. In short, he was the sort of bloke your mother prays you'll bring home for Sunday lunch.

So, could I fancy him? Could I hell!

Annie gestured towards the office enclave and asked if he worked from home.

'Yes. Mostly.'

'What do you do?'

'What would you guess?'

He included both of us in the question. My first thought had been something academic. I briefly considered school-teacher, but I doubted that the salary would cover the mortgage. Besides, the average class would have ripped him to shreds over the stammer. So I went for next dullest occupation I could think of. 'Accountant?'

'R-right first time.' He gave us both an apologetic smile. 'Bland and boring, that's me.'

'No, you're not. You shouldn't put yourself down,' Annie started in the voice of a woman with six younger siblings and a bossy attitude. She seemed to realise what she was doing and changed tack. 'Personally an accountant is just about the most interesting person I could meet at the moment. I'm trying to get some kind of business plan together for the agency.'

'Really. If you need any help . . . What sort of projections are you doing?'

And so it went on all through dinner. Profit and loss . . . cash flow . . . capital assets . . . turnover . . . loss . . . yatter, yatter, yatter. As he relaxed, Stuart's stutter became noticeably less. Occasionally I tried to steer the conversation back to the reason for our visit but Stuart shied away. The guy was getting cold feet.

Once we'd polished off the fish, warm chocolate tart, and Chardonnay, and were on to the coffee, I decided it was time to push it.

'So let's chat ghost. Or not, as the case may be. The one you think you may have killed?'

'Yes. No. Are you sure you wouldn't c-care for more chocolate tart?'

'Go on, then.' I extended my plate. The serving slice rattled against the china plate. At this rate he was going to have a total breakdown before we got to the point – and the deposit cheque.

Annie declined. 'Watching my weight.'

'Whatever for?'

'Oh, you know. Slight problem.' She soothed the loose crinkly shirt over the far from loose trousers.

'Rubbish. You look great. I've never understood why women want to look like ironing boards.' He extended the silver slice again – loaded with about five hundred calories of chocolaty gooiness.

Annie gave in graciously. 'If you insist. But then I think we really should get down to business, don't you?'

'Yes. You're right. There's no point in me inviting you here and then bottling out. Wait there.'

Given that we were both anchored to the seats by chocolate overload, we couldn't have done much else if he'd whistled up Marley's ghost at that moment. He lowered the lights and then produced a cassette and walked over to the entertainment centre.

'You'd better listen to this.'

4

'*Where are you, Joe?*'
    '*The lane.*'

'Which lane? Where is it?'

'Tyler's Lane.'

'Where is that?'

'On our land, ain' it? Can't leave her on our land. Got to move her.'

'Move who, Joe?'

'Her. Her. Oh, Jesus, oh, Jesus!'

'What's the matter, Joe? What's happening?'

'She spoke.'

'What did she say?'

'Ain' nothing. Just air coming out the body. My gran did that after she were dead. Saying hello to the angels come to take her to heaven, me mum said.'

'When was that, Joe? When did your grandmother die?'

'Five years back. Week after our Billie's seventh birthday.'

'Is Billie your brother, Joe?'

'Brother! She wouldn't thank you for that. She's a girl. Looks like a boy sometimes. Dad puts her in my hand-downs. Says there's no point in wasting money on girls' dresses when there's wear left in my clothes. She's got straight hair too. Stringy it is. She hates that hair. She wants curls, like Carol.'

'Who's Carol?'

'Billie's best friend. Her mum, Mrs Slack, runs the shop. Dad wanted to go courting there, she wouldn't have nothing to do with him. Don't blame her. It's hard, working the farm, for a woman. It's why my mum left, I reckon. She shouldn't have done that. Shouldn't have gone off and left us with him. I hate her.'

'How old were you when your mum left, Joe?'

'Twelve. Went after gran died, she did. Only stopped so we'd feed and house the old girl, my dad said. Cleared off after the funeral.'

'So you're seventeen now?'

'Yeah. Be eighteen next March. I'm near as big as Dad now. Knocked him down last month.'

'You had a fight?'

'Not a fight. Dad took the truck into Winstanton. Had a skinful at The Glass again. Tried to take a swing at us. I stopped him. I don't reckon Dad'll be bothering me again. Serves him right. Been asking for it. Should have seen his face when I put that fist in. Said I could clear out.'

'But you didn't?'

'Can't leave Billie alone with him, can I? Have to wait until she's old enough so he can't make her come home. We'll get a place together then. Me and Billie.'

'Is Billie with you now in Tyler's Lane?'

'No. I don't want to talk about that. I want to go home.'

'Why don't you?'

'Can't. Can't leave her here. They'll see her if they take down the wires tomorrow.'

'What are you going to do then, Joe?'

'Bury her. That's best. Get rid of her.'

'Who is she, Joe?'

'Can't say.'

'Why not?'

'I can't SAY. Understand. I can't SAY.'

'All right, Joe. Calm down. What are you doing now?'

'Looking at her. I wish it weren't full moon.'

'Why?'

'I can see her face. There's blood in her eyes. I want to close them. Stop her looking at me. Can't, though. Not with that blood. Can't touch that. Got to pick her up. She's still warm.'

'Does that matter?'

'It's like touching her when she's alive. She's soft. Smells good. Smells nice. Skirt's come up too. I can see her legs. Skin's all white above her stockings.'

Abruptly Stuart pushed down the 'stop' button on the cassette player. The silence in the room was so intense that when Annie and I both released our breath with an audible 'phew' it sounded like a rebuke.

Stuart walked over to the window and slid one side open.

31

The all-pervading 'hush' of the waves on the shingle filled the room, accompanied by the bitter scent of washed-up seaweed and salt-tanged wind.

'Who is Joe?' Annie asked. 'And how did you get the tape?'

'Tabitha gave me a c-copy. She gives me a copy after every session. I'm Joe.'

In which case I could see why he'd turned down the lights. I suppose in a way it was reassuring to find he didn't get his kicks watching women looking at – or in this case listening to – anything connected to sex or violence or any combination thereof. Or perhaps he just liked sitting in the dark imagining how we were reacting . . . ?

'When you say you're Joe,' I clarified. 'You mean, that's your voice on the tape?'

It seemed unlikely. There was a resemblance in the tone to Stuart's voice, but the boy on the recording was speaking with that slight touch of the old country accent you sometimes hear amongst older people around this area with its 'oy' sound instead of plain 'y' in some words and the 'Oi' instead of 'I', and there was no evidence of a stutter. He'd also claimed to be seventeen which made him about half Stuart's age by my reckoning. Unless it was an old recording. 'When was this made?'

'Four months ago.'

'When you were called Joe?'

'Yes. And no. Look, there's more on the t-tape. Do you want to hear it?'

Did I? I glanced at Annie. She gave me the slightest nod. I guessed she felt the same way as I did about the situation. It was probably all a load of self-delusional rubbish, but we were hooked. 'Fire it up.'

Stuart depressed the 'start' button and once again the unknown woman's voice whispered into the dark.

'What are you doing now, Joe?'

'Going back. Had to leave her. Go fetch something to dig with. I got a shovel they use for keeping the fire stoked in

32

the drying room. It was closer than home. Ain't sharp but it'll have to do. I got to hide her. I'll put her down by the huts. Lucky they've gone.'

'Who are "they", Joe?'

'That lot. The Londoners. Dirty lot. Thieving too. I'll bury her down there. There's soft ground by the pond. Had a toilet hut standing on there. Be easy to dig. And it won't matter if she smells a bit. They'll just think it's the shit they buried. There's lime down there too. Get rid of her faster. They won't think to dig this up again. Jesus, it stinks . . . I'm going to be sick . . . stinks worse than the pig pen.'

The sounds on the tape changed to sounds of someone panting and grunting as if he were digging. At least I hope that's what he was doing. And then there was a much louder groan of satisfaction.

'What's happening now, Joe?'

'Got her in. Rolled her in on her face. Can't see her eyes no more. The bitch will sleep nice and snug. Serves her right. Only got what she asked for.'

'Joe. Are you all right? Listen, Joe. I want to talk to Stuart now. Can I do that?'

'I don't want to go.'

'Yes, you do. I want you to go to sleep now, Joe. Breathe deeply . . . quietly . . . breathe with me . . . in . . . out . . .'

Stuart clicked the tape switch down again. 'The rest is just Tabitha bringing me back to this r-reality.'

Bully for Tabitha. On the evidence so far, the girl must have real talent.

Stuart turned the level of the dimmer switch up slightly. He seemed to be making an effort to hold his face in a deliberately neutral expression, as if he didn't want to influence our reaction to what we'd just heard. 'I'll make some more coffee. Or would you prefer a brandy?'

I would. Annie stuck to coffee since she was driving. His departure to the kitchen enclave gave us a chance to exchange looks if not dialogue.

Annie raised her eyebrows. I twiddled a forefinger beside

my forehead. With a frown she jerked her head towards the window and I realised that we were seated so that a reflected duplicate of the sitting room hovered in the night beyond the glass. Stuart didn't have to look in this direction to see what we were doing. He just had to glance to his left whilst he fussed over the work surface.

Trying to recover the position (not to mention the potential deposit fee), I put more enthusiasm into my voice than I intended when I called, 'So who's this Tabitha? I assume she's the other voice on the tape?'

'Yes. Tabitha Puzold. She's a hypnotherapist.' He returned with the cafetière, a balloon of brandy and the open bottle. 'I was t-trying to give up smoking. Without much success. A friend suggested hypnotism might help and recommended Tabitha.'

'And did it? Help, I mean?' I asked.

'Yes. It did, as a matter of fact. I haven't been able to touch a cigarette since. But unfortunately the sessions seemed to trigger a side-effect. I developed a t-terrible fear of flying.'

'Sort of trade in your old phobia for a brand-new model?'

'It wasn't funny, believe me. I got to the airport after the first session and I just c-completely lost it. I was sweating, my heart was pounding, I couldn't breathe. I thought I was going to black out. I couldn't get through the departure gate. I had to phone my client and reschedule.'

'I thought you worked from here.'

'Mostly. But sometimes I need to sort things out face to face. And these aren't the sort of people you ask to come to you. That's why this fear was so disastrous. I couldn't work if I c-couldn't fly out to them. I tried again a few days later. But it was the same all over again. And after that I started getting the nightmares. It was always the same. I'm in a plane and it's crashing. But not just crashing. It's on fire. I could smell the others burning. And see my own skin starting to bubble. It got so bad that I found myself fighting to stay awake.'

Annie reached over and put her own hand over his.

'What makes you think these attacks were linked to the hypnosis? It's not uncommon to suddenly acquire a fear of something that's never bothered you before. Look at how claustrophobia or agoraphobia sneak up on some people. In your case I dare say you were used to having a few cigarettes before you got on the plane. And this time you didn't have that crutch.'

'I wasn't sure at first. Frankly I didn't c-care. I just knew I had to get myself sorted out. So I went back to Tabitha. She suggested this fear could have been triggered by our sessions and that we should explore that possibility. I forget what the technical name for it is, I'm afraid.'

'Work creation?'

'Shut up, Grace,' Annie ordered. 'Go on, Stuart. She re-hypnotised you, I assume?'

'Yes. Only she couldn't break through the resistance. It's a sort of fence around my fears. The thing that holds them inside my head. That's when she said we should c-consider the possibility that this fear of flying was nothing to do with me as I was now – but rather it was related to an incident in one of my past lives.'

'Past lives,' I said. 'Like when people are convinced they used to be Galileo or Queen Nefertiti's hand-maiden?'

'That sort of thing, yes. Although in my case I was a farm labourer.'

'Who killed a woman and buried the body. Who was she?'

'I don't know.'

'You must. You were there.'

'You don't understand. When I go back and I'm Joe, I c-can't remember anything about this life.'

'And vice versa?' Annie asked.

'Yes. Tabitha says most people retain memories of their past lives once she brings them back, but some don't. Tabitha tried to regress me so that I could keep Joe's memories, but it didn't work. I can only remember frag-ments – smells, sensations, a brief glimpse of a place.'

'So what exactly is it you want me to do?' I enquired.

'Find out the truth. I want to know who this woman was. And whether I killed her.'

'You mean whether Joe killed her?'

'Is there any difference?'

'Sure there is. You get life . . . Joe gets a mention in an *Unsolved Crimes* production on cable TV at 2 a.m. one morning.'

'What Grace is trying to say—'

'What Grace is *saying*,' I interrupted Annie, 'is why does it matter if you killed someone in a previous life? I'm assuming this Joe is dead? He's not wandering around somewhere wondering where his personality went?'

'Yes, he's dead. He has to be for his spirit to seek a new home in me according to Tabitha. But that's not important. I'm the one who needs to know. Will you t-take the job?'

'It may not be such a great idea, Stuart. I mean, I don't believe in past lives. Maybe you'd be better off giving the job to someone who's a bit more gul . . . er, receptive to all that stuff. Annie?'

Annie hesitated. 'I've got a fairly busy schedule at present, but if I juggle . . .'

'No.' Stuart said firmly. 'I want Grace to do it. I want this job to be handled by a suspicious cynic. I want you to question every damn piece of evidence. I'll pay you on a daily basis, plus expenses. The usual arrangement.'

'How do you know it's usual?'

'Some of my clients have hired investigators. I see the invoices.'

'What do they hire them for?'

'To watch their wives and girlfriends. Sometimes both. And their kids. For obvious reasons I don't want to use a firm they've done business with in the past. That's why I chose you.'

'How *did* you find me?' Second sight, I thought cynically.

'*Yellow Pages*. Vetch's was the only investigators in the

area. So I guessed you'd have to work there. Will you t-take the job?'

For once I didn't leap straight in. Normally the idea of a continuous rolling expense account would have been irresistible. But there was *something* about this that didn't feel quite right.

Annie issued some gentle encouragement. It came via the toe of her shoe applied to my ankle-bone on Stuart's blind side.

Rubbing the sore area, I said, 'Okay. I'll do it. On one condition. Tell me why you really need to know, Stuart.'

5

'I'm not surprised you have trouble attracting clients. Have you won the lottery or are you just planning to make a habit of sending your career into self-destruct mode?'

It was so obviously a swipe at my previous not-so-glorious departure from the police that I snapped back with more force than I'd usually respond with to one of Annie's moans at my lack of professionalism.

'Listen, I'm self-employed, remember. That means neither you, nor anyone else, has the right to tell me what I do, or don't do. Where'd you park?'

I'd stalked back to the impossibly tight slot that she'd originally attempted to park in, only to find it occupied by a white van.

'Harbour,' Annie said stiffly before relaxing and saying, 'If you didn't want the job – fine. But you could have declined with a bit more tact. Particularly when you're dealing with a bloke who you last saw messing around on the edge of a potential suicide drop.'

'Sorry. But this whole thing is giving me the creeps. Anyway, I didn't decline.' I tapped the shoulder bag which now contained the tapes Stuart had handed over. Together with a very hefty deposit cheque. His reason for needing my services was quite simple: he was scared he might kill someone.

'Before, Joe had only "come out" when I was under hypnosis. But a c-couple of months ago,' he'd explained, 'I had a dream . . . a sort of dream. I was fourteen, just left school that summer . . .'

'I take it that means Joe was fourteen? Or did you bunk off from school?'

'No. I didn't. Joe was fourteen. I'd gone into Winstanton to find my dad. He'd not come home for two days. The local pubs had all banned him. He used to come into The Glass. I had to find him.'

'Why?' I'd asked bluntly. 'According to you, the bloke was a child-beating drunk. Why'd you want him back?'

'I can't exactly r-remember now. I think it was something to do with the landlord.'

'Of the pub?'

'I'm not sure.'

'Does it matter?' Annie had asked before telling Stuart to go on. 'Was he in the pub?'

'No. I looked in the door. I could smell the beer. And the smoke. I swear I could. As clearly as I c-can smell the fish I cooked this evening. So I went to the beach. He used to sleep it off on the beach. It was dark, just the starlight, and I was watching where I put my feet. There were more boats, pulled up on the shingle. More than now, I mean. And oyster baskets. I nearly fell over him. Vomit r-running out one end and worse c-coming out the other. And I knew when he sobered up he'd be worse. Maudlin and disgusting and swearing he'd never do it again. And I just saw this rock and I . . .' Bunching both hands above his head, he'd brought them down several times, pounding the life out of a section of air in front of his knees. The space was well and truly pulverised before he caught himself up and made a visible effort to relax. 'That's all I r-remember until I woke up in the morning here. I assumed it had all been a bad dream.'

It was Annie who prompted him again. 'Wasn't it?'

'Not all of it. I had an early start that morning. I was driving to meet a client. So I'd pressed a pair of trousers and polished my shoes the previous night.'

Ironing! Shoe polish! Oh, boy, was this not my sort of guy!

'When I went to dress, they were damp and stained with salt. I'd been out. I really had been on that beach.'

'And bashed someone's head in?' I asked. I'd thought I sounded professionally interested. The second kick from Annie suggested not.

'No. Of c-course not. But I looked. I walked the length of Winstanton beach trying to find a body. And all the time I was in the car, driving to my meeting, I had the news channel on. I kept expecting to hear that a body had been washed back on the tide. It was weeks before I started to really believe I hadn't killed someone.'

'Did you sleep-walk before, Stuart?' Annie asked. 'Before the hypnotherapy, I mean.'

'No. At least . . . I think I remember my mother tying the bedroom window shut so I couldn't c-climb out on the sill when I was about five. I suppose it could have been because I sleep-walked.'

'Could you check with her?'

'Both my parents are dead.'

'Brother? Sister? Aunts? Uncles?'

'No.' Despite the fact it was Annie showing the interest, he'd still asked me again if I'd take the case. 'You see, if we really are born again and again, then perhaps the good and evil in us are reborn too. Maybe Joe wasn't the first.'

'You mean you could have bashed in skulls through the ages.'

'Yes.'

'And if you have?'

'I don't know. Psychiatric help perhaps.'

'Take my tip here, Stuart. Cut out the middle-woman. Go straight for the touchdown.'

'Grace!' Annie glared.

'No. It's okay. That's precisely why I need Grace to do this. Shall I write out the deposit cheque?'

He knew the way to my heart. Even then I back-pedalled slightly, pointing out that Joe (surname unknown) from (location unknown) killing female (identity unknown) on an unspecified date wasn't much to go on. He could end up paying me for thousands of hours (please, God!) of work.

'That's not important. And I have more of Tabitha's session t-tapes that will fill in some of those blanks.'

So I'd agreed. I'd done my best to stop him wasting his money, but if the dingbat wanted to pay me to chase ghosts who was I to argue?

Annie nagged me all the way back to Seatoun on my lack of professionalism. Once she'd dropped me off at my flat, I negotiated my way around the large needle-sharp succulents that had been lurking by my front door for the past couple of months (despite the large PLEASE STEAL ME sign I'd hung round them), drew the curtains, switched all the lights on and tipped out Stuart's tapes.

To play or not to play? That was the question.

6

In the end, it wasn't the power of the supernatural that thwarted my efforts to join the ranks of the ghostbusters. It was the power of the AA MN1 500-LR6 battery. Or rather the lack of it. The cassette player proved to be deader than Stuart's supposed victim. I'd bought it at a car boot sale and the mains adaptor hadn't been included in the deal.

I hitched my bag and sorted out my car keys with the intention of using the player in the car. Since it was out of season, I'd managed to park in my own road – albeit down the other end. I was trotting along, bag in one hand, ignition key in the other, when headlights spilled over my shoulder, illuminating the tarmac road surface and picking out the basement railings. There's something about the engine of a police vehicle. Without turning round, I knew that the force behind those lights sported a go-faster stripe and a natty blue light. I kept walking.

They cruised level with me just as I cruised level with my car. I didn't recognise the officer in the passenger seat, but I'd have known the driver even if he hadn't chosen to pull up, lower the window, and bawl, 'Oi, Smithie, come over here.'

Constable T. Rosco; not so much a man, more a god who walked amongst women (in Terry's private delusions).

I took my time to slouch across and bend to their level. 'You called, oh silver-tongued one?'

Rosco's nose twitched. So did the other officer's. I couldn't say I entirely blamed them. Until that point I'd been immune to the effects of a bottle of Chardonnay, a couple of brandies and a Cointreau-lashed chocolate tart. Now the freshening night breeze blew a blast of my own boozy breath back into my nostrils.

'You ain't thinking of driving, are you, Smithie?'

'What, *moi*? Terry, perish the thought.'

'Only if you was, we'd have to nick you, wouldn't we, Nev?'

I smiled warmly at Nev. He was very young, very sweet and very desperate to look tough.

'It's an offence to be drunk in charge of a vehicle on the public highway, madam,' he said sternly. 'Even if the said vehicle is not moving.'

I widened my eyes. 'You don't say, officer.' I slid the palm of my hand down my trouser seam and felt the outline of the ignition key which I'd dropped into my pocket the minute I'd heard that engine swinging into the road.

'She knows that,' Terry said. 'She used to be in the job. She's the one I told you about. Grasses to pond-life.'

'You must have me mixed up with someone else, Terry. I have no interest in botany or biology, I promise you, Nev. My, aren't you cute?'

I was leaning with one hand on the car top. I used the free one to run a couple of fingers down Nev's fuzz-free chin. The poor kid jumped like I was attached to the National Grid. 'Knock it off. I mean, please don't do that, madam.'

'Push off, Smithie. And remember what I said. Touch the car – you're nicked. Let's roll up TED's, Nev. They get some top tottie up there.'

The Electric Daffodil (aka TED's) was a surprisingly upmarket nightclub for Seatoun and did indeed attract top tottie. Who knows, some of them might have even been drunk – or spaced out – enough to fancy Terry as much as he fancied himself. But they weren't going to get the chance tonight. My ears were sufficiently attuned to the patrol car's engine to distinguish it above the all-pervading shush of the sea and the desultory traffic along the promenade. Terry had parked up a mere turning away and left the motor running. I knew he'd come back in a few minutes and if I was sitting in my car with the ignition on, albeit simply listening to the cassette, he would arrest me.

It would never come to a charge, but he would waste several hours taking me up the police station, arranging to breathalyse me and carrying on an interview that would end up being binned. I had a busy day tomorrow, starting with the delivery of several court summonses. I needed my sleep. And I wouldn't get it in Seatoun's police station. The car cassette was a non-starter.

There was a general grocery store near the flat that sold batteries (and everything else) at exorbitant prices. But since they were going on Stuart's bill anyway, I decided to splash out. It wasn't until I saw the row of metal shutters reflecting starlight that it occurred to me to look at my watch. It was gone midnight.

Now I was on a roll, I was reluctant to turn back. I made my way down towards the sea with the intention of seeing if I could locate an open kiosk along the promenade. An unwelcoming row of steel grilles climbed the hill towards the harbour and shopping area, broken by the underpass leading to the amusement park and the steps to the Art-Geeko-style cinema. The only sounds were drunken shouts being bawled somewhere, the always-present roll and slap of the waves and the thrum of an occasional car or motorbike engine. In high season and school holidays, the arcades thundered with eardrum-splitting sound systems, the park's rides rattled and crashed, and the souvenir shops, cafés and fast-food kiosks stayed open eighteen hours a day under a garish illumination of liquid neon in swirling signs that flashed from dusk until 4 a.m. At twenty past midnight on a Tuesday at the end of October not even the cinema could be bothered to run a late show.

The temperature had plunged and sea breezes were piercing my triple X-sized silk blouse like needles. The alcohol was indicating it was time to lie down. I thought the whole job was a figment of Stuart's imagination anyway.

'Screw you, Terry,' I said to the night. Spinning round, I stalked home.

The court summonses were all real pains. By the time I'd finished getting close enough to their recipients to slap skin and pronounce them 'served' it was late afternoon. I'd brought Stuart's psycho-tapes along with me, intending to listen to them as I drove, but I'd ended up doing a tailing number on two of the jobs, so I decided to put them on hold until I could concentrate and take notes properly. Now I could, I still hesitated. I was due at Arlene's by six. There were five thirty-minute tapes. If they were full that was two and a half hours of listening. And if I had to keep stopping them to take notes, I'd be well past six. On balance it seemed sensible to postpone my date with Joe-and-corpses-I-have-known until after I'd waved Arlene on her way.

I went home, picked up a toothbrush, a change of underwear and the carrier holding Waterloo's bone, and headed out for Arlene's. Despite having known her for several years, I'd never been to her home before. It proved to be one of a row of half a dozen bungalows that stood alone at the very far end of North Bay beyond the built-up areas and Waterloo's favourite area for a spot of cliff diving. In front of the bungalows was a wide stretch of coarse hillocky grass that terminated in the wavering wire fencing at the cliff edge. The land behind had been the same once but a few years ago it had been developed as an exclusive golf course.

I crawled the Micra along the short road, reading house numbers. Each of the bungalows was painted a sugar almond shade. Arlene's proved to be the pale cream one that was second from the end. Her car pulled in behind me as I was parking.

'I'm running late, babes. Come in while I grab a shower and show you my best boy's things.'

The beast in question decanted himself out of her back seat, trotted over to sniff my trainer, lifted one leg – and thought better of it when he saw me draw back the other trainer.

Arlene opened the wrought-iron gate, led the way up the neat crazy-paved path and opened the front door. She scooped up the post from the doormat and indicated the case beside it. 'I'm all packed. Won't keep you waiting long. 'Ave a look round. Make yourself at home. Lounge is in here . . .' She opened the first door on the left of the corridor, clicked on the lights – and revealed a total surprise.

I'd fantasised that Arlene's home would reflect the donkey-jacket, bovver-boot personality that smashed iron bars into submission. But the room I was standing in was a delicate symphony of creams and gold. The walls and carpets were pale cream, the big windows overlooking the front garden were swathed in heavy ivory silk trimmed with gold edging and rope tie-backs, the sofas were plumply cushioned in clotted cream satins, the glass dining table was ringed by delicate chairs on spindly gold legs, the chandelier lights twinkled with crystal drops hanging from gold mountings. Even the child's high chair drawn up to the table gleamed under a coating of metallic gloss. I wondered who used it. She'd never mentioned a family.

'This is . . . lovely, Arlene. Did you get it all from the dump?'

'No, babes. I never bring anything home. I see enough of other people's rubbish all day. Only thing I ever brought out of that place was mumsie's best baby. Ain't that so, you little smasher?' Stooping on one knee, she took Waterloo's jaw between both palms and wriggled the loose skin before planting a kiss on his muzzle. 'Now, you be a good boy for Auntie Gracie-Wacie, won't you? Bedroom's down here,' she said, straightening up and returning to her normal brisk tone. She threw open the other door on that side of the corridor. The room with its fitted furniture and double bed continued the gold and cream theme. 'I changed all the bed linen for yer.'

'You want me to use your room?'

'You'll have to. The other's my baby's. Which reminds me. Don't shut the door on him at night, he don't like it.' She picked up a large vase full of white arum lilies and held it out to me. 'Is that water off?'

I took a deep breath over the vase rim and pronounced it okay.

'Chuck 'em if you don't like the scent. I know some people don't. It don't bother me. I've hardly any sense of smell these days. It comes in handy, working the dump.'

Must have been an added bonus when it came to sharing with the mutt too, I thought.

'Kitchen's here.' It ran along the back, taking up the space not used by Arlene's bedroom. She turned back towards the front and opened the first door on the right-hand side, which proved to be the bathroom. It was more cream and gold glitz, this time reflected through the tiling, ceramics, power-shower cubicle and sunken corner bath with its dolphin-shaped gold taps and jacuzzi. 'I'm just going to get out of me muck. Shan't be long.'

As soon as she turned the water on, I couldn't resist taking a look in the last room. It continued the creamy theme but was empty apart from a large chest labelled WATERLOO, a stainless-steel water bowl sitting on a plastic mat and a four-poster bed – dog size – complete with mattress, frilly lace-trimmed duvet and pillows, and swathes of muslin falling from a huge pink satin bow to form the curtaining.

Waterloo had followed me to the door. As I turned back to look at him, he dropped his head and refused to meet my eye.

'Well, who's a soft little wassock?' I murmured, re-passing him and closing the door.

I went back to the lounge and checked for a music centre that I could use for the tapes later. There wasn't one, but I discovered a cassette slot in the clock radio by Arlene's bed. Exploring the kitchen, I located a bulldog-shaped cookie jar, helped myself to a couple of chocolate biscuits and opened the back door to take a look.

Night was well on its way. There was just enough greyness left in the sky for me to make out the paler blur of the sand bunkers in the golf course beyond the wooden back fences. Each of the bungalows had a long narrow garden. Arlene's oblong was laid out with lawns and a narrow strip of flower bed either side of a central path that terminated in a small garden shed. It was the garden of someone who wanted to do little more than push the mower around once a week.

My view of the left-hand premises was obscured by a high fence, but the window lights falling over the garden on the right revealed bushes and shrubs grouped in different-shaped beds and rustic arbours covered with whatever plants climbed over arbours.

In the interests of establishing a friendly truce, I un-wrapped Stuart's bone and waggled it under Waterloo's nose. 'Look what I've got for you, eh? Fetch!'

I bowled it down the garden. It ricocheted off the shed

roof and soared into next-door's bushes. I could have sworn the dog sniggered.

'You ready, babes?'

Arlene had jettisoned the jacket and jeans for a tight-fitting cream jumper and matching flared skirt and a wide gold belt.

'Me train's at seven. I done you a list of what's what. It's got the hospital numbers on and everything. Shouldn't be in there more than three or four days, the docs reckon. Any problems with the house, Edith's got the numbers of me plumber or whatever.'

'Edith?'

'Next door.' She paused from coaxing Waterloo into the back of my car to jerk a thumb at the bungalow I'd just lobbed the bone into. 'Edith Halliwell. She's the original.'

'As opposed to what?' I enquired, pulling away. 'The Edith Halliwell clones?'

'Don't be daft. I mean she's always been here. Owned the house they pulled down to build the bungalows. Can you keep an eye out? She's nippy enough but you never know. The old girl must be over ninety.'

'She live alone?'

'Yeah. Family keep trying to get her to move to one of them sheltered flats but she won't have it. Comes over a bit posh school-mistressy sometimes and goes on about the past something chronic if you let her. Best to have somewhere else to go. I always say my baby needs to spend a penny. Don't I, baby?' She dragged the mutt off the back seat to give him another smacker. They kept up the mutual slobber performance until I pulled into the station forecourt and saw her out of the car.

'I'll ring the hospital,' I promised. 'Tomorrow. See how you're doing.'

'Say you're me niece. They don't give out much unless you're family.'

'Okay. See you then.'

'Yes.' Her glance slid round to Waterloo whom we'd left

47

shut in the car and who was now leaping all over the back seat, barking in disapproval of this arrangement. 'You'll take care of him, won't you, babes?'

'Trust me, Arlene. He'll be fine.'

'Yeah. Okay. I'll let you get back. I left some fillet steak in the fridge for supper.'

'Cheers, Arlene.'

'You have some too if he can't manage the lot. See you, babes.' She gave me a casual, brisk smile and trotted inside with her case. It was a brave performance that didn't fool either of us.

Life as a responsible dog owner proved to be more taxing than I'd anticipated. By the time I'd persuaded Waterloo he really preferred tinned dog food to fillet steak – I shut him in his room whilst I ate it; there's nothing like a choice between Chunky Cuts and an empty bowl for concentrating the canine mind – dragged him out for a run on the scrubby grassland, made the mistake of letting him off the lead and spent a further hour chasing him over the golf course and most of the next with a torch, a poop scoop and a plastic bag, I was pretty well ready to curl up in bed with a good book, preferably one entitled *The UK Guide to Animal Sanctuaries – A Thousand and One Places to Dump the Doggie*.

Locking up, I turned off the lights, hauled Waterloo into his girly pad, got myself a glass of red wine and curled up in Arlene's double bed. Tipping Stuart's cassettes from my bag, I spread them across the cream embroidered duvet cover and wondered where to start.

For the first time I noticed they had markings on them. In daylight I'd missed them, but under the artificial gleam of the bedside lamps, I caught a slick of rainbow. Picking one up, I held it at an angle under the lampshade. The figure '3', scratched in Biro on the shiny plastic casing, was just about visible. I checked the others and made out a '1', '4' and '5'. I'd kept the tape Stuart had played Annie and me last night in a separate pocket in the bag. Hooking it up now, I checked the front and found the figure '2'. Did the numbers relate to the sequence of Stuart's sessions with the inept Tabitha (Trade In Your Psychosis for a Brand-New Model), or were they simply left over from a previous use of the tapes? I guessed there was only one way to know for certain. Inserting number 1 into the clock radio, I pushed the 'play' button.

7

'Are you warm?'
  'Mmm.'
  'And sleepy?'
  'Not sleepy.'
  'That's good. Can you tell me your name?'
  'Joe.'
  'Just Joe?'
  'Joseph Gumbright.'
  'How old are you, Joe?'
  'Ten.'
  'Where are you, Joe?'
  'Rook Farm.'
  'Is it your father's farm?'
  'Well, it's Mr Cazlett's by rights, but moy dad rents it.'
  'What kind of farm is it, Joe?'
  'Ordinary sort of farm. Same as the others.'
  'No. I mean, what do you grow on it?'
  ''Ops. Mostly 'ops. Got a few apples but they ain't fruiting much.'
  'Ops?'
  ''Ops. For the brewery.'
  'Oh, hops. I understand. Is it a big farm?'
  'No. Haven't got our own oats. Have to use Mr Cazlett's.'
  'I see. Can you tell me what the date is?'
  'It's the end of April. They just started walking the stilts.'

49

'Why do they need stilts?'

'Stilts for the wiremen. For the bines. Don't you know nothing?'

'Right. Wiremen. Do you know what year you were born, Joe?'

'1921.'

'So this must be 1931?'

'S'right.'

'Where are you now, Joe?'

'Told you. At home. In bed.'

'Is anyone else there?'

'Gran's in the other bedroom. She don't come downstairs no more. She's sick. She smells. She's knocking on the floor. She oughtn't to do that. She knows it makes him madder.'

'Makes who?'

'My dad. He'll go on longer now. Don't let her die. Please, God, don't let her die.'

'Let who, Joe? What's happening?'

'Billie's come in my bed. She can hear it too. If we sing we won't hear. "Baa-baa black sheep, have you any wool . . . ?"'

'Joe, stop it. Stop singing.'

'I don't want to. We won't hear, we won't hear. Make him stop. He's killing her.'

'Who is he killing? Is it your grandmother, Joe? Is your father hurting her? What's happening now?'

'It's gone quiet. I can't hear nothing.'

'What are you doing?'

'Waiting.'

'For what?'

'He's coming. He's coming. Got to be quiet. Get under the covers. He's outside the door. Mustn't move. Breathe slowly. Pretend to be asleep. The door's opening. There's light through my eyelids. I . . .'

At that point an earthly howl of anguish jerked the hairs on the back of my neck to attention and sent ice-cold invisible ants skittering along my back and down my arms.

8

Once my heart had stopped bungee-jumping between my throat and my bowels and returned to base, I kicked my way out of the cosy nest I'd snuggled into under the duvet and padded across to the bedroom door. Ripping it open, I glared down at the source of my near-coronary.

'You howled?'

Waterloo yawned, displaying a jaw stretch that could have swallowed a small donkey. He pushed past me and padded into the room. Shimmying over to the bed, he heaved his forequarters up and then used his front paws and mouth to drag himself over the shiny coverlet whilst his back legs fished for a foothold.

'Oh, no, you don't! Get back to your own room!'

I grabbed his collar and attempted to heave him off. Waterloo twisted on to his back and wriggled. I tried dragging him that way but got worried I was choking him. Releasing him resulted in him flipping over and seizing a mouthful of duvet. There was no way the material would stand up to a tug of war with those jaws. Cunning was called for. In this case it came in the shape of a digestive. 'Look. Nice biscuit.'

Waterloo's ears pricked. I frisbeed the goodie into the hall. Waterloo sprang after it. I slammed the door after him. One to girl-power, nil to the canine.

Clambering back into the bed, I resettled the covers and depressed the cassette's 'play' button again. The room was filled with the sound of hissing static. I rewound to check if it was a fault, but apparently not. I'd already heard all there was on tape 1. Tabitha must start a new one with each session, which made sense, I suppose, if she needed to differentiate between what was said when. From what I'd heard so far it would seem that Stuart's sessions were probably classified by their position in the chronology of Joe's life rather than the dates of Stuart's appointments.

Otherwise why would she have been asking the seventeen-year-old Joe who Billie was when his ten-year-old self had already told her?

I grabbed hold of my thoughts. What the hell was I doing? Treating all this rubbish as if it were real, that's what. 'Oh, *please*,' I wailed out loud.

Beating up my subconscious was brought to an abrupt halt by an unearthly howling from the other side of the door. I ignored it. It increased in intensity. Was I going to be intimidated by a blackmailing canine?

Too right. After fifteen minutes I surrendered and opened the door.

'You sleep on the floor. Got it?'

Waterloo curled a contemptuous lip, hauled himself back on the bed and spun himself a comfy hollow. I had three choices – the floor, a quarter-sized four-poster or double-dating. I switched off the lamps.

'Don't you dare pinch my share of the duvet.'

I woke early because I usually did in a strange bed, and having four stone on my feet cutting off the circulation worked better than an alarm call. The first thing I did was throw open all the windows. I have to admit this wasn't an entirely unusual experience. But at least this time I could blame it on the dog instead of a late night detour via the local curry house.

Arlene's list of instructions indicated that her baby had to be let out first thing to attend to doggy matters. Dragging on jogging bottoms and sweatshirt over the T-shirt I'd slept in, I trotted across the road to the hillocky stretch of verge between the bungalow and the cliff fencing. It was just becoming light, with a greyness struggling to fight against a sea mist that was clinging in patches to parts of the headland. Without warning Waterloo attempted to drag my shoulder out of its socket.

At full charge and off balance, I couldn't stop. I had to keep running to avoid being dragged flat on my face into the dew-sodden grass. When we came to a halt we were half a mile downhill from the bungalow, my right arm had stretched several inches and I'd established the mutt had never been taught the meaning of 'sit', 'stay', 'whoa' and 'disembowelling'.

Sticking his nose down, he started sniffing and exploring every square metre in sight until I finally lost patience. 'What are you looking for? A luxury heated sod with quilted loo paper and automated flush? One tuft is exactly the same as the rest. Now squat!'

I put a trainer on his rump and pushed. After a token resistance, he finally dumped. Shivering in the early dew, I did the business with the scoop and plastic bag then hauled him home. Heading inside, I shook out some dried dog food for Waterloo and considered my options. A full – and varied – choice in the fridge was a rare treat for me since my shopping tended towards the desperate-and-grab-it style. I settled on cornflakes, followed by bacon and tomatoes and rounded off by toast and marmalade. Magic!

It was also time to get back to Stuart and his *alter ego*. Rather than play the rest of the tapes, I decided to make notes of what I'd discovered so far. Even if Stuart was totally off his trolley, there might be a germ of reality in his delusions. Taking out my notebook, I set down what I'd got so far whilst I spooned up flakes:

Joseph Gumbright/ Gumbrite(?)	: Born 1921
Billie(?) Gumbright	: Born 1926 (?)
Dad Gumbright	: Drunk by the sounds of it. Also violent.
Mum Gumbright	: Probably walked out on family around 1933
Gran ? (mother's mother)	: Probably died 1933
Rook Farm	: Gumbrights tenant farmers. Grew hops.
Cazletts/Cazlitts (?)	: Owned Rook Farm

Mrs Slack	: Ran village shop
Carol Slack	: Billie's best friend. (Prob same age?)
The Glass	: Possibly pub in Winstanton
Tyler's Lane	: Ran over Rook Farm
Unknown female	: Dead somewhere in Tyler's Lane

'So, on the evidence so far, Stuart wants me to investigate an alleged murder that occurred in 1938,' I informed Waterloo. 'Victim unknown, murderer, possibly reincarnated as mild-mannered accountant. Mulder and Scully, eat your heart out!'

Setting the frying-pan over a low heat, I went back to the bedroom. There was a small bookcase within the fitted suite but a quick check revealed that apart from a street atlas of the Greater London area and a book entitled *The Meaning of Names*, it held only paperbacks full of moist-lipped, bosom-heaving heroines and firm-jawed heroes who all seemed to be dynamic single millionaires. I recalled there was a squashy leather footstool in the front lounge – the sort that sometimes had a storage area inside – and went to investigate. Waterloo ambled along after me. As soon as we entered the room, he scrambled up into that kid's high chair I'd been wondering about and dribbled over the glass table.

At first glance the footstool appeared to be stuffed full of back copies of those celebrity gossip mags. I waded through various celeb couples showing us around their 'lovely home in Italy', 'fabulous home in Colorado', 'sumptuous home in New York' and 'magnificent home in London'. I excavated a bit further and struck gold in the bottom. In addition to the local telephone directory and *Yellow Pages* there were also several maps covering this and the neighbouring areas. I carried them back to the kitchen. The bacon was crisping up nicely. I flipped it and set out bottles of ketchup and brown sauce. Waterloo whined.

'What you need,' I informed him, 'is some healthy exercise to get rid of all that ugly fat. Mind you, given that that description covers just about all of you, you'd have to pretty well disappear up your own backside. But give it a go.' I opened the back door. Waterloo wandered out. Dog management – piece of cake.

I started with the directory. And came up against a blank wall immediately. There were no Gumbrights/Gumbrites listed at all. I tried any possible variations of the name but still came up with zilch. However, there were two 'Slacks' and Cazlitt proved even more profitable with two Casletts, one Cazlitt and three Cazletts. The *Yellow Pages* had nothing listed under 'Hotels and Inns' with the word 'glass' in its name, although I did find one public house trading under the name 'Half Glassed'. Since it was miles from Winstanton it didn't seem too hopeful, but I dutifully added it to the list in my notebook anyway. I had to have something to justify the fees I was going to charge Stuart and I had this perception of accountants as people who liked everything set down in black and white.

The fry-up had now achieved the blackened-round-the-edges texture I favoured. Sliding the lot on a plate, I did a samba impression with the two sauce bottles until the surface resembled a Damien Hirst collectible and prepared to dive in. Waterloo materialised at my knee. He whined piteously. I stuck two pieces of kitchen towel in my ears and unfolded the maps. Starting at Winstanton, I let my eyes move outwards in a circular pattern. If Pa Gumbright drank there, then logically Rook Farm shouldn't be more than a reasonable drive away.

At forty miles out I found what I was expecting to find – exactly nothing. There were no farms called 'Rook' or anything similar. Tyler's Lane was less certain because only the large ones were marked and it could have been any one of several hundred threads of colour wriggling over the contours. But I'd have bet money it wasn't.

Arlene's phone was an overly decorated ivory and gold

job located in the bedroom. Any further delving would just have to wait until I'd finished eating my grease mountain.

I toasted two thick slices of bread, spread butter and marmalade lavishly, poured another shot of tea, removed the kitchen towel from my ears and switched the radio on. Leaning my chair back on two legs, I stuck my feet up on another chair and contemplated the sun breaking through the clouds to glint off a golf bunker. It was a great life when you were living at someone else's expense.

Eventually I reluctantly arranged my dirty crockery and frying-pan over the tiled floor of the shower, stripped off, climbed in, turned the taps on as hot as I could bear and squeezed washing-up liquid over all of us. Five minutes later we were all grease-free and I was ready to exercise my dialling finger.

I rang The Half Glassed first. The landlord confirmed it had been called The Crooked Mile until recently. And in any event it had only been built twenty years ago. Posing as a tracer of my supposed family tree, I tackled the two Slacks next. Both were elderly and pleased to have someone to talk to. Neither had any relatives called 'Carol' nor could they recall an ancestor who'd run a village shop. They were, however, almost pathetically eager to help, dredging up endless possible connections, offering to contact distant relatives and forward all pertinent information. I gave them the office address. It had been a hard hour's work. My ear was sore. (Arlene would undoubtedly be even sorer when she saw her phone bill.) I decided I deserved a cup of coffee. And perhaps a few chocolate digestives?

The mist had been driven off and the sun was well up now. It was really rather pleasant strolling the back garden with my elevenses, watching the golfers teeing off beyond the fence and the gulls' spiteful squabbles over the remains of a packet of chips. The other gardens were empty and the row had the deserted air of nine-to-five workers' homes. Which might have been true for the rest, but surely the old girl next door ought to be in? It set my mind off on another possible path to Gumbright gulley.

I left the mutt shut in the kitchen and walked round to Mrs Halliwell's. My good idea came to nothing with no answer to my leaning on the bell. Putting it on hold for now, I returned to the task of racking up Arlene's phone bill. In fairness I rang Moorfields first to ask after her progress but got no more than that she was still down in recovery and to ring back later. Conscience cleared, I settled down to work through the Cazletts and similar.

One Caslett wasn't answering, the other was apologetic but they'd only moved into the area two years ago from their previous address in Northampton.

The Cazlitts were called Simon and Camilla and had duetted on a bright jingly answerphone message that conjured up steel and chrome sushi bars and endless dinner parties moaning about au pairs and ski resorts. I left a message asking them to ring me back.

The first Cazlett I dialled took so long to answer I was about to try number two on the list when the receiver was lifted and a female voice said, 'Yes?'

I launched into my prepared family-tracing speech again. Before I'd got thirty seconds into the spiel, she said, 'Yes. But wha' do you *wan*'?'

There was a plaintive wail in her voice that implied I'd interrupted a date with a bottle. I've always found that subtlety is lost on the plastered. 'Did your family rent out a Rook Farm to a family called Gumbright? This would have been in the late 1930s.'

'God, I don' know. Ask Greville.'

'I'd love to. Could you pass the phone over to him?'

'I s'pose so.'

There was the sound of something falling and breaking and the soft murmur of irritation. I waited. Nothing happened. Eventually I hung up.

The next Cazlett wasn't answering and number three thought it was unlikely her husband's family were the ones I was looking for since they'd come over from France in the 1950s.

It had been a reasonably productive morning. I rewarded myself with a leisurely dog-walking trip down into Seatoun for a visit to the bank and late lunch in my favourite café, followed by a call at the library to ask after old maps of the area. It turned out our small local branch didn't hold any and I'd have to try a larger branch with microfiched archives. I took Waterloo down on to the beach and strode along amongst the worm casts, drifts of tiny white shells and dried seaweed whilst he did his best to drag me into the incoming rollers. I was uncomfortably aware that I should have made contact with the office to pick up my messages and see if anyone else wished to offer me gainful employment. But I didn't want to. In fact, I'd caught myself deliberately avoiding it over the past few weeks. In hatching my brilliant plan to get Vetch to make Annie a junior partner in order to prevent her relocating to London, I hadn't considered the effect the new set-up might have on Vetch's Investigations. Streamlining, business plans and twenty-first-century efficiency weren't my style. I liked slobbing along. I wanted to slob into retirement. Slobbing was my *raison d'être*. In persuading Annie to stay, had I put myself top of the list to leave Vetch's instead?

9

By the time I got back to the bungalow, Arlene was back on the ward and 'comfortable'. I left a message that her niece had called and the baby was fine and eating like a dog.

Next I called Ruby, a local pensioner I knew, who was happy to spend hours in the warmth of the public library sifting out information for an hourly fee. I explained what I needed. 'Any reports in the local papers for 1938 about missing females, females found dead in mysterious circumstances or even females classified as natural deaths other than old age. Okay?'

'Righty-oh,' Ruby cooed in that drips-warm-honey voice that could have earned her a fortune on sex telephone lines. 'But the local library don't have anything older than ten years. Not the room, you see. I'll have to pack up a few sandwiches and catch the bus to a bigger place. Might have to make a few trips. Any time limit on this, Smithie, love?'

'None at all,' I assured her, recklessly spending some more of Stuart's money. 'In fact, treat yourself to lunch somewhere nice and stick the receipt in with the papers.'

'Ooh, lovely. Be in touch soon. Byeee.'

I shut the mutt in the kitchen and tried Edith Halliwell next door again. There was no answer to my first few rings and I was turning away when I caught the rattle of a safety chain being engaged.

Edith was surprisingly tall for her age, given the spine's usual habit of compressing and arching with time. Her wrists and legs had the bony thinness of old age, but her white hair looked to be still strong and thick from what I could see within the three-inch gap through which she was regarding me.

Her voice was firm too. 'May I help you? I should tell you I do not buy from the doorstep. Nor do I care to take part in surveys.'

'Really. I usually make up the answers myself.' I introduced myself as Arlene's house-sitter and mutt-minder.

'Of course, dear. She did mention you were coming. Do you have any news yet?'

I relayed the comfortable message. 'But I did want to pick your brains. If you don't mind?'

'That sounds interesting. Do come in.'

She ushered me into a lounge the same size as Arlene's. But it seemed far smaller due to the large old-fashioned pieces of furniture and the overwhelming plethora of photographs that were occupying every available surface and most of the walls.

'Do sit down. May I offer you some refreshment? Tea? Or a small sherry?'

'Whatever you're having, thanks.'

Thankfully she chose tea and left me to browse whilst she went to the kitchen to brew up. The place was wall-to-wall family occasions – confirmations, weddings, christenings, birthdays, holidays, schooldays, dancing classes. You name it and the Halliwells had recorded it for posterity in everything from faded sepia to glorious digital colour since Edith had started the dynasty back in the 1920s, judging by the flat-chested, unattractive wedding dress. The fading wedding photo showed a tall, plain girl with a handsome new husband. The thick hair was in much the same unflattering heavy-fringed, bobbed style as now, although it had been black then. Edith came in with the tea-tray as I stood browsing. I made suitable admiring noises and remarked on the size of her family.

'I have four children, nine grandchildren, twenty-two great-grandchildren and *two great-great*-grandchildren.' She said with that self-congratulatory tone people use when listing unfettered breeding.

She handed me my tea. It was all dead proper – embroidered tray doilies, bone china cups, milk in a jug, a plate of shortbreads, even real silver sugar tongs.

'And do you have children, dear?'

'No. I've got a couple of nieces,' I offered, since she looked disappointed.

'Oh, how *delightful*. I so wanted a little girl. But I had sons. Here they are . . . Frank, Cedric, James and Morgan.'

They were four glum kids bundled into short-trousered old-fashioned suits. I made more admiring noises. It was all the encouragement she needed to start detailing who was who; who'd married who; who'd fathered who; who was going to marry who . . .

I smiled, nodded and waited for a chance to jump in.

Eventually she made a reference to a photograph on the rear wall. It was one of the few non-portraits, showing a large rambling house with timber-framed balconies standing alone on a headland. It was possible to make out the far curve of the bay leading to Seatoun in the distance.

'Arlene said your house had been pulled down to make room for the bungalows. You must have been gut . . . very upset.'

'A little. My father had it built, you see. But it was my own choice. It really was far too large for one person and, of course, one can't get domestic servants any more.'

'Bloody hell . . .' It sort of slipped out before my brain could shout 'Zip it' to my mouth. I felt I had to elaborate. 'I've never met anyone who had a real servant.'

Edith assured me they'd *only* had a general cook and a daily maid.

'It was quite common when I was a young woman. We weren't *grand*, people had a maid in the same way they have a washing machine these days. Of course, the washing machine is more reliable but it's not nearly as entertaining. Our cook used to know all the local gossip.'

'Yeah, quite. I was sort of wondering if—'

Edith ploughed on. 'I do rather miss that. And having another woman in the house all the time. Well, except Wednesday afternoons, of course. Wednesday was the servants' half-day. They used to go to the pictures and then have a fish-and-chip supper. I should have liked to do that, but naturally they would never have invited me. Anyway, there wouldn't have been anyone here for the boys when they came home from school . . .'

'Could I just ask if—'

'But that was many years ago. When I sold the house I'd already shut up most of the rooms. My sons said they were unsafe. And it was so cold, bitterly so in the winter. Fuel is so expensive these days, isn't it? The central heating is a blessing and it only seems different if I'm looking in. When I'm looking out it really makes no difference at all.'

'I guess not. If—'

'However, having a smaller house does tend to make one aware of the *emptiness*. I suppose with the old house one's mind rather pretended there were still people in the other rooms. But the bungalow is so quiet. I used to have dogs. Fox terriers. Rollo was my favourite. He was *such* good company. But sadly he died. And I'm too old to get another one. It wouldn't be fair when I can't exercise him properly.'

I stuffed in several shortbreads and listened patiently whilst Edith rambled on about Rollo's amusing little tricks, plus his predecessors' equally amusing antics, all punctuated by her searching amongst the numerous frames for pictures of said treasures. Finally we came full circle to, 'I'm too old to get another one.'

'You could always get something else,' I suggested. 'A cat? Budgie?'

'Sadly I'm allergic to cats. And I have never been able to abide birds. They give me the chills.' She gave a slight shiver and massaged the tops of her arms.

I dived in fast before she could wander off down memory lane again. 'I was wondering . . . you must have been living here in the 1930s . . . could I run a few names past you . . . see if you recognise any of them?'

'Certainly you may, dear.' She folded her hands in her lap and sat up straight. In much the same way I expect she'd have done eighty-odd years ago when the teacher quizzed her in a spelling test.

'Gumbright?'

Her forehead puckered. Concentration unfocused her eyes. Eventually she shook her head regretfully. 'No. I'm sorry. What is it? A toothpaste?'

Now she'd said it, I realised it very well could be the sort of unimaginative brand name dreamt up by some early toiletries manufacturer. Was Stuart working out some long buried subconscious resentment at being forced to brush his teeth three times a day? Oh, hell – why did I ever take this case? Because you've just paid an extortionately large deposit cheque into your account, that's why, I reminded myself. I tried Edith on Rook Farm.

'No,' she said slowly. 'I don't believe I know that either. Is it a local farm?'

'That's what I'm trying to find out. How about Cazlett?'

'Oh? Oh, dear.' Something very like a blush passed over her papery cheeks.

'Old friends?' I prompted. 'Old enemies?'

'Oh, no, nothing like that. Not enemies. Not friends. More acquaintances. Nothing more. Really nothing more. We used to see them at social occasions sometimes. Dinners and dances. He belonged to the same committees and clubs as my father and husband, you see. Well, one did. It wasn't snobbery. It's just that people felt more comfortable mixing with those of the same . . .'

'Class?'

'Yes. I suppose so. It all sounds rather silly now, I dare say. But social connections were important. Medical treatment wasn't free then, you see.'

She'd lost me. 'The Cazletts were doctors?'

'No. Good heavens, no. Is that what I said? Oh, dear. I do get so muddled sometimes. My sons say I'll forget my head . . . No, it was Papa who was the doctor. Rather a well-known one. He had papers read out even though he was only a GP. And, of course, my dear Bertram came to be his partner. That's how we met.'

So Bertram had married the boss's daughter. Good move, Bertram. I asked if either of them had been the Cazletts' doctor?

'No, they lived too far away. I think Roderick did consult Papa a few times. But Papa didn't care for him. They quarrelled, I think.' She lowered her voice to a confidential whisper. 'Roderick didn't pay his bills.'

'What did Roderick do?'

'He was a farmer. A gentleman farmer, that is. He didn't do any of the labouring himself.'

'Did he ever rent the farm out?'

'Not Maudsley, I shouldn't think. Although they had several tenant farmers, I seem to recall. But I really can't remember any names. I'm not sure I ever knew them.'

'So I assume you're not still in touch with the family?'

'Oh, *no*. Not for years. Well, Lulu died, of course. Tragic for her sons. They weren't much older than my boys at the time. Not that she was what you'd call a proper mother to them. If I'd behaved—'

I interrupted ruthlessly. 'When was this? When did Lulu die, I mean?'

'I'm not entirely certain of the exact date. It must have been in the late 1930s because my sons were quite young. It was only a service, of course. Not a proper funeral.'

'Why no funeral?'

'There was no body, was there? I dare say they had a proper burial in the place that she died. But what I meant was, there was nothing for Roderick to bury *here*.'

'Where did she die?'

'Switzerland, I think it was. Or do I mean Italy? As I said, it was so long ago now and while I do pride myself on my memory, it's hard to keep things in order sometimes.'

'You didn't like her, did you?'

'Why do you say that?' Her cheeks coloured. For a second I thought I'd blown it. Then she relaxed. 'Is it that obvious? It's so silly. The things one reads in the papers these days . . . it hardly seems credible . . . I am not saying these things didn't go on, but it was done with discretion. One did not embarrass one's husband in public by behaving like a trollop.'

I was beginning to take to Lulu Cazlett.

'Roderick wasn't a happy bunny, then?'

'He was very good. He never reproached her openly. But one can imagine the effect that sort of thing can have on a man's pride.'

Oh, one certainly could. How about giving the missus one slap too many and finding yourself with a body on your hands one moonlit night?

'May I ask why you want to know about these things, dear?'

Frankly I thought she'd never ask. 'Genealogical research. Tracing family trees, you know?'

'I am perfectly aware what it means. Are you related to the Cazletts?'

She sounded doubtful. I guess I didn't look like an aristo fallen on hard times. 'No. It's a job. For a client.'

'A family member?'

'Possibly.' It wasn't entirely a lie since I knew nothing about Stuart's past.

'How interesting. One of my grandsons—' I'd learnt enough by now to cut across this trickle of a reminiscence before it turned into a full flood.

'Do you have any maps? Old ones, I mean. Pre-war?'

She wasn't sure. 'We had. But so much had to go when they pulled down the old house. I'm really not certain . . . perhaps the loft? There were some packing cases . . .'

She rose stiffly and this time she didn't seem quite so certain on her feet, instead holding on to the corners of the furniture as she fetched a pole from the kitchen, banged it vigorously against a trapdoor in the hall ceiling and hooked the loft ladder. I didn't offer to help. From experience with my dad I'd learnt that the last thing the infirm wanted was would-be helpers leaping in as if they could see USELESS imprinted over their charge's forehead. However, when Edith showed every inclination to climb up herself I intervened and suggested it would be easier if I looked since I knew what I'd find most useful.

I shinned up and shone the torch she'd offered across the dusty accumulation of Edith's past. It was full of things she plainly hadn't been able to part with – from broken toys and old furniture to leather hat-boxes and an articulated anatomy skeleton hung with a moth-ridden, fur-trimmed evening cape. There wasn't, thankfully, that much paperwork. Mostly it was old medical textbooks smelling of mould and carefully bound typed transcripts that were cracked and yellowed with age. Half an hour of rooting amongst *Advances in Psychopathology* and *The Uses of Subconscious Imagery in the Treatment of the Insane* by James Cedric Fisher M.D. unearthed a bundle of old maps. Scrambling back down into the hall where I could see them more clearly, I found Edith slumped in a chair in the lounge.

For one awful moment I thought she'd pegged out on me. Then I saw the gentle pulse in the soft crease of her neck. I stroked the back of her hand. She woke with a jerk and murmured her apologies. 'How rude of me.'

'I found some maps.' I caught the fractional confusion in her eyes. She hadn't remembered why I was here. And then she connected again.

'I'm glad. Oh dear, he's not very happy, is he?'

This last comment was aimed at the distinctive wail that resembled a constipated werewolf drifting from the direction of Arlene's.

'No, I'd best get back. Thanks for . . .' I waved the map bundle. 'I'll let you have them back a.s.a.p.'

'Keep them, dear. They are of no use to me.'

'Thanks. The place you mentioned . . . Maudsley? Where was it exactly?'

'Just outside Frognall D'Arcy. It was rather a grand house. Which was, no doubt, what made Lulu think she was better than the rest of us,' she added, the memory of some long-ago put-down plainly still rankling.

I remembered one more thing as she showed me over the doorstep. 'By the way, Mrs Halliwell, if you find a large cow bone in your bushes, could we have it back, please?'

Once I'd reassured Waterloo that I hadn't abandoned him, I carefully unfolded Edith's maps. The beiging paper was disintegrating at the creases and one map tore in two as I laid it out. The copyright symbol at the bottom said it had been printed in 1952, and disappointingly it was the earliest of the collection.

I scanned for the Cazletts' house and found it listed as Maudsley Hall just north-west of Frognall village. I let my fingers do the walking in ever-increasing circles around the stately pile. There was no Rook Farm, but there were plenty of isolated groups of two or three buildings that probably were farms, which this printer hadn't thought worth naming.

I opened Arlene's modern map and compared the two. Maudsley was still there. Or at least a building was shown in the same location although it was no longer named. Even a cursory glance over the area showed that dozens of isolated buildings seemed to have gone. Some – those nearest to the villages – had been swallowed up in modern estates. Others had vanished from the landscape. In fact, as I let my eyes roam, I could see the results of the modern farming methods that had been brought in during the past forty years. Hedges, fences, outlying barns, copses of trees, ponds – they'd all gone, replaced by huge stretches of featureless fields that gave easy access to those massive yellow farm machines that rolled across the land at sowing and harvest time.

I took out my list of Cazlett/Cazlitt traces from this morning and checked what I thought I'd already remembered: the address of the Greville Cazlett who appeared to be cohabiting with a drunk was listed in the phone directory as Maudsley Hall, Frognall D'Arcy. It looked like I'd hit pay-dirt in the matter of the Gumbrights' supposed landlords.

And in the meantime, there were three tapes left to play. I experienced that same uneasy reluctance to enter Stuart's other world. In the end I compromised. Dimming the lights and cuddling down with a cool Chardonnay and a hot dog, I inserted the next tape in the sequence.

'Where are you, Joe?'

'Up the Hall.'

'Which hall? The village hall?'

'Cazlett's.'

'What are you doing there?'

'Come to see Mr Roderick about the rent.'

'What about the rent?'

'Not paid it, has he.'

'Who hasn't? Your father?'

'Said he had. Knew he was lying. Boozed it away again, ain't he. Same as last quarter. Same as every bloody quarter. Mr Roderick said he'd have us out if it weren't paid on time.'

'What does he say now?'

'Don't know. He weren't here.'

'So you didn't see anyone?'

'Saw her.'

'Who?'

'Her. Mrs Cazlett.'

'Could she help you?'

'Said she would. Said she'd talk to her husband.'

'Did she say anything else, Joe?'

'She said . . . she said I was strong.'

'Strong?'

'She touched me. My arms and chest. Felt my muscles.'

'How did that make you feel?'

'Funny. Like . . . like I wanted to touch her back.'

'Did you?'

'She's old, isn't she. Like my mum.'

'How old are you, Joe?'

'Thir'een. But I'm big, though. Biggest in my class.'

'Have you got a girl, Joe?'

'No. Soppy, most of them. Always giggling and fussing with their hair, like Carol.'

'Carol who?'

'Slack.'

'You mean your sister's friend? But she's only eight, isn't she, Joe? What about older girls? What about the girls you go to school with? Do you like them? Do you like a special one?'

'They're the same as Carol and Billie. Always got their heads together, laughing. She didn't laugh at me.'

'Who? Mrs Cazlett?'

'Yeah. She said I was strong. She was soft.'

'Soft? Did you touch her back, Joe?'

'She made me. Put my hand on her chest.'

'Her breast, do you mean?'

'It was warm. Heavy. It made me feel funny. Down there. I wanted to hold her some more. Feel under her clothes. She felt so good.'

'What happened next, Joe?'

'She told me to stay there and she fetched some cream for my hands. It smelt flowery. Like her. I washed it off in the pond. Couldn't go home smelling like that. Made me stink like a girl.'

'What was the matter with your hands?'

'Been tying up the bines. Rushes cut 'em, don't they.'

'Rushes? I thought you grew hops?'

'Tie 'em up round the poles with rushes, don't you. Don' you know nothing? I do 'em before school. When I leave school next year I'll not do the training no more.'

'Why not?'

'It's woman's work.'

'Does Billie do it?'

'Some. But she's too little to do more than the right bottom ones. Dad lets her stop back in bed sometimes. But she don't like it. She cries.'

'Why?'

'I don't know.'

'Where are you now, Joe?'

'She said I had to go.'

'Mrs Cazlett, you mean?'

'Yeah. She said I had to go. She said to come back another time.'

'Will you?'

'Don't know. She's old. But the way she looks at me, it makes me feel . . .'

'Feel what, Joe?'

'Strong. Like I can do anything.'

'So you'll come back?'

'Yeah. Maybe I will.'

11

You can convince a drunk they've said practically anything. In this case it was going to be, 'Come round any time and talk to Greville.'

Maudsley Hall proved to be a large, square, red-brick building approached by a circular gravel drive that looped around a teardrop-shaped central bed planted up with a dreary huddle of rhododendrons before heading back to the black wrought-iron gates and a couple of gateposts crowned with depressed griffins.

I took a quick assessment. Eight large rectangular windows either side of the porticoed front door, same above, plus a circular one over the porch that looked out of place. And a row of far smaller windows strung like a row of square beads under the eaves. I leant on the tarnished bellpush.

The Charlie's Angels seventies-style mop of blonde flicks and fringe could have done with a trim and I wasn't overly taken with skin-tight leopardskin pants but, hell, who was I to complain about other people's fashion taste?

She spoke first. 'Are you from the magazine? I'm Prue.'

'Afraid not. I came to see Grev. You invited me yesterday.'

'I did?'

70

'Family tree research. I wanted to ask about a family who farmed locally in the 1930s. The Gumbrights?'

'God. What a ghastly name. Is it yours too?'

I introduced myself. Part-way through the pleased-to-meet-you bit, she turned and wandered off. She looked back at me. 'Come along, then.'

I allowed myself to be led into a room at the back of the house. It had a view over more gravel yard with a couple of garages, the roofless shell of a large outbuilding, its empty window-frames and door still blackened by the effects of fire, and a garden that was mostly given over to lawns and trees. An elderly gardener was raking slushed leaves into a red and gold pile. He was watched carefully by a couple of floppy-eared hounds who'd been tied to a garden bench. When Prue rapped on the glass they went into a frenzy of excited woofs. The noise set Waterloo off.

'Will you shut that thing *up*!'

I clamped as much of his jaw as I could fit in one hand. 'I'll just tie him up.' Escorting the mutt back to the hall, I looped his lead around one of the stair balusters.

She had flopped into a handy chair when I returned. All the furniture was old like Edith's, with its dark woods and heavy tapestries that soaked up the light and gave the whole place an air of dismal dreariness. The room had its share of family photos as well, but the Cazletts had gone one better by immortalising themselves in oils. The results were simpering around the walls, imprisoned for ever in tarnished gold frames and gradually being buried under a layer of dirt.

Pride of place had gone to a bloke in military uniform. Not the usual gold braid and ornate sword type of job that most posers favoured, but a businesslike khaki outfit. Since Prue seemed to have exhausted her hostess skills and was now leaning back with her eyes closed, I wasted time examining the Cazlett bygones. Military man was a real looker – but, boy, did he know it. Had he really not realised that the artist had caught that smug twitch of lip and thrust of jaw? Or had he just thought it was a justifiable reflection of his obvious superiority? A small engraved plate fixed to the base informed the world they were being looked down on by Capt. Roderick A. Cazlett, D.C.

So this was Roderick. The artist had achieved that trick of making the subject's eyes follow the observer's. As I looked up at Rod, I half expected him to drop one eyelid in a lazy wink.

He was flanked by two women. The brunette on the left had probably chosen the low-cut turquoise gown to show off her shoulders and bust, and to further draw the looker's attention she'd worn a blue stone pendant inlaid with the initial 'L' on a heavily ornate gold chain that came to rest between the swells. The blonde on the other side had, no doubt, gone for a white fitted brocade jacket in order to hide the fact she didn't have much of a bust to show off (we flat-chested sisterhood soon get to recognise the tricks).

Turning back, I discovered Prue had returned to semi-consciousness and was now watching me. 'Family?' I asked.

'My mother.' She waved an elegantly manicured hand vaguely in the direction of the blonde with the ironing-board chest. Judging by the curve of the orange jumper she was wearing, Prue had a lot to thank Daddy's genes or silicone valley for. 'For heaven's sake, remove your boots.' This last instruction was directed at the gardener who'd just wandered in and was transferring clumps of wet mud and squashed leaves from his wellingtons to the floor and rugs.

He thumped down in a high-backed chair next to the empty grate and started dragging off each boot. His socks came with them, sliding over bony dead white feet, the long toes covered in curling grey hairs. Hauling his left foot up, he rubbed a thumb over the ball. 'Another bloody verruca. I'm falling to pieces.'

He wasn't at his best, certainly. His skin had a pallor that emphasised the brown age spots on his face and the backs of his hands, and his boniness was accentuated by the fact he'd chosen to wear an over-large zippered jacket and old trousers held up by a belt that twisted around him twice. He looked to be in his seventies, so hopefully this was another source of information on the past history of the area should Greville prove as unhelpful as his flaked-out wife who seemed to be dozing off again.

Raising his elbows level with his shoulders, he flexed his shoulder blades and released them with a sigh of pleasure. 'That's the ticket. Needs a massage really.' He rotated the left arm with little grimaces of pain. 'Muscles knotting something spastic. Give it a prod, Prue.'

'You know I'm no good at massage, Grev. All those knobbly cords writhing under the skin. It just makes me . . .' She shuddered.

This tramp-like creature was the bloke I'd come to meet? 'Sorry,' I apologised. 'I didn't realise you were the gardener. I thought Greville was the owner.'

'I am,' he said.

'Ah-h,' I said.

He wasn't offended. In fact, he was so laid back about the whole thing, I suspected it wasn't the first time it had happened. When I explained my mission to investigate my – supposed – family's roots in the area, he obligingly said, 'Anything I can do to help then, me dear. Let's shift ourselves into the drawing room, shall we? Damn sight warmer. What about a spot of coffee, Prue? Sure our visitor would care for some. Didn't catch a name.'

'Grace Smith.'

'Would that be the nameless grace?'

'Is that one of those obscure literary references with which the well read like to let the rest of us ignoramuses know just how well read they are?'

'Naturally. Patronising the peasants is one of the few pleasures left to us nobs these days.'

He smiled at me. And I grinned back. It wasn't malicious. Just a game.

'It's from a poem, Nameless. "She walks in beauty". Byron.'

He led the way back to the front hall, padding barefoot, with his muddy wellingtons in his hand. Waterloo greeted my reappearance with a volley of yelps and barks that implied he'd begun to suspect I'd abandoned him. I ordered him to can it. And somewhat to my surprise, he did.

'Quite right. Got to let 'em know who's the boss. After you.'

He'd opened the door to the left of the front entrance. He was right about the drawing room being a damn sight warmer. Not only because of the small fire crackling in the brass grate, but probably because it faced south and the large windows overlooking the front drive let in the sun. It also had the psychological advantage of being furnished in golds and yellows, with lighter, more delicate pieces of furniture than I'd seen elsewhere. They were also, I noticed, sitting myself on a couch, in better condition. Fresh flower arrangements in vases added to the welcoming air. The heavy oil portraits had been replaced by a few abstracts and a couple of avant-garde-style black and white photos that seemed to be professional shots of Prue. It wasn't my style. I went for the lived-in, crashed-out look. But I made the right noises to make up for my earlier gaffe.

'Prue's handiwork. Thinking of becoming one of those designer types. Got 'em on every other television programme these days. Cover everywhere with paint and plywood. Now, what can I do for you, my dear Nameless?'

Greville settled himself next to the fire and dumped his boots on the hearth, whilst I went through my list of supposed family connections.

'Gumbright? Can't say it rings any bells. Certainly no one around by that name when I took over the estate.'

'When was that?'

'Thirty-six years ago. Year Dadda died. Been in the army before that. Didn't really care for it, but had to do something. Not enough money to keep me kicking my heels. Anyway, as I said, no Gumbrights.'

'Rook Farm?'

'Burnt down. Years back. I was away at school – that gives you some idea how long ago. Never rebuilt it. Parcelled the land out to the other tenants, far as I remember. We had five tenant farms. Three of them have been demolished and the other two have been converted. Don't own land any more. Don't own this house if it comes to that.'

For a horrid moment I had a fear that he really was the gardener. Perhaps he and Prue just played Lord and Lady of the Manor when the owner was out.

'Death duties,' he suddenly spat out. 'Bloody legalised robbery. Well, the Chancellor's not getting a penny of my money. Signed the lot over seven years ago, didn't I.' He tapped his forehead. 'Will power, me dear. Soon as the quacks gave me the news, I said to myself, You're going to fight this battle, old man. Don't let go until you've seen the Government off.'

So that was it. The too-large clothes and need for warmth weren't just down to eccentricity or old age. Greville was on his way to the final check-out. I felt the usual panic that always hit me when I was required to show empathy and sympathy – or any other 'pathy'.

Prue saved me by appearing with the coffee; not the family silver but three Clarice Cliff look-alike mugs on a stained old tin tray and an open packet of sugar with the wet spoon still in it.

'You ever heard of any Gumbrights, Prue?' Greville asked, shovelling three heaped teaspoons into his mug.

Prue denied any knowledge of the name. Ditto the Slacks and their village store. 'I don't think there was ever a shop in the village, was there?'

'Years ago. Remember one when Ralph and I were youngsters. Dadda used to give us a shilling each to run over and buy some sweets for the journey back after the vacs. Used to leave it until we saw the train smoke coming. Bit of a tease, see. Liked to watch us hopping around wondering if we were going to get it that term. Going back a bit now.' He exhaled through pursed lips over his coffee to cool it and looked at me over the milky ripples. 'Thing is, I was packed off to boarding school at seven and when the war blew up they evacuated us to Cornwall. After that there was the army . . . I didn't really spend that much time here. I dare say if you put a face in front of me I'd remember it, but the names . . . they've gone from here.' He tapped a forefinger against his skull. 'Pity we haven't still got the old estate books. We had a break-in a few years back. Stole whatever we still had that was worth anything and then burnt the office down. Bloody vandals. Any other names you'd care to run past us?'

'Tyler's Lane?'

'Mmm . . .' Greville's forehead puckered. He wagged a finger at me. 'Do you know, I think you might be in luck there. Shan't keep you a tic.'

Left with Prue, I was stuck for suitable social chit-chat. 'Hey, do you shoot up or snort up?' probably didn't cut it in these circumstances. She'd definitely been mixing something other than instant coffee granules in the kitchen. The washed-out sicky had been replaced by an alert sparkler with restless hands and pupils that were a shade too dilated given the brighter lights in this room.

'Lovely room,' I finally tried. 'Your husband said you designed it.'

You'd have thought I'd just asked whether she'd got the lot at a Slums-R-Us.

Anger shone through her skin and crackled in the air like static electricity. I half expected to see her hair shoot out at right angles with the positive charge. 'You know the bastard? What are you? Another trick that passed in the night?'

'Sorry, I think I've lost the plot here. I know a lot of bastards – which one are we talking about?'

'My husband. *Ex*-husband. Did he send you here?'

'Isn't Greville your husband?'

'Grev!' She stared. And then laughed. 'Grev! God, no.

Grev is my brother. Well, half-brother to be exact – same father, different mothers.'

I'd assumed that Grev had got himself a trophy wife even though she wasn't as young as I'd first thought. I'd put her down at mid-thirties in the hall, but in the better lighting it was possible to see the worn hands with their beginnings of pale fawn age spots. Clever make-up may have turned Prue's face clock back to thirty-five, but her hands were fifty-plus. Another piece clicked into place. The threesome in oils were their parents. If blondie was Prue's mum, then the brunette was . . . ?'

'That's right,' Prue agreed. 'Grev and Ralph's mother. They used to call her Lulu. She died. Then the old goat married my mother. He was years older than her, of course. She probably had visions of being the merry widow on the inheritance. Well, more fool her. She died three months before him. Cerebral haemorrhage. Went like that.' She snapped two of the elegantly manicured fingers in the air. 'Not that I really remember, of course. I was very young. Just a toddler.'

By my reckoning of her age, that meant Prue must have been the only toddling teenager in the pack. She must have been teased like hell at school!

Keeping a straight face, I said the family seemed to be really unlucky when it came to mothers dying young. 'Greville's mum, Lulu, did too, didn't she?'

'How do you know that?'

I explained Edith Halliwell and her long-ago connection with the Cazletts. The idea seemed to intrigue Prue.

'She must be absolutely ancient! Grev, listen to this. She knows someone who used to party with your mama and papa.'

Greville was too breathless to answer for a moment. He was staggering under the weight of a large frame which he leant against the wall with an audible gasp of relief. 'Didn't realise the damn thing was that heavy. Should have taken you to it.' There was a film of sweat on his greying skin and he gulped several mouthfuls of cold coffee with obvious relief.

I knelt before the glass which shielded a map drawn in brown inks and covering the immediate area. It mirrored a small portion of the one I'd already got from Edith, but the detail was far denser, with names scattered over not only houses and main roads but also lanes, copses, ponds and barns.

'Old estate map,' Greville managed to pant out. 'There's Rooks.'

The farm he was pointing out was the farthest from Maudsley. It was also called Windy Top Farm.

'Always called it Rooks,' he said. 'Don't know why. And there's your lane . . . Tyler's . . . just by the oast houses.'

I dragged Edith's map from the back pocket of my jeans and spread it out over the carpet. The lane he'd indicated was there but unnamed. Equally the miniature towers of the oast houses had been flattened to a square block on Edith's.

Something the ghostly 'Joe Gumbright' had said came back to me. Something about not having their own oats? Perhaps it hadn't been oats? 'Did the tenant farmers use these oast houses?'

'Had to. Wasn't another one around. This is the farthest north and east they planted the bines. All gone now. Grubbed them up years ago. Same with lots of the chaps. Breweries get the hops cheaper abroad. Is there anything else we can do for you . . . ?'

He'd turned a greyish shade. He'd plainly overdone it.

Prue was either indifferent to her brother's difficulties or so totally self-absorbed she hadn't noticed. 'Did you hear what I said, Grev? This Mrs Whatshername actually *knew* your parents. When they were young.'

'So did I.'

'Oh, you know what I mean,' she pouted, flouncing back the Farrah Fawcett to reveal gold hoop earrings. 'Children never see their parents as they *really* are. Aren't you in the least little bit curious about your mother? You can't possibly remember her at all well. You could invite this woman up to tea or something. It's not as if you can go out much any more,' she continued with breathtaking insensitivity.

'Why should I be curious about Mama? Barely saw her when she did live here. Lack of maternal instinct seems to be bred into our family.'

Prue's eyes sparkled with rather more than artificial stimulation. 'That's not fair. It was postnatal depression. It's a recognised illness now. Don't invite the old girl up, then. I was only trying to provide you with some kind of entertainment.'

Greville plainly needed to rest. 'Perhaps you could show Miss Smith out, Prue? Unless there's anything else?'

I asked quickly about this Ralph he'd mentioned. 'Your brother?'

Greville nodded.

'Is it possible he'd remember the Gumbrights?'

'Doubt it. He was younger than me, and I don't. Too late to ask him anyway, I'm afraid. Ralph died years ago. Went farming in Kenya. Bastards shot him.'

I bit back a flip retort that it seemed an excessive reaction to non-organic methods since he seemed more upset by that memory than any previous mentions of his parents.

'Had a son, though,' he said. 'Good chap. Runs a hotel in Switzerland. Going to turn this place into a health and beauty complex.'

I caught the soft exhalation from Prue's expensively lipsticked mouth and got the picture. Greville had signed over the property to this nephew and sis wasn't pleased.

'I've taken up enough of your time. I'll just leave my phone number if that's okay, in case you remember anything else. You've been really great. Thanks ever so much,' I gushed in my perfect guest mode. I gushed somewhat louder than normal because I'd been aware for the past thirty seconds that Waterloo was up to something in the hall. His whines and woofs had changed from 'poor abandoned little me' to 'bring on the Rottweilers – the killer's back in town'.

I found out why when Prue opened the drawing-room door. The hounds had got into the house and had fanned out to launch a two-dog attack on Waterloo. At present they were trying to stare him down. Waterloo dropped his head submissively. They advanced a few steps. Waterloo retreated as far as the lead and stair base would allow him. With the sneers of top dogs cornering a mutt who ought to know his place, the hounds closed for the kill.

Waterloo launched himself with a hundred-decibel roar and every muscle in turbo mode. The baluster I'd tethered him to ripped from the staircase with an almighty crack. I watched in disbelief as it hurtled at Prue in a move horribly like my assault on Stuart with the cow bone.

Unlike Stuart, she ducked. Behind her in the drawing-room Greville screamed.

12

Luckily Greville was reacting to a sudden spasm of pain brought on by his leap to field the spinning rod before it took out one of the front windows. Luckily for me, I mean, since I avoided an accusation of assault with a deadly mutt. I don't think Greville felt he was having one of his better days.

'Captained the school cricket team, you know,' he gasped, sinking back with a smile that was forcing itself on to pain-clenched lips.

'I'm so sorry,' I apologised. And I meant it. He'd plainly done himself some mischief and that was on top of whatever havoc Waterloo had wreaked on the family heirlooms. Out of the corner of my eye I could see what appeared to be the remains of several oriental vases that had disintegrated in clouds of dust and pottery fragments over the hall tiles. 'They weren't Ming or anything, were they?'

'Good God, we should be so lucky,' Greville gasped, his breathing becoming more even as the pain retreated again. 'Bad reproductions. If they'd been worth anything they'd have gone to the sale-rooms long ago, me dear. Fetch me a tablet, Prue, there's a good girl.'

'Haven't you had enough?'

'Bugger that. Fetch the bottle.'

'Oh, all right. Hadn't you better catch your dog?' she flounced through the Farrah Fawcett at me.

Waterloo was now hurtling around the front drive in a game of tag with the hounds. I snagged the lead as it whipped round and was forced to run half a circuit before I could get him to stop. The hounds dropped to their stomachs in response to an angry shout from the house and allowed me to lead Waterloo back to the car and bundle him in. Retreat seemed like the best option. With a cheery wave and beep of the horn I swept away as if the last ten minutes had been perfectly normal (well, okay, by my standards they had been).

I headed for the location of Rook Farm – even though it no longer appeared on my modern map. 'I could always look in the old rate books or something,' I told Waterloo. 'Or maybe old electoral lists?'

He was concentrating on chewing one of my rear seat belts in two and seemed unimpressed by my brilliance. I wasn't bothered. The Micra had been foisted on me by Annie. It was the sort of dull, reliable, unlikely-to-be-noticed car that a private investigator needs. My previous motors had all had personality (and dodgy engines). I missed those cars. Sometimes I fantasised that someone would steal the Micra and total it. I guess being eaten from the inside out by a demented dog would look just as good on the insurance claim.

It's hard to find something that isn't there. My map reading isn't too hot anyway and when you're cruising around a tangle of lanes amongst harvested fields that all look exactly the same, before long it starts to feel like you've fallen into a continuous time loop. Eventually I pulled over against a wire fence and pointed to a large acreage that rose in ploughed rows like brown corduroy to the horizon. 'I reckon it was up there.'

Waterloo yawned, rolled over and let go with enough methane to power a small airship.

'Oh, bloody hell!' Throwing open the driver's door, I dived outside. Since there didn't appear to be anything in the fields for him to worry (apart from me), I didn't bother to clip the lead on. Squeezing between two strands of wire, I set off up the slope.

The crumbly earth and ridges made it harder than it first appeared to climb the gentle rise and the sun was warming the air in a way that you didn't notice near the fresher coast. I was beginning to sweat and the backs of my calves were screaming a protest by the time I achieved the skyline. Waterloo wasn't too happy either and flopped with a look of deepest resentment at my feet.

I left him to sulk whilst I wandered, trying to find some evidence of buildings up here. There was nothing. Taking out Edith's map, I anchored it by kneeling on the base and leaning both hands on the upper edge. If I was in the right place, then there should have been a small ridge of trees on the other side of this rise that followed the line of a track down to a minor road. But there wasn't. In fact, the corduroy field on that side was a mirror of the one I'd just slogged up. Rook Farm had well and truly disappeared into the fog of the past. And it seemed to have carried the elusive Gumbrights away with it.

Up here alone, with just the wind skittering little clouds of cinnamon-coloured dust across the earth and a flock of crows foraging in an almost eerie silence, I suddenly got the chills again. From somewhere the memory that a bunch of crows were called a 'murder' came back. I didn't *want* to know if this Joe Gumbright had killed anyone, damn it. I didn't want to know if *anyone* had killed *anyone* a lifetime ago. The dead were dead and should stay that way, not start using the living as transmitters for e-mails from the other side.

I pulled myself up sharply. I was taking the rubbish seriously again. A definite no-no. Cynicism pays, I reminded myself. It had got me this job. 'If Stuart wants to contribute to my pension fund, who the hell am I to argue?'

We were only about five or six miles from Winstanton. This near the coast most of the land was flat, so that even from this very slight elevation I could see for a long way in all directions. Behind me were big, featureless, harvested fields. In front, towards the coast, the fields had been left in the old-fashioned small parcels and there were even some hedgerows and clumps of trees. Behind one copse I could make out whitewashed walls and red-tiled conical towers. The oast houses. The sharp tilt at the tip of the roof made them look like inverted and broken ice-cream cones.

Down there the Gumbrights had supposedly delivered their hop harvest for drying each season and 'Joe Gumbright' had buried a dead woman near Tyler's Lane. Maybe they'd kept records showing the names and addresses of their customers? There might be something down there to prove or disprove whether the Gumbrights had been tenant farmers at Rook Farm during the period that Stuart's fantasies placed them there. I called across to Waterloo. 'Let's go, kid.'

I set off down the other side. Waterloo's rump waggled enthusiastically in front of me. Now the gradient was downwards we were cooking. We slid and skidded down the too-dry, crumbling dirt until the fence posts brought us to a halt.

I reconsulted the maps whilst he shook dust over my jeans. The oast houses should be about half a mile down to the right. The older map showed a pond between my position and the oast, but on Arlene's modern version it seemed to have disappeared. From where I was now standing I couldn't see the oast houses or the supposed location of the pond because a large wall appeared to run from the road and arced around to cut off part of the farm fields. That was unusual enough in itself. Around here we didn't do walls. Walls were used in those areas of the country that had natural building materials that loaned themselves to stone building. In this neighbourhood the locals defined boundaries with old hedgerows or – more recently – strips of wire fencing. But this thing hadn't been put up to contain shy sheep or pole-vaulting pigs. For one thing it was over nine feet tall. It was constructed of modern brick but must have been up a fair time judging by the plants that had established themselves in the tiny crevices where they'd won a battle with crumbling mortar.

If I was reading the map correctly then the oast houses were inside this boundary. I walked the circumference, trying to work out where Tyler's Lane would have been. Like Rook Farm, its existence had been obliterated by changes in the landscape, but as far as I could ascertain it must have come off at an angle from the field we'd just walked down, crossed the track and then bisected the left-hand corner of whatever was behind that brick wall before joining up with another track on the far side.

The entrance to this gulag was guarded by an impressive set of black wrought-iron gates that were electronically controlled and sported an intercom system and security lighting. They'd been closed on my first pass, but as I was completing my circuit of the walls I caught the tail of a removal van just pulling inside. The gates hadn't closed behind it when I reached them. It felt like an invitation to snoop. I accepted.

Inside the gates a path curved away to the right lined by large bushes. A little further on I could see a meadowy area dotted with young trees creating dappled patterns. There was clear evidence that rabbits had been doing what rabbits do best judging by the explosion of desirable detached burrows. Waterloo switched to Great White Hunter as soon as he picked up the scent.

'Forget it,' I called after him. 'You couldn't catch one with three broken legs.'

He ignored me and dived into some bushes. I continued on the path. The trees to the left of the path were more mature as if they might have been there before the wall and beneath them the leaf mould was thick and cushiony. It was a peaceful sort of spot. Gradually the trees thinned out and the ground under my feet became stickier. Looking down, I could see the indentations of my shoes filling with water as I drew them up. I'd become slightly disorientated in amongst all the arborealness, but I could see the top of the wall again. In fact, I was aiming at the left-hand bottom corner. It seemed daft to continue. What the hell was I looking for anyway? A sixty-year-old corpse – grave unknown?

I'd started to turn back when a splash and a whirl of wings startled me. Two ducks rose into the air and shot past me. It looked like the pond was still there. But so what? Oh, what the hell. Hadn't Joe planted her near a pond within spade-collecting distance of the oast houses? At least I could truthfully write in my report that I'd examined the mystery corpse's burial ground. I pushed through the last of the reeds and dutifully stared at the pond.

It was a nice enough pond – as ponds go. It was certainly far bigger than I'd expected. I guess I'd been expecting something similar to the front-garden fillers you found in some of the more pretentious B & Bs in Seatoun with their plastic storks and toy-town wishing-well covers. But this thing was the size of a small lake. The green-tinged water was partially covered in scum, but I could see fronds waving below the surface and small life forms darting away from my shadow as it spread over them, so it wasn't totally stagnant. There were reeds and other water-plants just dying back, their tips dipping to touch the lake surface now. They even had water lilies. They weren't open at this time of year, but the cups of thick cream and pink petals must have looked pretty spectacular in the summer. At present the whole area was mostly green fading to beige.

At least they still had one splash of colour. Some kind of blue flower was drifting amongst the far reeds. I could make out its gentian-coloured blossoms just under the water's surface with a darker foliage drifting like strands of seaweed at one end. There was a bud or something too. It was nudging into the air a little way from the flowers. It was strange, it almost looked like a . . . !

'Bloody hell! *Help! Somebody!*'

13

It was a kid – face down in the water – her little fists curved like buds and her hair drifting like fronds of pond weed. I crashed in up to my thighs. The bottom was soft mud and the pliable plants wrapped my ankles. I jerked a knee up to tear myself free. I should have swum straight off the bank. I could feel myself becoming more and more bogged in this damn silt. It started to flow over the sides of my trainers and add to the problem. The wet had already swollen the laces and I couldn't heel them off.

'*Help!*' I bawled. '*There's a kid drowning in here!*'

With an effort I heaved my feet free and struck out. I didn't think she'd been in there for very long. Her fall had probably been the splash that had disturbed the ducks. If I could just get some air into her lungs quickly . . .

'*He-e-e-e-lp!*'

This time someone dashed to the rescue. Waterloo hit the water in a belly flop that sent a tidal pattern of ripples fluttering over the lake. He overtook me easily. Water cleaved out in front of him in a bow wave as his front legs paddled frantically. The movement put an added impetus behind the already spreading circlet of waves he'd set up with his dive. The first front swept under the kid, bobbing her up and down, the next set was deflected by a drifting branch that had been set into sail by the movement and came under the child at a sideways angle. The combination of the two different forces was enough to tip her round so that she was now floating on her side with one arm pointing towards the bottom and the other resting on the surface. It meant her nose and part of her mouth were now in the air. As she drifted out from the reeds into the main body of water she started to turn face down again. Her upper arm caught on Waterloo's head. He lifted his upper torso and kept her up until I breaststroked to their side.

Treading water, I let her head fall back over my left arm, pulled down her chin with the other hand and blew air into her lungs. She gave a little whimper and coughed up a gob of dirty water. Her eyes, though, stayed closed and she felt cold. My first-aid instructor had recommended warm blankets as a treatment for shock. He'd never actually explained how to find them when you're splashing around in the middle of a dirty great pond. Waterlogged jeans and silt-filled shoes aren't the greatest outfit for this sort of activity. I could feel my legs tiring and my heart racing. I was tempted to set down and pray the bottom wasn't too deep at this point, but I was scared of getting bogged down again.

The mutt was circling us in a doggy paddle. On his next pass in front of my nose, I grabbed his collar and flattened myself on the surface of the water as best I could. With the other arm hitched under the kid's so I could tow her on her back, my legs thrashing madly and Waterloo pulling, I headed for the reeds. The bank on the far side where I'd plunged in had sloped shallowly; over this side it climbed abruptly beyond the reeds. It wasn't particularly high, but it was slippery with mud and I had the kid to carry.

With her lying over one shoulder, I dug my fingers into the ground and used the toecaps of my trainers to get a purchase and haul us both up. Waterloo made an attempt to scramble after me but fell back with a soft splash after which he swam round in circles.

Someone shouted over my head, 'Here! Over here! I've found her.'

I was dragging myself over the edge of the embankment, so my view was confined to pink denim trousers trimmed with flowered braid, stained dark wine in places where wetness had transferred from the undergrowth.

'Is she dead?' Crouching, she snatched the child from my shoulder and stood her up. 'Emilie Rose. Wake up.'

'I think she's okay,' I gasped, sitting back on my knees. I spat the contents of my own mouth out. I could taste grittiness along my gums under my top lip. I desperately needed a gargle with a large glass of something alcoholic.

There were more rescuers rushing through the under-growth now. A heavy-set man in white shirtsleeves and black trousers won the race, closely followed by a woman in her mid-thirties who was handicapped in the sprint by the swelling bump of what looked like an imminent arrival. She dropped to her knees in the mud and drew the child into her arms, tucking her head on her shoulder and making sounds that were half soothing, half crying.

This was obviously Emilie Rose's mum. Maybe the pink-denimed one was a nanny – soon to be ex-nanny if she let the kid play 'walk on water'. Still, she could always get a job modelling for shampoo commercials. She was one of those girls with a perfect oval Madonna face and the spiritual effect was enhanced by a thick curtain of gleaming brown hair that parted in the centre and fell to her waist. When she swished you could almost hear the voice-over cooing the advantages of silken cuticles and healthy roots because she was worth it.

Mummy dragged off her cardigan and wrapped it around Emilie Rose, who'd now turned up the screams as the shock wore off. 'It's all right, *chérie*. Mummy's got you.'

There was a tinge of accent, a hint of mid-Atlantic. I suggested they ought to get the kid to a doctor. 'Whatever's in there doesn't taste too good.' I spat another mouthful out. 'And she wasn't breathing for a few seconds.'

She stood awkwardly, lifting Emilie Rose. The man tried to take her and she snapped angrily at him, asking him where the hell he'd been when her daughter nearly drowned?

'I'm sorry, Mrs Alaimo, I was watching the removers.'

'You are a bodyguard. That means you guard my daughter, not the bloody furniture. We must find the doctor. Where should we go, Melody? Where is the hospital?'

The shampoo advert swished. 'It's years since I lived here, Christina. I was a child . . .'

I started to issue directions but the bloke took charge. His job was on the line. He needed to re-establish his ability to handle an emergency. 'I'll find it. There's maps in the car. Let's go, Mrs Alaimo.' He swept her around, the kid still in her arms, and started fast-trotting her back towards the house. The shampoo ad and I were left staring at each other. She reminded me of someone I'd seen recently, but for the moment I couldn't think who.

'Do you want me to give you a lift to the hospital or something?' she asked.

'No. Thanks, but my stomach's had years of training with my cooking. It probably thinks the bugs are some kind of canapés. If I get the gripes later, I'll ring my doctor.' In the meantime, I had other responsibilities. I crouched on the bank, ready to help Waterloo out of the water. There was no sign of him. Frantically I scanned the placid surface of the lake. The ripples of our earlier excitements had subsided and whatever lived under the water had gone to ground, frightened by all our thrashing. There wasn't a flicker of life in there. Not even an air bubble.

'Waterloo!'

The girl looked torn between puzzlement and alarm. 'What are you doing?'

'Waterloo,' I yelled again. Don't tell me the stupid mutt had drowned while I was busy playing super-girl. 'My dog,' I explained. 'He was in there.'

'Oh?' She came to peer beside me. 'Can he swim?'

'He could five minutes ago.'

Hadn't there been tales of dogs staying afloat for hours after they'd been swept out to sea? How could he have sunk? 'Are there fish in there?' I asked the shampoo ad.

'I'm not sure. My father meant to stock it, but I don't know if he ever did after we left. Why?'

'I was thinking pike.' There wasn't a sign of blood or released gas anywhere. Surely something should be bubbling if he'd gone under. In fact, with Waterloo's digestive system, it ought to look like a sulphur lake out there. And smell like one too. 'Waterloo!' I bawled.

The bark behind us was so loud that we both nearly pitched forward into the water. Bounding from the undergrowth, he reared up to dance a line of muddy footprints down my thighs before backing off and shaking his coat vigorously. The resulting shower of mud spots left the shampoo ad looking like she'd just broken out in a nasty case of bubonic plague pustules.

'Oh – *pants*!' Brushing it resulted in her spreading the mess further over her pink blouse.

'Sorry.' I found my teeth were no longer under my control. Now that the adrenaline rush was wearing off the realities of standing around in soaking clothing were starting to alert my central nervous system to a few pertinent facts: we were cold; we were wet; we were a long way from the car heater. I didn't expect lifelong bonding for saving their kid, but surely they could run to a towel. 'I've left my car on the other side of the hill. Can I get dried off at the house?'

'Oh, sure. Sorry. Top mistake. This way. I'm Melody Alaimo. 'Spect you knew that.' She strode ahead of me, flashing a smile over her shoulder.

I nearly asked why on earth I would, but since I needed that towel, I stuck to giving my own name and remarking on the garden. 'Must take a lot of work – do you do it yourselves?'

'God, *no*. I mean my father designed it . . . sort of. It was in his ecology period. But nobody does it much now. I mean, we have a company come in to mow this bit . . .' She twirled a hand at the fledging wood we'd just come into. 'And do the flower beds. But you're not supposed to do the rest. That was the whole idea – back to nature, a wildlife garden.' Her stride had increased. Hands thrust in pockets, she bounced towards the house. I squelched after her. Every step squeezed a slick of pond silt over the sides of my shoes. It looked like four incontinent worms were trailing us.

They'd kept the three conical towers of the oast and the double-storey stone building connected to them, but even from that distance it was obvious that a lot of modernisation had been grafted around the original. I doubted if the hop driers had had a lot of call for the conservatory that jutted like a glass fungus from the modern wing on the right. And the stepped patio with its stone balustrade would have caused problems for any delivery trucks. Melody bounded straight up its shallow steps and headed for the front door. Waterloo would have gone after her if I hadn't grabbed his collar. He was slimy with muck from the pond.

'Can we get something to scrape him down with too?'

'Sure. Come in.' She waved us casually into the hall. 'You can go in there if you like.' She pointed to a door. 'It's what my father calls his goof-off hole. It's okay really. He'll be cool about it.'

She skipped up the stairs, oblivious to the muddy footprints she was leaving. I dragged off my own shoes and left them outside before padding into the room she'd indicated. It had been converted from one of the drying chimneys, its thick circular whitewashed walls and open-beamed ceiling no doubt meant to convey rural robustness. It was furnished with loose-covered chairs and sofas I daren't sit on and expensive audio and video equipment I was trying not to drip on. The wall decorations consisted of framed circular discs and glossy photos of rock concerts.

Waterloo didn't have my problem with making himself

at home. He bounded on to the nearest chair and deposited a muddy bottom print. 'Get off there.' I pushed him off, turned the dark red cushion over and plumped like I'd seen fanatical housewives do (personally I never plumped). I was standing in front of one of those discs as I thumped feather-down like it was bread dough. The engraving said it was a Platinum Award for 'Rancid Hounddog'.

'Looks like they've got your medal lined up,' I informed Waterloo. 'Wonder which one's mine?'

I padded across to the other frames, leaving dirty imprints of my bare feet across the floor. All the discs seemed to be awards for albums. And the pictures were all of the same bloke. Or at least the same bloke was generally there in the centre of a group of other musicians and assorted smoke and lighting effects. Gradually an idea started to form in the area of my brain marked 'developing tray'. It burst into full Technicolor as Melody opened the door carrying a stack of towels.

'Hey, this is Rick Alaimo's place, isn't it?'

Melody seemed surprised. 'Yes. One of them anyway. I thought you knew. Isn't that why you're here? It's okay. You don't have to kid us. Not after you saved Emilie Rose. Daddy will be knocked out. Anything you want . . . concert tickets . . . backstage tour?'

'No. Thanks. It was nothing.' I'd plainly been taken for a groupie who'd crashed the perimeter which was why they hadn't queried my presence in their lake. Modesty seemed more tactful than telling her I couldn't stand her dad's music. 'I didn't know he lived around here.'

'He doesn't very much. I mean, he uses this place maybe once or twice a year. But Christina wanted to move to Europe. We've been living in the States. That's where Daddy's recording company is.' She gave a little frown. 'But if you aren't a fan, then what are you *doing* here?'

'I'm a private investigator. I'm working a case.' That one always gets their attention. You can see them frantically reviewing their past mistakes, wondering which one you've sniffed out. A streak of sadism in me always lets them sweat for a few seconds before adding the explanation (slightly amended to cover the fact my client was most probably a fruit cake), 'I'm chasing up a client's family tree. He thinks he may have had relatives who lived around here. They were called Gumbright?'

I paused on an interrogatory note to see if she'd react. She shrugged. 'Never heard of them. And you think they lived here?' She raised both arms, palms flattened, like a kid who'd been asked to mime a tree.

'Not in this actual house.' I went through my Rook Farm routine, and attributed the mention of these oast houses and Tyler's Lane to some old family letters. I left out the bit about the ghostly body. 'I was hoping you might have some old records down here. The oast house account books perhaps?'

'I doubt it. I'll ask Daddy if you like.' She frowned. 'You really are wet, aren't you?'

It wasn't a comment on my softheadedness at taking on this daft case. I was puddling on her floors at an impressive rate as the jeans drained. Melody dropped the towels on to the mess. 'Listen, why don't you take a shower and I'll find you some fresh clothes?'

I thought she'd never ask. 'What about the dog?'

'Bring him.'

She led me upstairs and along an upper corridor. 'You can use this bathroom.'

It was tiled in orange and gold, with matching pale orange ceramic wear.

'We were going to have it restyled, but seventies retro is just so in at the moment and Daddy thinks it's just awesome having the genuine stuff instead of modern copies. It's neat, don't you think?'

I thought it resembled the set of a particularly low-budget TV soap.

'The shower works okay. I used it this morning. There's towels . . .' Melody opened another door inside the room

93

to reveal a neatly folded stack of towels. 'And robes.' She pointed out the folded dressing-gowns on the top shelf. 'I'll go sort out something for you to wear.'

My first problem was what to do with Waterloo. In the end I took the belt from one of the robes, and tied one end to his collar and the other around the shower's grab-rail. Once he was anchored, I turned the shower full blast on both of us. I expected him to give me a hard time, but surprisingly he sat under the torrent with what looked like a grin on his soppy face.

I found a tube of toothpaste and used a finger to rub it over my teeth and gums until I'd got rid of most of the taste of the pond. Finally I got us both towelled to a moist sort of dryishness, wrapped myself in a robe and raked my hair into its normal hacked-by-numbers style. Waterloo completed his grooming with a brisk shake that left his skin swinging long after the skeleton had returned to first base. There was still no sign of Melody. It seemed as good an excuse as any to snoop around a rock star's house.

In a way it was disappointing. There was nothing to indicate the place was a temple to sex, drugs and rock and roll. Up here it was all bedrooms and bathrooms. The décor was tacky sumptuous rather than kinky – not a ceiling mirror or concealed camera anywhere that I could see. It was all rather boringly suburban, given Rick Alaimo's reputation as a serial monogamist. He was one of those rockers who seemed to take pride in dumping the current wife/girlfriend as soon as her replacement was 'outed' by the paparazzi.

A view from a back window revealed more extensions around a courtyard. Through the entrance arch opposite I could make out the beginnings of more formal gardens plus a flash of blue that suggested an outdoor pool. The removal van I'd seen coming in earlier was parked below me next to a yellow convertible but there was no sign of their drivers.

I snooped onwards. At the end of a short junction I came across a flight of stairs leading upwards to a single door. It looked promising: fur-lined manacles and chandeliers designed for swinging in the attic perhaps.

It proved to be nothing more salacious than the nursery. Or soon-to-be nursery, I guess. The long low room wasn't furnished, but each of the cupboards along the walls was painted with rabbits, mice, fairies and other fantasy figures, and more story-book characters danced around the cream walls and flew over the sky-blue ceiling with its white puffy clouds.

A couple of window-seats looked down on the courtyard. A silver Mazda had joined the other two vehicles.

'Perhaps Christina's brought the kid back,' I remarked to Waterloo, who was snuffling along the floorboards like a trainee truffle-hound. 'It should be worth a packet of digestives if you play your cards right, my little four-footed hero. Come on.'

I padded down to the ground floor. There was no one around but I thought I caught the sound of voices from the rear of the building. With the robe hitched to ankle level I wove my way into a lounge that had overdosed on chintz. The voices were coming from behind a door on the far side. One was Melody's. The other was deeper but I couldn't hear the words.

Melody's voice carried more clearly. She was probably standing closer to that convenient keyhole. 'It's not too late, you know? I could still report you.'

Waterloo scuppered any eavesdropping by charging at the door with the apparent intention of hurling himself straight through the wood. When he found this wasn't feasible, he barked his little socks off instead.

'Pack it in,' I snapped, dragging him off by his collar.

The noise brought Melody out. 'Oh, hi. Sorry about your clothes. I had to take phone calls. Christina says Emilie Rose is fine, but they're doing a few tests. She says I must be absolutely *certainement* to get your name and address so she and Daddy can thank you properly.'

'Fine. Great,' I shouted over Waterloo, who seemed to

have completely lost it. His gymnastics caused the bath robe to fall open at the top. I took a hand off the collar to draw the lapels closed. Waterloo surged forward. I couldn't hold him one-handed. He swerved past Melody and straight into the room behind her.

I belted after him with nightmares of more smashed ornaments to talk my way around. He hadn't got far. The reason for his excitement became obvious. His nose was buried in the crotch of his new best friend.

'This is . . .' Melody said at my shoulder.

'We've met,' Waterloo's mate said. 'Hello, Grace, I didn't expect t-to see you here.'

That makes us even, sunshine, I thought grimly whilst smiling my hellos. 'Hi, Stuart. Small world.'

14

'You c-can drop the case if you want to.'

'I know I can.'

I didn't want either of us to be under any illusions about my loyalty. A hefty deposit cheque might have bought my soul – but it didn't entitle anyone to take the mick out of me. And it was beginning to feel like Stuart was helping himself to the Michael in mega-sized portions. What else was I supposed to think when he turned up smack in the middle of Gumbright-land and plainly very much at home?

The revelation that I knew Stuart had made Melody jump to the conclusion that my visit *was* connected to her father, whatever I might have said before. 'It's all right. I mean, you can tell me. I'm Daddy's personal assistant,' she whispered, drawing me back upstairs with her arm linked into mine whilst Stuart sorted out builders' invoices downstairs. 'I'll find out anyway eventually. It's not another paternity case, is it?'

Anyone who read the papers was aware that her father's generous distribution of sperm across the world had resulted in several public legal actions for maintenance. Melody had plainly got me down as a storm trooper for the next bimbo who'd scented a lifelong meal ticket.

'It's not about your father at all,' I assured her. 'I told you – I'm investigating genealogy, not panning for gold.'

She didn't believe me. I could see it in her face, but she dropped the subject for the moment and drew me into her bedroom. I had to admire her style. There are those who think I'm sluttish when it comes to housework, but this girl could give master-classes. Shoes and clothes were strewn in all directions – over carpets, wardrobe doors, bed and light fittings. What wasn't strewn was erupting instead from drawers and suitcases. The glimpsed labels I could recognise were all the ones that featured heavily in those glossy style mags. Melody displayed the chutzpah of a true slut by simply taking it for granted that everyone's bedroom looked like this and hence no apology was necessary.

'I don't know what might suit you.' She'd changed into a pink sleeveless dress that skimmed her legs at mid-thigh. On me it would have shown rather more than I was prepared to share with the world. Melody seemed to realise it was a problem too. 'You're awesomely tall, aren't you?'

I was five feet ten, not excessive, but at least six inches taller than Melody. She came up with the obvious solution. 'I'll get you some of Christina's things.'

She came back with a pair of black trousers, a maternity top and a plastic sack. We relocated to the bathroom. As we wrung out the soaking outfit and dumped it in the sack, she returned abruptly to the reason for my visit. 'Are you really not here about Daddy getting his rocks off with some bitch who's been flashing her tits at him again?'

'I told you – no.'

'Then how do you know Stuart?'

'He's a friend.' (I said it without a blush.) 'How about you? What's your connection?'

'He's Daddy's accountant. His *personal* accountant.'

She laid a significance on 'personal'. And in case I missed the point added, 'He writes out all the *personal* cheques.'

'Like the pay-offs? And the hush money?'

'Yes.' She was relieved I'd got the message. Hope lit her face. Was I about to confide the dirty details of Daddy's latest trip down mammary lane?

I wouldn't have if I could – I have my professional ethics (cue hollow laugh).

'Then you two probably know more than me. Seeing as how you're Daddy's *personal* assistant and he's Daddy's *personal* accountant. All I know about your dad is what I read in the papers.'

'If you told me, I could sort of . . . prepare Christina,' she coaxed.

'Unless Christina has been in suspended animation for the last twenty years, I should have thought she'd have a pretty clear idea of what she's taken on. I mean, she must be, what – Mrs Alaimo the fourth?'

'Fifth. My mother was the second. He had this house specially converted for her.' We'd left the bathroom by then. She pointed at the small flight of stairs I'd snooped up earlier. 'That was my playroom. Come and see.'

I couldn't very well admit I already had. So I let myself be taken on the tour again. 'Great decorations. Did you get it done up for Emilie Rose?'

'No way. These were mine.' She smoothed a wistful palm over one of the rabbits, tracing the lines of its jolly face. 'One of my nannies did them. She was really good, wasn't she? One of Daddy's more talented finds, I guess. Most of them only had a talent for one thing, if you know what I mean.'

'Your dad hired your nannies?'

Melody was moving around the room, touching and patting each fairy-tale character like they were old friends. 'Mummy didn't do that kind of thing. She didn't really want kids, I guess . . . When they split up, she let my father have custody . . . mostly, you know, they always give the mother custody . . . if she asks for it . . .'

'Not always.'

'Mostly.' She swished the hair in an I-don't-care-I'm-a-big-girl-now kinda gesture. And continued restlessly to open drawers and cupboards that must have held all her treasures when she was a kid. She swung open one cupboard door and pointed. 'See this . . . that's me. I wouldn't let them paint inside this one.'

Unlike the others, which had been painted pale blue inside to match the outsides, this one was the pale pink of an earlier decoration scheme. Down the edge was a series of short horizontal ink marks – the kind you make to measure each proud half-inch's progress towards being 'grown up'. With a closely packed set of annotations listing the measurements rising in a column beside them.

'I guess they'll have to start another one for Emilie Rose and the new bump now,' Melody said, leaning on the door and aimlessly rocking back and forth.

'I guess.' On closer inspection the faint annotations weren't measurements but letters in pairs: beginning with UC at the bottom and ending in LS at the top. There must have been about three dozen or so. 'Are these code or something?'

Melody giggled. 'No. Course not. They're all my nannies. Well, all the ones after we started making the height list. They were usually foreign, with funny names I couldn't say, so we just started using their initials. There's Uilemhin Connor down there at the bottom. Yousee to me. I can't remember most of the others. They went so fast.'

It was an impressive collection. Within the space of a foot's growth, she'd got through over thirty minders. 'What were you, the spawn from hell?'

'Probably. But it was mostly Daddy. He, well . . . you must have read the papers . . . everybody knows what Daddy's like. Used to be like,' she corrected herself. 'Until he married Christina. Not that I realised that when I was little. I just knew my mummy never seemed to like any of the au pairs much, but my daddy did. I thought that was because Daddy was such a friendly person. Sometimes I'd hardly met them before the yelling started and the latest nanny was being thrown into a taxi by my mother.'

'Wasn't that scary?'

'No. It was a blast. As soon as she got rid of Miss Spain, or Sweden, or Greece or wherever, Mummy would phone Auntie Cat and drag me off to London. The three of us used to stay in the best hotel suites and just hit the shops. It was a total absolute *high*. I mean, I was like seven years old, ringing up room service at two o'clock in the morning to demand chocolate shakes and tripping round Harrods and Harvey Nicks pointing at anything I wanted.'

'But all good things, eh?'

'Yes.' She sighed. 'I suppose in the end Daddy just went . . .'

'A bonk too far?'

'Yes.' She stood up abruptly, slamming the memories back in the cupboard. 'Let's get out of here.'

I retrieved my trainers from the front step. A small heap of sludge puddled on to the patio from one as I turned it over. 'I don't suppose you've any spare shoes?'

'What size?'

'Six and a half?'

It was no go. Melody was a four and Christina, despite her height, was a five. There was no way I could walk back over the hill in footwear that was three sizes too small. I needed a lift. Which was how I came to be sitting in Stuart's car arguing with him about whether I was going to continue with a case that was beginning to look increasingly like a massive wind-up on Stuart's part. And whatever perverted motives he had for playing out this I-have-lived-before scenario, I wasn't sure I wanted to play it too.

'You can see my problem, can't you, Stuart? You hire me to track down the Gumbrights of Rook Farm – a place you claim to know nothing about – and it turns out you can see the site from the window of your client's house. A house which, coincidentally, is constructed around the very oast houses that the Gumbrights used and is just a cuckoo's spit from where you . . . sorry, Joe . . . buried the body.'

Stuart drew in behind my car. 'I didn't know. I swear. What possible motives could I have for lying?'

'You tell me.' I relented slightly. 'Maybe you just heard somebody at the oast houses talking about the Gumbrights, without remembering it. And now it's all got mixed up with your dreams.'

'No.'

'Just that. No.'

Stuart released his seat belt and slewed around to face me. He'd combed his hair forward into a fringe so I couldn't check on the results of my earlier assault. 'That's not the answer, I'm certain. Rick has only spent a few weeks at that house each year since he and Melody's mother split up and I've only met him there twice. We didn't talk about local history. Rick doesn't even come from this area, damn it.'

'Fine,' I snapped. 'It's your money.'

'That's r-right. It is. Have you located any of those people on the tapes?'

'So far just the Cazletts. Who also live only a few miles from Rick's place incidentally. And seem to have been top-nobs around here once. Sure you didn't overhear that name somewhere?'

'Yes. What about the Gumbrights?'

'No go. In fact, even the Cazletts – who supposedly rented out Rook Farm to them – have no recollection of a family by that name.'

'That doesn't mean anything. Surely you are going to do more than just wander around asking questions? What about official records? You could check those.'

'So could you. Did you?'

'No. I'm paying you to do that. Unless you want to bottle out already?'

That's when he told me I could drop the case. And I agreed I certainly could.

'Only I don't think we will just yet,' I told Waterloo as we drove away. 'Whatever game Stuart is playing, I think we'll play along until we find out the rules – then we'll cheat.'

I dropped in at my flat to pick up more clothes and another pair of shoes and then went round to the offices of Vetch (International) Associates Inc. Which was a very posh title for a three-storey ex-boarding-house that had been converted into offices by our esteemed leader when he'd inherited it from his gran (allegedly the Martina Boorman of the bucket-and-spade trade).

Jan was packing up ready to leave when I entered. (It was the only time in the day she showed real enthusiasm.)

'She's mad at you,' she said, bypassing the usual 'hellos'. I didn't need to ask who 'she' was. Apart from me and Jan, the only other woman working out of here was Annie. 'You're supposed to keep in regular touch with the office,' Jan continued, stuffing the essentials of life into her shoulder bag (unopened can of cola, nail varnish, lip-gloss, hairbrush, mirror, etc.)

'Annie knows I'm based up at Arlene's bungalow.'

'Tried to ring you there. There wasn't any answer.'

'I was out.'

'Yeah, well, I worked that out, didn' I. She says you've got to have this.' From below the reception desk, Jan produced a boxed pre-pay mobile phone.

I was touched. Annie didn't normally hand out freebies. And she hadn't broken that habit apparently.

Jan held it out of my reach. 'You've got to pay me for it. Cash only, she said.'

'Supposing I don't want to?'

Jan frowned. 'She never said.'

'Let me know when she does. In the meantime, keep the phone. If I need to use one I'll do what I usually do.'

'Use somebody else's?'

'Got it in one. Anyone else looking for me?'

'No.'

'Any interesting cases come in?'

'I dunno. Annie takes all the notes, doesn't she. And she says she'll be dishing the jobs out too. Oh, yeah, you have to have one of these.'

She thrust a sheet of paper at me. It was a memo from Annie to 'All Staff'.

The turnover of Vetch's is insufficient to maintain a viable business during the next 12 months. If we are to survive it is essential we streamline operations and attract more clients. To this end I expect you all to come up with:

a) one idea to cut costs;

b) one idea to increase business.

Anchoret Smith

I met Jan's eyes. 'Bloody hell, this is serious. She's even signing herself Anchoret.'

'I told you to get her a bloke.'

'I haven't got one to spare.'

'It's okay, she's found one herself.'

'Who?'

'I dunno exactly. But she's got a date with him tonight.'

'Have you been listening in on the phones again?'

'How else am I going to find out what's going on around here? Nobody ever tells me nothing. I'm off, Vetch,' she shouted at the closed door of the ground-floor office.

I walked out with her. I'd left the mutt shut in the back of the car. When I opened the rear door Jan gasped.

'Gawd. How do you stand being shut in with that stink?'

'I drive with the windows open.'

'I was talking to the dog.'

Having got the last word in for once, Jan stalked away with a smirk on her face and a sway to her butt.

Driving back to the bungalow, I gave the mutt his dinner and slung my wet clothes and trainers in Arlene's washing machine before ringing the hospital to see how she was doing. This time they wheeled the phone to her bed.

'It's not too good, babes. They say there's an infection got in. Means I got to stay in longer. You okay to stay on?'

I assured her it was no problem and that Waterloo and I were bonding in a very special way (at thirty pounds a day my ethical goalposts were happy to shift themselves a little further into unknown territory).

'Put him on, then?'

'Excuse me?'

'Put him on the line. I want to talk to him.'

She wasn't kidding, she really expected me to stick a dog on the phone. I had to sit there holding the receiver to his ear whilst he woofed and slobbered. Eventually he stretched and wandered off down the bed. I wiped spit off the earpiece and said goodnight to Arlene.

'I need to ask a favour. Can you bring him up to visit me, babes?'

'Will they let him in?'

'Not inside, no. But if you give me a bell when you're outside, I'll sneak down to the doors. How about it?'

'When?'

'Tomorrow?'

I did a few calculations. If I went looking for the elusive Gumbright family in the local records I'd only find them if they'd had the courtesy to be born, married or had died in this district. On the other hand, the Family Resources Centre, which held that information for the entire country, was located in London. And, of course, it had the attraction that I'd be able to bill the entire trip to Stuart as expenses. It was an idea that appealed. 'You're on, Arlene.'

'You won't regret it. I'll make it worth your while.'

Two lots of expenses? Better and better. I rang Stuart to tell him the plan. And added a new twist just to see how much he was prepared to shell out on this ghost hunt.

'It could take most of the day. I don't like the idea of leaving the dog shut in the car for that length of time. I'll have to book us both into a hotel and leave him in the room. Are you on for the bill?'

'Let me think about it. I'll get back to you.'

'Chickening out,' I told Waterloo as I hung up.

After I'd fed us both, I let him out on the rough grass for ten minutes and did my routine with the poop scoop. There wasn't a lot to do in North Bay once the sun went down (well, not in public at any rate). I opened a bottle of red wine and turned the telly on in the lounge. I found I couldn't settle.

Spreading a sheet of my notebook, I jotted down details of who went where (and when).

BUILDING	SIXTY (ISH) YEARS AGO	NOW
Rook Farm (real name: Windy Top Farm)	Joe Gumbright Billie Gumbright Dad and Mum Gumbright Granny (mum's mum?)	No one. Building destroyed.
Maudsley Hall	Roderick Cazlett	Greville Cazlett (Lulu's son)
	Lulu Cazlett (1st wife) Greville & Ralph Cazlett (kids) (2nd wife – much later)	Prue Cazlett (2nd wife's daughter)
The Oast Houses	Tenants unknown (buildings owned by the Cazletts)	Rick Alaimo Christina Alaimo Emilie-Rose Alaimo Melody Alaimo (mum Rick's 2nd wife – whoever that was!)
Frognall D'Arcy village store	Mrs Slack Carol Slack (daughter)	No one. No shop in village any more.

My mind kept going over and over Stuart and his bizarre behaviour. What did he have to gain by claiming he'd killed someone sixty years ago?

'Curiouser and curiouser,' I remarked to Waterloo, who was lying over my feet. I kicked him off and went into the bedroom to get Arlene's Greater London atlas, intending to plan my route into London tomorrow. The small pile of cassette tapes Stuart had handed me were still sitting by the radio cassette.

I really didn't want to listen to more of Joe Gumbright's memories but, on the other hand, perhaps the answer to Stuart's behaviour lay in there somewhere? I slid tape number four in before I could change my mind and settled myself cross-legged up against the pillows. Waterloo scrambled up beside me and let go with a gas cloud.

'For heaven's sake. Out!' I shut him in the back garden where he promptly set up a howling that told the world he was just a poor lonesome dawggie without a soul to love him.

Ignoring him, I depressed the 'play' button on the cassette.

15

'Where are you, Joe?'
  'Home.'
  'You're at the farm?'
  'Walking in. Hitched a lift. Got a pass.'
  'A pass for what?'
  'Leave. Got a leave pass from Elsham. Funny seeing the places now. There's girls.'
  'At the farm?'
  'All over. Doing men's work.'
  'Has your father got a girl, Joe?'
  'Had two. They took them away. Billie wrote me. Got drunk, didn't he. They took them away.'

'Who took them away?'

'People who send the land-girls out. Tell 'em where to go. Gave them to another farmer. Serves him right. Billie says he can't work the farm properly. They'll take it away from him. He'll be directed.'

'Directed where?'

'War work. Serves him right. Drunken sod. Let's see him take a belt to me now. Let's just see him, eh? I'll sort him out. Sort him out good and proper. He'll never try it again.'

'How old are you, Joe?'

'Twenty-one.'

'Are you at the farm yet?'

'Just got there.'

'How is it?'

'Quiet. No one here.'

'Not even Billie?'

'Billie don't live here no more.'

'What about your father?'

'He's here. Drunken bloody bugger. Look at him. God, I hate. I hate him. I hate him. Why's he do it? Why's, eh? He knew I was coming. I wrote him. Why can't you stay sober, you bloody sod? Why don't you talk to me? Pretend you care what happens to me? Did you even notice I'd gone? GET UP!'

'What are you doing, Joe?'

'Kicking him. Letting him have it in the kidneys. How does it feel, eh, Dad? Does it hurt? Are you scared? Are you wondering if I'm going to stop this time?'

'Joe! Stop that. Stop it, Joe. Joe, listen to me. I want to talk to Stuart. Can I do that, Joe?'

'Stuart? I don't know no Stuart. I'll kill him, I'll kill him, I'll kill him.'

The tape spun into static at that point. It wasn't clear whether this Tabitha Puzold had turned it off at that point or 'Joe' had run out of steam.

There were ants with ice-cold boots crawling all over my

skin. It was like listening to a voice from beyond the grave. Except I didn't believe in such things, I reminded myself. And just to prove I thought the whole thing was a load of rubbish, I replayed the tape again. And again.

Joe was claiming to be twenty-one, so that would put us in 1942. Right, fine, it was just another date to be looked up at the Family Resources Centre. If Pa Gumbright had got himself kicked to death there should be a death certificate registered in that year. And there wouldn't be, of course. It was just a figment of Stuart's imagination. The guy wasn't just loony-tunes by the sounds of it, it was beginning to look like he could have periods of violence. I half toyed with the idea of breaking the habit of a lifetime and returning the deposit cheque. I knew hardly anything about multiple personality disorders but it did seem to me that it could be one possible explanation for Stuart's trips down memory lane. The other possibility remained that Stuart knew exactly what he was doing and for some reason I hadn't yet figured out, he'd deliberately set out to create this alter ego of Joe Gumbright.

Either way, the whole thing was beginning to give me a serious case of the spooks. I needed company. I'd just have to let in the only volunteer for house-mate around here tonight.

I bounced into the kitchen, not bothering to put on the light. Impetus carried me forward several steps before my brain registered several facts simultaneously: there was a draught coming through the back door that I knew I'd closed; Stuart was standing by the kitchen table; the moonlight was gleaming off a knife in his hand.

16

I belted him. It was a great move: legs apart and slightly bent at the knees, hands clasped together; bring them both back over the right shoulder and then S-W-I-N-G like you're hitting a baseball out of the stadium. It lifted him off his feet and sent him sailing backwards.

He hung on to the knife, though – which turned out to be a stainless-steel fish slice when I turned on the lights.

'Were you planning to flip me to death?' I asked.

'I s-snatched it from the draining board when I heard somebun cumbing,' he said through a split lip. 'It was subposed to be a knife.'

'Why? I mean, why were you sneaking in the back? I can work out the limited advantages of a fish slice for committing GBH myself.'

'We thought there bight be somebing wrong. We've been r-ringing the bell for ages. And the dog sounded distressed. So I climbed over the back fence to help you.'

'My hero.'

Sitting there on the tiles with blood spurting from that swelling lip, he no longer seemed scary.

'Der's dow deed to be sarcastic,' he said, trying to use the back of his hand to stem the flow.

'Sorry. I appreciate your charging to the rescue, honestly.' I bent to help him stand and discovered Waterloo hiding under the table. 'Some flaming guard dog you are.'

Stuart leant over the sink and started scooping cold water over his mouth. 'He ran inside as soon as I obened the door. Speaking of which, perhaps you'd better let Annie in? She's waiting out front.'

She was perched on one of Arlene's ornamental tubs and, for someone who thought her best mate might be in mortal danger, seemed remarkably relaxed about the situation.

'Hi, Sherlock. Didn't you hear the bell?'

I stuck a finger on the push. The box was high up in the hall and it remained stubbornly silent. 'Batteries must have gone. How come you haven't charged to my rescue?'

'Stuart insisted. He didn't want me to get hurt if you were wrestling with intruders in there. I thought it was rather sweet of him.'

It was also rather daft of him and showed he didn't know Annie very well. With her round face hidden behind big glasses, a cloud of mousy hair and two stone of extra weight larded over her five feet eight, people tended to dismiss her as an unfit, overweight nonentity. It was a mistake a lot of villains had made to their cost when she was in the police service. If a couple of low-lifes had been beating me up, I know who I'd have chosen to ensure their teeth were knocked down to their knee-caps.

And talking of beating people up. 'You hit him,' she said accusingly as we entered the kitchen to the sight of Stuart trying to staunch the bleeding with one tea-cloth whilst he wiped gore from his shirt with another.

'Just a tap. It'll draw attention from his head.'

Now he'd wetted the fringe I could see that the bruise on his forehead had swollen into a blackish-purple aubergine. The fat lip that was erupting below his nose should balance it up nicely.

'It's not funny,' Annie hissed. 'Where's the freezer?'

She wrapped a packet of frozen sliced carrots in another towel and left Stuart holding it over the swelling whilst we went in search of a first-aid kit. Actually, I didn't need to search because I knew there was one in the bathroom cabinet, but I wanted to get her on her own.

'What's with you and Stuart?'

'He's helping me to put together a business plan for Vetch's.'

She was wearing her black evening trousers, a black, bead-encrusted designer top, her best gold earrings and her current favourite perfume, which I happened to know cost sixty pounds an ounce. Definitely dressed for a hot night with the profit and loss columns.

What could I say? She was thirty-three years old and quite capable of looking after herself. Nonetheless I couldn't stop myself telling her to be careful.

'Thanks, but my mum had this chat with me when I was ten.'

'I'm serious, Annie. There's something a bit . . . odd . . . about Stuart. Just watch yourself, that's all.'

I knew I wasn't making much sense. And that assault had been a definite over-reaction. But I couldn't help it. There was just something about the voice on those tapes that totally freaked me out.

Back in the kitchen, we dabbed with cotton wool and disinfectant until Stuart called time and decided he'd have to stop off at his flat to change his shirt.

'Fine,' Annie agreed. 'Hadn't you better tell Grace why we dropped by?'

He drew a sealed envelope from his jacket. The contents felt knobbly. 'I've a flat in London. Normally I let it, but it's empty for the next week. I thought you could use it. A hotel might not let you leave the dog. You may want to t-take your own sheets.'

'Fine. Cheers.' I'd really have preferred room service, but what could I say? He was probably right about them letting Waterloo in for any length of time – unless the other guests collectively lost their sense of smell.

I walked them both to Stuart's car. As he sorted out ignition, lights, heater and seat belt, Annie thrust a box through the passenger window at me. It was the mobile phone yet again. 'Take it,' she ordered in a low voice. 'You need one.'

'They cost.'

'They certainly do. Believe me, I'll get the cost of this one out of you, Sherlock. And by the way, I've initialised it – so I've got your number,' Annie called out softly as Stuart swung the car into a U-turn and headed out of the cul-de-sac.

My plans to make an early start for London were thwarted by a couple of articulated lorries, a tanker full of corrosive liquid and a refrigerated truck of dairy products. The lorries both jack-knifed in the early hours of Thursday morning and collided with the other two vehicles, leaving the north side of the M25 blocked and bubbling and the south blocked and buttered. Commuters who regularly used this route around London had already started diverting into the main north-to-south roads across the capital, according to the traffic reports on the radio. It was going to be gridlock by seven o'clock at this rate. The only sensible strategy was to wait until the rush-hour had subsided. I made two mugs of tea, tipped one in the mutt's bowl, took the other back to bed and spent another hour reading Arlene's celebrity lifestyle mags.

Eventually I reluctantly hauled myself up, took a shower, loaded up whatever Waterloo might need for his trip to the big city and headed round to my own flat to collect my sleeping bag and a change of knickers. Waterloo trotted around my basement flat, sniffing with interest. Like so many other buildings in these streets, this had once been an Edwardian boarding-house. Someone had started converting this one into self-contained flats and then appeared to have abandoned the project. Everyone in the place was technically a squatter, I guess – but, hey, if no one asks for the rent, who goes looking for a palm to slap it in? Apart from the main room where I cooked, ate and slept, there was only a bathroom and a small room whose original purpose I'd never discovered. I called it the guest bedroom although, given its narrowness and total lack of windows, the only guest that would have felt at home in there would have been a vampire suffering from agoraphobia. Waterloo turned his ugly little mug up in a sneer.

'Listen, mate,' I informed him, dragging him back up the outside staircase. 'It may not rate a six-page glossy in the lifestyle mags, but at least I don't sleep beneath a dirty great pink satin bowsie-wowsie.'

It was still fairly dark and he had a long ride ahead, so I took him for a quick walk along the beach. The tide was coming in, the rush of dirty cream rollers breaking into a foam that spread out and connected the shallow pools that had been left behind. The breeze caught at my hair and slapped the short strands around; it stung my cheeks with salty spray and filled my ears with the rushing sound of the rollers streaming in from the horizon. I glanced back. The semi-circular sweep of the promenade with its harbour at one end and the rise of the town just behind it hadn't changed much over the past hundred years. The lower floors had been refitted to install modern shopfronts and electronic arcades, but at this time of day with the light just breaking all that was visible was the silhouette of the buildings with no detail to establish their time-frame. It could be any decade back there – the fifties, the sixties. Supposing I walked back into town and found myself in the past?

I shivered and told myself it was just the wind finding its way through my charity-shop-bargain padded jacket. After a while I plodded over the softer drifts beyond the high tide mark towards one of the short wooden staircases that led back up to the prom. I didn't take much notice of the pair of size elevens at nose level as I climbed. Their high polish reflected the lightening sky. Impressive, I thought, with all this salt and sand around most people's shoes had that delightful crunchy dirtiness that's *de rigueur* in cardboard cities.

My eyes slid upwards over the knife-sharp creases in the navy blue trousers. And I knew without even having to reach the slightly-fleshy-but-still-good-looking-if-you-were-into-tanned-tossers face. 'Hi, Terry. Thought you were on nights?'

'Overtime,' Rosco said.

He didn't look too happy about it. But then I don't suppose he had a lot of choice. Mrs Rosco had recently spawned mutants three and four: twin boys.

He jerked a thumb. 'What's that?'

'Well, let's see, Terry. It has a leg at all four corners, and it barks at the front end and wags at the other, amongst other things. What would be your best guess?'

'I can see it's a dog, Smithie. What's it doing on the beach after seven? That's against the by-laws.'

'So report me to the Council.'

I tried to walk round him, but he caught the lead near the collar. Waterloo reacted immediately, twisting his head round over his shoulder and snapping. Terry came within a millimetre of not being able to count past nine unless he took his socks off. He jumped back and swore. 'Did you see that? He's bloody dangerous.'

'Don't be daft. You shouldn't have grabbed at him.'

'He's an effing pit-bull. He's illegal. He wants putting down.'

'Oh, can it, Terry. He's a cross; his mum was a bulldog and his dad didn't stay around to introduce himself. I imagine you know the feeling. Excuse us.'

I stepped round him and headed to my favourite café, Pepi's, for breakfast. This was one place that *was* stuck in a time warp of red and white Formica, plastic squeezy tomatoes and a genuine 1950s jukebox that played the tunes that had Granny rocking in the aisles. It also served non-p.c. cholesterol-laden fry-ups that overhung the plates in greasy abundance and was run by a mate who sometimes allowed me to bum food for free. This wasn't one of them.

'Two-fifty,' Shane said, when I ordered the Colonel Parker Pig-out.

'Throw in a coffee?'

'If you like. But it's gonna make the bacon soggy. Divvy up, Smithie.'

I couldn't. It was against my religion to pay full price for anything. 'How about a couple of extra sausages for the mutt?'

'Go on, then. But keep him out of sight under the table.'

I settled into a bench seat for four by the window and pulled out one of Arlene's mags to browse whilst Shane fried up my order and bemoaned the fact that his girl was as skinny as a stick of macaroni as he swayed his jeans-clad butt to the thumping rhythms of the jukebox.

I'd got the one with an article on Rick Alaimo and the latest Mrs Alaimo. Curiously I turned to the relevant section and allowed myself to take up their invitation to explore their 'sumptuous home in New York'. It looked, to be honest, like just about every other 'sumptuous', 'luxurious' and 'fabulous' home those magazines photographed. Plenty of big, squishy furniture, loads of fancy paintings and antiques, huge rooms, terraces and stunning views over the city. I scanned the text. There was a reference to Christina's new pregnancy so the interview couldn't have been any older than last April. I was interested to see that she wasn't American, as I'd assumed, but French-Canadian. She'd also had a successful career as a restaurateur before her marriage.

'Bert Pratt,' Shane said, dumping a laden plate and napkin-wrapped cutlery in front of me.

'I ordered the Colonel Parker.'

'I meant him.' He pointed at the mag. 'Ricky boy. Real name Bert Pratt. He changed it.'

'Who wouldn't?' Shane himself had started life as 'Hubert'. He'd reinvented himself as Shane when he'd become the narrow-hipped, mean and moody rocker who sneered down at the customers from the black and white publicity shots around the walls. The thick greasy quiff of black hair had long ago slid backwards at an even faster rate than the belly had expanded forwards, but Shane could still rock it with the best of them. And did – with every record that clicked into 'play' on the jukebox. At present he was wondering aloud why he had to be a teenager in love.

'You must have a hell of a memory,' I said, doodling splurges of ketchup, mustard and vinegar, 'if you can remember that far back.'

'I'm not that old. I'm younger than Ricky-boy.'

'Really?' I stared at the colour spread of Rick and Christina draped over each other. He looked about half Shane's age.

'Played a gig with him once. This was back before he was Rick Alaimo, international superstar. Then he was just Rick Alaimo, pain in the arse and so-called super-stud.'

'Pulling back then, was he?'

'Me granddad could have pulled if he'd put on a leather jacket and guitar and called himself a musician. There's something about a bloke in a rock band turns the girls on. You could get as much as you could handle. Some of 'em used to follow the tours. Turn up every town you played. There was this one bird, she was a corker. I mean she really was *the* business . . . gorgeous figure, long blonde hair, blue eyes . . . every bloke on that tour reckoned they were going to have her. Only she took a fancy to one of my mates – drummer he was – and him and her . . . you know.'

'Shared a rare and beautiful moment of passion?'

'As far as you can in the back of a tour bus. Anyhow, soon after, Ricky starts laying it on thick. Fancy meals, expensive presents. So he pulls her, doesn't he.'

'Not a girl for long commitments, then?'

'Dunno about that. But the thing is, Ricky found he hadn't had first crack at her. He went *mad*. Made 'em fire my mate. He was top billing, see, so what he said went. Always had to be the big-mucker did Ricky.'

He sashayed off to serve a couple of new customers with bacon sarnies and a chorus of 'Great Balls of Fire'. I tucked into my fry-up and fed Waterloo his sausages whilst we played a new game called 'See Terry's fingers – bite Terry's fingers'.

By the time I was satisfyingly overloaded with cholesterol and the other customers were beginning to ask Shane if there was a problem with the drains, I figured the traffic would have eased sufficiently for me to head into London.

I'd left the car outside my flat. Rather than go through the back streets, I strolled along the promenade and followed the pedestrian area round the curve of the bay, intending to walk up the steps further along. The broad sweep of concrete between the cliff and beach was temporarily deserted. Except for one of the wooden beach huts apparently. I caught a muted squeal from inside as I passed, followed by the sound of something slapping rhythmically on the wooden planks. I'd have assumed it was a bit of early morning rumpy-pumpy and walked past, but Waterloo didn't have my natural tact. With a loud bark he threw himself at the closed doors.

'Will you *leave*?' I hauled, he panted and strained.

'Mmmmm*mmm*.' I stopped pulling and listened. It came again. From behind the doors a muffled yell as if someone had something clamping their mouth. It might be kinky sex, of course. Was I the sort of woman who barged in where she wasn't wanted? Are you kidding?

I flicked the doors fast. And I have to say it was a sight worth barging for. Who'd have thought Terry Rosco wore Peter Rabbit boxer shorts?

He was flat on the floor, with two girls pinning each arm, one on his chest and another sitting on his head with Terry's cap perched on her own long locks. The seventh was holding the bottom of his trouser legs and pulled them over his feet as far as his knees. Given Terry's usual offers to get his kit off for anything with an ovary, he didn't seem too happy with the scenario. With another muffled threat, he heaved, squirmed and kicked out. The girls laughed. None of them looked more than fifteen, apart from the one at the rear end who was in full slap and clubbing gear. She probably wasn't any older than her mates, but she could have passed for eighteen. It wasn't hard to figure out what had happened. Ms Eighteen-plus-and-legally-an-adult had lured Terry into the hut with some excuse – and with her in that outfit it wouldn't have taken much to persuade him – and the rest of them had pounced as soon as he was inside.

'Playtime's over, girl.' The trouser-bird started to front me up and then changed her mind when Waterloo growled threateningly and showed his dental work.

'Beat it,' she yelled.

With a lot of shrieks and giggles they began to scramble clear of Terry's prone figure. Red-faced and stuttering out threats, he floundered to sit up. Before the scene disappeared entirely I slid my mobile phone out of my jacket pocket. Annie had been so right. You just never knew when one might come in handy. And how lucky that she'd chosen such a slim compact model. Putting it to my eye, I mimed a shutter click.

Terry looked up from re-belting his trousers. 'What yer doing?'

'Just running off a few souvenir shots. Aren't you going to call it in?'

'When I'm good and ready.'

We both knew that was a lie. There was no way macho-man was going to report that he'd been assaulted and debagged by a bunch of schoolgirls. He started to stroll casually towards me. I wasn't fooled. I sprinted back the way I'd come with the sound of Terry's size elevens pounding the concrete behind me, and just managed to beat him to the main road. There was traffic up here and enough early morning arcade junkies to form a reasonable forum of hostile witnesses if he tried to grab my so-called 'camera' by force.

Grinning, I backed away, waving the phone and making certain he couldn't see much beyond a few inches of black plastic. 'You owe me, Terry. And I'll be collecting.'

I'd only intended to wind him up. I couldn't imagine that Terry Rosco would ever have anything I'd want or need. Which just goes to show how wrong you can be.

17

Despite delaying my departure, the heavy residual traffic left over from the earlier rush-hour chaos meant that it was nearly lunchtime before I managed to reach Moorfields Eye Hospital. Fortunately there was a public car park near by which, in return for handing over the defence budget of a small country, meant I didn't have to cruise for another hour looking for a free meter somewhere on the same latitude as London.

I rang Arlene on the mobile to announce our arrival.

'Bring him round to the outpatients' entrance, babes. I'll slip down.'

I checked my charge before we set off, buffing him up with a hanky before leading him across the road and staking out a square of pavement opposite the double doors. Even though I'd had fair warning of Waterloo's strength by now and was hanging on with both hands, he still managed to drag me over as soon as he spotted Arlene.

'Well, who's a naughty boysie-woysie? Has he missed his mumsie-wumsie?' Arlene cooed as the mutt reared up and licked everything he could reach.

'He talks of nothing else,' I panted, getting up off my knees. 'How are you, Arlene?'

'Not too good. The docs saw me this morning. Another week in here definite, they said. It's a real bummer. God knows what a mess Paddy will have got the site in.'

'It's a waste dump, it's supposed to be a mess.'

'There's mess and mess, babes,' Arlene said darkly, before switching to brain-rot mode again and cooing inanities at Waterloo. He flung himself on his back and wriggled in ecstasy and a large pile of London dust.

I looked Arlene over. Apart from the huge pad of dressing bandaged over her left eye, she looked okay to me.

Arlene confirmed my impression. 'I feel fine, babes, but they say if I leave before they get this infection sorted I could lose all sight in the eye.'

'Then you must stay.'

'Yeah, I know. But it's hard, because mumsie really misses her baby-waby.' She rubbed Waterloo's chops between her palms and they went into another orgy of mutual adoration. 'Don't suppose you could bring him up again, babes? I mean, I know you're busy and all that . . .'

I heard myself weakly explaining we'd be staying over-night so I could probably come round again tomorrow.

Arlene's eye lit up. 'Magic. Did you hear that, you lovely boy? You can come visit mummy again.'

I had to put up with another half-hour of nauseating dialogue and slobbering before Arlene finally decided she'd better get back to the ward before she was missed, leaving me free to dump the mutt and get down to business.

Stuart's flat was in Kentish Town. It proved to be the basement flat in a three-storey house that had been converted into separate units on each floor. Just like the site of *chez* Grace, the main front door was above pavement level and reached by a flight of scuffed steps whilst the basement had its own separate outside entrance.

I took a quick check and logged up a sitting room to the left, a bedroom to the right and a kitchen at the end of the hall. There was a door off it which proved to be the loo and a bath suitable for an anorexic pixie. The walls had all been painted the same shade of apricot. Here and there small flakes had been pulled off in square foursomes that said posters had been stuck up and pulled down. At least I didn't have to worry about Waterloo's habits as a house-guest. He'd probably bring a bit of class to the area.

Lugging in a sack from the car boot, I emptied out his blanket (for comfort and familiarity), water bowl (for drinking), dried biscuits (for eating), plastic bone (for play) and long rubber whippy thing (beats me but he was a consenting adult).

Once Waterloo was settled I locked him in and headed back down to the Family Resources Centre. Contrary to popular myth, birth and death certificates haven't been housed in Somerset House for years. They used to be stored in St Catherine's House in Kingsway, but they have now been moved to a purpose-built building in Myddelton Street – an area the map informs me is Finsbury.

It's an odd sort of neighbourhood. Red-brick and cream-tiled Victorian buildings are jostled up against dreary blocks of council flats, new office blocks, sparkling rows of terraced housing jazzed up with window-boxes and the bunting of Exmouth Market strung across the paved area dotted with stainless-steel café tables – in an apparent attempt to give the area that 'continental' atmosphere (an effort that was rather scuppered by the heavy scent of Indian cooking).

After my bag had been searched to check I wasn't smuggling in anything controversial – like a Kalashnikov or a cheese-burger – I was allowed to roam free in the inner sanctum.

The records are all housed in a large open-plan room, decorated with green soft furnishings and divided by large grey metal bookcases veneered in pale wood. There were big double-sided reading desks between each bank of bookcases, so that once you'd dragged the ledgers out you had somewhere to rest them before they pulled your shoulders out of their sockets. Believe me, genealogy is not for the weak. Each book weighs a ton, and once you've bagged one the chances are your reading slot will have been hijacked by a fanatic who's taken early retirement and now spends his life with a sheaf of notes, a packed lunch and the moves of a Sumo wrestler, tracing every trunk, branch and twig of his family tree. They take their lineage-prospecting seriously in these parts.

Taking out my notes, I started with Joe Gumbright. If there was any truth in Stuart's regressive ramblings, then Joe should have been born in March of 1921. Allowing for the fact his parents might not have registered the birth immediately, that meant I should probably check out the three quarters for spring, summer and autumn.

Each ledger is filed both by year and alphabetically. I heaved on the carrying handle of *Births A–G* for the first quarter of 1921.

I found him. Gumbright, Joseph Stanley. It wasn't until I heard myself swear under my breath and drew a ripple of frowns down the reading table that I realised how much I'd wanted to prove Stuart wrong.

That one single entry wasn't to say I hadn't, of course. There was nothing to indicate this was 'my' Gumbright. Apart from the date, the ledgers only provide the bare details of name and place of registration. You want detail, you pay. I filled out a requisition form to obtain a copy of the full certificate and moved along to the next person on my list. Five years younger than her brother, that put Billie's birth in 1926. However, if those five years were an approximation then it could be anywhere from 1925 to 1927. Perversely I slogged through the ledgers. It made me realise the futility of ever trying to trace my own ancestors; for every line of Sidebottoms there were a dozen pages of Smiths. But Gumbright was unusual. In some quarters there were no entries at all under that surname, which made the one in the summer quarter of 1926 all the more noticeable: Wilhelmina Irene. Billie to her friends, no doubt. I filled out another requisition before moving to the black ledgers of the deaths section.

It took far longer. Assuming they were both alive in 1938, I needed to examine all entries to the present day to discover what – if anything – had happened to them. I struck gold in 1942 – if you could call it that. Not the children, but one Stanley Gumbright, aged forty-four, had died in the same registration district.

Cold fingers teased my spine. I tried to shake them off. There was no evidence that this Stan *was* Joe's dad. Okay, he lived in the same district, Stanley was Joe's middle name and Gumbright was a really unusual surname, but did that mean I was unearthing evidence that Stuart had truly lived in another life?

I added Stanley's death certificate to my pile of requisition slips. It took a couple of hours to plough through the rest of the years up to the present day. There was no sign of Joe or Billie. In Billie's case that might mean she'd married, but unless Joe had died abroad then he was either still breathing out there somewhere or he'd died within the past two years and hadn't got himself typed up yet.

I was panting with the exertion of working out with those books and gasping for a drink. There was one more place left to check. When Joe/Stuart had talked of that visit to his dad in 1942, he'd said something about having a leave pass. They'd had conscription during the Second World War, I knew that much. Joe would have been called up into one of the armed services. For all I knew, there was some corner of a foreign field that was forever Gumbright.

It was back to black books. In a special corner that I always found particularly sad, the ledgers listing consulate deaths, deaths abroad, marine deaths, army deaths (officers and other ranks) and RAF deaths were huddled together in a sort of lonely tribute to all those who turned up their toes far from home and family. I found him in *War Deaths (RAF – All Ranks) 1939–1948*. Gumbright, J. S., Sgt., 1943.

Scribbling out the requisition, I went back to the marriage ledgers. At least I only had to work from 1942 this time, since Billie couldn't have married before she was sixteen.

She hadn't married at all, I discovered after another session of pumping ledger. At least not in this country. On an impulse and just for the hell of racking up Stuart's expenses, I worked back from 1921, trying to find his parents' marriage certificate. And unfortunately I did. A year before his birth Stanley Gumbright had married Irene Anne Springfield. I pulled myself up sharply. I had actually thought of it as Stuart's birth as if he and Joe were one and the same person.

'It's a con,' I muttered, spending yet another six pounds fifty pence of Stuart's money. It wasn't hard to find out these details, I'd just proved that. And as for the fancy details, such as Pa Gumbright's drunkenness or Ma's desertion, who was there to contradict him and say it didn't happen like that?

Same with Granny Springfield's death really, I reasoned. So one Wilhelmina Springfield died in 1933, aged seventy – big deal! I was certificate drunk by now. Sticking Granny on the expense account, I went looking for little Carol Slack from Frognall's local shop.

Because Slack wasn't as unusual as Gumbright, there were four Carols born in 1926. However, none had been squeezed into the world in Southern England. But what the hell – there went another twenty-six pounds of Stuart's money.

I'd finished with ten minutes to spare before they threw us all out. Placing my orders, I elected to collect the certificates rather than have them posted to me. It meant another trip to the metropolis, which was a pain, but at least Arlene would get another visit from her baby-waby. Speaking of which, I decided I'd better get back and see what the mutt had been up to in my absence.

It was easier said than done. London isn't the easiest of places to negotiate in the rush-hour, and when you're not quite sure of the route and regularly end up in the wrong lanes you can learn a whole new vocabulary of sign language. By the time I'd managed to get back to the flat and find a parking space I was in a hyped-up mood and ready for a bit of naked aggression. Which was lucky really because it looked like for once the fairies were going to grant my wish. A large tattooed yob was doing his best to kick in my door. Behind it Waterloo was barking his little socks off.

I had to yell to get Tattoos's attention. 'What's the problem?'

He let me know with the vocal equivalent of all those new hand-signs I'd just learnt that the problem was Waterloo. 'He's been banging on like that for hours. It's doing my head in. Is he yours?'

I denied ownership but shouted at Waterloo to belt up. 'We're just good friends. You live here?'

'Up there.' He jabbed a finger skywards. Even that had a ring tattooed around it. 'Ground floor. You Stu's new tenant? You don't look like a student. Mature, are yer?'

'No. Just nicely ripened.'

I'd stayed at pavement level – on the grounds it would be easier to make a run for it if he showed signs of transferring the boot tip from the door to me. Instead of walking up the basement stairs to me, he came forward a few paces, stretched up to grasp the stone handrail of the steps up to the front door, hauled himself up and vaulted over. He turned back to me with a smirk and a slap of his flat stomach. I got the message: me love machine, you lucky tottie.

Yeah, right. I smiled with admiration, just in case he could be pumped for a bit of information on Stuart. Sadly he couldn't, even though I stood around watching him flexing and stretching a few more pecs.

'Lived here for a few years. Didn't mix much,' Tattoos explained. 'I mean, I asked. Mix with anyone, that's me.' He dropped to the pavement to execute a few push-ups. 'The sad bastard was always working. Work . . . eighteen . . . work . . . nineteen . . . work . . . twenty. How about you? Fancy a beer? Got a couple of bottles in the fridge.' He sprang up and flexed his chest muscles in my face. His piggy eyes swept down from my dark roots to my disintegrating trainers and plainly wasn't impressed with what he found in between. 'Don't reckon you'll get a better offer.'

'You may be right. But if I'm seen out with you, it'll be in all the gossip columns tomorrow. It wouldn't be fair to put you under that sort of pressure.'

Uncertainty replaced smugness on the decorated face. 'You somebody, then?'

'It's sweet of you to pretend you don't recognise me. I've so wanted to be just a normal person. I won't forget it.' I kissed the tips of two fingers and extended them to him. 'And by the way, you miscounted – that was sixteen push-ups, not twenty. 'Night.'

I let myself in to a welcome from Waterloo that pretty well mirrored what Tattoos had had in mind for starters, I suspected. Drawing the curtains, I explored the flat's possibilities for a good evening in. They seemed to range from zilch to snowballs-in-hell. The kitchen was a food-free zone apart from a jar of coffee granules that had set solid.

There wasn't even a TV or radio in the place. It was a pain really. If only I hadn't told Arlene I'd bring the mutt visiting tomorrow I could have driven back to Seatoun that night.

I was half tempted to ring her and tell her I'd changed my plans, but I couldn't bring myself to disappoint her when she had no one else. In the end I wandered up and down the high street for an hour or so, doing a bit of people-watching before buying a pint of milk and fish and chips and carrying them home for supper. I ate cross-legged on the sitting-room floor with the greasy parcel in my lap and Waterloo tucking into a tin of dog food I'd brought with me.

It shouldn't have been that much different to being in my own flat really – but it was. The sounds were all wrong. All those night noises that I never consciously noticed when I was at home – the hush of the sea, the faint tinny sounds of the amusement park PA system, even the occasional shriek of a gull that had mistaken the bright neon lighting for daylight – they were all missing. In their place was the roar of London traffic and a continual argument overhead that seemed to be one-sided. It sounded like Tattoos was having a go at someone. Whoever the someone was they weren't answering back. Which made the sudden scream, followed by the crash of something overturning, all the more start-ling.

Waterloo erupted in a frenzy of angry barking. 'Shhh . . .' I smoothed a hand along his back and felt the muscles rippling. There were a couple more thuds. She didn't call out this time. That wasn't unusual. Screaming provokes some abusers. They either get turned on by it or take exception to their victim's whinging at what they see as justifiable punishment. Waterloo moved restlessly. He wanted to rush in and do something heroic. Past experience had taught me our help might not be appreciated. Getting involved with a beaten wife when I should have kept well clear was how I'd ended up leaving the police with a record for being in bed with the local low-life (metaphorically speaking).

It had gone quiet up there. I became aware that I'd been holding my breath and my stomach muscles were aching. I'd unconsciously pulled them in in anticipation of blows that weren't aimed at me. Waterloo's big brown eyes pleaded with me for a bit of action. He was up for it, why wasn't I? I told him to wait until he was asked.

His prayers were answered a minute later by a frantic knocking on the outside door. Waterloo's barking went into turbo mode. He flew down the hall and hurled himself at the wood.

I ordered him to back off. I didn't want Tattoos's punch-bag being confronted by a snarling mutt. I whipped the door open, ready to pull her inside and shut it fast before anyone could follow her in.

A blinding flash exploded in my face.

18

I lashed out with a fast kick. It made contact with a knee-cap.

Unfortunately it was the wrong knee-cap. The one connected to the pratt who'd just fired off a flash gun in my face was standing to the side of the door. Rick Alaimo had been standing directly in front of it. Now he was hopping in front of it instead.

'Sorry,' I shouted over Waterloo's noisy attempts to get a piece of the action.

'It's cool. Marlon, you bloody idiot, get that camera out of the chick's face and park your butt in the car.'

Marlon backed off hastily, muttering excuses, apologies and four-letter expletives in equal numbers until he reached the car drawn up at the kerb. It was big enough for him to take a jacuzzi in the back whilst he waited.

Rick lowered his weight back on to the leg and smiled warmly. 'Hi, I guess you're Grace. It's really great to meet you. After what you did for Em'lie Rose, I just can't tell you . . . I mean, well, heh, I guess you know what I'm trying to say . . .'

'Thank you?'

'That doesn't even begin to cover it. Can I come in?'

I'd got Waterloo cornered behind the half-open door. Now I had to stoop quickly and lock both hands around his collar. He wasn't happy about the situation. If there was a rumble going on, he wanted in. His paws scrabbled against the bare tiles as Rick edged his way inside.

The front door overhead crashed. I glanced up. A woman who was too old for the hairstyle of long plaits flew down the steps. On the pavement she looked in my direction for a moment. One of her eyes was swollen and closing; the other glared a challenge at me. We both knew I'd heard what had gone on; now she was daring me to interfere and offer some well-meant advice. She was quite safe. If she wanted me to point her at one of the professional agencies – fine. If she expected me to charge in and march her down there – no chance, darling. Been there, done that, got the T-shirt. Now I knew she was mobile and free to make her own choices, I left her to make them and returned to my visitor.

Rather than sit down, he was twisting in the centre of the sitting room examining it with interest. 'Stu said you were crashing at his place.'

So that was how he'd found me. It hadn't occurred to me to wonder before. Mainly because I didn't meet that many rock stars in the flesh and I was busy having a good look to see how he matched up to his publicity shots. The lean face and neck definitely had more lines and bags than those photos in his 'sumptuous New York home' had suggested. But it didn't really matter. Rick was living proof that men's faces wore in, whilst women's just wore out. A few crevasses in the tanned skin and a scattering of grey in the layered brown hair that just touched his shoulders added to the charm somehow.

'Never been here before,' he explained, finishing his rotation. 'Knew Stu had a place up here but we didn't hook up until he moved to Winstanton five or six years back. Last number-cruncher I had tried to rip me off. Then someone recommended Stu. He's a blast with the investment funds, isn't he?'

'I wouldn't know.'

'He's not your accountant, then? What's the connection?'

'Why don't you ask Stuart?'

'Gotcha.' He tapped his forefinger against the side of his nose. 'Keep it out. Fair enough. So where are you going to let me take you? Drinks? Dinner? You name it.'

He'd wandered close enough to slip an arm around my shoulder. It was just a friendly, well-met sort of a hug, nothing erotic. But it just so happens that I'm not keen on strangers pressing my flesh without an invitation. I shrugged him off and caught the faint surprise flashing over the brown eyes. But he recovered and switched the smile up a few kilowatts. 'So come on, Grace, let me say thanks properly. Em'lie Rose is our life. If we'd lost her . . . well, it just doesn't stand thinking about.'

'You've already said thanks. I'm glad she's okay, but I only did what anyone would have done. Anyway, it wasn't really me. You ought to thank Waterloo. A large joint – of the meat variety – would be acceptable.' I indicated the mutt, who'd parked his bottom and was watching Rick intently.

'The dog saved Em'lie?'

'Lassie is his role model,' I assured Rick. 'This dog does not know the meaning of the word fear.'

He wasn't too hot on 'sit', 'stay', 'heel' or 'do that outside' either. But I didn't want to spoil his moment of glory by mentioning his antisocial habits. I expected Rick to have a bit of a fuss, promise to send round a big box of doggy-chocs, and leave it at that. But I'd misjudged my superstar. Rick wanted to take us *both* out.

'I'm not dressed for it,' I said, giving him a look at the current outfit of scuffed jeans, *Save Trees (Eat A Beaver)*

T-shirt and oversized man's cardigan. 'And his best collar's in the wash.'

'No problem. Come to my party.'

I went just for the hell of seeing who'd let me in dressed like this. At least I had the satisfaction of seeing Tattoos standing at his flat window with his mouth hanging open as Rick's chauffeur ushered me into the back of the car.

And it was some car. It had thick-pile carpets on the floor and a drinks cabinet set into the back of the driver's seat. There was a CD player inside the leather armrest of the back seat. Rick inserted a disc. 'My new album. I'll autograph it for you later.'

As soon as his barbed-wire tones filled the leather-scented interior I remembered why I wasn't a fan. I was calculating whether it would be less offensive to scream at him to turn it off or just bail out the next time we stopped at a red light when Waterloo added his contribution. Flinging back his head, he gave out with his werewolf impression.

At least the mutt's intervention achieved one blessing. Rick killed the music when it became obvious Waterloo wasn't going to stop unless he did. The CD wouldn't eject from the player. He leant over it, trying to lever it free, and for a moment his head was at waist level and his hair was falling forward. The guy was wearing hair extensions.

He straightened up, flung the thick locks back off his face and gave me another one of those sexy winks. I responded with expected admiring simper, gave Waterloo a sly pat, and watched the night-life sliding past the car windows. Now my brain had stopped rattling inside my skull, there was room for a slight niggle to make itself heard again. It had been there ever since we'd left the flat. Something Rick had said was worrying me. But what? I tried to drag it back into my head whilst I attempted to work out where we were going. Marlon, the manic flasher, was seated up front, chatting away into his mobile phone. The glass partition between us and the front section appeared to be soundproof and he took no notice of us until Rick spoke into an intercom.

'Marlon, give the office a ring. Tell them to get hold of that chick from PR. Grace needs a dress for this evening. Meet us at the gig.'

I didn't know London well enough to follow our route. I thought I glimpsed the river occasionally, but the driver kept swinging away down tiny rat runs that took us off the main streets. Eventually we pulled into an underground parking bay. It was poorly lit and our footsteps echoed as we made our way over the concrete flooring. My skin started to creep and a coldness tickled my spine. Despite the fact I had no reason to be scared, I found myself watching for movements in the shadows and straining to hear signs of an ambush waiting behind the supporting columns. I was spooked for no good reason. Waterloo seemed to sense my panic. He pressed himself against the side of my leg. Who was supposed to be protecting who here I wasn't quite sure.

When the metal doors of the lift slid open and I found myself faced by several slabs of muscle clad in evening jackets, bow-ties and attitude, I was relieved. They were so obviously hired bodyguards. As one they stepped sideways to form a protected corridor between them so that we could all traverse into the lift. Heaven knows what they thought was going to burst through six inches of reinforced steel elevator wall but maybe they'd watched *Terminator 2* once too often.

The sounds of people, music and catering seeped through the door seals as we slid up the elevator tube. Waterloo was still uncharacteristically quiet. It occurred to me that this could be the first time he'd ever been in an elevator. We didn't have that many buildings that required one in Seatoun.

When the doors clicked back again we appeared to be in the midst of an office, but a temporary kind of place, set down in the middle of open-plan floors that cried out for classy screen dividers. Instead they had desks dumped at random, sofas scattered at angles, cardboard boxes in haphazard huddles, a couple of racks of clothing and, rather bizarrely, a row of doggy carrying cases holding mutts of the small yappy variety. The place seemed to be full of people yelling into mobile phones. One skittered over as soon as she saw us, still talking into her mouthpiece, whilst she fluttered a handful of neon orange nails at us.

'Rick, hi! Zoe's here and she's brought Sara which is whizz Noel can't make it, but Gwyneth is still a possible Melinda's a definite show if the bash at the Met doesn't go on past midnight Chris is a no-no But three of the music mags have got people down there and there's a couple of tabloids, including Matthew's which is *brilliant*, and one of the Sunday glossies might do a piece, she's getting back to me I think we'll stick to the timetable and go in thirty anyway You'll be Grace, hi Did Marlon get some good promo shots? Let's get you out of those togs I got you *the* most amazing dress It's going to be so you Is there anything you need to ask me?'

'When do you breathe?'

She smiled uncertainly. She looked about twelve. A tiny brunette in an orange leather miniskirt and a royal blue leather corset and knee-boots. It seemed to be a uniform. I could see another moppet behind her in a similar get-up with a reverse colour scheme.

She beckoned me to follow her. At the same time she hit the auto-dial button on her mobile and started jabbering away again. As far as I could tell, she seemed to be negotiating some kind of interview for Rick. I trotted along behind her as we wove amongst the rest of the chattering clones. A couple of kids were filling shiny carriers with the orange and blue logo 'The Hounddog Returns'. Each one was getting a CD, a T-shirt, pen and baseball cap. They all had the same eye-bashing design. My guide stooped and scooped one. She flashed bleached teeth at me. 'Rick's new concept album. Would you like one?'

'Not in a million years' didn't seem like the correct response in the circumstances. I tried to look suitably thrilled.

She steered me towards one of the freestanding clothes racks where evening outfits gleamed and glittered in the ceiling spotlights. 'Come see what we picked out for you. It's so cool. I mean you are going to die for it.'

Apparently several large boa constrictors already had. A subspecies of the breed I hadn't come across in any zoo since this lot bred bright pink.

'And we've got the matching boots too.' She whisked out a pair of shin-high snakeskin stilettos with six-inch heels.

'I was hoping you had.'

The irony was lost on her. She shepherded me towards a corral formed by boxing off sections of the room with curtains suspended from roof wires. 'You can change in here. Sorry it's a bit basic. We wanted the Met or China White, but it was such short notice we had to make do with this. Do you do your own make-up or do you want the stylist?'

'Stylist definitely.' Since I didn't have any make-up with me I could hardly do it. Anyway, I'd never had a stylist before. She was gone before I could ask what the occasion was.

The dress was a sleeveless poloneck sheath that fitted so snuggly I was going to look pregnant if I swallowed a pickled onion. The boots were size six and a half sadly, so I had no excuse to stick with the trainers and plead grunge-chic. The mystery of how they'd known my correct size was solved by Melody whisking in. She was continuing the leather theme in polished bronze held together with black bootlaces. She perched herself on a desk and swung a leg laced into knee-high thonged sandals.

'Hi! Daddy found you okay, then. I said I'd come pick you up, but he insisted on coming himself. He is just so grateful about Emilie Rose.'

'Don't mention it,' I said through gritted teeth. The boots

were real killers. I had to sit on the floor in an effort to wriggle my feet past the insteps. The dress promptly slid up round my hips.

'Those are La Perla, aren't they? Last seasons's?' Melody said casually. 'I buy their stuff.'

I dragged the hem back to thigh level. My underwear had been donated by a client with far more money than sense. As a consequence my lingerie was probably worth more than the rest of my flat contents put together – but that didn't mean I wanted to share my assets with the world.

'Sorry,' Melody apologised. 'Didn't mean to freak you out. I asked Daddy about those old record books for the oast houses you wanted. He said they never had anything like that.' Scooping up the long hair, she twisted it on to her head and frowned at her reflection in the mirror. 'Do you think I should wear this up for the party?'

Seeing her like that, I realised who she'd reminded me of that first time we'd met. She was the spitting image of the defaced brunette model in the glossy magazine ad on Stuart's living-room wall. The memory of Stuart suddenly brought back that uneasy feeling I'd had in the back of her father's limo. But this time I knew what had caused it. The time-frame was all wrong.

'Melody, your dad said Stuart started working for him about the same time he moved to Winstanton – is that right?'

'I guess so. If that's what he says. He used to have this accountant called Lisette before who looked like a super-model. Which is probably why Daddy hired her in the first place. Only it turned out she really *was* a whizz with the figures. Which was why they didn't notice she was ripping off her clients for ages. They think she skipped the country. Nobody's seen her since. Or the money. Daddy was really choked. He lost mega-dollars. Then he hitched up with Stuart.'

'When was that exactly?'

'Let's see.' Her pretty little face screwed up with concentration. 'Must be . . . six years ago?'

'Not two?'

'No.' Melody released her curtain of hair. 'Does it matter?'

'It might.' Stuart had told Annie and me that he'd lived in Winstanton for two years during that dinner party.

She slid off the table and smoothed the gleaming leather over her stomach. 'Can I ask . . . I mean, not my business, tell me to shove it, but . . . are you and Stuart an item?'

'No.'

'Oh, good.'

It wasn't an 'oh, good, I don't want to tread in anyone else's patch' – it was more of a 'thank God'.

'But a friend of mine might be. Why? Shouldn't she be?'

Melody tried to look nonchalant and failed. 'It's not really anything to do with me. It's just . . .'

She was interrupted by the arrival of the plumber – a muscular woman in dungarees who dumped a large metal toolbox on the floorboards with a crash and flicked open the catch.

It turned out she was the stylist.

Melody checked her watch. 'I must go. They'll need me downstairs. It's launch minus twenty.' She paused at the curtain. 'See you downstairs?'

It was an innocuous remark. But her large liquid eyes signalled something else over the stylist's head. She had something to tell me about Stuart. And she didn't want an audience there when she did.

19

An elbow dug into my stomach and a shoulder was rammed in my throat. The weight was enough to prevent my lungs expanding and claiming my share of the oxygen in the elevator. When the manufacturers had specified a maximum of eight passengers, they probably hadn't counted on four of them weighing a thousand pounds inclusively, plus a four-legged stowaway.

'Jeez,' one of the minders complained. 'We over the sewers here or what?'

'Quiet,' Rick snapped. 'I gotta stay centred.' Dropping his head, he massaged either side of his temple, circling two fingers over the flesh with tiny rotations. He'd changed from the suit he'd been wearing earlier into one which seemed to be lined with a darker-skinned cousin of my dress constrictors. It was TIME according to one of the witches in orange and blue leather.

'Are you okay, Rick?' she asked in hushed tones. 'Can you do this?'

He flexed his neck, gave her a reassuring smile and threw back his shoulders. 'I'm focused. Let's do it, people.'

The pressure on my solar plexus increased as the lift doors slid open. My bottom was practically welded to the lift walls so I had to watch Rick's entrance over the minder's muscular shoulder. Lights flashed, balloons descended, Rick's voice sang from a thousand speakers, the orange and blue witch pranced out ahead of him, clapping frantically over her head.

Rick stepped out. He waved and smiled; he punched the men's arms and kissed the women's cheeks. There was more frantic applause, squeals of appreciation, balloons exploding. Feet stamped, the leather-clad witches were jumping themselves silly, applause thundered from the speakers. It was HAPPENING! It was NOW! It was, to be blunt, manufactured hysteria.

Melody had come down ahead of us. She ran out from the crowd now and flung her father a hug and a kiss. Camera flashes went off. With what looked to me like a well-practised move, Melody swung to her father's side, one arm still linked around his shoulder, a leg thrust out to give maximum play to the slit up the side of her leather mini.

Now there was no chance of me barging out with the important people and gatecrashing their publicity shots, the minders abandoned me and surged out into the crowd. A couple of faces glanced curiously in my direction as if they might be trying to work out who I was. I didn't blame them. I could barely recognise myself in the mirrored walls of the elevator. The stylist had tousled my hair into that fashionable just-stuck-my-fingers-in-the-thousand-volt-socket look and layered on pink shades of eye-shadow until I looked like I had a bad case of conjunctivitis. When I'd protested she'd said, 'Trust me, love. If I don't put it on with a trowel, you'll look like a ghost in the pictures.'

I looked down at Waterloo who was staring up at me with an expression of total bemusement. 'Stay close,' I said. 'And let's knock 'em dead.'

I put my palms on my waist and slid them sensually down the seams of my dress whilst I sauntered out with an insolent slouch and the bored pout of a cat-walk super-model. Cameras went off all over the place. It was one huge room like that we'd just left above. Only here the supporting columns had all been swathed in orange cellophane and banners with the Hounddog logo were suspended from the ceiling. With my nose in the air, I ignored the *hoi polloi*, and headed for the most interesting site in the room – the bar.

I'd been right about being near the Thames. Unlike the upper floor, not all the picture windows had been curtained off and we had a clear view out over the yellow lights reflecting in the black water. Tower Bridge was way up to our left and what looked like Canary Wharf was down to the right. I dredged up what I could recall of my *London A-Z* and took a guess we might be in an office block somewhere around Bermondsey or Rotherhithe way.

Melody was still in the centre of a circle around her dad. There was no chance of separating her out yet, so I ordered a glass of champagne and a mineral water for the dog. The barman was bare-chested above leather trousers with his face painted to resemble a beagle's, nail extensions and a spiked dog collar around his neck. The water came in a proper dog's bowl. So did the champagne.

'You're kidding.'

'That's what they all say. It's these freaking PR lot. One stupid idea after the other. You've no idea. Give it here.' He whipped a glass from under the bar and shot the fizz into it. 'Nuts.'

This wasn't a further comment on the publicity department. All the bar snacks were in dog-feeding bowls. I took a handful. 'I can't see anyone I recognise.'

He shrugged. ' "C" list gig, isn't it, sweetie?'

'So what's all this in aid of?'

'Didn't they tell you when they booked you? It's the launch party, my darling. For Rick's latest album. He ought to retire. Can't afford to, though. Not with all those chickies to support. Think he'd tie a knot in it at his age, wouldn't you? Have you seen the latest? Think she's got anything on under that?'

Melody's bootlaced dress did seem to be slightly less well trussed than it had upstairs. Let's hope she didn't go sunbathing in it – she'd look like a griddle-seared raw steak. I aired my new closeness with the rich and famous. 'That's his daughter. His wife's at home, I expect. She's very pregnant.'

One of the leather-clad witches scampered over and grabbed my wrist. 'Is it true you saved Rick's little girl from *drowning*? Oh, God, that is so *cool*. I mean, it's absolutely *fantastic*.'

'It was hardly anything. I mean, okay, it was remarkably brave, and I had no thought for my own safety as I . . .'

The send-up was, once more, totally lost on her. She bounced away in mid-sentence and disappeared into the chattering crowds of party-goers who were nowhere near as famous as they were pretending to be. I wriggled the skin back to a decent length and sauntered out to see who I was partying with.

They were all in clumps, like oil drops in water, and they

all seemed to know each other. When one oily clump collided with another there was a mass neck hugging and lipstick smacking of the air. Whenever I happened to become tangled with one of the circles, I could see them all sizing me up to see whether I was a hug or a smack. Apparently I was neither. The barman had been right about this being the 'C' list of freeloaders. If this lot were famous it must be on another planet.

I saw one face I thought I recognised in the shifting masses, and then realised it was one of the kids who'd been loading the carrier bags upstairs. Only now she was floating around in a green leather evening dress from the rack, and had been 'styled' with the same reckless disregard for the world's make-up resources as I had. In fact, now I was looking for them, I found I could pick out quite a few of the lot who'd been milling around the upper floor. Judging by their outfits, somewhere there was a reptile house with a lot of chilly inmates. They all seemed to be clutching one of those yappy dogs from the carrying cases. They were working the floor, moving from group to group, chattering and laughing as if having the best time of their lives. Occasionally, if an area of room started to look deserted, they'd all congregate and have their own private little party – all with the same yells, squeals and look-at-us-isn't-this-just-the-most-FUN-ever.

Melody was temporarily alone. I started in her direction. Halfway there, the witch locked on to me again like a homing missile. 'I've got you a slot on breakfast radio.'

'That's very kind. But I wasn't really looking to change career at present.'

'It's an *interview*. About you saving Rick's little girl. That is just so *fantastic*. We can get major exposure with this. I mean, it's just so incredible it happening the very week we launch Rick's album.'

'You don't think they might have thrown her in on purpose?'

'What? No? I mean . . . no way. Is there?'

It was hopeless; she'd had a total humour extraction. I assured her I thought it was unlikely the Alaimos had tried to drown their kid as a publicity stunt.

'Top news. I'll book the car to take you to the studio for four o'clock, okay?'

She had to be kidding. 'Listen, even if I was prepared to do the interview – which I'm not – there's no way I'd be doing it at the crack of dawn. As it happens, they'd be talking to the wrong person. It was really Waterloo who saved her.'

I pointed to the mutt sniffing around her leather boots.

'The *dog* did it? Oh, God, oh, fantastic. That's just top banana.' She hurtled into the crowds again. I saw her make contact with her opposite colour scheme. They slapped hands and started jumping up and down in unison. The neighbouring groups seemed to think it was a dance moment. Everyone started bopping to the music. I couldn't have joined in if I'd wanted to in this outfit, so I tried circulating like the sociable little guest ready to mingle and make that new connection.

Nobody wanted to link up with me. In fact, most of them were speaking in a foreign language where things were win-win, holistic or blue sky. Melody obviously had pretension-speak down to an art. She flitted from group to group, laughing and chatting, but always ending up back at the circle around her father. It was irritating. There was no way I could have a private conversation with her in here. The level of noise meant it was necessary to put your head close to each other and then *shout*. And previous experience had taught me that as soon as you bawl under these circumstances, every single extraneous noise in the room closes down, leaving you yelling your closest secrets into the silent – but distinctly agog – void.

I tried to cut her out of the crowd around her dad but a rearrangement of guests left me tipping into Rick as I overbalanced on the six-inch heels. Sliding an arm round my waist, he asked if I was having a good time.

I wasn't particularly. As parties go, it wasn't that bad. If I'd been there with a few mates I'd probably have rated it a fair evening, but stuck on my own amongst those who generally seemed to regard me as sort of moving furniture – hired to stop the place looking empty – I was beginning to wish I'd stuck with the fish and chips and an early night. I gave him a noncommittal smile. And then noticed an interesting phenomenon. All those guests who'd previously barely acknowledged my existence were suddenly regarding me as if I were the sole carrot on Watership Down.

Rick squeezed my waist and dropped a casual kiss on my cheek. 'Catch you later, doll.'

He moved away. And so did my fan club. I snagged Melody before she could escape again and mouthed, 'The loos. Five minutes.'

The rest rooms were outside on the landing. My entrance didn't bother the nose-candy dippers at all. At least Rick's CD had come in handy for something. They'd torn and rolled the note sleeve and were using it to inhale through.

Melody came in a few minutes later. She seemed to find this use of the loo shelf entirely normal. 'I've been thinking,' she murmured in a low voice. 'Perhaps I shouldn't say anything. I mean, I promised I wouldn't.'

'Promised who? Stuart?'

'No. Myself.'

The little powder-puffers were finally flying. They soared out of the door and left us alone.

'Okay. So what's the problem?'

'I told you. It's Stuart. You said your friend liked him. Liked as in getting it together?'

'Possibly. Why is that a problem exactly?'

'It's just . . . oh, hell, I don't know if I should do this. It's so . . . regressive. I've left that cycle of my existence behind. Going back would just undo all the work.' She fixed those large doe eyes on me. 'I've been really proud of how strong I've been. Only, if I don't tell you, I'd be sort of *responsible* if it happened again, wouldn't I?'

'I have no idea, Melody. Unless you spit it out, how can I tell? What is it about Stuart?'

'He tried to rape me.'

20

'I think,' Melody added.

'You *think*?'

Tears filled her big eyes. Guilt fought the champagne in my stomach and produced a feeling of mild nausea. 'Sorry.'

She smiled through the moisture overload and wiped the back of her hand over her cheeks. 'I'm fine. I know it sounds really stupid. You've met Stuart. A pot plant could intimidate him.'

'Even one with low shelf-esteem,' I agreed. 'When did he turn into Mr Hyde?'

Melody swallowed her tears before saying, 'It was about a year ago. Stuart had flown over to New York for a few days to sort out some financial stuff for Daddy. Only Daddy and Christina had to go out of town so it was left to me to look after him. He asked me to have dinner with him . . . so I said okay. I mean, he was on his own, strange town, it seemed the friendly thing to do. It wasn't like I fancied him or anything. Only he seemed to think it was this big date scene. It was like . . . chauffeured car, champagne, candle-lit table. It was a bit . . . weird. Then he said could we go back to our apartment for coffee so he could sort out the last of the papers for Daddy.'

'And you agreed?'

'Yes. There was no reason not to. It wasn't like he'd tried anything. Or said anything like . . . sexy. We'd just chatted about this and that. Music and films and stuff. It's not like I led him on or anything . . .'

She sounded as if she was repeating something she'd told herself a thousand times before.

'Go on.'

Melody twisted one of the silky tresses around her forefinger nervously before continuing. 'He started touching. Only not really. I mean, if he'd groped me, I'd have hit him for sure. But it wasn't like that. He just . . . leant on me. Do you know what I mean?'

I did. If you said anything you were just a hyper-sensitive feminist – and if you didn't it was taken as encouragement to move on to stage two.

'I tried to be polite. And then I started getting angry. He was way out of order. I pushed him off and told him to go. His eyes were odd. It was like there was someone else inside his head, looking out at me. It gave me the shivers.'

Melody had crossed her arms over her chest. Now she started rubbing the skin between elbow and shoulder as if she could feel the goose-bumps. 'Then he started getting really heavy. He pulled at my clothes. I tried to fight him but . . . blokes are really strong, you know? And I was getting really *scared* . . . but it just seemed to get him more excited. Then, finally, I managed to get free. I just dashed into the bedroom and locked the door.'

'So what was his reaction to that?'

'Nothing. I mean, I listened for ages, thinking he was out there. But when I finally opened the door, he'd gone. He phoned me in the morning, said he was sorry if he'd got the wrong idea but I shouldn't have come on like that if I hadn't wanted him.' Tears squeezed over her lower lids and flowed in glittering streams over her cheeks.

'Forgive my scepticism here, Melody. But what the hell is this bloke doing still working for your dad?'

She sniffed back the tears and somewhere inside her I could sense a core of determination hardening. 'I didn't tell him. I haven't told *anyone*, apart from Auntie Cat. I mean, maybe he was right, and I did give him the wrong signals. I don't think Stuart has had many girlfriends. And I didn't feel good about starting trouble because he's been brilliant about sorting out Daddy's finances after his other accountant ripped him off and, well . . . this is strictly between us . . . right?'

'Right.'

'When I was at school there was this girl . . . She got dumped by this boy she really fancied for her best friend so she said he'd attacked her. I mean, she laid out the whole scene – rape and everything. He was arrested and his parents were just destroyed, you've no idea. Some of us – the girls, I mean – knew that she was lying . . . but nobody said anything because you don't, do you? I mean, you can't split on your friends . . . And then we heard his mother had taken an overdose. She didn't die or anything, they found her in time. But it was a real bummer. It made some of us own up . . . about what we knew . . .'

'How old were you?'

'Thirteen.'

'Okay, so you know it gets messy when someone cries rape. It doesn't mean you don't report it. Or at least tip off Daddy so he can find himself a new number-cruncher.'

'But it wasn't rape, was it? Nothing happened. And maybe I did lead him on. I don't know. I just kept going over everything I said and did in my head until I felt like it was going to *explode*. That's when I told Auntie Cat, and she said if I wasn't going to report it, I had to let go and move on.'

'You're fond of this Auntie Cat of yours, aren't you?'

'She's my godmother. She's lovely, my Auntie Cat. She was my mother's best friend when they were modelling.'

'What about your mum? Couldn't you have spoken to her?'

Melody snorted. 'Why would she be interested? She's never been interested in anything else I did. I talked to my Auntie Cat because she's always been the one who's been there for me. *Always.*'

'And she advised you to keep your mouth shut and let Stuart go on as if nothing had happened? Working for your dad? Seeing you every day?'

'It's not every day. Normally he's here and I'm wherever Daddy is. Auntie Cat said I should do whatever was best for me. I mean, she was right up for coming with me to the police if that's the way I wanted it. Only by that time . . . it was nearly a week later . . . and it wasn't like I was bruised or hit or anything. It would have been my word against his. And I could see how it would be, Stuart stammering away in the interviews and looking like he couldn't fight off a panic attack.'

'It doesn't necessarily follow you wouldn't have been believed.' Although privately I admitted to myself that her chances of getting a conviction would probably have been slight to nil.

'Well, I decided not to find out. Auntie Cat says other people can't make you a victim. You can only make yourself one if you give them power over you. So I decided Stuart wasn't going to ruin my life. It's not like he's the first bloke who's ever tried to take a shag too far, is it? It was just a bit of a shock because it was him.'

'Did it work?' It suggested a pretty strong personality if she'd pulled that one off.

'Not at first. My insides were heaving. I thought I was going to be sick. But it gets easier the more you do it. I wouldn't have said anything to you, but if your friend is getting involved, well, you know her best.'

I did. And Annie wasn't victim material either. Furthermore, she had a supportive family and a brother in the local police. Even Jack the Ripper could have worked out that wasn't good odds. I figured she was safe enough for now, but if she kept doing the balance-sheet boogie in her best evening wear then a bit of best-mate interference might be called for.

My meeting with Melody was brought to a close by the arrival of a posse of females giggling into the ladies. She extracted a whispered promise that I wouldn't repeat anything she'd told me before heading back into the party. I'd have gone in myself, but Waterloo flattened himself to the floor and whined a protest. He was partied out. And when I thought about it, I realised I was too. These people weren't my friends, I didn't want to see in the dawn with them. There was a set of stairs out on this landing. I took a chance they had access to the floor they were using as a temporary office/changing room and started up.

Two flights later Waterloo made it clear I was on my own. I tried heaving and pushing, but he wasn't budging. Eventually he compromised by letting me coax him through the double doors into this floor. With any luck I could walk through and reach the lifts at the far end we'd originally used.

Low lights had been left on throughout which made it easy to negotiate furniture, computer consoles, office partitions and a famous rock star with half-dressed girls in tow.

'Grace. Hi. We were just chilling out. It's buzzing downstairs,' Rick said.

It was probably buzzing inside his skull by now, I should have thought. Did he really think I hadn't noticed the drift of white dust down his lapel or the snuff box he'd just closed and dropped in his pocket?

His friends weren't nearly so discreet. One, who seemed unbothered by the drooping shoulder strap that was letting us see her 36D was all nature's work, was laying out a line over a mouse mat. The other was one of the kids who'd loaded the carriers with the promotion material. She looked younger than Melody. She also radiated vitality – of the chemically induced variety.

'Can't offer you any.' She grinned. 'I'm all used up and Rick won't share his with anyone. Will you, you old meany?'

She nuzzled his neck. He shrugged her off none too gently. 'You're not splitting, are you, Grace? I was going to take you out after this gig. Clubbing? A meal? There's a Chinese place we use.'

Chop-suey and coke at three in the morning? Not only

did I suddenly feel thirty – I was glad of it. 'I'll pass, thanks, Rick. Give my love to Emilie Rose. And Christina.'

If I was expecting the mention of his wife to embarrass any of this trio, I was way off target. The girls didn't react at all and Rick said, 'But she wants to say thanks. She made me swear to bring you round. You've got to come. She'll give me some real grief if you don't.'

And she wouldn't care he'd been snorting charlie with a couple of half-dressed kids? How unlike ordinary mortals' lives are those of the rich and famous.

'I'll drop in later, Rick. Got to split. Home calls.'

It could have been screaming its head off as far as the London taxi drivers were concerned. Once I'd shed the pink python skin and made my way down to the street, I found out a few facts of big-city life – viz. females who dress like doorstep dossers, with make-up from *Revenge of the Zombies*, and are accompanied by an aggressively surly mutt, become instantly invisible to cab drivers in the early hours of the morning. I finally got back to the flat at four a.m. The female from Tattoos's flat was sitting on the steps up to the front door. Her right arm was in a foam-rubber support bandage and her left eye was puffy with bruising.

I raised a hand and she acknowledged me with a small tight smile. Contact established, I asked if she was okay.

'I forget my key,' she said, her voice slightly raspy and heavily overlaid with a foreign accent.

She was wearing a thin jacket over a cottony flounced skirt and gypsy blouse. Despite the fact the Indian summer warmth was continuing during the days, the nights held the sharpness of autumn. She gave an involuntary shiver.

'Do you want to come inside and wait?'

She shook the plaits. 'No. Thank you. He'll wake up soon.' She huddled further into the jacket and stared at nothing. Her eyes were blank and defeated. If Tattoos had told her to stay out there until her feet fell off from frostbite, she'd have considered it a reasonable request. You can't argue with that sort of masochism.

In the end I chipped a few granules off the coffee lump and took her up a hot drink and a blanket.

She cupped her hands around the mug and murmured her thanks. 'You know Stuart, yes?'

'Yes. Do you?'

'No. Not really. He live here. Long time ago now.' She had the slight 'hurr' on her h's and roll on her r's of the Hispanic languages.

'How long ago?' I asked. 'Two years back?'

'No. More. Perhaps six or seven years. Why?'

'Just curious. You ever see him these days?'

'No. Sometimes he comes to the flat. But I do not see him.' She slid an oblique look at me from under her eyelashes. 'Are you girlfriend?'

'Nope. Just crashing at the flat for the night. Shall I say hi for you?'

'No. We had a big fight. He is very angry with me.'

'Really?' It was the second time in one night that someone had suggested that Stuart wasn't quite the mild-mannered little bunny he appeared to be. I tried a bit more shameless probing. 'That's funny, Stuart doesn't strike me as the hot-headed type. What happened?'

'It is best perhaps not to say. It was long time ago now. And he think I am to blame. Maybe he is right.'

'But you don't think so?'

'I have rights. Not to do if I don't want to do.'

'Did Stuart try to make you do something?'

She nodded.

'And he got mad when you wouldn't?'

'*Si*,' she said softly. 'He is very angry.' She shook the plaits, dismissing the incident. 'It is a long time ago. You will not say anything to . . . ?' Her glance slid to the windows of the flat behind us.

'Not if you don't want me to.'

'It is best. If *he* know . . .' Once again the dead eyes flickered in the direction of her own flat. 'Then there is more trouble. It is all forgotten. It is best.' Raising the mug to her lips, she winced at the movement. Seeing my expression, she said softly, 'He loves me. When he drink, he doesn't know what he do.'

You'd have thought the broken limbs and bruises might have given him some clue when he sobered up. But it was her funeral – and probably would be one day, unless Tattoos took a fancy to another punch-bag and threw her out.

I left her to her martyrdom and rolled myself in the sleeping bag. As soon as I closed my eyes I was woken up again by a persistent knocking on the front door and Waterloo's full-throated challenge to whatever was on the doorstep.

'Belt up,' I ordered him, blearily checking my watch. It said seven o'clock. I'd had three hours' sleep. If she'd stayed for the rest of the party so had the leather-clad moppet, but had it affected her bright-eyed, in-your-face cheerfulness? Unfortunately not.

'Hi!' she trilled. 'Can we come in?' 'We' were another female and two blokes, one of whom was touting the ubiquitous camera.

'Why?'

'We're here to do the interview, love,' one of the men called over her shoulder. 'Is it true your dog saved Rick Alaimo's kid from drowning?'

'Can we get a few facts?' the other female asked, bringing out a portable recorder.

'Help yourself.' I used a foot to nudge Waterloo over the front step where the empty coffee-mug was sitting on top of the neatly folded blanket. 'His vocabulary's a bit limited.'

'No. I meant from you. How long have you had him? What's he called? What breed is he?'

'Waterloo is a rare breed of Dutch mountain dog,' I assured her. Out of the corner of my eye I saw the camera being raised and managed to get the door partially closed and spoil the shot. He moved into a better position and I made sure it wasn't that much better.

'Can't I get a picture?' he coaxed. 'The readers will want to see you. Come on, Grace, just one shot. How about it?'

The leather-clad moppet suggested perhaps I wanted to get dressed first. I didn't. Neither did I want to be featured in their paper as the owner of super-mutt. So I ducked out by telling them Waterloo's owner was in Moorfields at present and I was just the dog-sitter.

It worked. An early morning call to Arlene fixed up an interview on the steps of the Outpatients entrance for her and old smelly bottom. The reporter got the whole heart-rending – and very saleable – tale of Waterloo's rescue from the tip, and Waterloo got to show off his best macho-dog poses. I stayed well inside the hospital reception area where they couldn't use the cameras.

'It's not that I don't think I done good,' I told the mutt later once we were riding back to Seatoun. 'It's just that this is just the sort of human interest story that's liable to be picked up and chewed over on all those slow-news days. And there are things a girl likes to keep private.'

In my case it was my ignominious departure from the police a few years ago. It had been in the days when I thought I knew it all when it came to battered spouses. Answering a call to the house of a minor villain with a history of domestic violence one night, I'd found the door open and his wife bruised and bleeding. It wasn't an unusual scenario at that particular address, but each time we'd taken a statement from the wife, she'd withdrawn the complaint before the case got to court, claiming to be terrified he'd get off and kill her. This time, though, she'd pleaded with me to say I'd seen him hit her. She'd sworn she'd go through with charging hubby if I'd back her up. So I had. It had seemed like a good lie at the time. So, it wasn't strictly legal, but the end justified the means, I figured.

Unfortunately at about the same time a plain clothes officer had been run down during a bungled drugs bust. There was a witness who identified the van driver, but he had an alibi: I'd put him fifty miles up the coast beating up his wife. As the officer hadn't appeared to be too badly hurt at first, I'd panicked and stuck to my story. When it became clear the damage was far worse than the doctors had originally assessed, I was well and truly in it up to my jugular. To make matters even worse, a large sum of money had mysteriously arrived in my bank account a few days later. There was no formal inquiry. They just called me into an office and invited me to sign my resignation.

I hadn't lived it down yet, but at least for a lot of people it was old news and they'd moved on to despising others. The last thing I needed was a bunch of reporters digging into the background of the co-saviour of Baby Alaimo.

'Any medals are all yours, kid,' I told Waterloo. He was sprawled on his back along the rear seat with an expression of dreamy contentment on his ugly mug and his fat stomach bulging with all the bribes he'd been fed to pose for his 'picky-wicky'. 'Maybe we should pop in on the way back and let Christina add to your big-headedness.'

It would mean a diversion, but with any luck I'd be there before the local press had got a sniff of the story. And once we'd done the 'thanks . . . you're welcome, anyone would have done the same' routine, I could concentrate on the increasingly bizarre details of Stuart's case.

Speaking of which – I still had one tape left to play. I slid it into the car's cassette player.

21

'Where are you, Joe?'
   'Garden.'
   'Your garden. At the farm?'
   'Don't be daft. Don't have a garden. It's her garden.'
   'Whose?'
   'Lulu's.'
   'Lulu Cazlett. Is that who you mean, Joe?'
   'Yes.'

'Is she with you? Is Lulu in the garden?'

'No. She's up at the house. They're having a party. Lots of fancy folks. Wouldn't have me at that, would they.'

'So what are you doing in the garden?'

'Watching.

'Watching who? Lulu?'

'Maybe. Some.'

'Why are you doing that?'

'I want to. It's my business, all right?'

'What's the party for? Is it someone's birthday?'

'New Year's Eve.'

'It must be cold outside.'

'It is. No worse than working the farm. You get used to it.'

'Why don't you go inside somewhere?'

'I'm waiting.'

'For what?'

'Lulu. She'll let me in soon, I know she will. She loves me. Those others, they don't understand her. Don't see what a special person she is. I'm going to take care of her.'

'Does she know you're waiting outside, Joe?'

'She saw me. I went and stood right up by the window. She saw me. She'll come out to me soon. She has to. I love her. I told her. It hurts. It hurts so much. I need to hold her. To feel her. I'm going to take her away. I'll get a job. Look after both of us.'

'How old are you, Joe?'

'I'm near enough seven'een. I'm man enough for her. I told her.'

'What did she say?'

'She laughed. Called me a sweet boy. But I'm not a boy. I love her. I'll make her listen to me. She has to listen. What they're saying about her isn't true.'

'What do they say?'

'That she goes with any man who asks.'

'Does she?'

'No! Don't you listen. She LOVES me. She wouldn't let

152

them do what I done to her. Not even her husband. He sleeps in another room. She told me so. And it's right, I asked the maid. That other bloke, he was a mistake. They're all leaving now. She'll let me in soon. Cars are starting. Why are they taking so long? Just go, will you? Oh, Jesus . . . !'

'What is it, Joe?'

'She's there. At the window. Over the door. It's like . . . like she's caught in the moon. Her body is silver. Beautiful, oh, Jesus, so beautiful. They're laughing. Why are they laughing? Can't they see how wonderful she is? It's for me, just for me. She knows I'm watching for her.'

'What's for you, Joe?'

'Her body. Her wonderful, beautiful body.'

'What's Lulu wearing, Joe?'

'Nothing. There's just her. With her whiteness and all those soft, warm places she shared with me. I love her. I've got to have her again. She must understand. I'll make her understand. She won't laugh at me again. I'll make her.'

22

The gates to the oast houses were standing wide open when I arrived. In fact, a large swathe of the garden to the left that I'd struggled through the other day was now wide open. Bushes had been uprooted and dragged aside; a couple of young trees were lying where they'd been felled, and much of the grass and reeds had been flattened under a temporary roadway of wooden duckboarding – laid to prevent the vehicles I could see over by the wall from sinking into the mud. I thought I glimpsed Christina behind a group of workmen. When I pulled the car over and switched off the engine, the silence was filled by the continuous throb of machinery.

I got out, trying to decide whether to drive on up to the house or walk across. Waterloo solved the problem by leaping out of the open door and belting away towards the scene of his big moment.

Before I could retrieve him, a dark blue Mercedes swung into the gates and braked so suddenly that its wheels skidded little puffs of dirt on the track before it came to a halt. Rick sprang out.

'What the hell's going on?'

He was looking at me and I assumed for a moment he was speaking to me until I glanced behind and saw that he was calling to Christina. She continued to walk serenely down the duckboards, apparently unworried by Rick's shouting. Emilie Rose was clasped to her mum's right hip, dressed in a set of blue gingham dungarees, with one bare foot resting on the swell under the soft folds of Mum's long skirt. I must say she'd cleaned up into a real cutie pie, with a cloud of dark hair, tilted nose and huge dark eyes that were currently regarding me with great solemnity.

'Hi, sweetie.' Christina slipped an arm round her husband's neck and brushed a kiss on his mouth. 'We missed you.' She patted her bump. 'All three of us.'

'Yeah. Me too. But, Chrissie, what the hell gives here?'

'I told you I wanted to make alterations out here, Rick. And since Emmy nearly died, I kicked a few butts to get them to move double-quick and get the pools drained and covered. The outside house pool has been boarded over until we can get proper covers fitted and they're fitting magnetic alarm locks way up high on the doors to the indoor pool room. So you can use it, but if the kids succeed in pushing it open all hell breaks loose. Now there's just this damn lake to drain.'

'You should have left it to me. I told you to leave it, Chrissie. There's an underground spring according to the guy who built the walls for me. It never dries out.'

'So we're finding. But you know me, Rick, I don't give up easy. I just hope you aren't here to take pics for the publicity, honey.' She smiled at me. 'We really aren't at our best.' She waggled a sandalled foot, muddied from tramping over the blitzed garden, and pushed back hair that was as thick and wiry as her daughter's.

She wasn't at all like the vacuous, silicon-enhanced blondes that were normally pictured with Rick. For one thing, she was about twenty years older. And for another she appeared to be capable of using words with three syllables. Rick reminded her of our last meeting.

'Oh, God, that was you!' She put the arm that wasn't holding her daughter around my neck and hugged. 'I am so *sorry*. I should have recognised you, but to tell you the truth I don't remember a damn thing between Mel shouting that she'd found Emmy by the lake and running into that hospital with her. It's like the whole hour has just been blanked out.'

'That's okay.' I gently disentangled myself from the hug. 'It's probably shock. Any ill-effects on Emilie?'

'No. I don't think she even remembers it, do you, darling? Kiss Grace thank you.'

She held the gingham bundle up, allowing the bemused poppet to shyly brush a kiss on the cheek of a female I'm sure she didn't know from squat. I refrained from pointing out, yet again, that her rescue was really down to Waterloo. Being forced to kiss the ugly little mutt could have screwed the poor kid up for life.

Speaking of which, 'My dog's in there somewhere. Do you mind if I go fetch?'

'Honey, our house is your house. Come on.' She linked the free arm through mine and drew me back along the duckboards towards the thrumming machinery and half-dozen boiler-suited workmen.

A large stainless-steel pipe ran from a tanker into the lake. They'd succeeded in pumping out most of the contents apart from a thick glistening layer of liquid mud that surrounded a bubbling pool about six feet in diameter in the centre of the lake floor. The retreating water had left a layer of plant life behind which was now rotting and releasing a foul smell to add to the general sourness of the mud. Guess who was romping around in the mess? He looked like the banana chunk after it had been dunked in the chocolate fondue. About the only parts of him that were distinguishable from the mud coating were his teeth and his eyes. I yelled at him to 'heel'. He responded by ploughing off in the opposite direction.

Christina said. 'They've been pumping for hours and still we can't get the damn hole dry enough for them to cap it off.'

'It was a farm pond, wasn't it?' I said. 'They were probably glad to have a constant water source in the summer.'

'How in the world did you know that? About the farm, I mean?' Christina asked.

Because this was the section of the garden that dissected Tyler's Lane where 'Joe' had supposedly buried that unknown woman's body, that's why. But professional ethics prevented me from explaining that her husband's accountant was an hallucinating sleep-walker who may have assaulted her stepdaughter. So I resorted to vague murmuring about researching local history. And since I was here, there was no harm in seeing whether another piece of 'Joe's' tape checked out. 'Were there any huts or anything around here once?'

'Yeah.' Rick looked impressed. 'There were. Up over in the far field. Hoppers' huts, they called them. Used to get hundreds of Londoners come down from the East End every year to pick the hops. You should have seen the places they put them. No water, no johns, no electricity. I mean, absolute basic living. You wouldn't keep a dog in them these days. They were pulled down when the garden was laid out. Should have kept them, I guess. They'd probably be listed buildings now. Say, is your dog okay?'

Waterloo was still romping in the sludge. But he wasn't romping with quite so much energy now. He reared up and tried to paddle with his front legs. His hindquarters came free with a 'gluck' sound and he managed to flounder a few more feet before he started sinking again. With more frantic movements, he tried to heave himself out of the glutinous embrace but just succeeded in sinking belly first. He gave a little bark. It wasn't his usual attention howl or Rottweiler-ripper challenge. He was scared.

'Keep still, you idiot,' I shouted. Before realising I was, once again, talking to a dog as if he understood every word I said. Without the water it was clear that the bottom sloped from the shallow end where we were standing to the deeper side over by the wall where I'd clambered out with Emilie Rose. It was even deeper than I'd anticipated. The mud wall must have been at least seven feet high but there was a ledge about halfway up which is what I must have got a foothold on. The first few feet of the bottom over this side were already drying and cracked under the daytime sun, but as soon as I reached the sludge it started to grab and cling to my legs.

'Hang on a minute, love.' A couple of the workmen were hauling a roll of the jointed duckboarding across to the edge. With a practised flourish they flicked it out. It unrolled like a carpet, bowling past me in the general direction of Waterloo. It stopped about three feet short of his front paws. He wasn't struggling any more. Instead, he lay on his stomach, sinking into the goo, plainly waiting for someone to haul him out. And guess who'd been nominated as the said mug?

Kneeling to distribute my weight more evenly, I crawled over on all fours. The mud and rotting vegetation oozed up between the slats, coating my trousers and hands. When I got to the end I had to lie full length and ease out to hitch my fingers under his collar. The movement completed my dousing by spreading muck across everywhere above waist level.

With me dragging, Waterloo managed to struggle over and get his front paws on the first duckboard. As he heaved himself free of the glutinous stranglehold, his face came within inches of mine. 'I'll get you for this,' I hissed in a low voice.

Unlike the wide boarding they'd used to give access to the vehicles, this strip was only about a foot wide. I wasn't going to try turning and pushing even further into the mud so I started crawling backwards with Waterloo padding after me. I was looking down so I didn't immediately see the cause of Christina's shout of, 'Look out!'

I looked behind in her direction at first. But she seemed to be staring over to the other side of the lake. I turned back. A section of the far bank appeared to be moving. At first it was so weird that my mind said it must be an optical illusion. Then a ripple of movement under the duckboards said it was real.

A whole chunk of the earth sailed forward like the prow of a ship. Behind it the earth collapsed into a widening rift and more dirt spilled down the sides of this canyon. From where I was crouching I couldn't see the whole picture, although one of the workmen said later it was like watching the earth unzip.

The force under the duckboards lifted them upwards and tipped me off. I landed flat on my back. Out of the corner of my eye, I saw the wave of mud surging towards me. It wasn't very high, but when you're glued like a fly on fly-paper, and facing being smothered, you tend not to think logically.

I screamed and tried to sit up. Waterloo responded by jumping on my chest and pushing me even further in. I closed my eyes and waited for death.

Luckily death stopped short by several inches and dissipated into a further layer of mud puddle. The mutt hopped off on to the slightly more solid layer of earth that had been swept down into the lake and scrambled away in the direction of the garden's new sunken feature.

'Well, thanks for nothing,' I shouted after him.

Floundering, I unglued myself from the sticky trap yet again. A couple of the workmen were wading out towards me and Christina was asking if I was okay.

'Flaming great, thanks,' I said through gritted teeth. I

pushed mud-soaked hair away from my mud-soaked face with my mud-soaked hands. Why wouldn't I be okay? There was many a hippo who'd give his potamus to be where I was now.

Waterloo came jumping back along the rib of solid earth. I had misjudged the mutt. He was grateful to me for my efforts to save his life. He'd brought me a present to prove it. Proudly he laid it at my feet.

It was a human arm bone.

23

'It means jail for sure.'

'Not necessarily. It could be a suspended sentence. Or probation.'

'Somehow, sweet thing, that does not fill me with a warm glow of reassurance.'

Flicking his indicator on, Vetch rejoined the traffic stream and waited for a gap in the oncoming cars that would let him turn right down to Winstanton.

It was nearly a week since the earth slip at the oast house had spat out the skeleton. We'd found the rest of it near the base of the garden wall. Unlike all those schlock-horror movies, we weren't confronted by a skull with elongated yellowed teeth grinning up at us. This body had been buried face-down which was great for those with a nervous disposition but not so hot for those of us who'd heard the spooky-voiced Joe Gumbright desperate to avoid the blood-shot eyes of 'his' corpse by turning her over. I even found myself looking for further signs of strangulation before reality kicked in and pointed out when they'd stopped stinking it was way too late to find the bruises. From the quick glance I'd taken, there was no soft tissue left, or any sign of clothing or personal effects – even rotted ones.

The drainage work had been stopped immediately. The police had thrown a cordon around the area and blanked any requests for information beyond the standard 'enquiries proceeding' line. Basically that translated as, 'Your guess is as good as ours at present, chum.' Until they'd established how long the skeleton had been down there, there wasn't a lot of point wasting more resources. The chances of the local boys apprehending the killer of some Victorian milkmaid were zilch. And if it turned out we'd simply stumbled across the site of an Anglo-Saxon burial, the only people who were going to be remotely interested were the local museum staff. In the meantime the press had christened the skeleton 'The Duke of Bones' after one of Rick's earlier records.

Stuart had seized on that 'Duke' tag with almost pathetic eagerness. 'If it is a man, then it c-can't be the woman Joe buried, can it?'

I'd gone over to Winstanton the day after my mud bath to bring him up to date on what I'd found so far and return his flat keys. Waterloo's find had made the late news the evening before, so Stuart was already in a state by the time I got there. The stutter was pronounced and he thought he might be sleep-walking again.

'Might?'

'I lock the door keys away before I go to sleep. So it's harder to get out. I don't think I've been b-beyond the front door, but in the morning there are things moved around in the flat. And I feel t-t-terrible. T-tired. Like I haven't slept at all.' He ran a hand through his hair, standing the soft brown mop on end and giving me the chance to observe that the purple aubergine had shrunk to a dirty yellow bump that blended quite well with the scab on the healing fat lip.

He looked like an overgrown schoolboy. Melody had been right: no one would have pegged him as a candidate for date-rape. And that included me. I wasn't daft enough to swallow her story without doing some checking of my own. So once I'd explained that the 'Duke' tag was honorary since they hadn't done the post-mortem and established the sex yet, I said casually, 'I went to Rick's launch party the other night. Thought you might be there.'

'No. I don't like those sorts of things. They're t-too c-crowded. Did you enjoy yourself?'

'Not really. They're not my sort of thing either. Melody seemed to have a good time.'

'Yes. She's a very social animal.'

'How do you get on with her? I got the feeling there was maybe an edge between you.'

He flushed. 'No. We're fine. What has she been saying?'

I shrugged. 'Nothing. Just that you had a date in New York and things didn't work out too well.'

I was prepared for him to deny that the incident in New York had ever happened. But instead he mumbled that it had been a misunderstanding. 'Mel and I are clear now. I'm surprised she mentioned it.'

Or hoping she wouldn't perhaps? 'Do you want me to go on digging?'

'For what?' he said sharply.

'The Joe Gumbright story. What else would I mean?'

'Yes. Sorry. Of c-course. Find out whatever you c-can.'

I intended to anyway. Not for his sake, but for Annie's. Whatever Stuart's game was, I intended to stay in play for now. And this way I was going to get paid for it. Saving your best mate from a possible rapist was all very well, but a girl's got to eat.

After checking in with Stuart, I'd spent a couple of sleepless nights tossing around trying to decide whether I should tell Annie what Melody and Tattoos's girlfriend had said about her latest squeeze. The fact I'd promised not to repeat what Melody had told me didn't bother me at all. As far as I was concerned, telling Annie didn't count. She frequently acted as my conscience anyway, so I justified it as no more than having a conversation with myself. Which was a definite improvement on the worryingly frequent chats I was having with the mutt.

At least I could use him as an excuse for dropping in on

her flat early one morning before she'd gone into the office and turned into Cruella the Career Bitch. I had my 'the damn dog dragged me out at dawn' moan all prepared and was already rehearsing in my head the rest of the conversation we were going to have. Unfortunately Annie hadn't been reading from the same script. For a start, in mine Stuart didn't open her flat door.

'Is there news?' he asked eagerly. 'Have they found out who the body is?'

'Not that I know of. We just popped round to scrounge breakfast.'

'Finally exhausted your credit at Pepi's?' Annie called from inside the flat.

'It's Monday. He's closed.'

'So I'm second in your soft touches for fried bread and sunny side up?'

'Since you ask – yes.'

She was curled on the sofa reading the morning paper in her striped pyjamas and pink towelling dressing-gown. It wasn't exactly seduction gear, but there was a self-satisfied glow oozing from her that said Stuart hadn't popped round with this year's company tax tables. It got worse when she cooked a full fried breakfast for both of us, added a few sausages for Waterloo and then sat serenely sipping black coffee and plain toast whilst we tucked in. Diets were always a sure sign that Annie was involved with a bloke, but in this case it wasn't even hurting.

I'd been practising celibacy for a few weeks – well, not exactly practising, I'd pretty well got it cracked actually – and until now so had Annie. Once Stuart had driven off I tackled Annie about her apparent change of heart.

'I figure you've got to grab your chances when they come along. He's kind, Grace. And he's a triple S – single, solvent and straight. Which, let's face it, is pretty much an endangered species over thirty.' She loaded hot water, washing-up liquid and greasy plates into a plastic bowl.

'But he's so . . . nerdish.'

'No, he's not!' Then she relented and admitted that perhaps he could come over that way. 'But that's only because it takes him a while to relax in company. Once he's comfortable with you, he's funny and interesting and comfortable to be with.'

'That doesn't sound like a whole load of fun. What about the phwoar-factor? You aren't seriously telling me this is the bloke you see in all those warm, fuzzy private fantasies you wouldn't even admit to your best mate?'

'No, I generally see Pierce Brosnan in those. Or occasionally Harrison Ford. Stuart is more the sort of bloke I see when I'm running my happy-ever-after feature.'

'Which is . . . ?'

'The one where I find a bloke who's strong and decisive enough to guard and protect me. But at the same time sensitive enough to allow me to be a completely free and independent spirit.'

'You know what they call women like you, don't you?'

'What?'

'Single.'

'I'm not picking out the honeymoon. I dare say it will just be a bit of fun in the end. But I want to enjoy it while it lasts, Grace.'

There had been slight pleading in her tone. Just enough to let me know that if I'd come round to tell her that Santa Claus didn't exist then she'd rather hang on to the fantasy for just one more Christmas, thanks. Which is why I'd had to put Plan B into operation a couple of days later.

It involved recruiting our esteemed leader, Vetch-the-Letch.

'Why me, sweet thing?' he asked, steepling his fingers and resting his elbows on the top of his executive-style desk.

'Because you have useful contacts.'

'True.'

'You are skilful and resourceful.'

'Indubitably true.'

'You care about Annie.'

'Mostly true.'

'It's not exactly going to enhance this agency's already shaky reputation if it comes out we were conned by a cunning psycho.'

'Very true. And . . .?'

'And I don't know anyone else to ask.'

'Just wanted to hear you say it, sweet thing. I'll pick you up at half nine. May I suggest a tight and provocative dress would be appropriate?'

'Whatever turns you on, Vetch. I'll be in jeans.'

Luckily Stuart was in. I'd already established Annie wasn't seeing him this evening, but there was always the chance he'd be out working or sleep-walking around the Middle Ages or whatever. He looked bad. The strain was cutting lines into his plumpish face and painting deep shadows under his eyes.

'Hi. I brought those copies of the Gumbrights' birth and death certificates I promised you. Have you met Vetch?'

'Er, no. I believe you were out when I c-called at the agency. Annie's spoken of you, though.'

'No doubt she touched lightly on my charm, genius and intuition.'

'No. But I think she mentioned your innate modesty,' Stuart said with an unexpected flash of humour.

'Must have been someone else.' Vetch moved forward a few steps, forcing Stuart to back up.

'Would you like to come in?'

'Just for a second,' I said. 'We're on our way to a job.'

We followed him up the stairs. We'd apparently disturbed him at work. He flicked the computer off before offering, 'Drink? Coffee?'

'I wouldn't say no to a small whisky if you have such a thing.' Vetch beamed. He looked around with interest. 'My, this place is a real piece of work. What a magnificent view.'

He walked over to the large picture window. Once again

the lights were creating an optical illusion of another living room hovering out there over the beach.

I declined the drink and passed over the photocopies of the documents I'd amassed so far. I'd driven up to collect them yesterday and taken Waterloo for another reunion with his mumsie-wumsie on the hospital steps. Stuart read through Joe's and Billie's birth certificates, the parents' marriage certificate and the grandmother's death certificate. 'There's no Rook Farm,' he said seizing on another one of those insubstantial straws.

That was true enough. The Gumbrights had been living in Winstanton when the kids were born. Their tenancy of the farm must have come later. And Granny's death certificate gave the family's address as Windy Top Farm. I kept the nugget that Rooks was the local nickname for the same place to myself for now.

I let him move on to the last document in the pile. Stanley Gumbright's death certificate. The cause of death ran to several lines and included such phrases as 'depressed fracture of the cranium' and 'subdural haemorrhaging' – or to put it another way, something had smashed something over his head hard enough to cause a massive bleed around the brain cavity.

I'd deliberately arranged the certificates in that order to keep the biggest shock until last and judge Stuart's reaction. It looked like genuine enough shock to me. But then, if that spooky, hate-filled voice on the tapes wasn't for real, Stuart was a hell of an actor and miming a suitable reaction to the confirmation that you'd bashed your dad's skull in in a previous existence would be well within his range.

I had one more little test lined up. 'There's something else. You said Joe was dead, but I couldn't find him in the regular death certificate lists. It sounded like he might have been called up in the fourth tape, so I looked in War Deaths, and came up with this.'

'He was in the air force?' Stuart whispered.

'A sergeant in 103 Squadron. That means bombers

165

according to the bloke I spoke to at an RAF historical group. Apparently they put 'Missing, believed Killed as a Result of Air Operations against the Enemy' on the death certificate if the body was never recovered. The date, 26 June 1943, ties up with the date of some big raid where a fair few planes were completely destroyed. And he mentions Elsham in one of the tapes. That was the base for that squadron.'

'They'd have burnt, wouldn't they?' Stuart said. 'If they were hit? The plane would have been on fire.'

'I've no idea. I mean, I guess it depends what happened.'

Stuart didn't appear to be listening. His pupils had dilated. Presumably we were meant to understand that he was reliving all those nightmares of crashing planes and burning bodies that had been haunting him in recent months.

Vetch and I exchanged looks over his head. Vetch tapped his wrist-watch and nodded towards the stairs. I'd just mimed back 'okay' when all hell let loose outside.

24

'That sounds like my car alarm!' Vetch tried to squint through the reflected room.

'That sounds like everybody's car alarms,' I corrected.

Stuart snapped the lights off. The outside scene sprang into focus. The phosphorescent lights of the ocean and the reflected slicks of the restaurant windows on the black waves were now augmented by the pulsating headlights and indicators of the vehicles in the harbour car park. As we watched another one sprang into life accompanied by the sing-song tones of its audible alarm. 'It's those bloody car vandals again,' Vetch wailed. 'If they've scratched my paintwork there will be murder done this night.'

He untangled his car keys from his coat pocket. I grabbed them. 'I'll go. I'm faster than you.' Two more cars had joined in the chorus. Stuart snatched up his own keys.

We both pounded outside and dashed for the harbour. The protesting wails were rising over the rooftops. Doors were opening as we ran past. The customers from the restaurant who had the least distance to travel got there first. The braver ones at any rate – the rest were standing watching the entertainment from the safety of the windows and the verandah that fronted the beachfront. Everyone was unlocking, disengaging alarms, checking contents and shouting anatomically impossible suggestions as to the fate of the next car thief they ran into (preferably in fourth gear and doing over eighty). I managed to get Vetch's alarm off and confirm that the windows were still intact before one of the restaurant watchers screamed with excitement.

'There! There! There's one on the beach.'

In the illumination from the looks-like gas lamps we all saw the black figure rise from behind the wooden groyne and hold the baseball bat aloft like some kind of challenge.

'Get him!'

Several of the drivers started to run. They were joined by some of the diners who'd got a lot braver now they could see the enemy didn't outnumber them.

I body-swerved through the parked cars, dodging wing mirrors and sweeping up Stuart on the way. The beach here was far narrower than Seatoun's, with shingly stone rather than sand. In the dark it was lethal for turned ankles and I saw a couple of the diners go down. The car-smasher leapt on to a wooden groyne, turned back and flourished the baseball bat again, eyes glinting through the face-covering mask. The whoop of derision was all the pack needed to redouble their efforts and flounder onwards. Rather than go directly forward, I dashed for the sea, with Stuart panting behind me.

'Where are we going?' he called.

'Tide's not fully in yet. Wet sand. Firmer ground,' I called over my shoulder.

Once we were down amongst the wavelets, we swung left

again and sprinted. The intervening groynes were slimy with weed and slowed us slightly. I nearly lost my balance on the top of one and stepped back to regain it. Stuart gave a shout of pain.

'What's up?' I asked.

'You t-trod on my hand.' He clasped his left hand under his right armpit and blew out several short breaths. 'It's nothing. Go on.'

Despite the hiccup, we managed to overtake the mob that were floundering over the stones and shingle. The beach was starting to run out. Beyond this point there was a large stretch of mud. It wasn't precisely quicksand, but it could be dangerous if you happened to stumble into the stickier areas of the morass when the tide was coming in. Our vandal had to turn soon.

Sure enough the dark figure twisted inland and dashed for the short climb from beach to scrub. There was a row of bungalows much like Arlene's about fifty yards from the front. The figure disappeared between two of them. I followed, with Stuart some thirty seconds behind me, and the mob coming a poor third.

By the time I reached the road the tiny enclave of half a dozen small houses and bungalows that stretched like tangled threads from Winstanton's western edge was serene and vandal-free.

'Where'd he go?' Stuart panted, staggering up to me.

'No idea.' I twisted, alert for any movements from behind walls or sheds. 'How's your car?'

'No damage. I think he just set the alarm off. How about yours?'

'Vetch's,' I corrected. 'Mine doesn't have a security system. It's fine.'

Those members of the pack who'd stayed the course all reported the same. Some were still for hanging, drawing and quartering of all vandals, yobs and bloody dole-scroungers, but mostly the chase had cooled them down, and the freshening winds were finishing off the job. We trailed back along the road into Winstanton town centre a breathless and chilly lot.

'It's a pity you didn't bring Waterloo,' Stuart said. 'I bet he'd have c-caught our friend.'

'I bet he would have too. But Vetch won't have him in the car. Anyway, he's got a booking tonight.'

Yes, indeed, folks, the flatulent mutt had become a media star. So far he'd clocked up breakfast TV, a radio slot, several newspaper paragraphs, a photo-shoot for the cover of a doggy magazine and opened a local fête in aid of the RSPCA. I'd declined to chaperon him on these trips so one of the orange and blue leather PR whirlwinds from the recording company generally did escort duty. They were called Chloe and Bo (I never found out which was witch), but with an album called 'The Hounddog Returns' to publicise, they regarded Waterloo as a godsend and were happy to take him off my hands whenever his public called.

When we trailed back to Stuart's flat, Vetch was sitting on the stairs with the front door partially open and my shoulder bag in his lap. 'Everything all right?'

'No problems.' I flicked his car keys at him and he caught them one-handed.

'We should go, sweet thing. We're going to be woefully late. Are you in trouble?'

This last query was directed at Stuart who was examining his left hand in the light from the hall lamp. The ring finger did seem to be somewhat larger than twenty minutes ago. I stared at the ballooning finger and then back at its owner. 'Did you want me to bandage it or something?'

The idea plainly alarmed him. 'No! Really. No n-need. I'll put it in some ice.'

'If you're sure. G'night.'

Vetch and I didn't speak until we were safely in the car and pulling away from the harbour.

'Which way, sweet thing?'

'Right.'

Vetch drove slowly down the streets the mob and I had

just walked. Once we reached the area where our vandal had disappeared I told him to pull over. A few seconds later we both felt a draught on the backs of our necks as the kerbside back door opened and closed. Without looking round, Vetch drove away and eventually pulled up on a relatively quiet stretch of coast road with just the scrub and the undulating swell between us and the cargo carriers riding at anchor out on the horizon.

Jan sat up, pulled off the woollen balaclava with eye slits hacked in it and grinned. 'Good, weren't I?'

'Where the hell did the baseball bat come from?' I demanded. She hadn't had it when we'd dropped her off just before we turned down to Winstanton.

'Had it down the leg of my trousers. I was getting into character.'

'You were supposed to be a car vandal, not a bloody bank robber.'

'I do hope I shan't find so much as a whisper of damage to my motor,' Vetch remarked. 'Otherwise I fear the cost will be coming out of your wages, Janice.'

'You don' pay me enough to pay for your repairs. Anyhow, I never hit anything. I just rocked them a bit to set the alarms off. I was gonna use the bat to sort out anyone who caught up with me.'

'For God's sake, Jan, that wasn't the plan.' We'd already agreed that if anyone did catch her, I'd lay into them and cause enough confusion for her to get away. Hence the need to sprint along that beach. 'I wanted a diversion, not a bloody accomplice in committing GBH.'

'I was improvising, weren' I. D'you crack it?' she asked Vetch, folding her arms along the back of his seat and craning forward eagerly.

'Naturally. Thank heavens for the paperless office. It's killed more trees than acid rain. There's a whole file full of printer-generated tax returns in the cabinet.'

'Is he rich?' Jan asked.

'I didn't have time to find out. One of those picks is

slightly twisted, sweet thing,' he said, returning my lock-breaking kit to me. 'It made relocking a challenge. I should attend to it if you intend to continue with a life of slightly dubious ethics.' Dialling on his mobile, he spoke briefly to whoever was on the other end and then read off Stuart's National Insurance number from where he'd inked it on the inside of his forearm. 'I'll be ready by the time we get back to the office,' he said, breaking the connection.

'Better buzz, then, in case any of the others gets there first.'

'They won't transmit until I give them the say-so. And a card number to charge it to.'

Yes, believe it or not, Vetch knew an official records blagger who took credit cards. Vetch himself had insisted on cash for my half of the fee. I handed the envelope of tenners over and told Jan we'd drop her off on the way.

'That's not fair! I'm on the team. I want to see what you've got on the mark!'

'Jan, stop reading trashy detective novels and revert to your normal activity of training for the World's Most Bored Receptionist Award.'

She'd have argued further if Vetch hadn't told her that if she couldn't obey orders he wouldn't be able to consider her for more leg work in the future – not that we would unless we both suffered a collective brainstorm. But when it came to snooping on the love of Annie's life, we just couldn't think of anyone else who was stupid enough to take it on. Her life wouldn't be worth living if Annie found out. Neither would ours.

Despite Vetch's assurances that no one else was going to be around, it was a relief to find the premises of Vetch (International) Associates Inc. were reassuringly quiet and empty when we arrived. Disengaging the alarms, Vetch rang his upwardly mobile blagger again, and then stepped over to the fax machine. Within seconds it started spewing out paper – the 'send' number that was normally printed on the top was conspicuously absent.

The Inland Revenue will track you from your first taxable penny to your last pension payout. In Stuart's case he'd started earning nineteen years ago at the age of sixteen. The records were generated in reverse order, so his present address and self-employed status were flagged first. Letting my eyes slide downwards, I found that he'd been telling the truth when he'd said he'd only lived in the sail loft conversion for two years. However, there was another address in Winstanton listed where he'd lived for the previous four years. Prior to that he'd been at the Kentish Town dump for five years. It seemed to have been at that point he'd gone self-employed. Prior to that there were about a dozen addresses scattered over various districts in London. That took us back to his twentieth year. The sixteen-year-old Stuart had apparently been gainfully employed for two years. Which left us with a gap between eighteen and twenty that wasn't accounted for.

It wasn't, as Vetch pointed out, all that significant. It was an age when a lot decide to drop out, chill out or check out. Possibly Stuart had been backpacking around India, finding himself in Tibet or researching a novel about beaches in Thailand. It wasn't a picture that was easy to formulate if you were holding a vision of present-day, diffident, stuttering Stuart in your mind. But maybe he'd been a real wild child before he'd discovered double-tongue grooving and laminate flooring?

Or perhaps the reason for those lost two years lay in by far the most interesting fact in the life and (abbreviated) times of Stuart Roberts. He wasn't Stuart Roberts.

His full name, according to the sheet of paper I was holding, was Stuart Robert Breezley.

25

'You're not only unprincipled, you're cheap with it.'
'I know. But if the cap fits, Vetch . . . ?'

'I am prudent. You are cheap.'

'What's the difference?'

'I make a reasoned judgement to hold on to my cash. With you it's a reflex action.'

'The result's the same. Neither of us is going to stump up the price of an illegal trawl through police records.'

'Well, I'm certainly not, sweet thing. And if you intend to go down that particular route, I think I'd prefer not to have a copy of your travel plans in advance.'

Having discovered that Stuart Roberts was Stuart Breezley, the next step was to discover if Mr Breezley's past was somewhat more colourful than balance sheets and DIY kitchen fitments. However, accessing police files carried with it certain inherent risks. Hence not only were such searches expensive, but anyone prepared to do one had to be convinced that you weren't working some undercover police sting but were a bona fide unprincipled snoop. I knew Vetch had such a contact, but he regarded this little treasure as a resource that was only to be used when we were at the crunch. And as far as he was concerned, my vague suspicions regarding Annie's current boyfriend weren't even at the nibble.

'I'll think of something.'

'Something that doesn't involve parting with cash, I'm sure,' Vetch purred, switching off the office lights and preparing to reset the alarm system.

I told him I'd lock up as I wanted to check my own office before I left. 'And I want to look someone up on the internet. Any idea how I do that?'

'You truly are a techno-Luddite, sweet thing.' Switching on Jan's computer, he demonstrated the mysteries of surfing the Web. It took me less than ten minutes to find what I needed. After which I ran up to my own office. It was one of three occupied rooms on the top floor, a dust-challenged tribute to my aversion to housework and haphazard approach to interior decor (i.e. if the paint's free slap it on, and to hell with the colour). There was a small pile of post sitting in the centre of the battered desk, which had presumably been left there by Jan. Needless to say, she hadn't bothered to tell me I had mail. Being helpful was way outside her job description.

It seemed an age since I'd been up here. Looking around it now, I felt a stab of nostalgia. I'd spent several happy years crashing out here, wallowing in free hot water next door in the bathroom left over from the days of Grannie Vetch's reign of terror, and nipping across the landing to Annie's beautifully-decorated office to scrounge coffee and chocolate biscuits. Now she wanted to turn us into a branch of Super-Efficient Snoops International. There may be no progress without pain, but I didn't see why it should be written into the deal that it had to be mine. I turned my attention to the letters.

Most were no more than junk mail inviting my subscription to magazines I didn't want and my purchase of cars, financial products and luxury holidays that I did want but couldn't afford. I binned them and turned my attention to the only two that looked interesting. I recognised the writing on the large brown envelope as belonging to Ruby, the pensioner who did our tedious library research. Presumably Jan had recognised it too, which was why it was still unopened, unlike the other, which was thick white expensive stationery with bold black lettering. Unusually it was addressed to the house number rather than Vetch's Agency. I lifted out a single sheet of paper. It was from Christina Alaimo, inviting me to dinner as soon as I could make it.

. . . I really feel I've never thanked you properly for saving Emilie Rose. First time all I could think of was getting Emilie to the doctors which I claim as reasonable behaviour in a mother seeing as how we get a whole new set of rules on manners as soon as they get us in the delivery suite (particularly when they get us in the delivery suite matter of fact!). However the second time that damn corpse got in the way and while I don't mean to sound unfeeling, I think one breathing daughter beats a collection of bones every time. I now have one working(ish) kitchen and a reasonably cop free garden again so please come to dinner so I can say thanks with more style than I did before? Give me a ring and we can fix a date soon.

Christina Alaimo

I saved Ruby's contribution until I'd got back to the bungalow and poured myself another glass of Arlene's claret. She really did have a very good selection stowed away in racks and cupboards – not that I can tell the difference between plonk or chateau posh. By 'good' I mean extensive. The more there were, the easier I felt about helping myself. With a bit of creative shuffling before I left, she'd never know quite how greedy I'd been.

Whenever there had been something she'd thought fitted my orders, Ruby had copied the entire page. The sheaf of papers enclosed consisted of no more than half a dozen sheets of A3. Nineteen thirty-eight had plainly been a slow year for unnatural female deaths. According to her invoice it had taken her three solid days of working nine to six to produce them – less an hour off each day for a hotel lunch at £11 a time ('Hope you don't think I was being greedy, Smithie, love, but the service here was fastest and I'd my bus home to think about'). I didn't begrudge her a penny of it – after all, Stuart was paying.

I was beginning to feel like my professional life was splitting and going down two distinct paths. The investigator down path number one was still working *for* Stuart and trying to prove or disprove the memoirs of his alter ego, Joe Gumbright. Whereas on path number two I was working *against* Stuart whilst I tried to find out whether this was some elaborate scam on his part – and if so, for what purpose?

So far the information I'd unearthed simply confirmed

the barest facts of Joe's life story. I knew the Gumbrights existed and had once rented Windy Top Farm and Lulu Cazlett had had a reputation as the local flirt. But so what? There was nothing there anyone couldn't discover by doing the same digging as I had. What proof did I have that Joe's dad had been a wife-beater? Or that his mum had walked out? That Joe Gumbright had really seen, let alone fancied, Lulu the flasher? About the only titbit of knowledge that was slightly unusual was that nickname of 'Rooks' for the farm. The extent to which that particular nugget had spread was something I'd have to check out.

I lay the sheets of enlarged microfiche entries across the kitchen table and started to read. I became aware of a niggling sensation that something was wrong. The house was too quiet. There was no one howling or whining for my attention.

I checked the time. It was gone ten. I went to the gate and strained to see if I could spot any headlights approaching. When I couldn't get a clear view from the front path, I crossed the road to the headland and shivered in the freshening sea breezes, trying to locate twin beams climbing the incline up from Seatoun Bay. Waterloo and Chloe/Bo had only gone to a guest appearance at a late night promotion in a record store twenty miles away, so what the hell was keeping them?

And what the hell was I doing? Pacing the grass worrying about what time a bloody dog got home, that's what! Stalking inside, I carried my drink and a plate of chocolate fingers to bed and spread Ruby's information over the duvet.

It was fascinating stuff. The reporting was curiously staid and unsensational compared with today's lurid prose. Mostly the death articles consisted of coroner's reports. I hardly needed to read the details; the headlines were enough to tell me I was on the wrong track. 'Death Follows Burns' turned out to be a sixty-seven-year-old who'd died of septic blood poisoning. 'Woman Dies in Tragic Accident' proved to be yet another pensioner who'd been knocked down getting off the bus in Seatoun. I had a brief flicker of hope over 'Woman's Body Discovered on Seatoun Beach'. Maybe Joe had decided night-time burial was too tricky after all. However, the next sheet had details of the indefatigable coroner's case. The beached corpse had been identified as Miss Ada Black, an inmate of the Comstock Institute, a private mental institution near Leeds.

'It would appear that this unfortunate woman escaped from those paid to provide care and companionship to her early on the morning of the nineteenth of October,' the Coroner had intoned in an oblique swipe at the standard of care on offer at the Comstock. He was pretty good at knocking without attacking directly, I realised. I read on with appreciation. 'She then took a taxi cab to the station and purchased a railway ticket to London and from thence another to Seatoun.' (Let her have access to money too, did you?) 'From the statements of witnesses who saw her later that day, she appears to have made her way on foot to North Bay. As we have heard from the medical examiner her injuries were consistent with a fall from the cliffs and we have heard evidence that the prevailing tides would have carried the body around the bay and deposited it on Seatoun beach. We have no way of knowing her intentions and must therefore assume that her death was a tragic accident.' (Even though we all know it was down to incompetence and indifference.)

This was great stuff but no help at all to me. I glanced through the rest of the sheets with fascination. It was like looking backwards down a telescope to a world that was getting further and further away. There were adverts for silk stockings next to ones for Pig Powders and small ads for third parlourmaids and prices paid for poultry feathers. My eyes, which had been gliding smoothly over the columns of newsprint, suddenly jolted off course just as a sharp rat-a-tat sounded on the front door.

Chloe (or Bo) returned the mutt with apologies for the

lateness and yet more thanks for the loan of the four-footed little photo magnet. Waterloo sauntered past me without so much as a 'woof', heaved himself on the bed and flopped with the exhaustion of a super-star who'd been working his public all evening. He managed to raise a weary head and sniff hopefully at the plate that had held the chocolate fingers when I returned from locking up.

'Forget it. You've been out stuffing your face all evening while I've been slaving over a not-so-hot career. Now shove over, fatso, and take a look at this.'

I turned back to the section of the paper I'd been reading before his arrival. It was an advert inviting patrons to sample Fine Ales and Best Bitter at The Spy-Glass Public House in Winstanton. Its address was 'off Island Wall' – which was the street fronting the area of shingle beach next to the old boatyard. One up to 'Joe'. Old Man Gumbright could have got smashed on a regular basis in a pub called the 'The Glass' and staggered out to sleep it off amongst the fishing boats.

'On the other hand, of course,' I informed the bloated mutt, I found this advert, so there's no reason Stuart couldn't have too.'

And looked at another way, I was holding a sheet of newsprint in front of a dog and expecting him to read it. At this rate I'd be as batty as Arlene. With any luck she'd be home this weekend before total and irreversible brain rot set in.

My luck was out. The infection had affected the original repair and the doctors had decided the only way to save her sight was to re-operate immediately. 'It means another week in here, babes,' Arlene said when I telephoned her the next morning. 'You will stay, won't you, and look after my baby?'

She was nearly in tears. I had to agree. And I even heard myself promising to bring him up for another visit soon.

'Tomorrow?'

I hesitated. Tomorrow was a Saturday and I'd planned a

visit to Frognall D'Arcy when I had more chance of catching everyone at home.

'Please, babes. They're gonna operate Sunday. Catch up on a backlog. If I don't see him before I go down for the cut . . .'

'Okay. Tomorrow.'

'Cheers. You won't regret it. I'll remember you in my will.'

Great. Waterloo and I could become the co-owners of a garbage-crusher. What more could a girl have to hope for?

I rang Christina Alaimo next to thank her for her invitation. I'd always assumed that the families of the rich and famous lay in late, but when I said I hoped I hadn't got her out of bed, she laughed.

'Honey, I have an eighteen-month-old daughter who rises before the damn lark and another break-dancing inside my belly. What would be your best guess?'

'In that case, you don't have to add to your problems by cooking for me.'

But Christina wouldn't hear of it. She enjoyed entertaining and she wanted a chance to try out her new cooker. 'I react to quadruple gas burners like other women hug diamonds. Come on, be a sport, give me a chance to shine?'

I recalled that she'd been a restaurateur. Maybe she really was one of those strange souls who liked to bond with freshly chopped coriander. 'Okay. When?'

'Let's see. Tomorrow's out, Rick's in town. How does Sunday sound?'

It sounded fine to me. We fixed on eight o'clock. In what I hoped sounded like a casual enquiry, I asked if there was any news on our skeleton.

'Not really. Your police play it pretty close to their chests. From what I gather, she's in bad shape – for a collection of bones, that is. They altered the natural drainage or something when they built the wall and garden. The lake waters have been leaking into the ground for years. I guess most of her just got washed away.'

I tried not to think about what I might have been doing the breaststroke in. With any luck boney's soft tissue had been flushed away years ago. However, I picked up on something else Christina had said. 'Why'd you call it "she"?'

'Because it's what the officers are calling her. It's definitely a woman's remains. Looks like they'll have to start calling her the Duchess of Bones. Listen, Emilie is playing splat the walls with her breakfast. I got to go. See you Sunday.'

I had a couple of other calls I needed to make, but I decided I might as well fix our breakfast first. The post arrived just as I was dishing up. Two bills for Arlene, a dozen letters and a parcel for Waterloo. Did I mention they'd started sending him fan mail? Generally addressed to the 'brave little dog who saved the little girl' or some such. I was now the unofficial secretary and only dogsbody of the mutt's fan club.

I opened the latest lot as we ate. The parcel was full of doggy treats including several packets of doggy chocs. I sprinkled a handful over my cornflakes and ignored Waterloo's indignant whine. If he wanted to snack, he should learn to open Sellotape. I delved a bit further and found a knitted blanket and jacket. I added them to the stack on the kitchen counter. For some reason, a section of Waterloo's fans seemed to think the coat nature had supplied him with was inadequate. They'd taken to purling and plaining jackets, bootees, bonnets and warmers to fit other parts of his anatomy – the sizing of some led me to suspect that there were a load of short-sighted old ladies out there who were feeding doggy chunks to Shetland ponies.

There was also a clutch who wanted him to mate with their bitches and had enclosed photos of the same – and several who'd enclosed self-addressed envelopes and asked for his autograph. They went into a carrier with the rest until I figured out how he was going to hold the pen.

Secretarial duties over for the day, I returned to the phone and dialled Ruby's number. Once I'd thanked her for the newspaper copies and promised to leave her money at Vetch's reception, I asked her to find another entry for me. 'It's 1942. The bloke's name was Stanley Gumbright, address Windy Top Farm, near Frognall D'Arcy. He died in September, so I guess you'd better work forward from then. I'm looking for a Coroner's Court report.'

'Right-o, lovey. Only you do know they didn't always hold inquests back in the war? Not if it was death by enemy action.'

'I think he may have had his head bashed in, so it definitely wasn't a friendly action. But I don't think it had anything to do with the war.'

On the other hand, how did I know? Perhaps he had been caught in an air raid or something. There was no way of telling from the bare facts on the death certificate. Anyone who wanted to invent a story around the Gumbrights could take the facts I'd discovered and weave their own fantasies out of them. Particularly when there was no one left to dispute them.

The final phone number I'd got from my trawl of hypnotherapist entries on the internet the other night.

I'd assumed it was Tabitha Puzold's private number but it proved to be a switchboard at a clinic. After a brief tussle with the receptionist they put me through to Stuart's own private mind-travel guide. I explained he'd handed her session tapes over to me and asked me to investigate the authenticity of the memories.

'I was wondering if we could talk. I mean, I expect you have to respect patient confidentiality and all that . . .'

'Yes. I think perhaps we should meet.'

It wasn't a reassuring response. I realise that I'd sub-consciously been hoping she'd laugh and tell me not to take Stuart seriously. But there was something about her flat tone of voice that was more warning than reassurance. 'Today is impossible for me, but we have a clinic Saturday. Can you come then?'

'Where are you exactly?'

The clinic was in Ealing in West London, which was fine by me since it meant I could go on to Arlene's afterwards.

'Which leaves us,' I informed the mutt, 'today to do a bit of local snooping into the lives and times of Mr Stuart Breezley, also known as Stuart Roberts and Joe Gumbright.'

26

In the interests of fair play I headed for Frognall D'Arcy first. Since Stuart was going to be billed for all my hours today I decided to root out the local gossip on the Gumbrights – former residents of that parish. (After which I had every intention of charging down path number two and digging up the scandal on Stuart Roberts/Breezley, former resident of a suspiciously large number of parishes.)

Frognall was about three miles further inland than the oast houses. How it had ended up with such a fancy name was a mystery. Like dozens of other tiny villages, it was nothing more than a collection of farm workers' cottages strung along a very minor 'B' road. The only unusual feature of Frognall was that it was split into two sections with a gap of about fifty feet in the central section. There were no shops, post office, school or church. Nor was there any public transport. At first I thought they hadn't even got that essential feature of village life – the pub – until I spotted a sign hanging from the side of the only building that didn't front the main street. Instead it was set at right angles to one of the last houses before the strange gap. It was called Frognall Halt.

It seemed as good a place to start as any. With my clipboard – which people seemed to find reassuring when accosted by strangers asking questions – I headed inside. Bad choice. The dark bar was no bigger than the average sitting room. The floor space was taken up by a small bar, three round tables and chairs, two wooden settles and a lot of shaggy hound.

The beasts from Maudsley Hall rose stiff-legged and showed their teeth to Waterloo. He was right up for it. Backing his stumpy tail against the wall, he prepared to defend his patch of floor.

'Flash! Gordon! *Sit!*'

Reluctantly the hounds sank back on their haunches in response to Prue Cazlett's command. Waterloo sneered before dropping on his own haunches in response to my boot on his rump.

Prue had come through from the door behind the bar. Lifting the counter flap, she stepped back into the main room and set down a cup of coffee. 'Hello. Did you want a drink?'

'Is this your place?' I wouldn't have pegged her as the local publican – and apparently I was right.

'No. Sheila's cooking out back. Do you want something?'

I opted for coffee too. She disappeared into what I assumed must be the kitchen and returned with another cup. My sixty pence was thrown into a box by the till before she took a seat at one of the tables. The Farrah Fawcett had been tied back from a bare face this morning and she was dressed in an oatmeal-coloured sloppy jumper and cord jeans. I preferred it to the leopardskin pants and skin-tight orange number she'd sprayed on for our last meeting.

I wasn't sure she even remembered that encounter until she said abruptly, 'Did you find those people you were looking for?'

'Some. I was going to ask around the village.' I waggled the clipboard. 'Am I likely to find anyone in?'

'Probably. Mostly females, although we have a few house-husbands. Some come in here lunchtimes if you're staying.'

I wondered if that was the attraction for her. There certainly wasn't much else to recommend the place.

Prue fished in the pocket of a battered wax jacket hanging from the corner of the settle and scooped out a packet of cigarettes. She flipped the lid and extended it in my direction.

'I don't, thanks.'

She lit up. From what I could see, nicotine seemed to be the only unnatural substance running round her blood-stream today. She appeared to guess what I was looking for and said, 'Sorry about the other day. I don't usually take anything now. I can't bloody well afford to. But I was nervous. A design magazine was coming to do an article on my work.'

'How'd it go?'

'They never turned up. Reassignment of priorities, they said. Didn't have the guts to say they weren't interested is what they meant. I shared a flat with their bitch of an editor for two years. You'd think sharing leg wax would count for something, wouldn't you? There were four of us. We were the wildest, hottest chicks in town. Got invited to all the best parties.' She blew a slow stream of smoke into the air and watched it curl and dissipate into wreaths of ragged mist. 'It wasn't supposed to be like this,' she said with no apparent reference to anything.

'What wasn't?' I asked.

'My life. We had it all planned in those days. A few years of partying then marriage to husbands that were rich, handsome and famous. Happy children, gorgeous home. Plenty of money. Glam lifestyle. That was the future.'

I began to get her drift. She'd never expected to have to earn her own living.

'What went wrong?' I asked curiously.

She stretched over and snagged a large brass ashtray from the bar, before saying, 'I got married and thought the rest would just follow on. It didn't.' She took another few lungfuls of nicotine and then continued abruptly, 'The husband was only loving insofar as he came back to my bed when he left the others. That was his definition of being faithful. I wasted years thinking he needed time to adjust to the idea of a happy marriage. Then I realised that *was* his idea of a happy marriage. The home, and the money, and the lifestyle were only available if I accepted that. Well, there's only so much bloody humiliation anyone can take.' She ground out the half-finished butt with a vicious scrubbing motion. 'Even the idyllic family turned into a bloody nightmare. I got postnatal depression – big time. They were pumping me full of uppers and downers. And when they weren't, I was filling in the gaps. By the time I came down from orbit a friend had hijacked the offspring.' She looked amused at my startled expression. 'Not literally. They just bonded, I guess. I wasn't wanted on voyage. How about you? Any children?'

'No.'

'Partner?'

'No. They always turn out to be married. Or have an urgent appointment – on the other side of the world. The last one suffered from a chronic case of lying. To me, himself and just about everyone he came into contact with.'

Prue squinted and threw me a shrewd look through the cigarette smoke. 'He was the one who got to you, wasn't he?'

'Yep. He was.'

She nodded. 'That's the worst, isn't it? When you find out they've been lying to you, and all that stuff about love and commitment and making a life together was just a load of shit to get what they wanted from you. Makes you start doubting yourself. You go over everything in your head, start trying to work out which were the lies. And if you fell for them because you were stupid, or just desperate to believe that someone loved you. Don't get me wrong. I haven't been living like a nun since my marriage ended. It's just that . . . well, you know . . .'

I had a fair idea. She'd needed someone to sit over the other side of the restaurant table and sign the bill, no emotional commitment necessary beyond a joint Gold

Card. And now it would seem the charge account had run out and Prue was stranded on the planet Pay-Your-Own-Way.

'It's a pity we can't do retakes,' she said. 'Take notes on where it went wrong and then play it again.'

'There are some who reckon you can.'

'You believe in all that reincarnation theory?'

Before I'd have said 'no chance' immediately. Now I hesitated; was this case eroding my finely honed cynicism on all things spooky? 'No,' I said firmly. 'I reckon it's just wish-fulfilment for people with dull lives. How about you?'

'The same, I suppose. I tried it with a friend, but I never went under, let alone back. Apparently I displayed a classic resistance to relinquishing control.'

A woman, presumably Sheila, came through from the back room and started to chalk up the lunchtime specials on the blackboard. There was a rather enticing smell of baking drifting over the bar which seemed to tie up with the 'scrumptious flaky pastry beef and onion pie with rich tasty gravy'. My mouth watered and Waterloo's drooled.

'Get much trade?' I asked.

'We're pretty busy lunchtimes, aren't we, Prue? And more so, we hope, once they done the alterations up the Hall.'

The hiss of impatient air fired through Prue's teeth at this reminder of evictions to come didn't appear to reach Sheila's ears. She chatted on happily whilst her chalk squealed over the board. 'I'm thinking trade will pick up nicely once they get the health place up and running at Maudsley Hall. They're bound to want a square meal after all that dieting and exercise.'

She pronounced it 'noicely' with that slight touch of local accent that was rapidly dying out along with most of the farming industry around here. It led me to hope that perhaps her family had memories of this area back in the days of Joe Gumbright's childhood. But apparently not.

She'd come from much further west a mere twenty years before.

Prue stood up. 'If you're going to be polling the village, I'll walk round with you. They're less likely to think you're a Jehovah's Witness and hide behind the curtains. Save me a portion of the pie, Sheila.'

Perhaps she wanted to find out what I might discover, but I was more inclined to think Prue was bored out of her mind and welcomed any diversion. As she'd predicted, with her in tow those that were at home were happy enough to talk about village history and any of their neighbours who weren't home. However, of forty houses in the village, thirty-five had no connections with it beyond the last twenty years. And of the five that did, only two could produce relatives who remembered the area pre-war. One of them was so far away with the fairies that she probably bedded down under a toadstool every night. The other recalled a farm in the location of Rooks, but couldn't remember the Gumbrights and frankly informed us that Prue's father was a 'bloody awkward bugger and a bloody useless farmer. Nobody stayed working for him if they'd any sense'.

'Was he?' I asked Prue when we'd left the last house and were strolling back towards the pub.

'Probably. He had a nasty temper and he could hold a grudge. I don't know whether he could farm or not. Probably not since we ended up selling everything. I never had much to do with the estate. It was Daddy's work, that was all. You just rather expect your parents to produce money, don't you? It doesn't occur to you to worry about where it's coming from.'

We were back at the Halt. The buzz of conversation inside indicated that trade had picked up. Waterloo and the hounds had formed a temporary pack. It headed confidently towards the open door. I called the mutt to heel and started the car engine. Prue asked if I wanted to come in.

187

'I've got more work to do. Thanks for your help. And good luck with the designing. I'm sure it'll be a big success.'

'Me too.' She smiled, just to prove I wasn't the only unconvincing liar around here. 'I have a couple of quotations for a full concept regeneration under consideration right now.'

To a girl who regarded colour-washing as pretty adventurous, she spoke a foreign language. But I kept up the big encouraging smiles and right-on positive vibes until I'd pulled away.

Having done my duty on Stuart's official investigation, I set off for the fun part of my day – snooping around his previous address in Winstanton. Nowhere in Winstanton is very far from anywhere else, but Stuart's old home was just about as far from his new one as you could get – in more ways than one.

It was an old house at the furthest edge away from the coast. Once this road had probably housed all the middle class who could afford properties out of whiffing distance of the fishing industry by the shore. Now events had turned full circle and the beachfront was desirable while these narrow, solid, detached houses, with their faint suggestion of an uptight curate hugging his cassock skirt to his knees, were now at the cheapest end of the market.

I walked the street, sizing up the area. The road sloped upwards, so that from the top end I could see the ocean glinting away on the horizon. Halfway down the street, outside number fourteen, the view was obscured by the intervening railway line and inner town houses and shops. The IRS printout had given Stuart's previous address as 14B which was the upper flat. They'd cut a door into the side of the house and presumably done internal alterations to give a separate entrance to the upper property. The paintwork was glossy, the brass fittings were shiny, the bell was unanswered.

Stepping back, I stared at the upper windows to see if I could catch out anyone hiding in case I was from the God Squad. It all looked quiet.

The gate to the back garden rattled open. 'They're out. Work. You gas?'

'No. That's the dog's speciality.'

She looked from me to the mutt and back again. 'Ugly little bastard, isn't he?'

From someone whose face could have given a toad the hots I thought that was pretty rich. A wave of defensiveness swept over me before I reminded myself that the mutt could no more understand 'ugly' than he could 'hold it until I open the window'.

'So what d'ya want, then?'

'Stuart Roberts?'

'Moved.' She started to close the gate again.

I whipped a foot in before Miss Congeniality could disappear completely. 'I know that. Listen, have you lived here long?'

She looked at me a tad more closely this time. I could sense she was sizing me up for something. Apparently I passed because she said, 'Ten years. Come in.'

The garden was much like Arlene's, a stretch of scruffy lawn and cracked path of an uninterested gardener. It must have been her territory since she had access to the back door. It led directly into the kitchen. There was a potter's wheel set up in the middle of the room like the one used by Demi Moore in *Ghost*. In this case Patrick Swayze would have been praying to stay dead.

Okay, so we shouldn't judge by appearances. But let's face it, we all do. She was shorter than Vetch, but at least our esteemed leader's inch-challenged body was in proportion. When she moved everything wobbled and waggled under the grey sweatshirt and leggings. But the oddest thing was the hair. It was henna-dyed and cut and gelled to stand out horizontally from the top of her head like an old-fashioned sweep's brush.

Rubbing clay-engrimed hands on a scrap of rag, she said, 'Martha, potter.'

'Grace. Private investigator.'

'I mean, my name is Potter.'

'Oh. Right.'

'What d'ya want Stuart for, then?'

I hadn't got any sort of cover story prepared, so I fell back on genealogical research.

'Didn't know he had a family. Never mentioned it.'

'It's a very distant connection. Did you get to know him well?'

'Didn't hang out together if that's what you mean. I wasn't his type. Not that I'm incinerating he was queer or anything. Look, is there any money in this?'

'Pardon?'

'Money. Cash. Shekels.' She rubbed fingers and thumb together. 'I've got materials to buy. This costs. How about buying something? It's an investment. They'll be collectors' pieces one day.'

Only if the collector happened to be driving the council garbage truck. There were examples of her efforts scattered all round the room – great chunky mugs, vases and plates, mostly painted bright purple with mystical symbols in black and gold.

I picked up a plate at random. 'How much?'

'A hundred and fifty.'

'You're kidding.'

'No. It's not just a piece of clay, it's a piece of my soul. When you take it away, you'll be carrying a bit of myself with you.'

'Couldn't you keep it and do me a discount?'

'This isn't about money.'

'Fine. So talk to me for free.'

'I'm artistic, not stupid. I've got bills to meet. Including the rent to your boyfriend.'

I let the implication that Stuart and I had more than a professional relationship pass for now. 'Stuart owns this flat?'

'Owns the whole house. You going to put out or get out?'

'Is it going to be worth my while to put out?'

'Might be. I mean, if you're thinking of hooking up with him, I know something he'd like to keep quiet. Course, I don't like to incinerate anything.'

'Yeah, well, air pollution can be hell.'

'What?'

'Never mind. What's cheapest?'

She detached a small cup from a hook. 'Twenty-five pounds.'

I set it on a work surface where it promptly collapsed to one side. 'Haven't you got one that stands up?'

'They're not *supposed* to stand up. It's a concept.'

I knocked her down to twenty quid. 'So tell me about Stuart's dark secret.'

She folded my notes into a jar before shrugging and saying, 'Like I said, I don't like to incinerate, but . . . he had a girl up there.' She pointed a finger stained with purple paint towards the ceiling.

'This is news? He is a grown adult.' In this life at any rate.

'I don't mean like that. Not a date or a one-night stand. Like I said, I've been here over ten years. He got me as a sitting tenant when he bought the place. When he first moved in, there was a woman lived up there. Only he said there wasn't. I invited them down, see. Thought we could have a meal, get to know each other . . . Anyhow he said he lived on his own. Says there's no one up there but him.'

'What makes you sure there was?'

'I heard them. Walking around when he was out. He said these old houses often made funny sounds, I mean, like I'm not going to know what the place sounds like? At first I thought maybe he thought I was prejudiced, so I said, if it's not a girlfriend that's fine, I mean, some of our greatest artists have walked a different path. But he's still swearing blind there's no one up there. Made some stupid joke about the place being haunted. Well, it wasn't a ghost I heard him having a ding-dong with.'

I looked upwards at the ceiling. It appeared solid to me, just like the internal walls. 'Sound carries well in here, does it?'

'Well, no.' At least she seemed embarrassed this time. 'I was out back at the bin that time. One of their windows was open a bit. I wasn't eavesdropping, but you can't help hearing, can you?'

'And you heard?' I prompted.

'They were having a row. Or not exactly a row because she was standing there taking it, the silly cow.'

'What were they fighting about?'

'I couldn't hear.'

'How do you know she wasn't giving as good as she got, then?'

'Do me a favour. She was whimpering. Or whining more like. And he was laying into her. He said . . .' She dropped her voice – plainly someone else who thought the mutt understood English since he was the only other person here. 'He said, "Do it or you'll be sorry . . . you'll be dead by this time next week."'

'I thought you couldn't hear what they were saying?'

'Just that. I didn't hear no more. I think they moved back into the room.'

That must have been a disappointment for her. I asked if she'd ever discovered who was in the flat.

'Yeah, I did. I found out why he didn't want me to see her as well. Couple of nights later, I was going down to the pub when I realised I'd cocked up and left my purse back here, so I turned round. And she was standing out there by the door to his flat. Soon as she saw me, she shot back and slammed the door. Not before I'd seen, though.'

The smug expression that tilted the toad's mouth invited me to press for further details. I pressed.

'Somebody had knocked her around. And I'm not talking a split lip here. I mean, this was a serious pasting. I'm not surprised he didn't want her showing that face outdoors.'

'Did you ask Stuart about her?'

'Not likely. Weren't my business. It goes to show you can't judge by appearances, though. Not that I didn't already know that. There's plenty of people who look at me and can't believe I'm artistic.'

Particularly anyone who'd seen her work. 'Did you see this woman again?'

'No. Anyway the footsteps stopped after that.'

'And that didn't worry you? Given the threat?'

The fat toad lip pouted. 'Listen, don't lay any of that guilt junk on me. If there'd been any funny business I'd have done something, but it's not like a body turned up, is it? Know what I think happened? Seeing me like that made her think and take me as a sort of role model. An independent, successful career-woman who doesn't need to rely on some man. I think the worm finally turned and got the hell out of there.'

Either that or someone stomped on it and squashed it into oblivion.

27

'I'd say he was a very dangerous young man. If I were hypothesising on the case you've laid out, of course.'

'Of course.'

Dr Tabitha Puzold and I exchanged small smiles, united by a common hypocrisy.

I'd kept my appointment with her that Saturday morning in order to dish the dirt on Stuart – but not before I'd handed a spade to another little helper the night before and ordered him to start shovelling an even bigger pile of muck – viz. police records.

I'd decided I needed a source that was thick and desperate.

'Hi, Terry.'

'What d'you want, Smithie?'

'That's not very friendly, Terry. We have the moonlight. We have the sea. Don't you find it all incredibly romantic?'

I slid along the bench towards him and smiled. We were in one of the four-sided wooden beach shelters that the council provided for those who wanted relief from the biting Channel winds that more often than not howled over the cliff-tops. I'd instructed Rosco to bag the seaward side so that we wouldn't be seen by anyone driving along the coast road. He'd been huddled in one corner when the mutt and I arrived and even without lighting his body language had suggested he was less than thrilled to be stuck out there on a chilly November night.

'That what you want, then?' he said. 'A snog?'

'Oh, Terry, you have such a silver way with words, how could any woman resist you? Although the graffiti in the ladies' lav on the promenade suggests some have. Well, practically all of them actually. Particularly Mrs Rosco. I'm surprised you could afford artificial insemination for all four kids.'

'Artific . . . What you talking about? Somebody been saying I'm a jaffa? Those kids are mine. And the wife hasn't got no complaints.'

'You mean she doesn't mind you playing bondage games with schoolgirls?'

'So that's it. Out to make another wedge of dirty money, Smithie? Once dirty, always dirty.'

'You should be so lucky, Terry. I promise you I don't want a penny for the postcards.'

'What postcards?'

'The ones I'm having made from the negatives. Those Peter Rabbit shorts look so cute. I thought I'd send a few to the station, the section house, the football club . . .'

'You bitch!'

Terry lunged along the seat and stopped quickly at the sound of Waterloo's growl. In the darkness he'd been invisible crouched behind my legs.

'You've got that pit-bull off the lead again.'

'I keep telling you, he's not a pit-bull, he just doesn't like you. He has taste. Now, if you want to keep your nearest and dearest from seeing Peter playing with all those under-age girls, here's the deal . . .'

Next morning I discovered I'd rather over-estimated my ability to negotiate the London streets with just the *A–Z* and faith in the borough planners to give clearly marked direction signs. By the time I managed to get into Ealing on the western reaches of London the car clock said ten minutes past one.

Tabitha Puzold had said they opened Saturday morning. If I didn't find them soon, I'd have to do this all again on Monday. In my rear-view mirror I glimpsed a cab pulling away from the kerb. Slamming on my brakes, I indicated and reversed in one movement. It's a manoeuvre only recommended for those who have skins like a rhinoceros or are deaf and blind (according to all those driving behind me, I qualified on all counts).

Hauling Waterloo out, I set off at a fast trot for a pair of semi-detached houses that were in need of some exterior painting and repairs.

The front was unlocked. Inside it was smarter than I'd expected and some effort had been made to make the wait-ing room welcoming. A woman looked up from tidying the magazines on the coffee-table and asked if I was Miss Smith.

'Yes. Are you Tabitha?'

'*Dr* Puzold is in her office. Come on.'

I followed her to the back room. With a perfunctory knock, she stuck her head in and announced, 'She's arrived . . . finally. I'm off, then.' Stepping back, she jerked her head at me, indicating I could go past her now. Plainly a graduate of whatever course for receptionists had forged Vetch Investigation's own Miss Charm.

Tabitha Puzold was busy relocking a wall safe. My initial impression was a forgettable collection of worn floaty muslin and washed-out denim – a rock chick who'd faded into a comfortable mumsy hen. We'd hardly pressed palms before the door burst open again and Jan's clone stuck her head in. 'I forgot to say. Anscombe and Ringland rang. You can see the Docklands flat at four. And the one with the roof garden at six. Bye again.'

Tabitha retrieved the spectacles hanging from a chain on her chest, perched them on her long nose and scrawled the times on a couple of estate agent's leaflets, then excused herself in order to put the lock on the front door before we talked. I took a quick gander whilst she was gone. Both the flats were selling at two hundred grand plus – there must be more money in sifting through neuroses than this unimpressive clinic suggested.

Apart from the desk, chair, filing cabinets and numerous framed certificates attesting to her qualifications, Tabitha's office contained a couple of big easy chairs and a couch grouped around a low table that held plants and smoothly polished stones. Nothing was tatty, but nothing was too new or clean either. It was cosy casual. It reminded me of the section of Annie's office that had been designed to put nervous clients at ease and loosen their tongues. It was an impression that was confirmed when Tabitha suggested we move to the couch and make ourselves comfortable. I did. She took the chair that let her see my face. Waterloo settled under the table.

'Now, Grace, you want to talk about Stuart Roberts, is that right? You must understand that I can't discuss a specific client's case notes with you.'

Then what the hell was I doing here? 'Could you just bend the rules a bit?'

'Certainly not. That would be unethical. I would never do such a thing.'

Tabitha's wide lips pressed together, no doubt indicating disapproval. I'd have pegged her at being in her sixties if it hadn't been for her hair: it was black, long and tumbling, with several strong grey streaks through it. I figured if it hadn't completely lost its natural colour yet, she was probably younger than the heavy lines in her face suggested – fifties maybe. Her best feature was her big treacle-toffee-coloured eyes. She turned them on me now, brimming with reproach. 'Perhaps if we were to discuss your concerns on a purely hypothetical plane?'

'We can discuss it on a 747 for all I care, providing we get to the nitty-gritty. How do you want to play this?'

'Why don't you put a hypothetical case to me and ask what kind of treatment I might prescribe?'

I was plainly in for a session of double-speak. I sighed. Waterloo sighed in sympathy – unfortunately from the opposite end. I said quickly, 'Suppose someone wanted to stop smoking?'

'I'd confirm that it was their own choice – rather than something someone else had forced on them – and then I'd hypnotise them.'

'Just like that?'

'It's not as difficult as you may suppose. To a properly trained therapist.'

'How does it work? I mean, if you were doing me right now?'

'I'd spend perhaps an hour getting to know you and encouraging you to relax, talking to you in a deep, soothing voice like this.' Her voice had changed imperceptibly as we spoke. It now had a comfortable rhythm, rather like floating in a warm bath. 'And then I'd spend another fifteen minutes on the induction, deepening the hypnotic state so that I can speak to the subconscious mind. And then, in the final quarter of an hour, I'd send the message to your subconscious – the dangers of smoking, the damage to your health, the unsociable smells.'

'That's it?'

'That's it. One session is usually sufficient, although I do insist on a boosting sealing session a couple of weeks later. Just to reinforce the message.'

'And if they came back with another problem? Fear of flying, for instance?'

'Essentially the same. Although in the case of phobias I'd talk them through it first, ask them to assign a number to each aspect of their fears. For instance, crashing would be a hundred, whereas taking off might be twenty-five and the actual flight only ten. Then I'd work through each aspect, starting with the lowest number and reducing the anxiety for each section until they were completely cured. That takes a little longer. Perhaps three or four sessions.'

'Do they know what's happening to them? I mean, how much can they remember when they snap out of it?'

'Everything. They're not unconscious. Merely in a mild trance-like state.'

'What about regression? You know, telling them they're Cleopatra's hairdresser or something?'

'I don't tell my patients anything beyond the fact they are back in a life before they were born.'

'And you'd use it to cure a phobia?'

'Possibly. If, for instance, the subject was showing resistance to hypnosis. Normally that has a simple explanation – fear of losing bladder control is a common reason – but if I already knew that not to be the case . . .'

'Because you'd already hypnotised them for another reason?'

'Precisely. In those circumstances I might choose to ask them to explore other personalities to see if we could find an underlying anxiety they weren't aware of in this life. But, of course, my first concern is always the well-being of the patient. Once . . . I mean if . . . I realised that such an action was making the condition worse, I'd cease treatment immediately.'

'Is it dangerous?'

'To whom?'

'To anyone who comes in contact with the patient.'

'If the treatment were to trigger some deep-seated psychological problems, or even reinforce some previously learnt patterns, then it is possible the subject might start to regard their own actions as normal behaviour, almost inevitable, in fact.'

'Which, in layman's language, means what?'

'They might start to repeat certain cycles of behaviour whilst at the same time distancing themselves from the results of their actions.'

'It wasn't me, someone forced me to do it?'

'On a very simplified level, yes.'

'So, for instance, if this hypothetical person was in the habit of beating up girlfriends, he might do it again?'

'It would certainly be unwise for anyone to become too close to him.' She gave me a deeply significant look.

'Would these cycles include things they *could* remember? Nightmares, sleep-walking, that sort of thing?'

'Certainly. Think of them as the subconscious's attempts to break through and gain our attention.'

Well, one up for the good old subconscious – Stuart's had certainly got my full attention.

I thanked her for her help and wished her luck with the flat-hunting.

'Thank you. I think my only difficulty will be in choosing which one I like the most.' She scooped the leaflets and her lips curled in pleasure. 'It's been a long trek, but I have always had faith that my talents would provide their rewards in the end. Good luck to you too. And take care.'

My navigational skills were even further challenged by the journey from West London to the north-east section of the city where Moorfields was located. At one point I found myself driving past the market at Camden Lock. Amongst the crowds waiting to cross the main road were Stuart's former upstairs neighbours. Tattoos's arm was linked around his girlfriend's waist and one of hers was clasped across his back whilst the other was cradling a bunch of dahlias. He whispered something in her ear and she smiled, turned and pressed a kiss on his lips. To a casual observer they must have looked like just another happy couple out to do the Saturday afternoon shopping. It was a fantasy that would, no doubt, continue until he started in on the bottles of booze I could see peeping from the supermarket carriers dangling from his other hand.

He didn't see me. But the girlfriend's eyes met mine briefly as I was forced to stop by a car waiting to turn right. The flash of alarm across her face was enough to halt my half-raised wave. I was an acquaintance who hadn't been approved by the boyfriend; there was no sense making her life even more miserable than she was making it herself. I drove on and eventually arrived at Moorfields more by luck than judgement.

Arlene had started a scrapbook of her baby's press cuttings. She brought it down to show the little star whilst I looked her over. She was already starting to look thinner and washed out, confirming my theory that hospitals are no good for your health.

The run home to Seatoun was relatively trouble-free, but nonetheless my neck muscles were cramped and my head was aching from all the map-reading, driving and traffic fumes. I could have done with a chill-out evening of giant-pizza-to-go, a bottle of wine and a video designed to insult the intelligence of an amoeba. Instead I got a message on the answering service from Rosco instructing me to meet him at Pepi's that evening.

'I got the info on that Breezley bloke and it's dynamite. Be there, Smithie, and pretend you don't know me until I give you the wink.'

When I got to Pepi's there was no sign of him amongst the packed tables. I looked around at the crowded room. It seemed busy, even for a Saturday night. In fact, the whole of the front had as I'd driven through it. 'Something happening?' I shouted at Shane over his jive and fry routine.

'Bonfire Night tomorrow, ain't it. Some of us are starting early. Seen me specials?' He nodded towards the menu, detailing such delights as 'Crispy fried Guy Fawkes guts' and 'Boom – you're (fried) bread'. 'You ordering?'

'Later. If Terry Rosco turns up tell him I'll be back. And be sure to wink at him.'

I took a stroll along the promenade. Despite the chill, the bars and amusement arcades were buzzing. A small window of hope had appeared in the long dark hell of Low Season. Most of the local traders had seized on the fact that November the fifth fell on a Sunday this year to turn the whole weekend into a last-second profit-fest.

Wandering amongst the tinny music, looking into souvenir shops and drinking in the smell of frying hot dogs, burgers and onions and warm yeasty beer, I realised how much I'd missed the tatty dump. Life on Arlene's headland was too remote for me. I needed noise and people outside the windows, if not in my life. At the top of the street, I turned to saunter back and glanced across to the beach side. The Council hadn't yet removed the coloured lights that were strung between the lampposts in high season and there was sufficient illumination over there to make out the features of those wandering down the broader pavement beside the sands.

Not that I needed to see Annie's face to recognise her. She and Stuart were strolling with their arms around each other and her head on his shoulder. I watched as he said something and she lifted her face and laughed. Hand in hand they made their way to one of the short flights of steps that led to the sands. It was almost a rerun of the touching little scene between Tattoos and his girlfriend that afternoon. Remembering how I'd expected that little drama to play out later made me want to heave. I knew Annie could take care of herself on the physical level, but what if he landed a knock-out in her emotional gut?

'She's a big girl, she can handle it,' I said to the mutt. 'Let's go find you a leg to chew on.'

Terry was huddled in a seat near the counter when I marched back into the steamy, jumping-joint atmosphere of Pepi's. Sashaying over, I plonked myself opposite him and winked suggestively.

Rosco shrank even further into his coat collar. 'Pack it in. Act casual.'

'I am. Have you got a sore throat?'

'No,' he hissed hoarsely. 'I don't want nobody hearing this. Let's make this quick. I've left the wife and kids on the beach.'

'Are you hoping for a high tide?'

'What yer talking about? Council's having a firework do down there tonight. You got those negatives?'

It took me a moment to remember I'd bribed him into this appearance with lies about incriminating postcards. 'They're safe. For now. Information first and if it checks out I'll hand them over. I take it you've found out something interesting on one Stuart Robert Breezley of the birth date supplied?'

The expression on his face said it all. Self-satisfaction flowed over the just-on-the-turn fleshy good looks. He'd got the dirt on someone and was just dying to share it with someone, negatives or no negatives (which in the circumstances was just as well).

He puffed even further with self-induced importance and then whispered hoarsely, 'He's been pulled for murder.'

He let this information sink just far enough in, before adding the final killer blow.

'Twice.'

28

After Terry's bombshell that night, I'd hung around, intending to watch the firework display, check out the barbecue on the beach and do a bit of long-distance chaperoning of Annie and her psycho-date. Waterloo had put paid to my plans as soon as the first rockets soared up and exploded in a shower of emerald starbursts.

He didn't actually howl because a macho-mutt like him had a reputation to keep up, but several of his lily-livered cousins set up a furious barrage of barks and whines from various cars and flats along the front. The next rush of golden fountains hissing beyond the kids' paddling pool had him thrusting his head between my knees. I ended up having to take him home and spend the evening behind drawn curtains with the telly playing full blast.

Neither of us slept much that night. Between the late-night bonfire parties, the nightmares and the tossing and turning, we both ended up tangled in duvet and sweat at five o'clock in the morning.

'Up!' Standing on the mattress, I rolled the mutt out of the sausage roll he'd formed out of the bedclothes. I stripped the entire room, added the collection of Christina Alaimo's clothes that I'd acquired after my trips to the oast house and pushed the lot in the washing machine whilst I sorted out breakfast. I'd be able to return them to her tonight, always assuming I got back from digging the dirt on Stuart in time to make the dinner invitation.

The plan fell at the first hurdle. Terry had only managed to pick up the slenderest information about Stuart's murderous past – mainly, I suspect, because he'd been snooping in a panic and had barely snatched a look before logging out again. He'd got the names of the victims – Clifford Breezley and Nyree Williams – and the dates. The deaths appeared to have occurred within a fortnight of each other some seventeen years ago – which tied up with the start of those 'lost' two years in Stuart's National Insurance records. It didn't explain why he'd been back on the scene after a mere two years, of course. Had he been released on appeal, or had he never been convicted in the first place, and if so where had he been?

The best place to start asking was Stuart's home town at that time. Except I couldn't remember where the hell it was. I'd memorised the date of his birth and that last address in Winstanton, but the long list of former addresses I'd simply speed-read. Beyond the fact that a lot of them were in London, I couldn't dredge up more than the odd few lines. I needed the fax from Vetch's IRS contact, but I didn't have it. I'd turned out the pockets of the clothes I was wearing that evening and emptied out my shoulder bag before I had a flash picture of Vetch folding it into his jacket pocket as he'd left me surfing the Web at the office that night.

He wasn't answering at home or on his mobile number. I left messages that I needed to talk to him urgently. Whilst I ate, I flicked through the Sunday papers. My mind was all over the place. When I'd read the same paragraph a dozen times I gave up and slumped in front of the TV until the wash cycle whirled to a noisy finish.

The sky was just lightening from graphite to a rose-dipped pearliness when I stepped out back with the laundry basket. The smoky acridity of last night's celebrations was still caught in the air. I kicked a spent rocket off the path and started pegging. Waterloo had wandered out after me. He sniffed the blackened ends of the firework, flattened his ears, whined and ran back to the kitchen.

'Chicken!' I clucked at him and flapped chicken elbows.

After another couple of hours of trying to raise my favourite lecherous gnome on the phone, I drove down to the office on the offchance he was working today. I drew a blank. Even Annie – who'd taken to checking in seven days a week since her elevation to boardroom status – appeared to have given it a miss this weekend. I needed that address. I spent the afternoon collecting more clothes from my flat, walking the mutt and ringing Vetch ever half-hour. Zilch.

'I just hope he hasn't gone off on a job for the next few days,' I remarked to the mutt. 'When I don't want to see the smug little gnome, I fall over him at every turn. But when I need him for once, where is he? And I'm talking to a bloody dog again.'

For want of something more constructive to do, I collected up all the 'Joe' tapes and replayed them.

Sitting cross-legged on Arlene's bed, with the light dying

outside and just the sounds of the sea and the birds and the wind rising around the headland, was, I'll admit, spooky. It wouldn't have been so bad if the recordings had genuinely been sixty years old. Listening to someone possibly confessing to a murder committed six decades ago might have been okay. But it was the thought of someone reaching out from the past to take over the body of someone living that was really chilling. It raised the subconscious fear – if Stuart, why not me? Was there someone swirling around in the spooky soup just waiting to take up lodgings in my head?

Angry with myself for being so gullible, I hauled the mutt up beside me and cuddled up to his furry coat whilst we listened to Joe burying the body, hearing his mum being beaten up, being propositioned by Lulu and kicking his dad to death. The final tape of Lulu's flashing had only been partially rewound.

'They're having a party. Been playing silly games. Silly games.'

That wasn't right, was it? I didn't recall anything about games. Ejecting the tape, I flicked on the bedside lamp and twisted the plastic casing under it. There was no inked '5'. I flipped it. And there it was. There was a further recording on the reverse of this tape.

I wasn't sure I wanted to know, but a sort of morbid fascination made me rewind to the beginning and press 'play'.

'Where are you, Joe?'

'At the farm.'

'Your farm? Rook Farm?'

'Out in the fields. Got up real early. It's a hop-picking morning. Misty and damp first out. Then sun comes up. Be burning out here by dinnertime.'

'And is that what you're doing? Picking hops?'

'Start next week. Pickers are coming down. Been helping to get the huts ready. Have to limewash 'em and fetch the faggots up.'

'What are faggots?'

'Wood. Bundles of sticks. They put 'em on the beds. Don't know much, do you?'

'How old are you now, Joe?'

'Fif'een and a half.'

'Are you still living at Rook Farm?'

'Yeah. Not for much longer. I'll soon be old enough to get a farm job with a cottage. Then me and Billie will go live there. Stop her crying so much.'

'Why does she cry?'

'Dunno. Won't say. I reckon he works her too hard. Makes her do all the cleaning and cooking and washing. It's not right. She's only a kid.'

'Is she with you now?'

'Yeah. Been keeping out of Dad's way. He's mad at the lot up at Maudsley.'

'Why?'

'They're having a party. Been playing games. Silly games.'

'What kind of games?'

'Kids' games. Hide and seek. Blind man's buff.'

'How do you know? Did you see them?'

'Yesterday. She said to come up yesterday. They had tea out in the field. Cornfield. Had proper tables and chairs. I helped carry them up. It was real funny.'

'Why? What was so amusing, Joe?'

'Wood pigeons. Cornfields full of 'em after they finished harvesting, aren't they. They were flying all over the place. Some of them landed on the table. They were only after crumbs. But there was this one woman, she went mad. Screaming and waving her hands around. Said they were in her hair. They weren't. Pigeon wouldn't be that daft. Everyone laughed at her. Then she went to sit back down again and the chair fell over. It was really funny.'

'Did she think it was?'

'Doubt it. She sort of laughed a bit, but she wasn't pleased. Thought she was going to blub. Big gawk of thing she was. Not pretty like . . . like . . .'

'*Lulu?*'

'*Yeah. She wanted me to help. They're having a treasure hunt today. Gave me these envelopes to hide.*'

'*Hide where?*'

'*All over. In Frognall. Oast houses. Fields. That's why Dad's angry. Says they'll ruin crops, trampling around the fields. Why should he care? Half our fields aren't even strung properly. Bines are rotting on the ground.*'

'*Did you touch Lulu, Joe?*'

'*She said I could . . . She . . . she . . .*'

'*Go on.*'

'*She let me kiss her. And touch her . . . She touched me . . . until . . .*'

Thankfully the tape cut out at that point given what I presume Joe was doing for the next thirty seconds or so. I was letting it spin to the end when Tabitha's husky, coaxing voice filled the dark room again.

'*Are you still in the fields, Joe?*'

'*Up Maudsley Hall. Been watching the treasure hunt. They found all the clues. Some bloke won.*'

'*What bloke?*'

'*Don't know his name. He's married to the gawk, I think. Don't know who they are.*'

'*What's happening now?*'

'*She . . . Lulu . . . she said he deserved a prize for winning. Said she'd give him something he really wanted. She's taking him into the hop field. He's laughing, pulling back like he don't want to go, only he does really. You can see he does.*'

'*What are the others doing?*'

'*Nothing. Just sort of looking . . . couple of them . . . they don't look right . . . like . . . like they've been caught doing something they shouldn't . . . They're going away now . . . back to the road . . . except her . . . she's still watching . . . only now . . . she's going after them . . . going back down to the cars.*'

'*Who is? Lulu?*'

'No. The other one. The gawk. Lulu's in the hops with him. I'm going in too.'

'Won't that annoy her? If she thinks you're spying on her?'

'I don't care. She won't see anyway. I'm going down the next line. It's dark in here. Hops are right over the top. Hardly no light at all. It's just like walking down a big green tunnel filled up with the smell of hops. I can hear something.'

'What?'

'Not sure.'

'What are you doing now, Joe?'

'Lying down.'

'Why?'

'To see. There's a hole down the bottom of the bines. There's a spider's web over it. Got dew on it. Sun doesn't burn it off in here. I can see her.'

'See who? Where?'

'Lulu. Bit of bine hasn't grown over the top in her tunnel. She's got sunlight on her. Not all over. Just a little bit. It's like when the sun comes in the church. Just one little bit through the glass. I can see her skin. It's really white . . . she is so beautiful . . . and he's ugly . . .'

'The man? Where's he?'

'On top of her. He's . . . he's . . . Why . . . She knows I want her . . . He's hurting her . . . but she likes it . . . I can see . . .'

'Go on, Joe. Can you still see them?'

'He's gone. She's still laying there. She's smiling. She's looking right at me through the spider's web. She's smiling at me. She knows I'm here. I hate her . . . I hate her . . .'

The cassette click jerked me from a 1930s hop field back into the present day. Jumping up, I shot around the bungalow, drawing curtains and switching on every light in the place. When I'd finished, I checked the first four tapes to see if they'd also been recorded on both sides. They hadn't. I relogged it as numbers five and six in the sequence.

More to make me feel in charge than for any practical reason. Then I watched the noisiest, trashiest programme I could find on TV until it was time to leave.

29

The fireworks had started early this evening. Even with the curtains closed and the radio on, the mutt was obviously putting a brave face on it. In the end I took him next door to Edith's and asked if she'd mind.

'It's just a few hours. Unless you're going out to a firework party?'

'No, dear, I went to one last night. That's quite sufficient at my age. Are you going somewhere nice?'

'Dinner. At Rick Alaimo's.' I waited for her to be impressed with my connections to the rich and famous. She wasn't. She'd probably never heard of him.

'Would you care for a little something before you go?'

It seemed crass to dump the mutt and run so I accepted a thimbleful of sherry. It arrived in crystal glasses.

'Did you find any of those people you were seeking?' Edith asked.

I told her about Greville Cazlett and his half-sister, Prue.

'A daughter. I wonder how Roderick cared for that? He seemed indifferent to his sons. But then men weren't expected to take much notice of their children until they'd started shaving. The boys, I mean. Is the Cazlett girl pretty?'

How could you call a fifty-plus woman a girl? 'Prue's sort of . . . Helen Mirrenish?'

Edith inclined her head over the rim of her sherry glass to indicate she knew who I was talking about this time. 'I saw the second wife once or twice at WI meetings. Attractive little thing, but incredibly dull – hadn't an original word to say for herself. Not that I imagine that bothered Roderick, it would simply give him more time to exercise his own voice. Besides, I dare say he found it something of a relief after Lulu.'

'I gather she liked to party?'

'Lots of people like to party. Lulu's behaviour was . . . quite disgusting at times.' She extended the sherry. I pleaded the need to drive later to refuse. It tasted like sweet cough mixture. Edith helped herself to another slug with evident enjoyment. The rim of the bottle rattled against the glass and some of the liquid slopped over the edge. She was remarkable for her age, but I was afraid the family would get their own way and haul her out of here in the end. 'One New Year,' she said, continuing a conversation that I thought had come to an end, 'they had a party at Maudsley. We didn't go, we'd had a family bereavement, but several friends of ours attended. Do you know what Lulu Cazlett did?'

'What?' I asked, whilst my subconscious pleaded, Don't say it, please don't say it. That cold water was running down my spine again.

'Did you happen to notice a large circular window over the main doorway?'

Now I was damn sure I didn't want to hear this. 'Looks out of place?'

'I always thought so too.' Edith smiled her approval. 'Well, this particular night, she waited until the guests were leaving, then she went up to that window and removed all her garments. Everything. She was completely naked. Please don't misunderstand me, I'm not a prude. The point is, it wasn't the nakedness that shocked everyone . . . but she was *playing* with herself . . . do you understand what I mean? Up there, blatantly, in full view of her husband's friends. I'm a great believer in preordination. I think our life is laid out for us from the very beginning. We carry our destiny with us. Fate or whatever you wish to call it sees to it that wherever we go our good deeds are noted, and all the bad ones are found out eventually. It's a horrible thing to say, but I think it was probably something of a relief to Roderick Cazlett when Lulu died abroad.'

To put it mildly. But was it a relief because she was dead? Or because nobody had suspected she'd actually been killed months earlier and hastily buried out at the oast houses? What if Roderick had lashed out after she'd provoked him once too often then dumped her somewhere away from Maudsley Hall? And Joe Gumbright had come across the body and decided to get rid of it rather than have it discovered on his dad's farm? Roderick was hardly going to start making enquiries as to what had happened to it, was he? Much better to make up some story about Lulu travelling abroad and then kill her off a few months later.

Or what if Joe had killed her in a fit of temper when she'd sexually teased him once too often? Supposing Roderick had found them? Would he have wanted a messy trial with the smutty stories about the lady of the manor and the teenage farmhand? She'd already made a laughing stock of him for years. Why not offer to keep his mouth shut if Joe got rid of the evidence?

'I must go. Thanks for the sherry.'

I reached the oast house by twenty to eight, a fact which seemed to surprise Christina. 'In this country if you say eight, folks seem to think that means wander in around eight-thirty for drinks.'

'Sorry. I can drive round a bit if I'm in the way.'

'No way. I like people who show up for meals on time. Comes from owning restaurants, I guess. Late shows can be a real pain.'

'How many did you own?' I asked. She'd invited me into the basement kitchens to watch her putting the finishing touches to the meal. New stainless-steel appliances were jostling with fresh paint and half-finished tiling. Christina was working around the mess with the easy fluid movements of someone who'd done this a thousand times before.

'Six,' Christina replied. 'Not all at once. When I married Rick I had a two-hundred-seater in Manhattan.'

'Have you still got it?' I snagged a peeled carrot and nibbled.

'I sold up when Rick and I married. Lease was running out and I was offered a really good deal for the name and the goodwill.'

'His idea or yours?' I pulled myself up. 'Sorry. I'm snooping. It's habit.'

'No. It's okay. I've been asked the same thing a dozen times by journalists. All dying to put a "Rick Alaimo weds gold-digging bimbo number five" spin on the story. It was my choice. I didn't want the worry on top of . . .' She patted the swelling bump. It seemed to have grown in the brief time since I'd last seen her. 'When you're starting out on this route at forty plus, it makes sense to concentrate on the project in hand.'

Pinching the tip of a chef's knife with two fingers, she chopped a bunch of herbs in a chequered pattern with a speed that was breathtaking whilst I made a mental note that she was six or seven years older than I'd estimated.

Since she didn't seem to mind nosy questions, I asked her straight up why she'd married Rick.

'With his track record you mean?' She scraped the herbs into a simmering pan. 'No mystery. I wanted kids before it was too late. And I happen to think marriage goes with that. Catholic guilt trip, I guess. On my forty-first birthday I promised myself I'd marry the next guy who asked. Rick was the next guy. I'm not blind to what he's like. Hell, we've been friends for twenty years. But the way I see it, if he's chasing women like me, then he's not looking for a clubbing chick. I'm prepared to give him a chance. And if he blows it – he's out.'

Christina whisked the sauce. 'I don't plan to be dependent on him by becoming a full-time stay-at-home mommy. It's just a question of rearranging your working life to accommodate new routines. Running a restaurant might not be an option at present, but I can set up a consultancy. There are loads of places that have a catering function, secondary to their main business.'

I thought I'd got the general picture – Christina was nobody's bimbo.

'As a matter of fact, there's someone coming tonight I'm hoping is going to give me my first contract. He's a bit of a dish himself. I've only seen him over a video-link but . . . mm, *mmm*.' She laid out plates and started arranging slivers of veg in artistic patterns. 'I'll sit him next to you, shall I? He could prove to be a very tasty dessert.'

That was when the first niggles of panic set in. I made a noncommittal noise and asked if she'd mind if I used the phone.

'Sure. There's one . . . Oh, darn, I wish people wouldn't do that,' she concluded as we both registered that the receiver was missing from the wall-mounted base unit. 'There's one in the study. I'll show you.'

'I know where that is. If it's okay to wander?'

'Make yourself at home. I'm going up to check on Emmy-R.'

I took her at her word. After I'd found the phone and I'd confirmed that Vetch still wasn't anywhere I could get my hands on him, I mooched around the house, checking out those areas that hadn't been included in Melody's initial tour for more insights into the lifestyles of the rich and famous.

The left-hand side of that courtyard extension was locked tight. Frustrating to a woman who regards locked doors as a challenge. Thwarted, I located the entrance to its twin on the other side of the main house – and struck gold. Through the glass wall, the water undulated inside a blue-tiled pool and sent light patterns rippling over the other three walls decorated to imitate a Roman fresco. Rick was swimming lengths with a lazy crawl. He didn't react when I tapped on the glass. There was no slap from the waves lapping the tile edges or hum from the air-conditioners that must be running to deal with the condensation. Soundproof, I decided. Gripping the handles, I dragged the heavy sliding door open.

Rick flipped, spotted me and dived. I was left standing on the edge, wondering if he was trying to break the under-water breath-holding record, until he finally surfaced in a splutter of coughing and trod water.

'I didn't know anyone had arrived yet. Chris should have called me. She get you a drink?'

'I'm fine.'

'Pour me a scotch, then, sweetie.'

Biting back a desire to point out I wasn't a Snickers bar, I looked round for the drinks cabinet which was surely a feature of every pop star's swimming pool complex. There was no sign of one.

'Straight back the way you came. Third door on your left,' Rick called. He was still treading water in the centre of the pool. His breath was coming in shorter pants now as if he wasn't comfortable with all this exercise. You'd have thought he would have swum over to the side and climbed out.

I had a fair idea why he wouldn't. Through the distortion of the water, I could see his circling legs. The skinny white limbs were roped by cat's cradles of blue and mauve varicose veins. The rock legend wasn't wearing so well after all and he didn't want to get out whilst I was there.

The room he'd directed me to in my other guise as poolside drinks attendant was another that Melody had missed out on the house tour. It was part of the older oast house, still retaining part of the circular tower at the far end, and was decorated in a rather bizarre shade of avocado. All of which I took in in a blink, before the biggest horror hit me.

In the centre of the avocado carpet was a dining table. It had been recently polished – I could smell the waxy aroma of beeswax mixed with lavender – and was now laid with the full paraphernalia of formal dining. I stared at all those place settings of silver cutlery, crystal glasses, candle-holders and flower arrangements and realised I'd screwed up again. This wasn't a quick nosh with the Alaimos, it was a real, grown-up dinner party. I would be expected to sit around sipping Chardonnay, nibbling on sun-dried toma-toes and having witty conversations about the best websites for supermarket shopping and orgasms. I wanted out!

30

I was starting back with the chunky tumblerful of whisky and ice-cubes that Rick and I both knew he didn't really want when Christina reappeared. The loose black cotton dress she'd been wearing to cook in had been swapped for deep aquamarine silk trousers and overshirt. She'd even found time to knot her hair up in casually tousled tendrils and put some slap on. My second-best jeans with their flowered inserts in the flares started to feel a tad under-dressed.

She had four more guests in tow; their body language made it clear they were two pairs rather than a quartet. Christina seemed less relaxed than she had been in the kitchen. She introduced the first couple with a slightly too bright smile.

'This is Bernie Crossfield, Rick's manager. And this is Winona.'

Bernie was a running-to-fat, sixtyish, balding bloke in a conventional suit. Winona was an anaemic-looking blonde in some kind of designer sari in spice colours. She said in a high plaintive voice, '*Why*-No-Nah.'

I pegged the second man immediately as the dish Christina had been trying to fix me up with. He was one of those forty-somethings who'd worn into interesting facial lines, distinguished flecks of grey in dark hair and broad shoulders under a real dinner jacket. His dinner partner was Prue Cazlett.

'Raoul's a hotelier, he's planning to relocate here from Switzerland soon,' Christina informed the room, whilst dropping me an imperceptible wink in case I'd missed the point that this was *the one*.

He had one of those sexy little Continental edges to his accent as he wished us all good evening. 'I hope you don't mind that I bring my hostess? How could I resist bringing such a deliciously beautiful aunt?'

'Of course not, Raoul,' Christina said in a tight voice. 'Great to see you again, Prue.'

It clicked. This must be the nephew to whom Greville had signed over Maudsley Hall in order to avoid death duties. The one who was going to turn the place into a health farm. Perhaps Prue was hoping to retain her claim on the place via a bit of bedroom bonding. Did step-aunt/step-nephew count as incest? And why hadn't she mentioned she knew the present owner of the oast houses when I was asking Greville about the place?

Christina was still doing the introductions. She flashed that strained smile at Prue and said, 'You know Bernie, of course.'

'We go way back. Hi, Bernie.' Prue was gathered into an embrace. Bernie squeezed her buttocks like a careful shopper checking out the citrus display. It made you wonder just how far back she and Bernie had gone.

'And Winona?' Christina enquired.

'*Why*-No-Nah.'

Prue ignored her. Everybody ignored her.

'And this is Grace, who saved—'

'We've met,' Prue said abruptly. Her face was neutral. She was trying to figure out what I was doing there. That made two of us.

There was a definite odd undercurrent of tension in the air that I couldn't pin down. I was still trying to work it out when Rick and Melody joined us.

Rick was wearing a dinner jacket too. Melody was in a silver and red slip dress that was designed to look good on great legs, a taut stomach and butt and 34B breasts. She had the full quartet, darn it. She hugged me like a long-lost sister, greeted Bernie as 'Uncle Bernie' and looked through *Why*-No-Nah to schmooze a sensual 'hello' at Raoul.

He shook her hand but surprisingly enough seemed slightly embarrassed at the flirting. I revised my forming impression of middle-aged lecher. Perhaps Prue was in with a chance after all. She'd rather wisely foregone the leopard-skin pants again in favour of a plain navy dress, although the Farrah Fawcett was back in all its flicking, curling glory.

She flicked it out of her eyes now as Melody said, 'What are you doing here?'

'Raoul invited me.'

'You mean you didn't give him a choice.'

'Does it matter who invited who?' Christina intervened. 'You're very welcome, Prue.'

'No, she's not. I don't want her here.' Melody pouted.

Curiouser and curiouser. There was definitely something I didn't understand going on here. Perhaps dinner would be more entertaining than I'd been anticipating.

'Then it's lucky it's my house, isn't it?' Christina snapped.

For a moment the happy step-mummy/step-daughter veneer slipped. They fronted each other up. There was a brief second of embarrassed silence whilst we held our breath and waited for the natural referee to give his verdict.

Prue said, 'Well, Rick? Do you want me to go too?'

'Christina's call. How about a drink, Bernie?'

Christina suggested we all move into the next room for drinks whilst she finished the table.

'Do you want a hand?' I asked. In my world, napkin-folding rated way up there over canapé chit-chat.

'I can manage, thanks.'

'No, you can't,' Rick interposed. 'You shouldn't be toting stuff around in your condition. I thought Melody was helping?'

Melody tossed the shampoo ad locks and announced she'd had to change. 'What can I do now, Christina?'

'Entertain the guests. I'll be fine. I've only got to fetch in the starters. Don't make a fuss, Rick. I'm having a baby, I'm not sick.'

She plainly wanted our space rather than our company. Rick threw open a set of adjoining double doors, led the way into a sitting room and shut us in again. It was the room that had been chintz town on my last tour. In the brief spell since my visit, it had been redecorated. The squashy sofas had plain throws to hide the chintzy horrors, there was a real fire crackling in the big fireplace and various assorted vases of casually arranged flowers and family mementoes had been placed around the room. It was stylish but comfortable at the same time. A home rather than a showpiece set.

'Classy,' Bernie said. 'You get a designer in, Rick?'

'No. Christina organised it. It's pretty damn good, isn't it?'

'So what was wrong with it before?' Prue demanded.

'Apart from looking like an illustration from a magazine in a doctor's waiting room?' Melody asked.

'Well, what the hell do you expect? The place hasn't been touched for twenty-odd years. I can give it any look you like. Did you get my portfolio? Rick?'

Rick had turned away to fiddle with the drinks cabinet. There seemed to be one in every room apart from the swimming pool. The place was a paradise for a lazy dipsomaniac. Not looking at her, Rick muttered that he'd passed it across to Christina. 'It's her choice. This is her home now.'

An expression I couldn't quite place flitted over Prue's face. With a small, tight smile she managed to murmur, 'Of course. I'll chat with her later. Maybe we could do lunch?'

The back of Rick's neck was visibly relieved. He waved bottles and raised an enquiring eyebrow. It was whiskies all round, apart from me. I hate the taste of the stuff.

'Listen, girl-friend,' Melody said, giving me another little hug. 'Daddy, in fact all of us, decided you deserved a reward for saving Emmy.' She drew a large silver-wrapped parcel tied with big glittery scarlet ribbons from behind a sofa. Eyes sparkling, she handed it to me. 'I really wanted to get you a "must have". Something that lit fires for you.'

Two dozen double cheese-burgers or the world's largest box of matches? I weighed the package in my hands. Tough guess.

Everyone was looking expectant. I was plainly supposed to open it there and then. I waded through the wrap to a large plain cardboard box. Under the lid was a mound of fluffy pink tissue. I parted it and stared. Coiled inside were the raspberry snakeskin, ankle-turning, toe-crushing, shin-high boots from the launch party.

Melody shook the hair cascade. 'They're Galahad Montez. They're signed, see?' She displayed the flourishing signature inside. 'He is so cool.'

He was also a masochistic transvestite if he owned these beauties. I forced a smile and enthusiastic thanks through clenched teeth.

After that, conversation was stilted to say the least. Rick and Bernie were talking about bands and tours most of us had never heard of; Raoul was trying to be polite and not look like he cared; Prue had a determinedly bright-little-guest expression stapled in place which was negated by the way she constantly fiddled with her glass; Melody had switched off and somebody had forgotten to switch Winona on.

The mutt had started to look like scintillating company by the time Prue said, 'I need a pee.' She flung back the rest of her drink in one, stood up and glared around in a challenging fashion. 'I remember the way. Unless Christina's remodelled that as well?'

For something to say in the awkward silence that followed her departing flounce, I said to Melody, 'Prue knew the oast house before, then?'

'The whole place was designed for her, wasn't it, Daddy?'

'Yeah. She wanted to live in this area. God knows why. It's not like she had any fond memories of it. But I guess it sort of stuffed it to that brother of hers. Her having a better pad than his, and right under his nose. Sorry, Raoul, I forget Greville's your uncle. No offence. It's just how Prue was.'

Raoul gave a shrug that combined acceptance with charm. I wrestled with an idea that was forming. The reason for all the weird hostile currents that had been crackling around ever since the other guests had shown up suddenly dawned on me. I swung round to face Melody who was perched beside me. 'Prue's your mother!'

'Yes. Of course she is. Didn't you know?'

No, I didn't. I wasn't a fan of her dad's. I had vague recollections of a constant stream of identikit-blonde wives, live-in girl-friends and live-out girl-friends passing through the show-biz gossip columns on his arm over the past twenty-plus years, but I couldn't have put faces and names to any of them. And I certainly hadn't known that one of them was called Cazlett. It tended to clarify why Prue had reacted so aggressively when I'd mentioned her ex-husband (given Rick's reputation for loving 'em and dumping 'em) and I could definitely see that Christina might not be too thrilled to find herself entertaining one of her predecessors. However, solving those little mysteries raised an even bigger one: how likely was it that Stuart hadn't known that the ex-wife of one of his biggest clients was called Cazlett?

I was still brooding on the answer to that one when Christina pushed open one of the double doors to the dining area and announced that everyone could take their seats. 'And our last two guests are here, Rick.'

She pulled the other door open. And revealed Stuart and Annie in their best evening clobber – a silky skirt and the black beaded top she fondly imagined was slimming in her case, and a dinner jacket and bow-tie nattily accessorised by a finger splint in his.

I ended up in the middle of the table with Stuart on my left, Bernie on my right and Raoul opposite with Prue beside him. It was the perfect position from which to observe her heightened breathing and slightly dilated pupils. She'd had a hit in the loo.

We weren't a mix that gelled. There were long pauses in conversation filled by over-enthusiastic praise for the food. Although I must say it *was* good.

'And you truly have no help? You do everything yourself, Christina?' Raoul asked, clearing his plate of garlic and herb mash.

'I'm interviewing trained nannies and housekeepers, but I can't see any point in hiring just for the sake of having someone around. We had a so-called chauffeur and body-guard, but I fired him.'

'Trained nannies,' Prue said. 'That will be a novelty. Why not just go out and pick wannabe singer trash, Rick? They work far cheaper,' she informed Christina. 'Why, some of them will do it for the price of a new pair of knickers. What size are you? An 8?' A lack of reply from Christina didn't bother her. She crashed on regardless. 'Insist he gets the correct size slut. I found one three sizes too large parading around in my best lingerie once.'

There was a short embarrassed silence before Christina picked up the previous conversation as if Prue hadn't spoken. 'I've done fifty covers on my own before now. It's just a question of organisation.'

'And yours is magnificent. I look forward to our collaboration in the club,' Raoul said.

'Collaboration?' Prue said sharply. '*She's* going to work at the Hall once it's converted to a health complex?'

Christina ignored the accusatory tone and said evenly, 'I'm opening a catering consultancy. I faxed over my proposal to Raoul as soon as I heard he was starting up around here.'

'And you hired her? Just like that?' Prue snapped two bronze-tipped fingers. 'When you wouldn't give me a contract?'

Raoul slewed on his seat to face her, taking her hand in an intimate gesture. 'Prue, please, we will discuss this later . . . yes?'

'No.' She snatched her hand away. 'Let's discuss it now. Tell me why you've given her a job . . . as if she bloody well needs it . . . and you won't let me do the interior design at Maudsley?'

Raoul sighed audibly. And then bravely jumped in. 'Because Christina has experience and an established reputation. Your efforts, they are charming, but . . .'

'Not good enough?' Prue finished tightly.

'As you say. I have offered you a job . . .'

'A receptionist! A sodding trainee *receptionist*. It's a joke – and it's your damn fault,' she flung angrily at Rick. 'If I'd had a proper divorce settlement . . .'

'You did.'

'It's not enough.'

'It's all you were worth, sweetheart. Now can it. Or clear out.'

Prue was very near to tears. Her chest heaved. Around the table we were all holding our breaths, with the exception of Winona who was chewing with the placidity of a cow masticating cud.

With a visible effort, Prue caught herself, swallowed the anger and forced a smile. 'You're right. This isn't the time. Sorry, everyone.'

We all returned the smile. And wondered what the hell we could talk about now.

'Are we having fireworks?' Winona asked. Her face was expressionless. It was hard to tell whether it was subtle sarcasm or plain boneheadedness.

Christina rejected the whole idea of Bonfire Night. 'What the hell's the point of celebrating burning a guy to death? It's bizarre.'

'We always had fireworks when we lived here, didn't we, Daddy?' Melody said.

'Did we? I can't really remember.'

'You still living with the old man, sugar?' Bernie asked.

'Natch. I'm his PA.'

'That doesn't mean you need to live in the same house,' Christina said.

'Are you saying you want me to leave?'

'I'm saying most people want to cut loose from their parents. I know I did. Didn't everyone else?'

'I did,' Annie agreed. 'But then I have six younger brothers and sisters so the nest was distinctly overcrowded.' She was across the table from me, caught between Raoul and Christina so that I hadn't had a chance to talk to her, but even so I'd caught a hint of bubbling happiness behind the big gold-rimmed glasses. And I was preparing to trample all over her new romance.

'How about you, Stuart?' Christina enquired. 'Didn't you want to get out from under?'

It was a casual remark intended to keep an awkward conversation flowing. Sitting next to him, maybe I was the only one who noticed the slight shake to his hands and the increased pulse in the side of his neck as he said, 'It wasn't r-really an issue. My parents died when I was quite young.'

'Of what?' I asked. I knew it was a crass thing to ask, but with Vetch out of communication, I couldn't let the opportunity pass to dig out more information on Stuart's background.

He turned a strange look on me. Our eyes were only eighteen inches apart. His were hostile. Definitely not the cuddly accountant who'd employed me. I felt elation that I was on the right track coupled with a large lump in my chest. One way or another it looked like Annie was going to get hurt.

'My mum was ill. My dad had an accident. Could we change the subject, please?'

Embarrassment triggered several voices at once. Because

Bernie's was the loudest, he caught the ball. 'How they getting on with Duke, the bundle of bones? They figured out who he is yet?'

'It's a woman, Uncle Bernie. That's what the police are saying. They've been squidging through the muck looking for clues for days.'

'I felt real sorry for them,' Christina said. 'It was disgusting out there. They were crawling through liquid mud in places. You've no idea.'

Annie and I exchanged looks over the table. We both knew the joys of dredging through piles of dirt and garbage praying there was nothing contagious or lethal hidden in there. 'Have they said anything to you?' I asked Christina. 'About a possible identity?'

Christina started serving chocolate torte and raspberry coulis. 'Not to me. Why should they? I've not been here long enough to remember the post code without looking it up and she's sure as hell been down there longer than that! They talked to Rick.'

Rick rested his elbows on the table and looked at us over the rim of his wine glass, rocking it fractionally so that the burgundy liquid slipped from one side to the other. 'Seemed to think she'd been down there a good while. Thought she could be a stranger – died somewhere else and hidden out here. Place is empty most of the year.'

It was a reasonable theory on the police's part. Thanks to the flat nature of the landscape and removal of the traditional hedgerows to form large, easily farmed fields, there weren't that many places to bury a body in peace around here (as a former acquaintance had kindly pointed out as she mused on the best way to get rid of my body). The secluded corner of a rarely used garden would have made an ideal hiding place.

Rick continued, 'Seems it happens more than you'd think. Runaway kids, drifters and loners. Nobody misses 'em.'

'That is very sad,' Raoul said. 'To be buried without your

name. With no one to look at your grave and remember your smile. Or the sound of your voice.'

There was a silence around the table, broken only by Winona's steady chewing.

'Caught one of your flicks on the movie channel the other night, Prue,' Bernie said with that sort of false heartiness that said the atmosphere was getting to him too.

'You were an actress?' Annie said. 'That must have been fascinating. What were you in?'

I knew her tones of voice well enough to translate this as a game effort to keep the conversation flowing. Prue took it at face value and elaborated.

'Cat and I did a few movies and television. I was usually cast as the English-rose type, she got all the dark, sultry foreigners. She was good at voices and accents.'

I added my contribution to the forced chit-chat. 'That's your godmother, right, Melody? You mentioned she . . .' I was about to add 'came on the shopping binges to Harvey Nicks every time your mum and dad had a fight' when it occurred to me that wasn't going to add much to the general feel-good pot. So I finished with the lame, 'Was very close to you.'

'She is. Like a mother, in fact.'

The challenging tone and raised chin were a challenge to Prue. Presumably Cat was the friend who'd 'hijacked the offspring' during her postnatal depression.

She didn't rise to the provocation. 'We could have done a lot more but Cat decided to change career and I got married and had other responsibilities.'

'Responsibilities! Give it a rest, Prue,' Rick snorted. 'You both had walk-ons when the director wanted some tits and bums on screen. How many lines did you have in your whole career, darling – three, was it? Or four?'

'Shall we have coffee next door?' Christina asked. 'If you've finished, Winona?'

'*Why*-No-Nah.'

'Yes. Right.' Christina stood up. Her movements were

jerkier than before. As successful dinner parties go, this one was pants – big time.

Rick disappeared upstairs to check on his youngest daughter. Prue announced she was off to the lav. Judging from Raoul's anguished expression, he'd already caught on to what she was doing in the privacy of her own WC. The rest of us were left to shuffle into the sitting room and wonder how long before we could make a run for it.

Stuart muttered he should find a bathroom and went out.

I, too, clutched at the gathering's favourite excuse for bolting. 'I think I need the loo.'

I felt the need to put some space between me and this dinner party for ten minutes. I walked quietly upstairs, intending to lock myself in the bathroom I'd used after my impromptu swim last time. There were voices coming from behind one of the doors. They sounded angry. So I did what any good investigator would do – eavesdropped.

'I'm not accountable to you,' Rick hissed. 'I pull the strings, you jump. Just remember that. You were nothing when I picked you up.'

My first guess – he was talking to Prue – was squashed by the reply.

'I was an accountant. A very g-good accountant. That's why you picked me. And while I'm working for you, I shall do my job the best way I know how. The ac-count is nearly empty. It should have over three hundred thousand in it.'

'It's my cash. Don't sweat it, Stu.'

'I have to. And technically it's not your money, it's Christina's. Does she know where it's gone?'

'Hey – for richer, for poorer, remember? It's between Chris and me.'

'No. It's not. You know the deal. A lot of that money was already committed to other creditors.'

'They'll keep. Hold them off. Duck and dive a bit. It's like you say, you're a great accountant. Be creative.'

I caught the sucking inward breath that I'd come to identify with Stuart attempting to overcome his stutter.

Rick forestalled him. 'Gotta go. Need a slash. Hang in there, Stu. It'll come right, you'll see.'

I darted away from the door just before he opened it. Safely lurking in the room opposite, I heard him move away and a few seconds later Stuart followed. They were going in my direction, so I went the other way. The idea to use one of the *en suite* bathrooms was thwarted when I found all the doors had been locked. I took the charitable view that they didn't want Emilie Rose wandering amongst the renovations rather than suspecting we might nick a bedside lamp. At the foot of those stairs leading up to the nursery I saw the door at the top was open and could hear soft hiccuping sobs. Just in case the kid had gone walkabout I figured I'd better do my responsible-adult bit and go round her up.

It wasn't Emilie Rose. I clicked on a wall light and found Prue was perched in one of the window-seats. Her hair was fast degenerating from tousled chick to rat's tails and her make-up was giving up. She added to the problem by scrubbing away tears with the base of her thumb.

'Hi,' I said.

'I blew it again, didn't I?' she said bleakly.

'I'd say so.'

'I'm scared.' She hugged the tops of her arms. 'Nobody wants me. I've got nowhere to go.' She half turned to look at the unlit half of the nursery. 'I was happy here. Some of the time. But it all goes, doesn't it? In the end they all lie. It just comes down to money. Everybody wants money. I did. And I wanted to be the star's wife. You've no idea what a buzz that is.'

I remembered that brief taste of being taken for Rick's latest squeeze at the launch party. Suddenly I'd been a VIP. Imagine having that high for years? It could prove to be the biggest addiction of all. No wonder some of these rock chicks were prepared to put up with any amount of humiliation in order to hang on to it. 'Did you love him?' I asked curiously.

'No. I sort of kidded myself I did. I used to kid myself I loved them all. It was . . . I don't know . . . my way of convincing myself I wasn't a tramp. Some of the girls on the circuit, they just used to collect lays. I had to believe I was in love. I wasn't. I was only ever truly in love once in my life. Trouble is, I forgot what a powerful aphrodisiac money is. My true love didn't so much walk out as dance a frigging lap of honour to the bank courtesy of Rick's cheque-book. Would you believe I'd actually gone out to Ibiza to find us a place? Somewhere cheap where Ellis and I could live together?'

'Ellis being the one who was even better than being the star's wife?'

'Oh, yes. Being with Ellis made me feel a thousand times more . . . alive . . . than being Mrs Rick Alaimo. I'd have given up everything for Ellis – the fame, the money, the easy life. I didn't have any illusions about the divorce settlement I'd get from Rick if I dumped him, but I just didn't care. We'd talked about it, me and Ellis, living simply somewhere in the sun. Growing a few vegetables, painting a bit – souvenirs for the tourists, you know – sunset over the beach sort of thing. I used to be a pretty good artist. We both were. Maybe have Melody out for the holidays if she'd have wanted to come. I loved Ellis so much . . . it hurt . . . and then I got this phone call at the hotel in Ibiza. "Sorry, baby, it's all off. Your husband's come good. No hard feelings, but twenty grand is twenty grand and easy lays are ten a penny."'

'Sounds like you were well out of it.'

'I know. In here I know.' She tapped a finger against a disintegrating hairstyle. 'But it doesn't stop me feeling stupid and ugly when I think about it. Rick wouldn't take me back, of course. And I had to make out I was divorcing him for jumping on one too many hot little cats. Save his bloody male pride.'

'Did you care?'

'Not for a fucking minute. But it was that or his slimy

lawyers would tie up my divorce money for years. As it was I had to sign an agreement not to talk about what happened before I got a penny out of him. It's not enough. It's why I had to move back in with Grev. It's just bills . . . all the time . . . sodding bills. There's nothing left for *nice* things . . . clothes, a decent car, holidays . . . everything's bills.'

Tell me about it.

'I *need* money. I'm broke and I'm lonely and I'm so unhappy . . . and I'm just about ready to do something desperate.'

32

I drove back to Arlene's. Dialling 1471 confirmed that no one had rung since her last call. I couldn't find the mobile. Eventually I located it in the boot of the car. The messaging service told me nobody loved me. Where the hell was Vetch? If he didn't resurface soon I'd have to start considering other police contacts. There must have been a home address listed when Stuart was charged with those two murders. I'd managed to grab a few minutes alone with him before we left the oast houses and he'd resolutely denied knowing that the maiden name of one of Rick's former wives was Cazlett.

'Do you ask the maiden name of your c-client's wives?' he stuttered, plainly understanding I was accusing him of pulling a fast one somehow. 'They've been divorced for t-twenty-odd years. And she s-still calls herself Prue Alaimo. Ask Melody.'

I had. And he was right. Prue probably used it as a last-ditch attempt to hang on to some of the rock-star glitz. Nonetheless I still wasn't convinced Stuart's supposed ignorance wasn't part of some twisted plan. I really needed that previous address for him so that I could start snooping in earnest.

I could try to con Rosco into getting it for me but, given his eagerness last time, I had a nasty feeling he was seeing himself as Seatoun's answer to Dirty Harry – a sort of cut-price Slightly Grubby Terry. If he got a whiff that Stuart Breezley was now in this vicinity, he'd probably start nosing around with all the subtlety of Waterloo after he'd spotted me hiding the chocolate digestives. Speaking of which, I supposed I'd better rescue Edith from the burping bottom so he could get a good night's sleep before his next date with the cameras.

Vetch rang me at three o'clock in the morning.

'Sweet thing, I gather you wish to talk to me?'

'I've been after you for hours.'

'Be still, my beating heart. Are all my fantasies about to come true?'

'I doubt it. And will you get your nose out of my arse?'

'Have I called at an inopportune moment, I hope?'

'I'm talking to the dog.'

'Even more bizarre. I had no idea your tastes were so exotic.'

'Knock it off, Vetch, and listen. I've got a major problem. It's about Annie and her latest . . .'

When I'd finished, I'd chipped some of the archness from his tone. I heard the crackle of paper as he unfolded the fax from his IRS contact. 'This shows his first address in Park Street.'

'Park Street, London?'

'No, it's just shown as Park Street, Hertfordshire. There's a road address as well.' He reeled it off. 'Perhaps the street's off the road or something. There doesn't appear to be a town given. Then he seems to have moved into London a couple of years later after that unlisted period in limbo. Which is when his name change occurs.'

'Maybe a double murderer was depressing the property prices in limbo.'

'Whatever the reason, sweet thing, I sense you are

planning to charge off and ask probing and tactless questions. I think it would be best if you placed your curiosity on hold until I can contact a few people. I'll ring.'

He hadn't by the time I'd fed us both and taken the mutt for his trot and dump routine that morning. I managed to remember the washing and take it in off the back line. It all had a rather interesting smoky scent. Jan turned up at nine-thirty to collect Waterloo for his appointment. The local paper had asked if they could take some pictures of him and Jan had volunteered for chaperone duty. Principally, I suspected, as part of her plan to be 'be famous'. Any publicity – even as the best pal of facially challenged mutt – was a help.

'Was Vetch okay about giving you time off?'

'I dunno. I never asked. I'm working for you, aren't I? You'd better get a move on, or we'll be late.'

'What's this *we*? I thought you were taking him to the newspaper offices?'

'Yeah. But I need a lift.'

The newspaper was located in a side street just off the main town square. I dropped Jan off and told her I'd be somewhere along the beach.

After the brief fillip of Bonfire Night, the blight of low season had well and truly settled on Seatoun. The weather had caught the general depression by plunging ten degrees and coating the sky with a sooty layer of moody-looking clouds. Huddled down in my padded coat and woolly gloves, with a knitted 'West Ham Forever' cap pulled down over my ears, I felt draughts in places I'd forgotten I had as the wind whistled amongst the shabby sixties shopping colonnades that the planners had grafted on to the older town.

Along the promenade the melancholy was even worse. At least in the town the shops made a pretence of expecting to see a customer before next May. Down here most of them didn't bother. The arcades were still open but the souvenir shops, rock emporiums and general-tat-for-the-beach kiosks had pulled down the metal shutters and plastered notices indicating they'd be back next Easter. Even some of the cafés and burger bars had called it a day until spring. I found one that hadn't and bought a large coffee to go. Carrying my caffeine fix down the wooden steps, I made my way over the beach to the firmer sands and wandered along watching the white horses crashing in on the seal-grey rollers and losing myself in the roaring boom of the water that acted like white sound drowning out all other noises. White wasn't the right word for it, I decided, sipping scalding liquid to stave off hypothermia. In Seatoun the horses were teeth-rot yellow.

The wind and spray coming off them was so fierce that it was impossible to breathe if it hit you full in the face. I tucked my head down and walked parallel with the strand, occasionally turning my back on the ocean altogether to snatch another mouthful of coffee. It was cold, miserable and uncomfortable. Which meant I could blame my present mood on the location rather than admit the truth to myself. I was worried to death about the effect all this was going to have on Annie. Only I couldn't quite decide whether I was worried because she was going to get hurt – or because it would probably cause irreparable damage to our friendship and leave me without a best mate.

Emptying out the dregs into a handy tidal pool and setting a starfish on the road to caffeine addiction, I tramped back to the promenade and huddled in a wooden shelter until Jan eventually returned leading the mutt.

I went through the routine of trying to get hold of Vetch on the phone again. But once again he'd disappeared into wherever gnomes went when they wanted to get away from the rest of us average-height humans. I stared moodily over the iron balustrade to the sand particles skittering over the deserted beach. I couldn't go into the office because I might run into Annie and she had an uncanny knack of reading my thoughts. I couldn't hide in Pepi's because it was

Monday and Shane closed the café on Mondays. That just left my flat.

It was as I'd left it – untidy, dusty and guarded by that damn tub of spiky succulents that no one wanted to steal. I shared a biscuit with the mutt, ditched all the accumulated junk mail and rang the hospital to confirm that Arlene was okay. And Vetch still hadn't surfaced with the dirt on Stuart.

Finally, in desperation, I pulled out my driving atlas, spread it on the floor and scanned the section of Hertfordshire with no clear idea of why I was doing it. 'What kind of inefficient jerk can't list the town?' I asked Waterloo, who was now nose to nose with me across the open pages.

I scan-read all those tiny villages and 'B' roads and then – *pay-dirt*! The reason there was no town listed for Park Street was simply because it was a place in its own right. It was little more than a smudge sandwiched between St Albans and the M25 motorway. 'Zoom up, catch the motorway, metal to the floor, we could be there in ninety minutes. Couple of murders . . . bound to be somebody who remembers, don't you think?'

Waterloo didn't answer. This was something of a relief. The day he started talking back I'd know I'd definitely gone loony-tunes.

Park Street proved to be a collection of thirty or so small streets and closes caught between the North Orbital Road and the M25 motorway, but still within sight of the farmland that they had once bisected. It had a rail station, a few small shops and a row of industrial warehousing along the main road, but there was no discernible village centre. In fact, it was hard to work out where the place began and ended. There were a few ancient cottages but most of the buildings looked reasonably modern, post-1950s anyway. The address Vetch had for Stuart was a curve of identical brick semi-detached houses. Neat, bland

and unremarkable, they certainly didn't look like the spawning ground of a mass-murderer.

Number seven had a pale blue door, new white double glazing, a neatly mown and fenced front lawn – and no one at home.

Number nine had a black and white cat with an ability to high jump that should have qualified it for the gold in the moggy olympics. Quivering with fright, it huddled on top of the fence to the back garden whilst the rest of its eight lives had nightmares about Waterloo's teeth closing a millimetre from its fur.

'Come here, you bloody pest!' I leapt the small fence dividing the two gardens and dashed to retrieve Waterloo before anyone saw us. From the corner of my eye I caught a glimpse of a startled face at the front window and knew it was too late to sneak out.

'Sorry,' I apologised to the woman who opened the door. 'He's got lousy manners, but he's not really danger-ous.'

I was having to hang on to his collar with both hands. She didn't look entirely convinced. I asked if she knew when number seven would be in.

'They're away. Can I tell them who called?'

'It wouldn't mean anything to them. I'm really looking for information on some people who used to live there. The Breezleys?'

Her next question confirmed that all had not been forgotten in the case of Breezley versus two corpses. 'Are you a reporter?'

'Private investigator.' Risking taking one hand from the mutt's collar, I delved in my back pocket and extracted a business card. As soon as she'd read it, I took it back again. The prices some of these printers charge are scandalous. 'I'm doing genealogical research for a client. Looks like he might have some connection to the Breezleys. Did you know them?'

'Yes.' She stood back. 'You can come in if you like.' A kid

wailed inside the house. She looked at Waterloo. 'How is he with children?'

'I don't think he could manage a whole one.'

I shut the mutt in the car and then rejoined my new acquaintance. She was picking brightly coloured plastic toddler-type toys from the carpet while their owner sharpened his teeth on a feeding cup and displayed everything he'd got below his rotund tum.

I sat on a sofa. All the seats and the carpet were covered with assorted blankets, sheets and rugs – mostly stained with multicoloured blotches.

'Sorry about the mess. He's taken against his nappy. Screams the house down if I make him wear it. And he can get the cap off that so-called childproof mug.'

Please, God, I prayed silently, let the dampness seeping through my bottom be orange juice.

'So what should I call you?' I asked.

'Poppy. I'm Poppy Ingram now. But I was Poppy Turner back then. You know what you're dealing with here? About the deaths?'

'My client had heard rumours,' I said in my best professional voice. To reinforce the dispassionate bystander persona, I got out my reporter's notebook and pen and pretended to consult former notes. 'He was hoping for a bit of detail. You'd be amazed how many people like a bit of spice on the old family tree. Sheep stealers and transportation to Australia are *very* popular. A highwayman is like winning the lottery.'

'Yes. I can see how that would be okay. I mean, it's history, right? But this isn't . . . I mean, what happened to Mr Breezley was . . . sick-making.' She shuddered and looked like she might really vomit.

It was hard to peg her exact age, but she could only have been a very young kid seventeen years ago. 'You remember it clearly, then?'

'I don't have much choice, do I? I found him.'

33

'Ten,' Poppy said, in answer to my question. 'I was ten. You *see* things wrong when you're a kid, don't you?' She struggled to find the correct words to explain herself. 'I mean, you look at what's there, but you have to make sense of it with what you already know.'

'Like what?'

'Mr Breezley. It sounds really daft now but I thought there were two of them. I had this kid's book with identical twins in it – one was good and one was really bad, and I decided that was who lived next door. Nice Mr Breezley and Nasty Mr Breezley. Nice Mr Breezley used to tell me jokes and give me chocolate.'

'What about nasty Mr Breezley?'

'He was gross. He smelt. He'd get really angry. He was always threatening to kill Sugar and string her up.'

'Sugar being . . .'

'My cat. That was her granddaughter your dog chased just now. Sugar used to scratch up his flowers and poo in the beds. He said he'd kill her. I told nice Mr Breezley about it once. He laughed. Said sugar was bad for little girls' teeth anyway. I really did think he was another person.'

Had the inhabitants of Frognall thought the same about Joe Gumbright's dad? I wondered. Had the old boy been a little charmer when he wasn't getting legless in Winstanton? *Pack it in*, I ordered myself. *There is no connection. Stuart is not a reincarnation of Joe Gumbright, hence Stuart's dad is not a reincarnation of old man Gumbright. It's all a con – remember? Besides, you don't even know that Breezley Senior's problem was down to drink. Maybe he was just nuts.*

'What was his problem?'

'The offy. He couldn't pass one. But nobody tells ten-year-olds about alcoholics. He was never falling down legless. He didn't throw up in the gutters or kick in people's windows. I guess if he had, the grown-ups might have talked about him more. But it all went on behind closed doors, as they say. It wasn't until years later, when I was turning things over in my head, that it finally clicked the old boy had been a drunk.'

Okay, I conceded. *He drank. Doesn't mean he wasn't a pussy-cat when it came to the wife.*

'I never caught on that he must have been knocking his wife around until quite recently,' Poppy chattered on. 'She was always quiet. Never opened her mouth mostly. And she was accident-prone. Amazing how many times she'd be having falls or cutting herself on the tin-opener or catching herself on the hot rings.'

All right, he drank, but so what? Did she do a bunk like Joe's mum, eh? Go on, ask her that! I did.

'She walked out in the end. Went home. Back to Ireland.'

Well three up to the old rebirth theory. What about Billie, though? Hasn't mentioned a daughter, has she? Ask her that.

Poppy shook her head, setting the blunt cut dark hair swinging across her round face. 'No girl. They had a son, Stuart.'

'Yeah, I know.' It slipped out before I recalled she didn't know Stuart was employing me. I hastily reconsulted the notebook. 'And a daughter, it says here.'

'No. You must have got the wrong person. There wasn't any girl, just Stuart. He was weird.'

'Weird how?'

'He had this awful stutter. I mean, he could hardly talk with it. Not that he tried much, he just sort of looked at the ground when he had to say anything to you.' She ducked her head and tipped it to one side, staring at a spot to the left of my knees. It was the classic pose of those whose self-esteem wasn't so much on the floor as tunnelling towards the earth's core.

'Was he violent?'

'Violent?' Poppy looked at me with surprise. 'No. Why'd you ask that?'

'Just a rumour I picked up. Not true, then?'

'No way. Stuart was a plonker. All the kids used to tease him. He was older than us. I mean seven or eight years older, but we all had a go at him. I suppose he was a real easy target. He was such a jellyfish.' Her big brown eyes widened. 'I guess his dad was beating him up too. God, I never thought of that before. That's awful, we were real little shits to him too. That's why I wasn't scared when I found him, I guess. I mean, it never occurred to me he might want to bash my head in.'

'Is that what he did? Cracked someone's skull?'

'They said he did. I saw him, you see. Sugar got into their garden. I spotted her from my bedroom window. I used to have the back bedroom then. Charlie's got it now.' She looked fondly at the offspring who was bent double staring up at places most of us don't get to see unless we fit floor mirrors. 'It was real early one morning. I was sure nasty Mr Breezley would get Sugar, so I crept downstairs and round to their back garden. It's funny, I can still remember the smell of the wet grass. I couldn't see Sugar, but the door was open a bit and I was scared she'd gone inside the house, so I pushed it a little wider . . .' She mimed the action without being aware of it. 'And I saw him.'

'Stuart?'

She nodded, her lips pinched tightly together as those long-ago pictures re-formed in her mind. 'He was standing over his dad with this hammer in his hand and there was blood and stuff splashed all over the floor and the cupboards and everything. Sugar was licking at it. That was what upset me. Funny, isn't it? I was worried my cat would get sick. She was just inside the door so I scooped her up and ran home.'

'Did Stuart try to stop you?'

'I don't think he even saw me. He was staring down . . . like he was in a trance. I was frightened I'd get into trouble for sneaking over like that so I just kept my mouth shut and went to school. Eventually, after the talk started about Mr Breezley being murdered, I couldn't resist telling my mates what I'd seen. You know how great it is to know something the others don't? Anyway, it got back to my parents and I ended up talking to a policewoman. Then they took Stuart away in a police car.'

'And stuck him in jail?'

'I guess. We broke a window round the back of his house. We used to dare each other to go inside and take something. I took a stupid little statue. I had to throw it away in case my parents saw it. And then he came back. I mean, one day we went round the back and he was just there . . . standing in the kitchen . . . It scared the hell out of us.'

'They released him?'

'Yep, see . . . Charlie, *No*!'

Charlie was piddling on the floor. I had to wait whilst she stuffed the soaked rug into the washing machine and re-covered the area with more blankets. 'Lucky you've got so many spare,' I remarked.

'We buy them in bulk, from the Oxfam shop. Where was I?'

'Stuart was running free again.'

'Oh, yeah, well, the house on the other side of theirs, number five, there was this woman lived there, Auntie Nyree we called her.'

The other supposed 'murder' charge Terry Rosco had dredged up against Stuart had involved a woman called Nyree. I visualised the notes I'd written up on it and came up with a surname. 'Nyree Williams?'

'Yes.' For the first time suspicion flitted over Poppy's features.

Trying to retrieve the situation, I waggled the notebook. 'Old electoral list. I jotted down a few names. So tell me about Auntie Nyree. A real aunt?'

'No. We just called her that. Like you do with grown-ups who are friends of your parents. I thought she was incredibly glamorous. Almost more than Barbie. She had all this blonde hair and really exciting clothes. And she always wore make-up. She probably looked like a tart, but when you're ten the Dolly Parton look is a real turn-on. And when you're seventeen apparently. She gave Stuart an alibi. Told the police he'd spent all night with her. Not that I knew that back then. It was years later, when I was talking about it with my mum. She was telling me the facts of life . . . about three years too late, bless her . . . but she was using Auntie Nyree as a warning of what can happen to women who put it about. They end up dead. They found her strangled in her bed.'

'Stuart?'

'I don't know. The police took him away again. And this time he never came back. The house was sold and my parents just clammed up when I asked about it. They were both a bit anally retentive when it came to discussing sex, if you know what I mean.'

'Are they around?'

'They're dead. That's why I moved back here. They left it to me.'

'Oh? Well, how about the neighbours? Someone a bit older who might fill in a few gaps on the Breezleys for me?'

'There's no one in the street who used to live here back then. They've all moved away. Or died. Anyway, what else do you want to know?'

Preferably chapter and verse on what they'd done with Stuart. He must have been somewhere during that 'missing' two years in his IRS record.

'I suppose,' I suggested resignedly, 'if she had her own place, Nyree was a bit older than Joe – I mean Stuart?'

'A bit!' Poppy snorted. 'She must have been in her thirties at least. Maybe even forties. She had a husband around somewhere. He didn't live there but he came round sometimes. He wanted her to come live with him again but she kept telling him to leave her alone. He was the first grown-up I'd ever seen cry. It was quite scary in a funny way, if you know what I mean.'

I did. The first time I'd seen my own dad cry it had rocked my safe little world. Dads weren't supposed to behave like that. Dads were solid rocks that nothing could hurt.

'She didn't leave any relatives behind here if that's what you're thinking,' Poppy said.

It wasn't. I was thinking of the age gap between Joe Gumbright and Lulu Cazlett. And that remark in his description of moving her body that her eyes were full of blood. One of the classic signs of strangulation.

I stood up, thanked Poppy for her help and gave her my mobile number in case she remembered anything else. 'Good luck with house-training the kid.'

'It's just a phase. I think he's growing out of it.'

Given what he was doing behind his mum's back, I wouldn't have laid bets on it.

'He makes you look like a real sophisticate,' I informed Waterloo. He was slumped on the back seat after a quick run around the South Mimms Service Area before we headed homewards. 'The question is . . . where the hell do we go from here?'

The answer was about two miles down the M25. Caught amongst three lanes of stationary traffic and an indicator board flashing all lanes closed. I took another stab at my new game called 'Let's see if we can find Vetch'. I lost.

As a consolation prize, I rang Arlene.

'They say it went like a dream this time, babes. I should be home by the end of the week. How's my best baby? Did you get my birthday card?'

'My birthday's in August, Arlene.'

'Not yours. Mummy's best boy. Vet reckoned he was about thirty weeks that day I pulled him out of the crusher. So we counted back. And we always celebrate on the sixth of November. Didn' he get me card?'

'The post hadn't come when we left this morning. Do you want a word with him?'

Leaning between the seats, I held the phone up to Waterloo so he could bark his news down it. Looking up, I found the occupants of the Jaguar in the next lane staring in amazement. Anyone would think they'd never seen a talking dog before.

When I reclaimed the phone to say bye to Arlene, she said anxiously, 'You will do him a birthday party tonight, won't you, babes? He'll expect it.'

Not only could he talk, he could read the date on the calendar. This was one hell of a smart canine. I promised Arlene gourmet doggy heaven would be his tonight. And then I made the call I didn't want to make.

'Why can't you tell me now?' Annie asked.

'Not over the phone. Can we meet?'

'Tomorrow?'

'Tonight would be better.'

'Okay. But I can't say when. I've got an appointment early on.'

'Stuart?'

'No, it's a client.'

'Thank God for that.'

'What's that supposed to mean?'

'Nothing. Can you come to Arlene's?'

'Looking forward to it already, Sherlock.'

With a sick feeling, I broke the connection.

34

By the time I'd cleared the blockage on the motorway and got home it was gone seven o'clock. There were no messages. In the circumstances there was only one thing to do: party.

'So what do you think? Invite a few of your mates over and order in pizza and six-packs? And then maybe we could hang out? Check out a few of the local lamp-posts?'

Waterloo yawned. Plainly not. 'Something more sophisticated? Fair enough.'

I opened his cards for him (he'd got three – one from Arlene, one from his vet's office and one from a mail order pet's catalogue) and then shut him in the back garden whilst I organised his surprise.

What did one need for a birthday party? Booze. I had no idea whether the mutt was allowed alcohol or not. In the end I decided to compromise – he could watch me drinking it. Food. Three courses minimum – I knew how to be a classy act. Atmosphere. Until now we'd been eating in the kitchen, but in honour of the day I opened up the front sitting room and used the dining table. With subdued lighting, smooch-pooch music on the radio, the table laid with place mats, Arlene's best china and a couple of candles, it looked pretty good.

I changed into something appropriate for the occasion (clean jeans and a vest with just a lick of make-up) and then opened the back door and ushered the birthday boy inside. 'Dinner is served. If you'd care to take a seat?'

He hitched himself into that kid's high-chair immediately, confirming my guess that this was his usual routine when Arlene was home. I poured myself a glass of wine, lit the candles and toasted him. 'Cheers!' With a wuff of appreciation, he stuck his front paws on the table and slurped from his water bowl.

'First course coming up. Don't go away.'

It was oxtail soup – fresh from the tin. I carried the steaming dishes in and invited him to get stuck in. Watching him slopping liquid over the glass table surface to the accompaniment of loud slurps and gurgles I suddenly had a vision of evenings spent with a previous boyfriend (well, several actually).

'I've done fillet steak for the main course. Medium grilled with packet mash, frozen peas and instant gravy for me.

Raw with a side order of dog biscuits for you. I hope you approve?'

We munched through the main course in companionable silence and then I fetched the desserts. I was rather proud of my efforts: ice cream on a base of dog-biscuit crumble sprinkled with doggy choc-chips. Delia, eat your heart out!

Annie arrived as I was making the coffee. 'Bad timing?' she asked.

'No. Why?'

She indicated Arlene's coffee-pot. 'Fresh ground coffee. Smooth music in background. Plates for two in the sink. The aroma of scented candles. A trained investigator notices these things, Sherlock.'

She sounded light-hearted. Normally I'd have responded with a flip remark of my own, but this time I had a lead lump sitting in the middle of my diaphragm that had nothing to do with the wall-filler texture of the mashed potato. 'It's nothing. I mean no one. Have a seat. Drink?' I was clutching the bottle I'd opened for dinner. I was surprised to find it only had half an inch left in the bottom. 'I'll fetch another.'

'Don't bother on my account.'

I wasn't. I grabbed the nearest bottle of red and filled two glasses to the brim. I sank most of mine in one slug. When I emerged for air the kitchen was slightly out of focus.

'That bad, is it?' Annie asked, shoving a chair into the back of my legs.

I collapsed into it and nodded. 'It's about Stuart.'

She was wearing the large, red-rimmed specs tonight. The kitchen light was reflecting in the lenses so I couldn't see her eyes, but I saw the muscles tightening at the edge of her lips and knew this was going to be as difficult as I'd anticipated.

It was about ten times worse. I expected her to argue, but instead she just sat in silence as I outlined everything I'd found out about Stuart's past prior to the move to the sail loft. I wanted her to shout and yell and tell me I'd lost it.

Instead she just racked up the lip compression several turns and heard me out. It was like standing in front of the Head, trying to explain why you'd been snogging in the boiler room when you should have been revising French in the library.

'And what exactly do you think this all means?' Annie asked in her best head-girl's voice when I finally trailed to a miserable halt.

'Oh, come on. It means Stuart has a few problems in the loose-screw department at best.'

'Does it? All right, he was picked up on suspicion of two deaths – according to you. He was also plainly released again. The police do make mistakes, as we both know. After all,' she muttered, 'they recruited you.'

Oddly enough, this blow below the belt cheered me up. Bitchy I could handle. 'So what about those missing two years after he disappeared from Park Street? Where was he?'

'I have no idea. Hitching around the world?'

'Or locked up somewhere. Supposing he'd been found unfit to plead to this Nyree Williams death? So they stick him in a secure hospital, two years later he's pronounced cured – and off he trots into the wide blue yonder.'

'And fifteen years later he decides to hire you to poke into his past and bring it all to light. Good plan.'

'I don't think he had any choice. Did you know he lived in Millrun Road when he first came to Winstanton?'

'Yes.'

'Did you know he lived with someone?'

'No.' She shifted slightly. The overhead light no longer glinted from her spectacles. I could see her eyes. It wasn't a reassuring sight. 'But it's hardly news, is it? Thirty-five-year-old bloke has past?'

'She was only there for a few weeks. And she never went out during the day.'

'So what's your theory here? That Stuart dates vampires?'

'It's not funny, Annie.'

'Am I laughing?'

Unfortunately – no. My relationship with my best mate was rapidly going into meltdown. I was tempted to call a halt to the whole thing – pretend it was all a joke in very bad taste, and give Stuart his deposit back. But I couldn't. It wouldn't solve the problem. Annie would still be dating psycho-man.

'Her face was marked. Bruising. Swelling. Well, you know the form, you've seen enough battered significant others. And she was scared. Badly scared.'

'Says who?'

'Stuart's downstairs neighbour at the time.'

'And did the neighbour happen to catch a name?'

'No. But she did notice that Ms Battered disappeared a few weeks after Stuart moved in. In fact, Stuart denied she ever existed.'

'Really.'

'Want to know what I think is going on here?'

'Do I have a choice?'

'I think he lost it, found a dead body on his hands and buried her out at the oast houses. It's okay the police theorising those bones were stashed by a stranger, but we both know you don't go trawling the country with a dead body in the hopes of hitting on a deserted property. It had to be put there by someone who *knew* the oast was un-occupied for most of the year. And who better than the owner's very own *personal* accountant? He probably thought she'd be left undisturbed for a lot longer than this. After all, that area was planned as a back-to-nature garden. It could have been decades before it was dug up again. And then one morning he gets a call and finds out that the latest Mrs Alaimo has jumped on a plane and moved in. It's too late for him to move skelly by then, so he does the next best thing . . .'

'Which is?'

'He starts manufacturing his defence.'

'How clever of him.'

I could have quick-frozen molten lava on her tone by this time. I ploughed on. 'He might have got away with acting the retarded crazy at seventeen, but it would have been a bit tougher this time. I mean, the guy's got three properties, a successful accountancy business, glamorous clients. It's gonna be a lot tougher to prove he wasn't in control of his actions this time around. Not to mention having a lot more to walk away from. So he starts laying the groundwork – just in case the police make the link between him and the body. He invents this whole other persona – Joe Gumbright – and then hires me to dig out all the parallels between the two lives. Parallels which I'm damn sure he'd already researched himself. And then if he does end up in the dock, it's a case of wheeling out the defence, "It wasn't me, m'lord, I was possessed by the spirit of one of my former lives." The jury's gonna love that one. They'll have him committed before you can say "psychiatric ward – short-stay bed only". He could be out in a year if they have a run on the crazy beds.'

'That is quite ridiculous.'

'Is it? So what's your theory? That Joe Gumbright has been reborn?'

'No, of course not. But I know Stuart isn't a violent person.'

'Well, you would say that, wouldn't you?'

'Meaning what?'

'Oh, come on, Annie, you know what I mean. *Lurve* can shoot your judgement to hell. We've all been there.'

'I'm going now.'

'To Stuart's?'

'That's not really any of your business, is it?'

'Yes. No. Look, just be careful, Annie.'

'If he starts laying out the harvesting implements on the duvet I'll be sure to call you.'

'It's not funny.'

'No. It's not. And can I suggest you don't start sharing

any more of this rubbish unless you can afford an expensive slander action? It might reflect on the agency.'

Her voice had now acquired the ability to freeze the whole of Mount Etna.

'Don't be like that, Annie. Please. It's only because I'm worried about you. I know you haven't had a lot of luck with blokes lately. And Stuart must seem like, er . . .'

'My last chance for water before I hit the desert?'

'Er. Sort of. At least ask Stuart about those missing years. And his parents. He said at the dinner party his mum was dead, remember? Yet according to Poppy Ingram, Mrs Breezley went back to Ireland. At least that's one fact that doesn't tie up. And tell him I know.'

'Safety in numbers?'

'Something like that.'

'I'm going now. Goodnight.'

She stalked to the front door with me trailing behind. I'd blown it. She didn't believe me. She still believed in Stuart. Behind the sitting-room door, Waterloo was kicking up a racket at being excluded from his natural role as guardian of his mumsy-wumsy's property. I opened the door fractionally to let him race out and check I hadn't let in a gang of burglars. His rump caught the door and jerked it from my grip. It swung open to reveal the intimate dinner à deux scenario.

Annie's expression twisted from icy to contemptuous. 'Well, at least I'm not that bloody desperate!'

She slammed out. I stared down at the mutt. 'That went well, didn't it?'

35

I spent the next morning watching a selection of brain-numbing morning TV programmes. This will give you some idea of how desperate I was *not* to go into the office. I knew I ought to drop by to check if any work had come in and generally show a bit of 'corporate spirit', but I couldn't face the idea of running into Annie.

In between DIY and cookery programmes I made further fruitless attempts to track down Vetch by racking up Arlene's phone bill.

'He ain't here,' Jan said. 'He must have come in early because he's picked up his messages, but he ain't here now.'

'Does he know I'm looking for him?'

'I dunno. You want me to tell him?'

'That might justify you parking your bum in reception, don't you think? Is Annie in?'

'Yeah. But she ain't half in a mood. It's like being trapped with a Rottweiler in specs. You want a word with her?'

'*No!*'

'Okay, don't shout. You thought of your idea to put Vetch's on the map yet?'

'My what?'

'You know . . . it was in that memo from the Rottweiler I gave you the other day. I bet you chucked it away.'

I had.

'I've thought of a real belter,' Jan said.

'It doesn't involve putting a big cross on the street map marked VETCH'S IS HERE, does it?'

'No, it don't. I'm not daft. It's gonna help make me famous as well. Wait until you see it.'

'With baited breath, Jan. Tell Vetch I need to talk to him pronto. And tell Annie I've emigrated.'

I tried taking the mutt for a walk along the beach but got fed up with his constant attempts to drag me into the breakers. In the end I took him into the amusement park and we wandered aimlessly looking over the empty rides. They always leave some running with the lights flashing and tinny music blasting out – presumably to stop the staff slipping into terminal depression. It wasn't working. Finally I gave up and headed for the one place in Seatoun where I could be certain of finding noise and company.

Shane was semaphoring with the frying-pans like he was directing a jumbo jet to take-off position whilst he treated the half-dozen customers to the news that he was walking back to happiness.

'Can you take a detour via the cappuccino machine?' I yelled over the jukebox volume.

'For you, Smithie, no road is too long.'

He jived back, his stomach jiggling over his jeans waistband, and deposited a frothing mug in front of me. 'That copper catch up with you yet?'

'Is one chasing me?'

'Fancies himself. Sharp togs, blunt mush.'

'Rosco.' The prat was still after those non-existent negatives of his humiliation at the hands of the teenage jail bait. 'Tell him I've not been in.'

'Can't do that, Smithie.'

'Why not? Have you been sprinkled with truth powder by the honesty fairy?'

'Nope. But I'm about to be visited by the local plod.'

I'd taken a booth next to the steamed-up window. Making a dash for the back door wasn't an option. Rosco was in.

In the café. In a foul mood. Intent on rattling my teeth.

He leant both palms on the Formica and bent forward into my face until we were nose to peak. 'I thought it was you, Smithie.'

'Good to know that Observation Course for Slow Learners hasn't gone to waste, Terry.'

'I want those pictures.'

I patted his slightly-running-to-flesh chops and cooed, 'Now, I told you, the special ones have to be imported. And you have such . . . unique . . . tastes. You'll just have to be patient. They'll be worth it – I promise.' I winked.

He looked blank. And then realised that we had an audience. And he was still in uniform. With an angry glare round the rest of the café, he sank into the seat opposite me. And then leapt up again with a frightened yell. Under the table Waterloo gave a rumble of satisfaction.

'You've still got that bloody pit-bull!'

'Mutt, Terry. Mutt. And he's a hero. Haven't you been reading the papers? He saved Rick Alaimo's daughter from drowning.'

'That was him?' Terry looked cautiously under the table. Waterloo growled warningly. 'He looks bigger in his pictures.'

'So do you.'

That brought another hiss of anger from between Terry's fleshy lips. He was so agitated he even took his cap off. This was serious stuff. He loved that uniform. 'I need those photos, Smithie. I came up with the info on Breezley, didn' I?'

'Not much of it, Terry. What happened to Stuart Breezley after he was pulled in for those two deaths? Did he get sentenced? Locked in a padded room? Invited to join the local anger management forum?'

'I don't know. It was a sensitive file. I had to duck and dive. Get in and out of the computer fast.'

'You mean you bottled it.'

'What's it matter anyway? Is he around? You reckon he's been at it again?'

'Not that I know of,' I said with fingers crossed.

'Maybe he did Lucky.' There was a smug little tilt to his mouth. His usual expression when he wanted me to know he had inside information on a case.

I played along. 'Lucky being . . . ?'

'That bag of bones they dug up at your mate Alaimo's place. The team's calling her Lucky.'

That would certainly fit in with the macabre in-house humour of the CID. Just in case there were any useful snippets hidden behind Terry's self-satisfaction, I looked impressed at his inside info and leant a little closer. 'Been down there for years, the Alaimos were saying at dinner.'

'You eat at their place?' Now it was Terry's turn to look impressed. 'I was up there the other day,' he whispered.

'Turning the ground over. Evidence of identification, you know?'

The thought of Terry slogging through a landscape that resembled a First World War trench was a warming picture. 'Find much?'

'Nah. Rotted near clean away.'

'Not so lucky, then.'

'That's not why they're calling her that.' His superior smirk invited me to probe further.

I shrugged. 'Don't pretend you know more than you do, Terry.' I drained my cappuccino and started to go.

He grabbed a wrist. 'I found a clue. A necklace.'

I frowned, trying to recall the moment I'd first seen that skeleton, after Waterloo had decided to play 'fetch' with her arm bone. I'd only taken a fast check, but I was damn sure there hadn't been anything caught around the vertebrae below the skull. Perhaps it had come undone and fallen into the mud underneath her? 'Where was it? Under the body?'

'Few feet away.' He shifted into belligerence. 'Doesn't mean it ain't hers.'

'Doesn't mean it is, either. Is that what makes her lucky? You retrieving her jewellery ten years too late?'

I'd hoped he wouldn't be able to resist the opportunity to put me right on the skeleton's burial date as well, but he managed to suppress his natural inclination to strut his superiority this time. (That, or he didn't know.) He did, however, put me right on the nickname. 'It's from her necklace, ain't it?'

'Is it?' That would certainly narrow the time-frame down. Those neck chains with lettered girl's names or attributes (lucky, sexy, hot stuff, etc.) were a fairly recent product. I didn't think they'd been around in Lulu Cazlett's day. And if they had, I couldn't see her wearing one.

'Had an initial on it. Big gold "L". Big fancy chain too. Worth a bit.'

I was beginning to get a funny feeling down my spine

again. I had a flashback to my visit to Maudsley Hall and those three oil portraits of Roderick Cazlett and his two wives. I also remembered how I'd suspected at the time that Lulu had worn that heavy gold pendant as a way of drawing the viewer's attention to her seriously impressive bustline. 'This initial, on its own, was it? Or was it set into something? A blue stone for instance?'

'Lapis lazoooli, they said. Here, how'd you know that, Smithie? Withholding information . . . I could nick you for that.'

'No, you couldn't. I'm not withholding, am I, seeing as how nobody's told me about that necklace. Officially, that is.'

Indecision flitted over his fleshy features. On the one hand, he'd been blabbing about what he shouldn't. On the other hand, if he got cosy with me, he might bag himself a great big CLUE. And put his side one-up in the age-old battle between uniform and CID.

'Go on, then, Smithie. You and me are mates – yes?'

'No.'

'Still, you'd want to catch whoever done her, wouldn't you? I mean, if you was to know something . . .'

I made him pay up for another cappuccino before laying out the information regarding Lulu Cazlett and her supposed death abroad.

'Sixty years?' Terry visibly slumped. 'They'll all have snuffed it by now, then. Won't be no one left to nick.'

'Still, in the interests of truth and justice and all that . . .'

It was plain that truth and justice didn't do it for Terry. He was more into screaming car chases, hurling the suspect to the ground and slapping on the handcuffs whilst yelling 'You're nicked, sunshine!' as the TV cameras rolled and the flash-bulbs went off. 'Who'd you reckon did it, then?'

Who did I? On balance I thought my money would be on Roderick Cazlett. After all, there was nothing on the Joe Gumbright tapes to suggest Joe had done it. Just that he'd disposed of the body.

'The husband. Roderick. He was the one who claimed she'd died abroad and arranged for the memorial service to be held in Frognall D'Arcy. That was one hell of a deception. I figure it must have taken one hell of a secret to launch it.'

'Makes sense.' Rosco resettled his cap. His shoulders went back. His chin went up. Action man was about to strut into action. 'We'll be in touch. Don't leave town.'

'What about my Great-Auntie Gertie's birthday party?'

'What about it?'

'I'm expected home for it.'

'Well, okay – I expect you could go to that.'

'And my dentist. I'm thinking of using a new one in Winstanton.'

'Yeah, well, Winstanton would be all right.'

'And I've gone in for this free draw for theatre tickets for London. If I were to win would I need a police escort?'

He finally caught on. 'Stow it, Smithie. Nobody loves a smart-arse.'

'You must be crushed to death by friends, then,' I murmured as he stormed out.

I hung out there for a few hours until Shane indicated that the mutt's contribution to the methane mountain was seriously affecting his client turnover. I knew what I had to do. I went back to the office to find Annie. I figured I owed her an apology. Not a big one – Stuart was still on the hook as far as his dodgy past was concerned – but if that *was* Lulu they'd dug up then his ex-girlfriend couldn't have been buried out at the oast houses.

'Which isn't to say,' I remarked to the mutt's waggling rump, 'that she isn't dead and buried somewhere. But let's give him the benefit of the doubt for now. Although I want it clearly understood that I don't buy this reincarnation rubbish. However – and why ever – he found out about Joe Gumbright, I'm not subscribing to the hot-line-to-the-other-side theory.'

I said as much to Annie. She received the news with the

same stone-faced calm that she'd been putting out last night. Forget freeze-drying volcanoes, this woman could have frozen small suns.

'Thank you for telling me,' she said when I trailed to an awkward halt. 'Could you go now, please? I have a lot of work to do.'

She was using her own newly redecorated office on the top floor of Vetch's again. Sitting in the pink and blue room, with its tasteful pictures and plant arrangements, all designed to create a restful, confiding atmosphere, I'd experienced a brief warm flash of *déjà vu*. It was just like the old days when we'd wandered into each other's offices to scrounge, bitch and commiserate together. All I had to do was grovel, plead and declare Stuart to be the greatest thing since low-fat chocolate and maybe we could get back to those easygoing days.

Only my personal little demon wouldn't let me do it. Instead I heard him asking if she'd tackled Stuart about his past. 'You know, his mum being dead rather than born-again Irish? And his dad being killed? Not to mention Nyree the neighbour? And those missing two years after the deaths?'

'He didn't want to talk about it.' Her voice was still icy but she didn't quite manage to control the tremble on her upper lip before I saw it.

'Tough call?' I suggested.

'No.' She gulped. 'He didn't want to discuss it. I can respect that.'

'No, you can't. I bet you want to shake him until his teeth rattle.'

'And his tongue falls out,' Annie said through gritted teeth. 'Are you satisfied now?'

'Don't blame me. It's Stuart who's been twisting reality. At least if it *is* Lulu's skeleton we know he wasn't trying to establish a crazy-defence *vis-à-vis* the girlfriend who disappeared from the Millrun Road flat. Unless he buried her somewhere else, of course.'

'Perhaps we should hire a bulldozer and just plough up the entire neighbourhood.'

'There's no need to get uptight. Remember, it was Stuart who hired me to dig in the first place.'

'Perhaps that was another facet in his cunning plan to appear mad. I mean, let's face it, you'd have to be to hire an investigator who assaults you at every meeting.'

'Accidents will happen.'

'They will if you stay any longer.'

'I was trying to help.'

'You're not. Shove off.'

At least that sounded more like the old Annie. I mooched over to my own office opposite. I'd shut the mutt in there. Big mistake. I threw up the window and watched the herring gulls lift off from the roof with squawks of annoyance. The stiff breeze coming off the sea caught them, and they hovered above the house like white and yellow kites. Waterloo padded over and walked his front legs up the wall until he could rest his paws and chin on the window-sill and stare out too.

'What now?' I asked him. 'I think perhaps we owe the Cazletts a call. It's not like we're tipping off a murderer, unless Roderick is still haunting the place. And Greville *is* terminally ill by the sound of it. Having the police tramping around accusing his dad of murdering his mum could be fatal. Well, fatalish,' I amended, because I couldn't really see Greville as the sort to keel over just because there had been a spot of in-family *crime passionel* six decades ago.

You just want to know if it is Lulu, Waterloo taunted.

That's when I realised things were definitely getting out of hand on that front. I'd started to imagine the damn mutt's thoughts. It was just as well Arlene would be reclaiming him in a few days.

It was dusk by the time I reached Maudsley Hall, one of those lowering, depressing dusks that precedes a cold autumn night. The house looked deserted. The only light came from my headlights. As soon as I switched them off we were left in the lonely stillness where dried leaves somersaulting over the drive sounded like skeletal feet trying to sneak up on me. Goose-bumps rose over skin as that icy-water sensation tickled my spine. I told myself to get a grip and I did. On the mutt's lead.

The front door was unlocked. I took a few steps inside and tried an exploratory whistle. From somewhere out back, the hounds responded immediately. Waterloo wriggled his rump, blew himself up and howled a challenge. The echoes reverberated around the hall.

The racket drowned out all other sounds. It was the change in light and cessation of the draught on the back of my neck that warned me the front door had been closed. I swung back and found Greville leaning against it, cradling a shotgun.

'Hello, Nameless. I hear you think my dear Mama doesn't lie in a foreign cemetery at all. In fact, you seem to have given the police the impression Dada lied through his teeth when he claimed she'd pegged out in Italy.' He smiled slowly and snapped the gun into a firing position with a decisive click. 'Do you know, my dear, you were quite right.'

36

'It's a fine piece, don't you think?' He stroked the steel barrel with smooth, even strokes. 'Twenty-first birthday present from Dada. He had a pair made for my brother and me. Haven't used them for years, but Raoul fancied a shoot. That's my nephew, you know.'

'We met. Dinner party at the Alaimos.'

He was still between me and the great outside. And you can just never tell how people will take a spot of slandering the family name. I could feel my heart starting to speed up and my breathing becoming shallow. Guns had that effect on me. I don't want to be shot. I've always suspected it's nothing like in the movies when they stagger up, holding a hand to a small shoulder hole pumping gore, and shrug it off with a casual assurance that it's 'not as bad as it looks'. Personally I had a hunch that it would hurt like hell, and if it ever happened to me I intended to scream my damn head off whilst they carted me off on a stretcher.

My stomach muscles had sucked in so hard they shook hands with my backbone. I must have looked terrified.

'No need to panic. It's not loaded.' He broke it again to show me the empty chambers. My stomach said ta-ta to my vertebrae and promised to be in touch next time we were in mortal danger. 'Why's it so dark in here?' Greville clicked on the hall lights. 'Been fetching this from the cellar. Got a bit lost amongst the memories. Amazing what you hang on to, isn't it? Well, I dare say Raoul will have a bonfire with the lot when he opens the health complex. Come through, see what else I've unearthed.'

He led the way to the back of the house and into the kitchen. The hounds greeted his arrival with an ecstasy of tail-waving and slobbering, before turning their attention to the business of checking out Waterloo with a bit of serious butt-sniffing. The room was much as I'd have fantasised a kitchen in these old houses to be: well used and furnished with appliances and furniture bought for their durability rather than their charm. The floor tiles were cracked and the walls emulsioned to paint over the dirt rather than make a style statement. The only thing that was out of place was the microwave oven. I liked it. It was my sort of dump.

Greville laid the gun over the table next to a collection of dusty glass cases. They were the sort normally used to display stuffed fish or birds, but this lot had handguns instead.

'Are they real?'

'I would assume so. Don't think we had any sharp-shooters in the family so one of the ancestors must have picked them up somewhere for wall decoration.'

I peered in the cases out of a sort of morbid curiosity. Shotguns are fairly prevalent in the countryside, but handguns are a different matter. In the police you have to apply to be authorised to carry arms – personally I'd never had the slightest ambition to be one of those privileged to do so. I figured if I had a gun they'd send me into situations where the bad guys shot at me. But this lot were nothing like the neat, modern handguns the cops waved around. They were big silver beasties with revolving chambers, elaborately decorated handles and huge barrels.

'Do they work?'

'Doubt it. Probably decommissioned. Some of them must be over a hundred years old. I'm damned sure they're not licensed. But you won't report me, will you? Would you care for a cup of tea?'

'Thanks.'

'Splendid. Make me one while you're there, will you?' He started to pull bottles of gun oil and polish out of his jacket pockets and line up the guns to be cleaned. I let him get away with it since he was ill, and put on the kettle.

I was itching to ask about that cryptic remark that I'd been right about his father lying when he'd claimed Lulu had died in Italy, but I find you often get more out of people if you let them ramble at their own pace rather than go for the direct interrogation technique. 'You're looking well.'

'I'll never be well. But this is one of my better days. Have you come to give me the pleasure of your company? Or did you want Prue? Or Raoul? Good-looking chap, ain't he? His father was too.'

I ducked the implication I might be after his nephew and reminded him he'd told me his brother Ralph had lived in Kenya. 'Raoul's Swiss, isn't he?'

'Mother was French-Swiss. Took him home after Ralph died. Invited her to bring the boy here, but she preferred her own people. Still, turned out well, hasn't he?'

'Sounds like he's got it together okay,' I agreed, trying to locate cups. The mugs Prue had used on my last visit were sitting in the sink, so I rinsed a couple of those out and added a shot of milk. 'Did you know he was thinking of giving Christina Alaimo a catering consultancy?'

'Was he now? I dare say that explains why Prue is in an even more irrational mood than usual.'

'She's scared. No home. No job. No bloke.'

'I know.' He looked steadily at me as I put the mug in front of him and took the seat opposite. 'You think I'm being heartless, don't you, leaving this place to Raoul?'

'No. Well, a bit.'

He lobbed several heaped spoonfuls of brown-damped sugar from an open bowl into the tea and stirred vigorously. 'I didn't have any choice. It was that or sell it, assuming I could have found a buyer. If he'd have had to pay even a fraction of inheritance tax, Raoul would have passed. As it was, I had to talk him into taking the place on. It's going to take a tidy lot of investment to make a go of this health club. But at least the house will be left standing. It's ridiculous really, I had no idea how fond I was of the old place until I had to face the idea of losing it.'

'Maybe Prue feels the same way.'

'No. She doesn't. Doesn't give a damn about it. But that's not the reason I cut her out. Fact is, she can't afford to run it. And whatever she managed to sell it for, that daughter of hers, Melody, and her witch of a godmother would have picked clean.'

'You're not a fan of Melody's, then?'

Greville blew derision down his pinched nostrils. 'Melody! Pretty name. Pretty face. Morals of a bloody weasel. I take it you've met her? Friend of yours?'

'Not really. Waterloo pulled her baby sister out of the lake.'

'That was him, was it?' Greville said, lifting his chin to peer at the mutt, who was sprawled on the tiles like the middle section of a capital 'I' whilst the two hounds formed the crossbars at either end. 'He looks bigger in his pictures.'

'It has been mentioned. Why don't you like Melody?' I asked curiously.

'Because she's a manipulative little piece of trouble.' He smoothed a rag over the shotgun. The room smelt of gun oil, dog and male sweat. 'I'd blame it on that father of hers, but frankly I think we should give credit where it's due. If you're raised by a woman with a need to control then it stands to reason some of the milk will go into the whelp.'

For a second I thought he was talking about Prue. Then I gave credit where it was due – to the 'friend' Prue claimed had 'hijacked' her baby during her own postnatal depression. 'Auntie Cat?'

'Auntie Cat,' Greville agreed, gulping tea thirstily. 'Melody's godmother. Met her?'

'No.'

'Sly. But smooth with it. Hides a lot of festering behind a soft voice and a concerned smile. And she's trained our little Melody well. D'you know she accused some poor boy of raping her? Pure spite because she couldn't get him for herself.'

'I thought that was some girl she'd gone to school with?' That was what she'd told me. I could hear her soft voice, just trembling on the edge of tears, as she'd explained why she hadn't wanted to cry rape after Stuart's supposed attempt in that New York hotel.

When I was at school there was this girl . . . she got dumped by this boy she really fancied for her best friend so she said he'd attacked her . . . He was arrested and his parents were just destroyed, you've no idea. Some of us . . . knew that she was lying . . . but nobody said anything because you don't, do you . . . you can't split on your friends. And then we heard his mother had taken an overdose . . . they found her in time . . . It made some of us own up . . . about what we knew . . .

'No,' Greville said. 'It was dear little Melody. Wanted him for herself, but he wasn't interested, so she set him up. Cold-blooded about it too. Took her months to plan. She

261

made a best friend of his girlfriend. Found out what underwear the other girl wore – and then found out when they'd been tumbling each other. When she was ready she stole a pair of the girl's panties from the school laundry and replaced them with an identical pair. Then she cried rape. Didn't overdo the torn clothes or bruises, just quiet tears and protests that she hadn't led him on. When he denied ever touching her, she waved "her" used underwear around as evidence. Police tested them for semen and what did they find? Poor, tearful Melody had been telling the truth. It nearly destroyed that poor lad. His mother tried to commit suicide. It was only when the other girls decided they couldn't stomach any more of our little Melody's lies that they caught her out. And she wasn't the slightest bit ashamed of what she'd done by all accounts. Her father had to pay out to hush things up. Luckily she was too old to be inflicted on some other unsuspecting school.'

'At thirteen?'

'Whoever gave you that idea? Melody was a few weeks short of her eighteenth at the time. And quite old enough to know what she was doing. Any more in that pot?'

Topping up the tea, I asked if there was anyone else who wanted one.

'No one else here. Raoul's gone to town. Meeting with his architects. And Prue's gone to see Cat. Hoping to bag a room in her flat when she has to leave here.'

'So they wouldn't have spoken to the police, then?'

'Police?' Greville looked blank.

My subtle attempt to steer the conversation back to the subject of his dead mum seemed to have hit a brick wall. I dumped subtle.

'Mystery woman interred at oast houses. Gold necklace found nearby. Appeared in your mum's portrait.'

'Oh, that. Some officers did turn up as we were finishing lunch. Wanted to know about Mama's death. Seem to think she hadn't died of typhoid fever in Italy. Well, she hadn't, of course. Bloody stupid story. Can't think how Dada got away with it. Right out of some Victorian novel. But it was a different world back then – moved on a wink and a dodgy handshake. Doubt you could get away with fudging an inquest these days.'

'Fudging how?'

He poured the remains of his tea into a dish on the floor before answering. There was an eager scuffle to reach the goodies first. Waterloo came last due to his vertically challenged legs. I felt obliged to soothe the little guy's feelings by pouring him his own offering in another dish.

Whilst I was busy Greville had taken something from an old tweed jacket hanging behind the kitchen door. He passed it across to me as we sat down again. Unfolding the yellowing paper, I found myself reading the death certificate of Louise Ada Cazlett (also known as Ada Black). According to this she'd drowned on 19 October 1938 in Seatoun. The name nudged a memory. The coroner's reports that Ruby had dug out for me. One of them had been a *Miss* Ada Black who'd washed up on Seatoun Beach after she'd escaped from a private mental institution. '*It would appear that this unfortunate woman escaped from those paid to provide care and companionship to her early on the morning of the nineteenth October . . . she purchased a railway ticket to London and from thence another to Seatoun . . . she appears to have made her way on foot to North Bay . . . her injuries are consistent with a fall from the cliffs . . . we have no way of knowing her intentions and must therefore assume that her death was a tragic accident.*'

'Leeds,' I said. 'She came from Leeds.'

'How did you know that?'

'Research. Old newspapers. The name stuck. So what's the big deal? Why the mystery death in Venice?'

'Naples actually. Fact is . . . my mother had nymphomania. The policeman to whom I had to explain this had precisely the same smirk as you are displaying.'

Desperately I tried to rearrange my face. He was right. I

had grinned. I hadn't meant to, but just the word raised mental images of tacky blue movies.

'I know everyone finds it amusing,' Greville said calmly. 'Men in particular seem to imagine that marriage to a nymphomaniac must be paradise on earth.'

'And it wasn't?'

'No. Nymphomania is a mental illness, not a super-charged libido. My mother put my father through a private hell. Ralph and I were packed off to boarding-school as soon as possible. Nonetheless we couldn't be entirely shielded from the sniggers and rumours. One of the symptoms was a total breakdown of what would be called morality in those days. My mother's behaviour was becoming the talk of the district. Eventually her condition became so severe that she had to be confined to a mental institution under her maiden name.'

'Not in Naples, I take it?'

'Yorkshire. She came from that area originally. The Italy story was concocted for the benefit of Ralph and me. It was felt that having a mother confined to a lunatic asylum would have a serious effect on both our chances of a career and snagging a suitable filly for breeding purposes.'

'I thought a dash of lunacy was almost obligatory in the upper classes.'

'Eccentricity – perhaps. Proven lunacy – no. Anyway, our family is hardly that upper class. I dare say Mama could have swung naked from the town hall chandeliers had she been a duchess, but in our case a fast night passage north and a smokescreen of Italian travels was called for. Unfortunately – or fortunately perhaps – she escaped a few weeks later and tried to make her way home. Or so we assume. Her mental faculties had disintegrated by then to a point where it was uncertain whether she knew where she was, or what she was doing.'

'Like chucking herself in the sea.'

'Yes. The coroner was charitable enough to record it as an accident. For her sake I hope it was.'

So much for my theory of the jealousy-maddened husband/lover planting poor old Lulu in the ground.

'The coroner and, indeed, the local newspaper editor were both acquaintances of Dada's. They were kind enough to provide a sanitised version of the matter, shall we say? And, of course, the death certificate my father would have needed to show when he put his status as "widower" on his second marriage lines.'

There was a gentle irony in Greville's voice that told me he'd more or less guessed what I must have been thinking and was pointing out the flaws in my theory. There was also enough humour in his tone to tell me I'd provided him with a considerable amount of free entertainment. At least I had the consolation of knowing my ability to act like a prat had comforted a dying man.

'Dada kept up the fiction of foreign travels for a couple of months until people had lost interest in "Ada Black's" drowning and then announced poor Mama's death.'

'Did you know the truth?'

'Not then. He didn't tell us until many years later. Although, to be frank, I doubt we'd have cared much. We scarcely knew her, you see. My strongest memory of that event is cold feet and watching my breath freeze at the memorial service because the damn church boiler had packed up. Let you into a secret, shall I, Nameless? You're not the first to have imagined Dada burying the body one dark stormy night. Apparently it was a favoured theory in the district for years after Mama left.'

'And nobody told the police?'

'If they had, Dada would have shown them the certificate I've just shown you, wouldn't he? But I doubt if they did. I suspect the village rather enjoyed having their own un-detected murderer living in their midst. Gave the place a certain cachet. Ironic really, isn't it? In saving us from being the sons of a lunatic, Dada turned us into the sons of a murderer. On balance, though, it was probably the best deal. Murder is generally more acceptable than lunacy.'

That still left the necklace. I asked Greville if the police had mentioned it.

'Showed it to us. Apparently you'd identified it from a portrait? It was passed on to my stepmother along with the rest of Mama's jewellery. And then Prue had it. Lost it years ago when she lived out there with the rock-star garbage.'

Which would explain how Rosco had managed to unearth it from the garden. Another dead end – literally. The unknown female was still very much unknown. And since it would seem Lulu Cazlett was safely buried under her maiden name in a Leeds cemetery, that brought us neatly back to Stuart – the twice-arrested murder suspect – whose girlfriend had disappeared a few weeks after their arrival in Winstanton.

37

I wanted Vetch. A rare enough event for me to feel annoyed that he was still playing hard to get. Exasperated, I lobbed the mobile over my shoulder into the back of the car. There was a scuffle from the mutt, and he squeezed through the gap between the front seats with the phone clamped in his jaws.

'We're not playing fetch, you idiot.' I idled the car around a bend, unsure where to go from here.

Waterloo dropped the mobile on the passenger seat and sniffed it. He nudged it towards me with his nose and whined. When that didn't work, he stepped up the volume.

'Oh, for heaven's sake.' Grabbing it, I slung it into the back again. With a yelp of exuberance, Waterloo bounced after it. This time there was a suspiciously snapping sort of crackle. He wriggled back into the front again and laid the remains of the phone down with a laid-back, nothing-to-do-with-me-guv expression.

'It's lucky for you I haven't paid for that. The question is, whither now? I ought to see Stuart and tell him he's off the hook on the Joe Gumbright thing and that Lulu Cazlett has been safely tucked up in a Leeds cemetery for sixty-odd years rather than mouldering away by the oast houses. On the other hand, if this is just a con to establish an unsound-mind defence when they finally trace the oast house skeleton back to him, he's going to know that anyway.'

Waterloo whined. I took it as encouragement.

'What we really need,' I suggested, 'is to talk to Vetch about the background to those early arrests in Park Street. And to find out more about this mystery woman who lived with Stuart when he first came to Winstanton. And since Vetch is currently unavailable . . . that leaves us with Stuart's downstairs tenant, doesn't it?'

Winstanton it was, then.

Martha Potter looked like she'd been caught in a bomb blast in a paint factory. She greeted me with the query, 'Have you got a car?'

'Yes, thanks.'

'Great. You can save me calling a cab. Take this.'

She dumped a cardboard box full of newspaper-wrapped lumps into my arms. Glimpses of her excruciating pottery peeped from gaps. Martha hooked a hand inside the cut-out carry-handles of two larger cartons on the kitchen floor and started shuffling backwards, dragging them with her. Even with her head upside down, the gelled, sweep's-brush hairstyle remained rigidly horizontal. Her impressive butt was spreading inside a pair of raspberry-pink leggings. I saw Waterloo eyeing the wobbling buttocks with a con-sidering gleam and threw him a warning glare.

'Where are you going?' I asked as we heaved the load into the Micra.

'The Town Hall. I'm setting up my exhibition. Did you want something?'

'No, providing a free taxi service is my contribution to world feel-good day.'

'Fine.'

'I was being sarcastic,' I said.

'More fool you. What did you really want?'

'Extra information on your landlord's former girlfriend. The one with the extensive line in facial bruising and the ability to disappear into thin air. Remember her?'

'No.'

'What do you mean – no? It was you who told me about her in the first place.'

'Did I?'

'Has someone got to you?'

'Nope.'

I glanced sideways at her. She was staring unconcernedly through the front windscreen. There was a smear of blue paint behind her ear and more streaks of it in the circular hair. She sure didn't look like a woman under threat of violence. More like a smug pink toad who'd just spotted a fat juicy fly in tongue-flicking range.

'How about bribery?' I suggested.

'What you offering?'

'Not me. I meant, has Stuart bunged you something to keep quiet?'

'Why should he? Go round the back.'

This last instruction related to the Town Hall. It was several streets away from the front, but close enough for us to catch the sea breezes and hush of the waves sweeping the shingle as soon as we stepped outside the car. A fire door at the back of the building had been propped open and a hand-painted sign was marked EXHIBITORS THIS WAY – NO ADMITTANCE TO GENERAL PUBLIC – EXHIBITION OPENS WEDNESDAY.

'Grab the other side of this.' Martha latched her fingers under one side of the first carton and stood waiting for me to help her out with it.

'What did your last slave die of?'

'Not obeying orders fast enough.'

Game to her. I told the mutt to 'guard' and together we staggered inside with the first wave of Martha's contribution to the cultural life of Winstanton.

They'd set aside about half a dozen rooms on the ground and first floors. It seemed to be a general hotchpotch of anything that could be considered vaguely artistic. Martha was sharing a room overlooking the front street with a bloke who sculpted driftwood into objects that looked remarkably like driftwood, a woman who made patchwork and a photographer who specialised in moody black and white shots.

I went to look. Martha called, 'Next carton, come on.'

I clicked my heels. '*Ja, mein Kapitän.*'

If I hadn't been certain she was hiding something about Stuart and his late flatmate, I'd have left her flaming cartons in the road. As it was, I had to help heave the rest of the horrors in and pray no one thought they were mine. It all seemed well organised. Trestle tables and hanging frames had already been set up for the displays and a female with a yellow tabard annotated OFFICIAL was handing out glossy rolled posters to the exhibitors whilst chanting the mantra, 'Blu-tack only, no pins.'

The photographer unrolled his poster and started attaching it to the wall behind his corner. 'Michael J. Halliwell – Sponsored by Weekes Estate Agency & Furstons Frozen Foods.'

The patchworker was sponsored by a bank and the driftwood had got the local DIY warehouse to stump up. Martha was busy unwrapping lopsided crockery. Her own posters were sitting on the end of a trestle. Idly I pulled the tight roll, wondering who on earth would be daft enough to sponsor her. And I got my answer to that and an earlier question: 'Martha Potter – Sponsored by S. Roberts Accountancy Services.'

She looked up and we locked glares. 'It wasn't a bribe. He appreciates my talent.'

'For what?'

'That's typical. I bet you get orgasmic over stupid watercolours of fluffy puppies.'

'Not since they threw me out of the print section of John Lewis. Come on, Martha, do you really expect me to believe Stuart has suddenly turned into an art lover? When did he offer to put the dosh up – recently?'

'Fairly.'

'Before or after you happened to mention you'd been talking about the mystery flatmate to me?'

'Why don't you ask Stuart?'

'Ask Stuart w-what?'

He was right behind me. 'I thought that was your car outside, Grace. Can we talk?'

'Sure. Walk?'

Fate had decided my next move for me. Who was I to argue? As we headed for the door, Martha came after us and thrust an untidy parcel in Stuart's hands. 'For you. To say thanks. Hang on to it. I'll be worth a packet some day.'

Stuart disentangled a large wonky platter, painted in a swirling pattern in shades of royal blue and gold. 'That's generous, Martha. Thanks. Good luck for tomorrow. Grace . . . ?'

I left the car where it was, but retrieved the mutt. I let Stuart set the direction but didn't say anything. If he wanted to talk he could choose the subject. Winstanton wasn't very large; it didn't take long to work out that we were heading for his flat. Just what I needed – to be locked in with a possible multiple murderer. I must have paused without knowing it. Waterloo stopped in response to the tug on his lead and looked up enquiringly. Stuart did the same.

'Problem?' he asked.

This was no time for false bravery. Why be embarrassed by cowardice when it keeps you alive? 'I think I'd rather stay out here until you've answered a few questions, Stuart.'

'Like what? Why did I sponsor Martha?' He examined the plate in the light from one of those repro gas lamps. 'It r-really is terrible, isn't it?'

'And some. So why throw money at it?'

'Because she really and truly believes in it. It's her whole life. Her passion. Ever since I've known her. Normally I wouldn't have wasted money on something so hopeless. But she caught me on a high. I was happy. I wanted everybody else to be happy. Don't worry, I'm over it now. I won't be throwing any more money at hopeless causes. It only happens every six years or so.'

'What cured you?'

'Annie. I thought, you know, maybe . . . I've not had a lot of relationships. My own choice. But Annie sort of gets under your skin, doesn't she?'

'How do you expect me to answer that one? Annie's a mate, but I've never been attracted to women in that way. I got the impression last time you came up in our chats that the pair of you had had a row about your past. Or, to be exact, you telling her to keep her nose out of it.'

'I didn't say that. Not exactly. It's just . . . I've been trying to bury that part of my life for years.'

'Literally?'

'What do you mean?'

'Oh, come on, Stuart. I'm sick of wading around in the history zone – yours and Joe Gumbright's. You hired me to find out whether you'd strangled Lulu Cazlett in another life. Well, good news . . . Joe's in the clear, but I can't say the same about you.' It was too late to back away now. I might as well finish what I'd started. 'What happened to the woman who moved to Winstanton with you? Or, to put it another way, did what was left of her surface at the oast houses the other week?'

'The oast . . . ? Is that what you think? That the skeleton is Benita?'

'Who the hell's Benita?'

'She's . . . Oh, look . . . c-come back to the flat. Please.'

I hesitated. I had the mutt to look after me, didn't I? I glanced down at him. He was staring at Stuart with the same expression of soppy hero-worship he'd worn at the time of their very first meeting on that cliff edge. It was no good looking to him for protection. Come the chainsaw, he'd be helping Stuart wrap me into handy-sized parcels.

The narrow twisting alley that was Sailmakers' Row was

even spookier than I remembered. Hairs rose on the back of my neck. I heard light footfalls behind me and heard the distinctive sound of breathing rising and falling. When I glanced over my shoulder there was no one there. Waterloo could feel it too. There was a down-droop to his ears and a lack of wiggle in his rump.

'Is this place haunted?' I asked the back of Stuart's neck. I'd whispered without realising it, until he reflected my lowered voice back to me.

'They say it is. But I've never seen anything. Why do you ask?'

'No reason,' I hissed back.

We were nearly at his house. The front door was hidden deep in the almost solid shadow caused by the overhang and lack of any star- or moonlight. I thought I glimpsed someone under there. Told myself it was imagination. And then let go with a whimper when part of the shadow detached itself.

'I've been waiting for you. I think we need to talk, Stuart,' Annie said. 'Hello, Grace.'

'Hi. Stuart was just about to fill me in on all those little bits of his past that have been so intriguing us recently – you know, the bodies, the lies, the reincarnations.'

'So you'll tell her, but you won't tell me?' Annie asked.

'That's different. I don't c-care what she thinks.'

'And you do care about me?'

'You know I do, Annie.'

'I don't know anything of the sort. It seems to me if you truly care about someone, you want to share your life with them. And I don't mean sharing a double duvet here. If you can't trust me with your past, why the hell should I want to trust you with my future?'

'Is this the bit when I make a tactful retreat?' I asked.

'Tactful got left out when they brewed you, Sherlock.' Annie had moved into Stuart's chest. Her arms were linked under his armpits and her hands were massaging his shoulder-blades. Sexuality was tingling in the air.

'Put him down, Annie. You don't know where he's been. But he's just about to tell us, aren't you, Stuart?'

38

'Where should I s-start?'

'How about with the flatmate that never was?' I suggested.

He'd dimmed the wall-lights and left the living-room curtains open so we could admire the view of phosphorescence darting over tar-black waves tipped with ripples of milk and the glittering ferry sliding across the horizon. We were all nursing glasses of red wine. Mostly to give us something to do with our hands.

Stuart took a quick swallow and said, 'When you were using my flat in Kentish Town, did you meet the guy who lives on the ground floor?'

'Tattoos?'

'Yes. He's addicted to getting a skinful – in more ways than one. He had a girlfriend – Benita.'

'Long dark hair and "walk all over me, please do" stamped all through her?'

'She was quite pretty when I first moved there. Came to this country as a mother's help. That didn't work out and she ended up with the tattooed lunatic upstairs. I know it's fashionable these days to portray wife-beaters as charming, intelligent professionals in designer suits – but that doesn't mean the thick, tanked-up thugs have all joined embroidery circles. I despised him. But I despised her more for not doing something. Not fighting back. Not walking out. Just accepting as if she had no choice.'

'Because of your mother?'

'You found out that too, did you? You're good.'

'Save the compliments for the references. What went down with Benita? Did you and her . . . ?'

'No. I never had anything to do with her. I told you. Then

273

the day I was moving down here to Winstanton, I found her in my c-car. Crouched under a blanket in the back seat. Her face was pulped. She begged me to take her. She said she'd not run before because she was certain he'd track her down and kill her, but he'd never guess she'd gone with me.'

'And you agreed?' It sounded like an unlikely scenario.

'Not at first. But then she said they both knew I found her pathetic. I guess I gave away more than I knew the odd times I had to speak to them. Benita said he r-regarded that as normal, another man seeing her as weak and useless. That was why it would never occur to him that I might help her. I suppose what she said . . . it made me feel . . . guilty. It brought back all those snubs when all anyone ever saw was the stutter – never the kid behind it. And it made me realise what a thin line there was between him and me. So I turned the ignition on and went for it. She wouldn't let me take her to hospital . . . even in the new flat down here, she was terrified. She used to watch the street for hours. Convinced he was going to c-come for her. She made me swear not to tell a soul that she was up there. She wouldn't go out.'

'She did once. Martha saw her.'

'I know. That was the only time. It was near the end. I guess she was getting a bit stir crazy by then. We were so broke. Buying the house had taken all my cash. We were sleeping on the bare floor.'

'When you say sleeping . . . I realise it's none of my business,' Annie said.

'I really mean sleeping. Nothing else. At first she didn't know what she wanted to do. It was like she'd used all her strength just getting away. She even started t-talking about going back to him. That made me really angry. I told her she had to leave, get far away. If we went back she'd probably be dead in a week. I just managed to raise enough to buy her an air ticket to Madrid and give her some cash to tide her over until she got a job. I drove her to the airport. She said she'd write, let me know how she was getting on.

But she didn't. And then when I went back to the Kentish Town flat to sort out new tenants – guess what?'

'She and Tattoos are into the old bonking and bashing routine again?' I said.

'She'd phoned him from the airport. To say goodbye. Can you believe that? After all she'd said.'

'Let me guess . . .' Annie helped herself to another slug of claret. 'He really, *really* loved her. And he'd never, *ever* raise a finger to her again. He couldn't manage without her. Come home and he'd treat her like a princess.'

'Pretty well. What's the matter with you women? Why do you do it?'

'It's not only women, Stuart. Men do it too. Sometimes being with an abuser is better than being alone.'

'Then you're all welcome to it. I swore then that's the last time I help. If you're stupid enough to want your brains rattled to a soup, be my guest.'

'I don't. And if you ever try it on me, Mr Roberts, I shall knock you into next week.'

'And she's the girl to do it,' I agreed. 'Blinding left hook.'

'You're too kind, Sherlock.'

'I wouldn't do that. I c-couldn't hit a woman.'

'Then why did you hire Sherlock here to find out if you did? Albeit when you were wearing Joe Gumbright's skin?'

'Because I had to be certain. I mean, I'm certain *I* wouldn't, but if someone else possesses me . . . I don't remember making any of those tapes. The person on them . . . that isn't me . . . and he is so angry . . . Did you listen to all the recordings? He beat his dad to death . . .'

'Possibly.'

'He smashed the drunken sot's head in. You don't know how often I dreamt of doing that to my dad.'

'We all have violent fantasies sometimes, Stuart,' Annie said quietly.

'With one exception in my case.' He slung back the rest of his wine. 'I'm beginning to think I d-did kill my dad.'

It's a bit of a conversation-stopper, that one. I mean, how do you respond to an announcement like that? Murmur reassurances of the 'there, there, I'm sure you're exaggerating' variety – or check the steak knives are out of reach? Annie's phone provided a welcome diversion. From the half-conversation, I gathered it was for me. Our esteemed leader had finally decided to make contact.

'Sweet thing, your phone is unavailable.'

'The dog ate it. I've been leaving messages for you for God knows how long.'

'God may not, but I assure you my message service does. It was awash with desperate pleas when I finally got my phone back.'

'Where did it go?'

'Down a drain grate. Someone I was trailing turned nasty and dropped a large number of my personal possessions into a sewer. I've had to pay the council to retrieve them. I'll tell you the whole fascinating saga some time. In the meantime, has your harassment to do with the background to the reincarnated Mr Roberts?'

'Annie and I are round at Stuart's place at the moment.'

'I see. Can you talk?'

I glanced up – and met two pairs of eyes who weren't even bothering to pretend they weren't listening. There didn't seem any point in prevaricating any further. If it was soul-baring time, then we might as well have Vetch's contribution.

'Can you come over? We're running over Stuart's past at the moment.'

'Try not to totally flatten the beast before I can join the party. Twenty minutes.'

'Go on, Stuart,' Annie said gently after I'd relayed the message. 'You were going to tell us about your father.'

'He was . . . ordinary. You wouldn't have been scared of him. Not like the one Grace calls Tattoos. When he wasn't drinking he was just . . . normal.'

'And when he did?' Annie prompted.

Stuart put his wine glass down with an abrupt gesture, as if the surface had suddenly become electrified. 'He t-turned into a monster. He didn't go down the pub. He used to bring it home. Hide it around the house. Mum and I, we'd find it – pour anything left away when he was out cold. It didn't stop him. Nothing stopped him. He just used to . . .'

Unconsciously he raised his tightly squeezed fist and started slamming it on to his own thigh. It must have hurt, but he didn't stop until Annie reached across and captured the pistoning fist. With an effort, he got control of his voice again.

'If the bruising got too bad, he'd keep me off school. Otherwise he'd make my mum write a note saying I'd tripped over or walked into something.'

'Didn't anyone get suspicious?' Annie asked. 'Social Services? Doctors? The neighbours?'

'If they did, they did nothing about it. Perhaps they b-believed it. My stutter was far worse then. I could hardly communicate at all. I had a reputation as a thicko. A bit of a retard. Clumsiness went with the label. I couldn't do much about it. I couldn't do anything except lie under the c-covers listening to him hitting my mum and praying he'd exhaust himself and wouldn't come looking for me. I used to dream that we'd run away, her and me. Go somewhere safe where he couldn't hurt us. And then one day she did. But she left me behind. With him.'

Even though the betrayal was twenty years ago, the pain was still there . . . raw and fresh in his voice.

'You said she'd died,' I reminded him.

'I wish she had. As far as I'm concerned, she is dead. I'll never forgive her for leaving me with Dad. I used to fantasise about killing him. Grabbing that scrawny neck and slamming his face into the wall . . . again and again. I was so lonely. I didn't have anyone to t-talk to . . . even assuming I could have got the words out. And then Nyree moved in next door. She was a lot older than me but she was lonely too. Girls were never interested in me . . . and when you're seventeen and sex is on offer . . .'

I assured him we all got the picture. He'd dived straight into every seventeen-year-old lad's sexual fantasy – the experienced divorcee. 'So where does your dad's death come into all this?'

'I found myself standing in the kitchen one morning and he was there . . . on the floor . . . and there was blood everywhere . . . and a hole in his head . . . and a hammer lying by him. It was so like my dream . . . it didn't even feel bizarre or anything. It was almost like I expected to see it. I was so certain I must have done it. I tried to clean up. Hide what I'd done. It was stupid. It was a mess. And what c-could I have done with the body? In the end I called the police. At first they were okay. And then they arrested me. I wasn't surprised by that – just that they hadn't done it at once. Apparently the kid next door had seen me with him or something. The solicitor told me to say nothing. As if I could have. I was in a terrible state. I couldn't get a single word out. The Court remanded me to prison. Prison has a smell, you know. I don't remember much about that time. But I remember the smell. And then they released me – not proceeding with the charges.'

'Why?' I asked, even though I thought I already knew the answer.

'Nyree told them I'd spent the night with her.'

'Pity she didn't think to mention it sooner. Any idea why she didn't?' I challenged Stuart.

He lowered his head in that shy, upward glance that hadn't been in play since he'd left it behind with the awkward kid he'd once been. 'Because it wasn't true.'

'Are you certain? Your memory seems to have gone a bit dicky around that time.'

'Oh, yes. Nyree t-told me. She said she was sure I was innocent, so a little fib didn't matter. But it did. What was the point? I still thought I'd done it.'

'They wouldn't have dropped the charge simply on the

basis of your girlfriend's belated alibi,' Annie said with quiet assurance. 'Didn't they tell your solicitor why they'd done it?'

'No. I mean I never asked. He wasn't really mine. They gave him to me at the police station. Duty solicitor. I saw another one the next t-time I was arrested.'

'*Next* time?'

I'd forgotten Annie didn't have the full picture on Stuart's past. Her faith was getting a tad punch-drunk here.

'When Nyree d-died. I found her in her bed. It was indescribable.'

'Try,' I urged. Annie flashed a 'button it' glare in my direction.

'Her eyes were wide open. Looking at me when I came in the room. Just looking. But there was blood in them. They were all blood. And there was more, dried around her mouth and nose. I tried to wash it away. It made her look so ugly. Like she had a moustache. That's the last thing I remember until . . . until months later.'

'So where'd you go?' I asked. 'Did they bang you up again?'

'I . . . I'd rather not say.'

'It's a bit late for coyness, isn't it?'

'Belt up, Sherlock. It's all right, Stuart. If you'd rather keep it private, we understand.'

'No, we don't. I'm nosy. I want to know even if you don't.'

'Grace, will you – answer the door?' Annie concluded as the chimes set Waterloo into his 'I'm ready to eat the first trespasser through the door' mode.

39

It was Vetch. Pointy ears at attention and archness cranked up – sure signs usually that the little gnome knew something that we didn't.

'Do I intrude, people?'

'Not at all,' Stuart said politely. 'May I get you a drink?'

Vetch let himself be pressed to a half-glass. I had the other half – it kept my full measure company. Stuart and Annie opted for mineral water this time.

Stuart said, 'I didn't drink at all. I used to be t-terrified I'd end up like my father. But that was handing him control. So now I *choose* when I take a drink.'

'Stuart's dad was a drunk,' I told Vetch.

'I know. I had quite a long chat with my contact in Hertfordshire. Who, incidentally, sweet thing, has been on holiday and not contactable until tonight.'

'And now you are the fount of all knowledge?'

'I couldn't have put it better myself. Where should I start?' He steepled his fingers and touched the tips to his lips.

'Stuart's sexy neighbour. Dead in bed. Enlighten us. As briefly as possible.'

'Ex-husband. Heard rumours of affair with neighbour. Jealous. Decided to smother passion. Regrettably smothered ex-wife with it. Gassed himself in car few days later. Left admirably detailed suicide note.'

Stuart looked sick. 'Then it was my fault? Nyree was killed because she and I were . . . ?'

'You? Lord, no!' Amusement inflated Vetch's puff-ball cheeks. 'I doubt it occurred to hubbie she was getting hot and sweaty with a teenager. Naturally his suspicions were centred on the only adult male in the house.'

'Dad!' He jumped to the logical conclusion. It didn't take an Olympic long-jumper to reach it. 'Nyree's husband killed my dad?'

'Officially, no. Not enough evidence. The file is still open. Unofficially, all bets are off. Your father was booted into the after-life by Nyree's misguided ex.'

'Why don't you know any of this?' I asked Stuart. 'If you were in the house at the time, beating someone to death isn't a Trappist monk sort of thing . . . you know, plenty of screams, lots of crashing and pleading?'

Stuart looked stricken. Vetch looked smug. 'Apparently the cadaver drained O-positive – ninety proof. A sort of built-in anaesthetic. Stuart's father would have been unconscious when hubby was using his head as a bongo drum. There wouldn't have been much noise beyond a few thumps?' The implied question was directed at Stuart.

'Dad fell over things when he was drunk. I tuned it out. Maybe I did hear him being killed. I don't remember. To be honest, I don't c-care. Why did they decide I hadn't done it?'

'They'd already begun to suspect that someone else had been in the house that night. They just didn't know where to look until Nyree William's intervention. They never believed the night-of-passion alibi, but at least she set them on the right track. Sadly, any evidence to arrest her husband eluded them, so he was left free to pop back and strangle her. It would seem they did warn her to take extra care.'

'So, while Stuart was sitting in prison, they already knew they had the wrong person?' Annie said angrily.

'Suspected, partner. Not knew. And I think Stuart was regarded as . . .'

'Not the sharpest tool in the box,' Stuart finished bitterly.

'At least they owned up to their mistake,' Vetch reminded Annie. 'And they only took him into custody when he turned up in the remarkably unlucky Nyree's bedroom. More for his own safety, I think. They never charged him.'

'Wow!' Annie exclaimed. 'Their magnanimity knew no bounds, did it? That must have made a dent in the arrest quota that month.'

I was beginning to feel left out of this. Annie shouldn't be slagging off the police. That was my job. I raised a finger. 'Where'd you go, Stuart? I mean, the people in Park Street reckon you never came back after they carted you out of Nyree's house. So if you weren't in the chokey, where were you?'

'You're fishing, Grace,' Annie objected.

'Of course I am. Am I going to hook anything?' I raised my eyebrows at Stuart.

'I was sectioned,' he said through clenched teeth. 'The last thing I remember is standing over Nyree trying to clean up her face. I don't r-recall much after that, until about six months later. When I snapped out of it and grasped I was in a secure mental unit. They gave me drugs, I think. I'm not sure. It was all so confusing. I know I asked about Nyree . . . and Dad, I suppose. And they kept saying I shouldn't worry about that any more. It wasn't my fault. It's like a bad dream now. Sometimes I think it was. I'm sorry, Annie.'

'What for?'

'An ex-mental patient isn't most women's dream date, is it? That's why I didn't want to tell you.'

'And a possible mass-murderer is?' Annie asked.

'It's preferable. Ex-murderers write best-selling books. They get invited on chat shows and to celebrity parties. People get a kind of vicarious thrill from being in their circle.'

'That's ridiculous, Stuart.'

'No, it's not.' I thought he might have a valid case. Hadn't Greville made much the same point about his parents? 'Serial-killer has a certain cachet to it. Whereas crazy is just like having BO with a psychotic twist.'

'Sherlock.'

'Yes?'

'Shut up before I hit you.'

'But she's right, isn't she?' Stuart blurted. 'Multiple murder is cool. Mental illness isn't. I'd have been t-treated better if I *had* been a mass-murderer. At least I'd have got some respect. As it was, they just shunted me from unit to unit. I suppose I could have just walked away from it at any time, but you don't. You lose yourself. You just do whatever you're told. You become a kind of automaton.

'Finally they put me in this sort of halfway house. Where

they teach you to live an independent life. The other patients there were nice, b-but they were . . . well, they *were* mentally impaired. I mean, they couldn't make the beans make five. And I looked round and I thought, I don't belong here. I knew if I stayed I'd become like them . . . institutionalised. So I pushed what I could in my pockets and took that . . .' He nodded towards the 'Posh Drinks Ad' with its George Clooney look-alike up to his neck in sports car, air-brushed bimbos and exotic Monte Carlo location that had intrigued Annie and me on our first visit.

'I t-tore it out of a magazine. It sounds stupid now, but I decided that was who I was going to be. Smooth, successful, in control. I was going to reinvent myself. I changed my name. Took miserable jobs, two or three at a time. I lived in some unbelievable dives . . . and I studied until I passed my accountancy exams . . . then I set up on my own. You've no idea how hard it was. Working all the time . . . no friends . . . no time . . . learning how to c-control the stutter . . . be someone clients could trust . . . And then one day I did a job for a guy in the music business who was in a tax muddle. I got him sorted . . . and suddenly I was hot property. People wanted me . . . I didn't have to hustle for the work . . . it found me. One day I looked in the mirror and I saw the sort of man that people invited to the party.'

'And you never went back to the Park Street house?' I asked.

'No. I suppose the building society repossessed it eventually. I don't know. I never dared to go back. I had this fear that if I ever t-tried to then Stuart Roberts would disappear and I'd become clumsy, useless Stuart Breezley again. Irrational, I know. And then I heard those tapes . . . someone I didn't recognise, but living my life sixty years before I was born. It was like I was going mad. My head felt like it might explode. All those old memories whirling round and round. I *knew* I hadn't killed Nyree and Dad . . . but part of me started to wonder . . . maybe I had, perhaps

I'd just forgotten. Maybe the police had made a mistake and they *should* have charged me. Or perhaps when the doctors said it wasn't my fault, they'd m-meant I wasn't responsible for my actions.'

'You would,' Vetch drawled, 'have saved yourself considerable anguish – and investigator's fees – had you simply gone back and asked someone.'

'Or even,' I added, 'told me about your past when you hired me.'

'How could I? What would I have told you? I didn't know what the truth was any more. I thought if it's going to keep happening, if I'm going to keep dying, keep coming back and killing Nyree and Dad . . . over and over again . . .'

'Then you'd rather chuck yourself over North Bay cliffs?'

'Something like that. But then I realised that would just start the cycle again. I'd have c-come back as someone else, not Stuart or Joe but someone else who'd kill his dad and an older woman . . . so I didn't do it. I got myself laid out by a crazy woman with a bone cosh doing dodgy Abba impressions instead. I hired you to find out the truth. Whether it turned out I was mad or a killer, I had to know. And do you know the worst thing of all?'

It was a general question, so we all felt obliged to shake our heads.

'Over the past couple of weeks, I've found myself hoping you'd discover I'd killed them all. It was so much b-better than being told I was mad.'

Annie caught his hand between her palms and made him look into her eyes. Very clearly, she said, 'You're not mad. Do you understand me, Stuart? You are not mad.'

He nodded.

'And you didn't kill any of them, did you? Neither this Lulu Cazlett person in a past life nor your father or this Nyree in this one.' Annie straightened herself into her brisk, big-sister, don't-you-kids-snivel-when-I'm-minding-you voice. 'So whatever's going on here, it's not down to some spirit from the past taking up residence in your head, Stuart.'

'There's still a spare skeleton out there looking for skin,' I reminded them.

'Not our problem, sweet thing,' Vetch said immediately. 'As I am constantly reminding our happy little team, the police do murders, private investigators do not. You have established that they are not the remains of Stuart's lover – either in this life or the last – and therefore Annie may safely be left in his company without fear of being trussed up and strangled – on an involuntary basis, that is. I think it is now time for us to make a tactful withdrawal.'

Annie was quivering. Not with desire but indignation. 'You've been censoring my dates? I haven't let my mother do that since I was sixteen, so you sure as hell aren't going to, Sherlock. Buzz off.'

She slung a cushion at me. It missed and hit the mutt, who'd been enjoying a snooze under the dining table. With a snarl, he bravely took it on. Lumps of polystyrene filling showered over the polished wooden floor. Vetch was right – definitely time to go.

I had to hitch a lift back with him since I couldn't risk driving with an alcohol level over the limit. Ever since I'd been 'invited' to leave the police my car had been on a sort of unofficial check-it-out list that meant it was stopped if there was the slightest hint things were not as they should be.

Vetch pulled a couple of envelopes out of his jacket. 'These were on Janice's desk. I thought it wise to rescue them. She seems dizzier than ever these days.'

I examined the letters. One was from Ruby and must be some more information I'd asked her to research for me. I couldn't think what for the moment, but it would wait. I squinted at the other. It was a pale blue envelope addressed in a spidery ballpoint. I didn't recognise the handwriting. I stuck them both in my bag and settled back to enjoy the drive up to North Bay. I was feeling pleasantly full of self-satisfaction and red wine. The car smelt of leather, recycled air and dog. 'Thanks for digging up the info on Stuart. But it still doesn't explain how he knew all that stuff about the Gumbrights.'

'He probably read it somewhere, sweet thing. It's surprising how much the subconscious retains without us knowing.'

'I guess.' It was the simplest answer but somehow I wasn't happy with it.

I forgot about the letters until I was climbing into bed. Ruby's proved to be a photocopy of the report on the inquest into Stanley Gumbright's death. I'd forgotten all about asking for it and it seemed redundant now, but I glanced down the column rows anyway. It was dated 30 October, 1942 so the Coroner's Court must have sat soon after the death.

The body was discovered by the deceased's son, Sgt Joseph Gumbright, who was on leave from his squadron, his daughter Wilhelmina Gumbright and Mrs Joyce Slack, the proprietor of the local store, with whom Miss Gumbright has lodgings.

Sgt Gumbright had called at the shop to visit his sister and the trio decided to walk across the fields to visit Mr Gumbright that afternoon. On arrival at the farm, they found Mr Gumbright in the kitchen. The deceased appeared to have fallen and hit his head on an iron anvil. An ambulance was summoned immediately but they were unable to assist Mr Gumbright who was pronounced dead on arrival at hospital.

Sgt Gumbright gave evidence to the Court that his father was in the habit of using the anvil as a doorstop to prop open the back door during the warmer weather. Miss Gumbright stated that her father had visited her the previous evening and he had seemed in good spirits.

Medical testimony stated that Mr Gumbright drank a

large quantity of crude home-brewed alcohol prior to death which had probably contributed to his unsteadiness. In the doctor's opinion he had probably been dead since early morning and any efforts to render assistance would have been meaningless.

The Court extended their sympathy to Sgt and Miss Gumbright on the tragic loss of their father. A verdict of accidental death was given.

'That doesn't tie up with Stuart's tape. Joe didn't mention anyone being with him when he found his dad.'

Waterloo yawned. He was bored with the Gumbrights. Life had more to offer – bitches, chocolate biscuits, a good back-scratch. Turning belly-up, he wriggled his backbone into the duvet.

The second letter was postmarked Tunbridge Wells. I tore it open, half assuming it was a potential client to whom I'd been recommended (it does happen sometimes).

Dear Miss Smith,

I apologise for taking so long to write back to you with the family history that I promised to help you with. As you have probably guessed, Slack is my married name and so I had to contact my late husband's relatives to see if any of them had any information to assist you in your research.

It was from one of the elderly Slacks I'd spoken to at the beginning of this investigation. I felt slightly guilty at the wasted effort she'd plainly put in on my behalf.

A cousin of my husband has recalled that her father had a younger brother called (she believes) Albert or Alfred, who moved to Nottingham shortly after his marriage and became a partner in a garage in that city. Tragically he died when quite a young man. His widow moved back south and ran a general grocery shop in Frognall D'Arcy for some years. They had one child, a little girl called Carol.

I shuffled the birth certificates I'd ordered from the Family Resources Centre. There she was: Carol Slack. Born: Nottingham. Dad: Albert. Mum: Joyce. Great. Now I didn't need her any more, I'd found positive proof of little Carol Slack's existence. Whatever Stuart had been reading about local history it must have been amazingly detailed. I couldn't figure out why he didn't remember where it had all come from.

As a matter of interest the cousin's older sister wrote to Carol as a penfriend for some years. Unfortunately the sister is dead herself and all the letters have long disappeared so I'm afraid I can't pass them on to you. From the few details that the living cousin can recall, the Slack girl married and moved to South Africa where her husband had some kind of job with the railways. She believes they had two children, both born out there. The first was a boy called – she remembers particularly – Leo, after the lions because the mother was very taken with the wildlife of the country. Similarly the daughter was named after a deer, although she can't remember the exact name.

I'm so sorry not to be able to provide more information for your family tree, but I should be so interested to see a copy when it is finished.

Yours sincerely,
Margaret Slack (Mrs)

'Well, she's out of luck there, isn't she?' I said to Waterloo.

I pulled myself up sharply. I was talking to a dog again. I looked round for a diversion. Arlene's *The Meaning of Names* book was handy, so I hitched it over. Could anyone really saddle their kid with a deer's name? What had they called the poor girl? Bambi?

Bambi wasn't listed. I scan-read the index at the back of the book. A former client had once told me my name meant 'God's favour'. Annie's full name of 'Anchoret' was 'much loved'; Stuart was a steward in Old English and . . . my eyes fell on the word 'gazelle'. Bloody hell . . .

40

There's nothing like a shot of self-righteous indignation to make you hyper. I was up at six and raring to go. Only to remember I'd no means of going anywhere. The car was still stuck in Winstanton.

By six-thirty I was bundled into warm clothing, dragging the mutt over the headland towards the nearest bus stop. It was still dark and the wind was sharp on my cheeks and nose. I could taste salt on my lips and hear the deeper booming crash of the breakers smashing into the base of the cliffs.

'Year's drawing in,' I shouted to Waterloo's rump. 'It'll be Christmas before we know it. Where does the year go? Oh, God, I'm sounding like my mother. Step it out, fatso.' I yanked him away from his paw-wiping ritual and ran him to the stop. The service to Winstanton ran every two hours. The first one was at seven. I decided to take the nine o'clock – the parky weather had dampened the hyper-action mode into 'food first, fanaticism second'.

Which left me a couple of hours to waste. I had never used Arlene's luxurious sunken corner tub with its gold dolphin taps and jacuzzi option. And today could be my last chance.

I can recommend a hot tub as the ideal location for a fried breakfast. When you've finished take a deep breath and a jacuzzi on turbo-charge strips the greasy, buttery, marma-lady, sticky residue from every pore. I lounged for a while. I was feeling good. There was so much to look forward to – a return to my place, a big fat cheque for minding the mutt and a couple of hours of kicking arse. Life didn't get much better than this! In the end, I reluctantly hauled my butt out of the cooling water and swathed myself in several big soft towels.

Snuggled cosily, I examined the lotions on Arlene's shelves. There was stuff to smooth, silken and turn my skin sensuously soft. Was the world ready for this? Only one way to find out. I was unscrewing and sniffing when I heard the footsteps. Or paw-steps to be pedantic.

In the wall-cabinet mirror, I caught a blur of beige and brown hurtle through the door. It soared off the floor, used the bath-stool as a launcher to bounce even higher, and then seemed to hang suspended over the tub. Frozen to the spot, I watched four stone of dog belly-flop into forty gallons of water.

Two seconds later, with perfumed liquid lodged in every orifice, watching the steady drip of water from the ceiling, the curtains, the light fittings, the towel rails, the walls and every other surface in the room, I wondered idly what the technical term for murdering a mutt was. Canicide?

Waterloo was sitting in the bottom of the tub in six inches of water, with a pleased expression all over his fat little mug and a blob of foam sliding over one eye.

I coughed perfumed sludge from my throat and nose. 'I suppose you think that's funny, do you?' My voice sounded very far away.

He stood up and wagged his stubby little tail. He was saved from sudden death by the realisation that the ringing in my ears wasn't down to water hitting eardrums at the speed of an express train. The phone was ringing.

I lowered my face near the mutt's. 'I'll be back.'

It was Arlene, brimming with slap-happy joy. 'It's definite, babes, they're throwing me out tomorrow. I'll be home with mumsie's best baby by tea-time. Is he there?'

Where did she think he was? Getting in a fast round of

golf before the morning rush? I glanced across the passage. 'He's just stepping out of the tub.'

'He didn't do his high-diving trick, did he?'

'Bit of a habit, is it?'

'He loves his swims. Any water and he has to jump in it. He's not hurt himself, has he?'

Waterloo had regained the floor and decided to dry off with a few vigorous shakes. Now I had showers of water droplets flying off horizontally as well as dribbling vertically. 'No, he's not hurt himself. That's my job.'

'What?'

'Nothing. Call me when you get in. I'll pick you up from the station.'

I walked through the pattering curtain of fine drops to where Waterloo was licking his coat into shape. Kneeling, I clasped his jaws in either palm and turned his head until we were nose to nose.

'It's all been a great big con, hasn't it, you four-footed, fur-covered gas generator? You didn't dive in that pond to save Emilie Rose. She just happened to get tangled up in your doggy paddle. All those interviews? All that fan mail? All those presents? Pure fraud.'

Waterloo slurped a very wet tongue from my chin to my forehead.

'Crawling won't help, you fake. I said you were a great, soft wassock the first day I came here and I was right. Now haul ass into the garden until I come fetch you.'

By the time I'd mopped and polished the bathroom into a fit state it was close to nine, and the freshly scrubbed state of that room rather emphasised the general sort of grubbiness of the rest of the bungalow. I put righteous indignation and butt-kicking on hold whilst I made with the vacuum and disinfectant sprays and eventually just made the eleven o'clock bus. It deposited us both by Winstanton harbour from where it was just a short trot to the Town Hall.

My car was where I remembered leaving it the night

before. I didn't remember the wheel clamp. A ticket on the windscreen informed me it was going to cost me sixty quid to get it removed. 'Sod it. And a pox on your cox, guys!'

'Very c-colourful. I didn't know you had a talent for verse.' He'd materialised on my blind side whilst I was checking to see whether the clamp lock was pickable.

'Verse and worse if I get my hands on them. Hi, Stuart. Couldn't loan me sixty pounds, could you?'

'I don't have that much cash on me.' He bent to pet Waterloo with his splinted finger. It didn't seem to be healing up as fast as the forehead lump and split lip.

'It says on the ticket they take cheques.'

'Then why don't you write them one?'

'Didn't bring my cheque-book with me.'

'Annie mentioned your phobia over parting with cash.'

Great, my best mate was warning the world not to lend me money. Was there no loyalty left in the universe? Not to mention soft touches with ready cash. 'Is she around?'

'She was. She had to dash back to the office after the local paper arrived. Have you seen it?'

'Nope. Why?'

'Come have a c-coffee. I'll buy you a copy.'

I'd rather have had the clamper's fee, but plainly a mite more buttering up was called for. I let Stuart lead me to the La Lune Bleue Bistro (formerly the Cosy Kettle Café) in the High Street. We collected a local rag from the newsagents next door, took a seat and ordered two frothed double-caffe with a cacao sweep (strong cappuccinos with choc powder to the rest of us).

Stuart opened the paper and folded back page three. It was headlined THE HERO OF NORTH BAY with a smaller subhead, 'Rock Star's Daughter meets her Waterloo'. At first glance it was just another puff of the little fake's supposed heroism. Until you got to the accompanying pictures. They'd given them a full page. Possibly because they thought the shots of the mutt, grinning his smug mug off, were cute. But more likely because Jan was posed behind him. She was wearing the sort of see-through number favoured by Hollywood actresses showing off their latest plastic surgery and Prime Ministers' daughters-in-law showing off their PR-savvy. Jan's pictures were rendered just about acceptable for a family paper by the letters sewn over the sheer netting. Across the front it read, VETCH'S AGENCY – SATISFACTION, and on the rear shot of her bum was the word GUARANTEED.

'Bloody hell.'

'Annie put it rather more strongly. She did wonder whether you'd put Janice up to it. It is your dog?'

'No, he's not. Our brief relationship has been based on a lie. Like most of my relationships, now I come to think of it. Can I borrow your mobile?'

'Didn't you have one?'

'The dog ate it. Pretty please?'

The agency's number was engaged. I tried six redials and then gave up and called the clamping company instead. Even if I did manage to wheedle sixty pounds out of Stuart, it was a two-hour wait before they could get round to me.

'Do you have an urgent appointment?' Stuart asked.

'Sort of. There's someone . . . I mean something . . . I want to sort out in London.'

'I'll give you a lift, if you like. There's someone I'm planning to sort out t-too.'

Our eyes met over the coffee-cups. 'I'm not stupid, Grace. I've worked it out. And I made a telephone call this morning to check out how it was done. Are you coming?'

'I guess so.' An uncomfortable thought struck me. 'Just because you've worked it out, I still get paid – right?'

He drove at a speed that was going to get him big-time penalty points if any of the speed cameras had film in them. We screeched into the one and only available parking space with a panache that scared off the black taxi trying for it. Throwing himself out of the car, Stuart strode off with fast strides towards the clinic.

I was handicapped by the necessity to untangle the mutt

from the back seat and get his lead on. By the time I reached the front door, there was no sign of Stuart. A notice announced the clinic was closed for the afternoon. The internal lock was on but one of the front windows was open. I scrambled into the waiting room. Waterloo howled the howl of the abandoned. There was nothing to tether the lead to and I couldn't risk him wandering off. I had to climb out again and bunk him over the sill.

He dashed into the hall and disappeared whilst I was halfway through the gap. When I reached the back office, Tabitha was backed against the far wall and Stuart was settled in a visitor's chair, arms folded across his chest and a grim smile on his face.

'Get him orf.' It was funny how pronounced that touch of accent – evident in the 'orf' rather than 'off' – was now that I knew to look for it. Or perhaps it was simply that she normally put on a voice that matched the slightly absent-minded professional persona.

'He just wants to be friends.' I hauled the mutt away. 'Hi, Doc. Hope you don't mind us dropping in, but I got this really interesting letter and I had to share it with you.'

'What letter?' Stuart asked.

I handed him Margaret Slack's note. 'Guess the Arabic word for "gazelle".'

'Tabitha?'

'Give the man a cuddly toy. Did you know that, Doc? That your mum christened you after a deer? You do remember your mum, don't you, Tabitha? The one who started life as little Carol Slack from the village store in Frognall? She of the cute curls that Billie Gumbright would have sold her soul for? Did she still have the curls when she married Mr Puzold?'

If I'd hoped to shock her into embarrassment with my snappy investigative technique it sure wasn't working. Tabitha was all cool reason.

'She had tight curls all her life. She hated them. Thought she looked like a white kaffir. Auntie Billie now, her hair thinned older she got. Wore a wig in the end. Must have fried her brains like a tea-cosy summertime in Jo'burg, but she wouldn't leave it orf.'

'Billy Gumbright moved to South Africa too?'

'My grandma Slack adopted her after her father died. They both came out to live with us. I grew up listening to stories of back home in Frognall.'

He must have known the answer, but still Stuart had to ask. 'Including Joe's affair with Lulu C-Cazlett? And the way his dad used to beat him up? And the way his mother walked out on them?'

'Oh, yes, all that.'

'And Lulu's romp in the hop tunnel after the treasure hunt?' I enquired.

'All perfectly true. Although I must admit it wasn't Joe who saw her but Auntie Billie. She was hiding in there from her father. Luckily it wasn't quite the shock it might have been to most eleven-year-olds. Her father had seen to that. Do you know, Stuart – apart from the lack of a sister, I couldn't believe how similar your story was to Joe's. It was like a sign from the Lord.'

Tabitha was visibly regaining her composure and taking control of the situation. She sat herself in the chair she'd used on my last visit, hands folded, ankles crossed, sympatico gene idling in standby mode. Only the slightly malicious tilt of one mouth corner spoiled the overall impression.

'Not quite the same,' I pointed out. 'Stuart's neighbour, Nyree, was killed by her ex-husband. Lulu ended up in the crazy farm and drowned herself.'

'Really? Fancy that. My ma and Auntie Billie always used to tell how she was murdered and buried somewhere around Frognall by her husband. They used to scare me and my brother with tales of how he'd cut her up in pieces and sneaked out to bury each bit. Quite the bogeyman was Roderick Cazlett.'

'You put it all in my head,' Stuart said. 'All that stuff I

had nightmares about – the hops, and Rook Farm, and the Gumbrights – you put it in there first.'

'Very true. It was a very helpful experiment actually. Some of my clients feel quite bereft if they don't have a truly fascinating past life. I've always been a little wary of implanting a scenario in the past. But now I know it works so effectively . . .'

'You can get them to spew b-back all your poison and listen to themselves doing it,' Stuart said bitterly.

There was something about her face that said that wasn't quite right. A sort of smug twinkle that screamed, haven't quite reached the endgame yet, sucker.

Which left one other possibility. 'It's not Stuart on the tapes, is it?'

Her voice deepened and acquired the husky local account of Joe Gumbright. 'That past loif regression lark is a bugger to control. You can't be sure where they'll go back to each time. And we wanted to be certain Stuart recorded all the juiciest toims. So he could listen to them . . . again . . . and again . . . and again. Oi'm good at imitating voices. Always have been. And in this case, well, who knows what Joe sounded like? Joe sounded loik I chose for him to sound.'

'But . . . why?' Stuart asked. 'Do you r-realise you nearly drove me insane?'

'What of it? It's not like you haven't been there before.' Her self-possession was almost eerie. She wasn't ashamed of what she'd done. She was gloating over it.

'B-but *why*? What have I ever done to you?'

'To me? Nothing. No, this one was for Melody. To teach you that you can't use her and dump her.'

'Sorry.' I raised a finger. 'Can I butt in here? She knows Melody?' I ignored Tabitha and swung in my seat to face Stuart.

'It was Melody who recommended her.'

Another piece clicked into place. 'Tabitha? Tabby? Tabby-cat? Auntie Cat? *You're* Melody's godmother. For God's sake, Stuart, didn't it occur to you it might not be too bright to get yourself zombied by the godmother of a girl who's going around telling people you near as damn tried to rape her?'

'Raped? What are you talking about? Mel and I only had one date. And it didn't work out. She said we could still be friends.'

'And recommended you to her nice Auntie Cat to cure your smoking, right?'

'She recommended me to a Dr Tabitha Puzold. I didn't know it was her godmother. I'd never met her godmother. I thought that "Cat" was short for Catherine.'

Well, fair enough. I'd made the same mistake myself. However . . . 'When you came out with a brand-new fear of flying this didn't ring the ding-bat alert?'

'No. I m-mean, she said I would remember everything that had happened in our sessions, and I believed I had. I didn't think I'd told her anything about my family. But I spoke to another psychotherapist on the phone this morning. Apparently there's a technique called memory substitution – they can take something they don't want you to remember and substitute another memory so that the time sequence appears to be continuous to you. There's no way of knowing what I really told her when I was under.'

We both swung back to stare at Tabitha. She'd taken off the glasses, sleeked back her hair and was calmly applying bright red lipstick. With a decisive snap she closed the mirror case and grinned. The lipstick on her white teeth looked like blood. 'We were going to leave it at the fear of flying, but you were *so* receptive, sweetheart, we couldn't resist having a little fun, seeing just how far we could go. It was so satisfying, watching you *wriggle* on the hooks we baited. I must say you've done remarkably well. Who'd have believed you'd unearth all that information on Lulu and the Gumbrights? I'm impressed. I'm also running a little late. Do you mind if I change while we chat?'

She hooked a hanger from behind the door, unfolded a bamboo screen and stepped behind it.

Stuart didn't seem to quite believe what he was hearing. 'You and Melody are both mad.'

'Why? Because we refuse to be pushed out of the way when it suits you? Melody is worth more than that. Of course, I gave up expecting anything more from men years ago. A lot of people assume I'm a lesbian too. But the truth is I've simply found that celibacy has many advantages. You hurt my Melody so I hurt you, a perfectly reasonable reaction I'd have said.' The denim and muslin ensemble appeared on the top of the screen.

'I didn't hurt her. I don't know what she told you, but it was nothing like that.'

'So what was it like?' I asked.

Stuart flushed. 'I'd r-rather not say.'

'Force yourself. It can't be any worse than the rest. What did you and the apprentice psycho get up to on this date?'

'Dinner. A club.'

'So far nothing incriminating. Unless you took her to some rat-infested dive? Or made her pick up the tab?'

'No! They were the best places in New York. I . . . I read up in those gossip columns where all the important people went. It had to be the best.'

A sniggle of an idea had started to take root in my imagination. 'The magazine picture.'

He blushed an even deeper shade of crimson. 'It sounds really pathetic now. But I really wanted the whole fantasy.'

'And Melody is a dead spit for one of the models in your fantasy. But – and forgive me for being totally blunt here – it doesn't explain why she'd play along. To be frank, Stuart, you ain't no Keanu Reeves.'

'I didn't understand it either. I mean, I couldn't believe my luck when she said yes. It was like the whole fantasy was c-coming to life. I thought I could do anything.'

'Including having sex with my Melody,' Tabitha hissed from behind the screen.

'Yes. No. Oh, look, it wasn't like that. I knew before we

298

were halfway through d-dinner that it was all wrong. It was like a really sumptuous play. Okay when you're watching from the audience, but when you get close to the scenery it's all illusion. We had nothing in common. Melody might have looked like the girl in the picture, but I wasn't that man. And I didn't want to be. I wanted a woman I could talk to. Feel comfortable with.'

'So what happened? Did you dump her?'

'No! I *would* have called it a night. But she was doing all the pushing. It was like she r-really wanted to be with me. It was her idea to go back to the hotel. She was going for the full seduction bit. Music, soft lights, sexy strip-tease. It was amazing.'

His expression suggested it hadn't been too difficult to live with either.

'And then . . . just when I was going to . . . go for it . . . she pushed me away. And then she laid it out – what she r-really wanted.'

'Which was?'

'Money. Melody doesn't understand the words "credit limit". She was being hassled by half a dozen stores she owed. She wanted me to write her cheques on Rick's account.'

'Why you? I mean, why not her dad?'

'I write the cheques on Rick's accounts. It's the arrangement we have with his banks.'

'So you bounced her? No pun intended.'

'In a way. I wrote the cheques. But I wrote them on an account I knew was empty. Then I had sex with her.' He looked me straight in the eye. 'She deserved it.'

'Who's arguing?'

'Next morning I c-called the bank to apologise for the mistake. They were very accommodating.'

'So what you're saying is Melody didn't know she'd been raped until the cheque bounced?'

'We r-ran into several people she knew in the hotel lobby when she was leaving next morning. She was all over me.

The security cameras caught it too. A bit difficult to call it rape after that.'

'She didn't tell her dad?'

'Tell him what? She was prepared to act like a hooker to pay off charge accounts she was supposed to have closed months back? She was threatening all sorts for a few weeks. She was bloody furious. But then so was I. Then she calmed down. She c-came to see me. Said she'd been scared they'd put debt collectors on to her. But she realised how badly she'd behaved and she hoped we could forget it and be friends.'

'And you fell for it!'

'Yes. Why not? She *had* behaved badly. I thought she was being . . . honest. Straightforward. It became a bit of a joke between us after that. You know, a sort of catch phrase . . . "I can still report you, you know?" '

His sad lack of experience was showing. He was so unbelievably naïve it was frightening. I had to lay it out for him. 'Women are not honest or straightforward when they think they've been conned into bed. We brood. We rage. We slag him off to our girl-friends. In desperate circumstances, we dump paint-stripper on his car or slice up his favourite jacket. It's your hard luck you picked the one who really knows how to hold a grudge and has Fairy Freaky as a godmother.'

On cue The Godmother re-emerged from behind her screen. The haphazard vaguely scatty look had been replaced by skin-tight black pants and sweater cinched at the waist by a large belt, high-heeled ankle boots and a waist-length bright yellow jacket with a stand-up collar. With her hair coiled and her eyes hidden behind stylish smoky glass, she looked sharp, sexy and totally in control of the situation.

She was looking at us like we were a pair of laboratory mice performing for her amusement. Stuart trembled. The fingers on his unsplinted hand curled and uncurled. For a moment I thought he was going to smash Tabitha in the face

– an activity I was quite prepared not to see if necessary. Instead he said, 'You're a disgrace. I'll report you.'

'To who? One of the joys of practising as a psychotherapist in this country is that you don't need to be licensed. You don't even need to be qualified. Oh, sure, it helps to have a few certificates on the walls, but you can always buy those. You can even get a doctorate if you can scratch up the fee to some mail-box college. Then just screw your brass plate up and—'

'Start screwing the clients?' I finished for her.

'Most of them deserve it. You've no idea how tedious they are. But I make them pay for boring me.'

'Through the nose, I'd have thought. Any of the new flats pan out?'

Tabitha paused in the process of snapping on a chunky gold watch to say, 'The Docklands property was more than fine, thanks for asking. I'm just orf to take some measurements. So you can both leave now.'

'Leave!' Stuart sprang up. The movement woke up the mutt, who shook his skin, yawned and looked for the excitement. 'Just like that! Do you expect me to forget this? Just walk out and let you get away with it?'

'What else can you do?'

Put like that, she was right. What the hell could we do about it? Messing with someone's mind might qualify as harassment, but even if we could get anyone to take it seriously, how did we prove it? I was damn sure Tabitha hadn't kept any records that could incriminate her. And what did we have? A few tape recordings that weren't even in Stuart's voice. Just an accent practice session by an ex-bit-part actress. Real Old Bailey stuff.

I caught Stuart's eye and could see he was thinking the same thing. 'I'll make certain your other c-clients hear about this,' he said.

'Go ahead. If they leave, there's always another bunch of sad cases ready to embrace the latest fad and be convinced it's going to solve all their problems. Let's face it, if they'll believe they can change their life by shifting their furniture around, they'll believe anything. Well, as I said, I have plans, so unless you'd like *me* to call the police, you'd better go now.'

Her self-possession was almost admirable. We'd just caught her out for the vicious, lying cow that she was – and she didn't give a toss. However, before we crawled out, there was something I had to ask.

'The day Joe's dad died. How come you changed the story? In Stuart's – I mean your – rantings, Joe comes home on leave and finds his dad alone at the farm and – we were meant to assume – bashes his head in. That doesn't tie up with the inquest report . . .' I unfolded the copy Ruby had found and spread it out. 'According to the evidence Joe and Billie and your grandmother gave to the Coroner's Court, Joe called in at the shop first, and the three of them discovered the old man's body together.'

'So they did, the second time.' Tabitha was locking filing cabinets as we spoke. 'Haven't you worked it out yet? Auntie Billie killed her father. He'd been abusing her for years. That's why she moved out as soon as she could. Got a room over my grandma's store. He tricked her back up to the farm with some story about her mother coming. Soon as she was there, he locked her in. Told her it was her duty to "look after" him – in all departments. She showed a bit of spunk for once. Waited until he was sleeping orf the rot-gut booze he'd brewed up, and then dropped the anvil on his head. Then she ran back to my ma's and told her what she'd done. Used to say the Lord must have given her the strength that day. She'd hardly been able to move that anvil before, but she got the strength to lift it clear orf the floor from somewhere.'

'She told you all this?' I asked.

'Endlessly, towards the end of her life. She was proud of it. As she should have been. It's simply akin to shooting a mad dog. Quick and clean. No sense in being sentimental about it.'

'But the police might not have taken quite such a pragmatic view, hence the three witnesses the second time around?'

'They fixed it up to look like a drunken accident. It was lucky in a way that Joe came back on leave that day. A uniform was almost a sign of probity in those days. One look at Joe in his RAF uniform and I'm sure the Coroner's Court was prepared to swallow any story he produced. She missed him, you know.' For a brief second a softer expression flitted over Tabitha's angular face. 'All her life, she missed her brother.' The compassion was roughly shaken away and replaced once more with that brittle, glittery smile. 'But the truth wouldn't have been any good for our little game, would it? Stuart had to believe he was a born-again murderer, not a born-again perjurer.'

'You,' Stuart said slowly through gritted teeth, 'are a very sick woman.'

'Am I?' Tabitha's smile increased by a thousand watts. 'Then why are you the one who ended up in the psychiatric ward, Stuart? So, I think we've covered everything haven't we . . . ?'

'Not quite,' I reminded her. 'Who the hell is the body in the Alaimos' garden?'

41

'Do you really expect us to believe you haven't the faintest idea who our bundle of bones is?'

Tabitha shrugged. 'I don't much care if you believe it or not. But it's true. Melody picked the spot for Lulu's "burial" by the pond because we thought it might be amusing to get Stuart grubbing around in the mud, not to mention hard to explain to Rick and Christina. I mean, for goodness' sake, if I had an accountant who started excavating lumps of my garden, I might start to wonder if he was . . . dare I say it . . . crazy?'

'So I wasn't just supposed to go mad, I was supposed to lose my c-clients too?'

'Mmm.' Tabitha made a rocking motion with her open fingers. 'We were flexible. That's the essence of creativity, isn't it? Throw the essential ingredients together, add a catalyst and stand back to see what develops. Believe me, we were as surprised as you when a real body popped up. Still, it must have given you a glorious shock. Well, as I said, people to meet, windows to measure . . .'

She was holding the office door open. There didn't seem to be much left to do here except trade insults. Personally I had nothing against a good slanging match, but Stuart had gone all tight-lipped and dignified on me. She let us out the front door. The office phone was ringing as we left.

Neither of us spoke until we were speeding west out of London. I queried why we were heading in the opposite direction to home.

'I'm going to cut down the M4 and then pick up the M25. It w-will be quicker than cutting through London t-traffic. After which I'm going to the oast houses to tell Melody what I think of her. I'll drop you off first if you want.'

'Are you kidding? Let's go, tiger. I've got a few things to say to Mel myself. And I bet she knew I hated those snakeskin boots.'

'Pardon?'

'Nothing. A personal matter between me, Melody and my corns.'

'Do you believe Tabitha?' Stuart asked, weaving between lanes. 'That she doesn't know who the skeleton is?'

'It does seem to be stretching coincidence into the realms of the ridiculous. On the other hand, if Tabitha knew it was there, I can't see any point in her getting you to "discover" it.'

'Maybe she d-did it. Killed the woman and buried her out there. Melody told me once that her godmother and mother shared a flat before she married Rick. You'd invite a girl-friend to stay after you married, wouldn't you?'

I couldn't imagine ever being in a cosy joint mortgage

somewhere with Mr Right, arranging flowers in the spare bedroom before my guests arrived for the weekend. It was my sister's sort of scene, not mine. However, rather than admit to this lack of normal thirty-plus female gene, I pointed out I'd probably notice if my house-guest lugged a corpse in along with her weekend case and asked where we kept the spades.

'I can't see there's any mice in it for the Tabby-cat, to draw attention to the body if she'd got away with it, can you? Anyway, she said that Melody put the "X" on the map. God, what a piece of work she turned out. Oh, bloody hell . . . !'

'What?'

'Emilie Rose. That day. It was an awful lot of garden for a very small girl to toddle through.'

'No, Grace. That's just s-sick. You can't think even Melody would try to kill her own sister.'

'Stepsister. And, no. I doubt she intended to kill her. Just scare Christina away perhaps? I get the impression Melody's happiest when it's just her and Daddy. And she *was* the first one there after I did my famous rescue act. Not that we'll ever prove it now.'

Waterloo, who until then had been sitting in relative quietness on the back seat whilst he watched the sights zip by, suddenly started barking his little socks off as we approached the Heston Services.

'You should have gone before we left,' I called over my shoulder.

'Didn't Tabitha say she was heading for her new flat?' Stuart shouted over the racket. 'In the Docklands area?'

'Yep. Why?'

'Because she s-seems to be going in the opposite direction. And in one hell of a hurry.'

We were currently travelling in the middle lane; across in the outside lane, a white two-seater sports car hurtled past, going at a speed slightly in excess of Concorde's take-off velocity. Tabitha was hunched over the wheel.

'Perhaps she's doing the same as us. Using the south of the M25 to cut round London?'

As soon as her tail faded in the distance, the mutt shut up. He was probably trying to impress with his hot-shot spotter dog act, but since we had a lot of motorway ahead and I didn't fancy walkies on the hard shoulder, I made Stuart pull into the service area and followed the damn dog around with the poop scoop for ten minutes. By the time we got back on the road, the traffic had thickened and we got stuck behind a bunch of Hartley's and were jammed in for most of the journey.

We reached the oast houses as dusk was falling and Stuart's headlights were picking out hedges and the scuttle of night creatures twisting away in fright as we illuminated their world. The iron gates to the drive were standing wide open and when we rolled up in front of the house Tabitha's car was parked on the drive.

'Perhaps she dashed down here to warn Melody the avenging accountant was on his way?'

'W-wonder why she didn't telephone.'

I shrugged and leant on the bell. When that didn't seem to raise any interest inside, I thumped flat-handed on the door. Waterloo added a few deep-chest woofs. Nothing again.

Stuart scanned the windows. 'There are plenty of lights on. I know they're in there. *Open up!*' He rapped loudly and insistently on the boards.

'Shut up, I think I can hear something.'

We both stood, holding our breaths. Waterloo panted but it wasn't loud enough to quite cover the miserable insistent wail of a toddler somewhere inside the house.

'Emilie Rose,' Stuart said. 'There must be somebody with her. *Rick! Christina! Hello!*'

'Has it occurred to you,' I asked, watching him trying to beat the door to death, 'that Rick might not see this your way? If you start slagging off his precious daughter, you could find yourself a celebrity client short of the full balance sheet?'

'I d-don't care. I don't need him. *And I'm not going away!*'

He thundered angrily on the surface. Waterloo decided to go for it too. He howled with enthusiasm. When that didn't work, Stuart stormed over to Tabitha's car and leant on the horn, pumping out a loud staccato version of Beethoven's Fifth: dah da da *daaaah*. Dah da da *daaaaah*.

The house still remained unresponsive. But Stuart wasn't in the mood to postpone. He headed for the side of the house. 'I'll see if I can get in round the back.'

I shouted to him to wait. 'There's something happening on the other side of this door.'

Stuart sprinted back in time to confront a three-inch sliver of Rick peeping out from the crack. 'I can't see you now Stu, mate. Check back later.'

'The hell I will. Where's Melody?'

'She's . . . out.'

He tried to re-shut the door. Stuart stepped back and kicked hard with his left leg. John Wayne couldn't have done it better. However, I couldn't help feeling that John's response to finding a foot of gun barrel pointing at his head might not have been to stick his hands in the air as Stuart was now doing.

'Come in,' Prue ordered. 'And don't do anything silly like trying to run.'

She shuffled back in the hall, one of those cowboy six-shooters from the display cases at Maudsley held two-handed. I was surprised she could hold it. It looked like it weighed a ton.

We both came inside and she ordered Rick to close the door again. 'Now put your hands on your heads and walk ahead of me.'

One of us should, no doubt, have done something clever like kicking the weapon out of her hand. Nobody apparently felt that clever. We marched in line, with Rick leading the way and me with one hand on my head and the other towing the mutt, to the indoor pool room.

The steamy, hot, chemical smell hit us full in the face as soon as we stepped inside. I started to sweat. Tabitha was ahead of me by several pints. The coiled hair was descending in damp tendrils and her make-up was sliding chinwards. She was tied with thick duct tape to the handle of one of the windows that gave on to the internal court-yard. Melody was tied to another. She looked scared to death. Which fitted the theme of the party pretty well. The only person who seemed unconcerned was good old three-syllable Winona. She was tethered to the handle of the pool steps by her wrists and was unconcernedly flicking wavelets with one bare foot. Part of her coolness was probably down to the fact that – unlike everyone else – she was only wearing a swimsuit and a chiffon cover-up – the belt of which had been used to tie her up.

'Look who's here, everyone!' Prue trilled, like the perfect little hostess introducing the next wave of incomers to the fun. 'It's Rick's accountant. That seems appropriate, doesn't it? Mind you, I don't know what we're going to do with you.'

She frowned at me. I offered to leave if I was surplus to requirements.

'Don't get silly. You know I can't let you do that. But I want you to know I like you. And I'm really pissed off that I have to do this to you.'

Great – that made me feel a whole lot better about getting shot!

She levelled the barrel directly at my chest. She was dressed as I'd first seen her, in leopardskin pants, orange sweater, Farrah-Fawcett hairstyle, glittering, chemical-in-duced eyes.

Waterloo whined. The barrel swung in his direction.

'Quiet. This is no time to get brave.' I adjusted my grip slightly to get a firmer grasp on the lead. Before I could he shot forward, jerking it out of my hand. He charged the threat to me. Prue backed away. I saw her fingers whiten as she increased the pressure on the trigger.

'Don't fire!' I flung myself at the trailing lead. And missed.

He was within inches of Prue's legs. She turned her head away slightly, screwed up her eyes and aimed.

From where I was lying – prone on the floor – I waited with sick dread for the inevitable explosion of blood and splintered bone to fountain over the white tiling, and sent a silent apology to the charging butt. I'd misjudged the mutt. He was brave. He was trying to save me.

Waterloo shot straight past Prue without a glance. Launching himself in a belly-flop, he hit the pool and set off on a leisurely lap of the turquoise waters. So much for heroes.

'Get up,' Prue ordered.

I got. She flicked a roll of duct tape at me and told me to tie Stuart to the other side of the pool steps.

I spun the tape like a juggler's quoit. 'You know, Prue, I was thinking. Greville said those guns had probably been decommissioned years ago. And even if they hadn't, they must be upwards of a hundred years old. I mean, hundred-year-old ammunition must be in pretty short supply. I'm betting here that you're waving an empty gun around – right?'

The sound of the shot was amplified by the excellent acoustics in the pool room. Pieces of toughened glass from the shattered recessed ceiling light peppered the tiling like a noisy hail shower. Melody and Tabitha both screamed. The recoil knocked Prue on to a recliner chair but she hung on to the gun.

Over my heart's attempt to beat-for-Britain, I dimly heard Stuart remark, 'That d-didn't go too well, did it? Any more bright ideas?'

'No. I think that was pretty much it. Put your wrists up.'

Once he was tied up, Prue used a small penknife to slice the tape end and then ordered Rick to tether me to a fake palm pot. Its width meant I was crouched on the floor, with my arms at full stretch, hugging the damn thing (which weighed a ton). If I wanted to get free I'd have to either topple it or stand on the pot to get my arms up over the palm top. Either way, Prue was going to have plenty of warning.

'How'd she get in?' I murmured to Rick as he looped the sticky plastic around my wrists.

'She was waiting when Mel and me got back from the hospital. Said she'd brought a present for the baby. Soon as she got inside she just flipped. She's had us trussed up for freaking *hours*. She made Mel call up Tabitha and pretend big emergency, pronto action required.'

'Where's Christina?'

'Hospital. She started.'

'And you aren't with her?'

'The docs said the kid wasn't going to make its appearance for hours. All that medical stuff gives me the willies. I came home to get my head together. Birth is a stressful time for the father. I don't think you girls realise what we go through. When my other kids were born it was, like, major trauma to my creative vibes.'

Prue had caught his reply. She let go with a high-pitched laugh that was definitely out-of-her-skull material. 'And Winona was kissing the creative vibes better, was she?'

A plaintive wail drifted from the steps. '*Why*-No-Nah.'

'Winona came over to stay with Em'lie. She's up there all alone, remember. Probably terrified. You gotta let me go to her.'

'Oh, shut up. The only bit of fatherhood you were ever interested in was the conception. You hate children. The only reason you kept Melody was to spite me.'

'If you wanted her all you had to do was apply for custody.'

It seemed as if she hadn't heard him. Her mouth was twisted with misery and her eyes were all over the pool room. The gun was wavering. Rick stepped towards her. Her eyes jerked back into focus at the same time the gun jerked up to level at his chest. 'You stay where I tell you, you bastard. Strip off.'

Rick's smile became more self-assured. 'Sure, sweetheart. But let's go somewhere a little more private, eh? How about one of the bedrooms? Just you and me, eh? What do you say?'

'The idea makes me want to vomit. Now get your clothes *off*!'

'Mummy, pleeeese,' Melody hiccuped through tears. 'Let me go.'

'Shut up.'

'Prue,' Tabitha coaxed in her soothing sympathetic therapist tones, 'why not let one of us slip upstairs and see that little Emilie Rose is safe? Think how frightened the poor little—'

'*Will you shut the hell up!*' The gun barrel waved erratically and swept the room. We all drew in a collective noisy breath and then expelled it with relief when she targeted Rick again. 'Are you still dressed?'

He threw his jacket over the pool lounger. The snuff box fell out and spilt its contents in a small snowy heap under the chair. Unbuttoning his shirt, Rick said, 'What's this about, Prue?'

'As if you didn't know. I saw the necklace, *sweetheart*. The initial necklace. The police brought it to Maudsley. Wanted to know if I recognised it.'

Rick dropped the shirt and started on the trousers. 'What did you tell them?'

'That I'd lost it years ago. When I was the lucky Mrs Alaimo the Second. Although, technically speaking, I guess I was Mrs Alaimo the First. You were still a Pratt when you married Number One. And you haven't changed a bit have you, you lying, cheating *bastard*!'

This time the shot gouged a large chunk of tiles and concrete out of the poolside. Rick heeled his shoes off and stepped out of the trousers in one smooth movement. But then he'd had a lot of practice over the years.

'And the rest.' Prue moved the barrel in tiny circles. It was pointed at the relevant area of Rick's anatomy. 'Come on, you've never been shy about flashing your *creative vibes* before.'

Trying to keep his front to the wall, Rick wriggled off his underpants, revealing a pair of white wrinkled buttocks that frankly resembled a couple of anaemic elephant's jowls.

'Oh dear, who hasn't been using the gym weights recently? Turn around, Rick. Let everyone see what all the fuss is about.'

No doubt we should have tactfully looked elsewhere. Did we? Did we heck! We all checked out the well-travelled Alaimo pecker. He wasn't going to be in the market for any of the mutt's surplus knitted warmers.

'Now sit down . . . there.' She jabbed the gun at a sun lounger. Rick lowered himself, trying to keep his knees together. Prue slung the tape at him. 'You know the routine. Ankles first. Left side.' When he looked like he was going to argue, she cocked the gun. We'd all heard it a hundred times in the movies. It was amazing how much more threatening it sounded when it was in the same room.

'Do it, Rick,' Stuart called. 'It may be your house, but Prue's the one with the l-loaded gun.'

Her breathing was getting noticeably shallower, the pupils were so dilated that her blue eyes looked black, and she didn't seem able to keep still. Whatever she'd taken, she'd gone for the mega-sized serving.

'Now, just a few more adjustments.' She scrabbled in a sports bag and emerged with a new plaything. A large, lethal-looking pair of scissors.

She opened and closed the steel blades with a sharp snap and smiled. It wasn't a pleasant sort of smile. 'Now, *sweetheart*, let's see what the rock legend can manage without, shall we?'

'Prue, no, please . . . I beg you . . .'

'Don't worry, Rick. The blades are razor-sharp.' She ran

a thumb down one blade. 'I kept them that way especially for you. I promise you, I'll hardly feel a thing.'

42

'One snip, two snip, three snip . . . four,' Prue sang in tuneless rhythm as she clipped.

The pile on Rick's chest grew. She dangled another hair extension teasingly in front of his nose before letting it coil into the nest. Somewhere in the house a phone was ringing insistently.

Rick started to speak and she shushed him. Her tone was almost comforting, like a mother hushing a baby. 'Not much more now. There!' She dropped the final strand into the heap. 'Now, let's have those teeth out. Open wide!'

Rick's impulse to clamp his jaws shut was swiftly cured by the sight of the gun barrel pressed up his nose. She extracted two dentures, dropped them to the tiles and smashed her heel on each.

'There, isn't that much better? Alaimo *au naturel*.'

'Mummy, please. I've got to *go*.'

Prue sauntered across to her daughter. Using the tip of the barrel, she forced Melody's chin up until they were eyeball to eyeball.

'*I – DON'T – CARE.*'

Stuart raised his voice. 'Prue! B-be careful with the gun. It could go off accidentally. You wouldn't really want to shoot your own daughter, would you?'

Her head on one side, Prue appeared to consider this statement. Then she delivered her verdict. 'Never loved me. Always Daddy, Daddy. When it wasn't Auntie Cat. Screw her.' She wandered away a few steps then whirled, both arms extended like a real sharpshooter. This time the barrel was pointing at Tabitha's chest. Melody screamed. Prue laughed. '*Now listen, you don't speak until I tell you to. I'm not telling you again. Understand?*'

They both nodded mutely.

Prue drew in the gun again and blew imaginary smoke off the barrel. 'This is fun. I should have got a gun years ago. People take notice when you've got a gun. Did you know that?'

She looked round vaguely. Fortunately she failed to notice that Winona was working at the knots around her wrists with her teeth. Unlike the duct tape, the chiffony belt had some play in it. God knows what she could do if she managed to get free.

'Tell me about the necklace,' I yelled.

'What?' Prue shook the Farrah Fawcett out of her eyes.

'The necklace,' I repeated, willing her to come towards me. 'Lulu's old necklace, remember? With the lapis lazuli and the gold initial "L"? You told the police you lost it. Did you?'

'No. But I didn't see why the police should have all the fun.' She started to wander back, but stopped at the spread-eagled Rick's lounger. 'You know what I did with it. Tell her.'

Prompted by that gun barrel aimed at his *creative vibes*, Rick lisped, 'She gave it away.'

'To?' Her fingers were going paler as they tightened on the trigger again.

'Ellith,' he screamed in a falsetto. 'She gave it to her threaking girl-thriend. The bloody nanny. Can you believe that? Not only doth my wife turn out to be a clothet dyke, but she'th letting one look after my little girl.'

Girl-friend? Several pieces of the kaleidoscope whirled crazily and then settled into an understandable pattern. It wasn't 'Ellis' – it was 'L.S.' The last set of initials scratched on Melody's height chart in her old nursery upstairs.

'You were going to set up home in Ibiza with the nanny?'

Prue ignored me. I doubt whether she even heard me. She was still glaring with cold contempt at her ex. 'You chose her, Rick. Remember? You always chose them. All those little slags on heat. It was fine for them to take care of your

daughter when it was you they were screwing, wasn't it?'
She brought the gun barrel nearer. Rick struggled to wriggle
up the lounger but the taped cuffs were holding him fast.

'Prue. Sthweetheart. Pleath. Whatever you want. We can
work it out. Jutht tell me what you want.'

'What do I want? Hmm . . .' Prue considered the
question. She ran the tip of the gun down a leg, tracing the
outline of a prominent varicose vein.

Winona was free. Slipping out of her chiffon cover-up,
she slid silently into the water and started to breaststroke
smoothly to the far end where Waterloo was having a fun
time paddling in circles.

I glanced over at Tabitha and Melody. They were both
staring intently at the swimming figure, silently egging her
on. For God's sake, it would only take one look, and Prue
couldn't fail to notice.

I had to shout again to be sure of penetrating the
chemical fog. 'So you think the body in the garden is L.S.?
What does the "L.S." stand for?'

Prue's face twisted once more and this time she started to
cry softly. 'Lucy Simons. It was a joke, see? L.S. Our special
name. Would you like to see a picture?'

I summoned up an enormous smile. I oozed eagerness
from every pore. It had the right result. Prue gave a watery
smile, sniffed back an enormous snootful of tears and
dragged a very battered snapshot from the waistband of
the spray-on leopardskin pants. It showed an averagely
pretty twenty-something standing in front of the oast house
with her hands resting on the shoulders of a little girl.

'Is that Melody?'

'Yes.' Prue dismissed her daughter. She rubbed a wistful
finger over the young woman's face. 'I knew she wouldn't
leave me, but then I got that phone call . . . "Sorry, baby,
it's all off. Your husband's come good. No hard feelings,
but twenty grand is twenty grand and easy lays are ten a
penny." And when I got home, she'd gone. And *he'd* got his
lawyers on the job. And they had a little message for me.

The divorce courts don't like dykes. The divorce courts don't give lezzies big settlements. So be a good little ex, Prue, and sign these papers if you want to be taken care of.'

'And you signed?'

She nodded. 'I didn't care. She'd gone. I trusted her. I loved her with all my heart, and she'd betrayed me. What the hell did the rest matter?' She sank to her knees in front of me. 'You understand, don't you, Grace?'

Winona was nearly at the far end. Any minute now she'd be hauling herself out and running for the phone.

'But she didn't leave you, did she, Prue? Not in that way. What do you figure happened?'

The hair had slipped over her face again. She turned her head fractionally, so that she was peering at Rick through lank strands. I got a sudden mental flash of an old illustration of a mad woman in a French lunatic asylum. 'Why don't you tell Grace what happened, Rick? Go on, tell her!'

'It'th like you said, Pru-pru. She left. Walked out. She muth have dumped the necklace on the way. Or maybe she losht it.'

She whipped the gun up and fired. The kick hurled her over again. A dozen tiles crashed off the upper half of the wall and shattered around Rick.

'You don't need to shoot, Prue,' Stuart said loudly. 'You've got six hostages tied up in here. You don't need to fire the gun. We're c-completely helpless.'

Thanks for reminding us, I thought sourly.

Prue scrambled back to her knees. She ignored Stuart's interruption. 'Tell her!' she screamed at Rick. 'It was you. I know it was you. Tell her the truth. *Tell her!*'

'It wath a mithtake,' Rick shrieked. 'I didn't mean to kill the bitch. She laughed at me. She said you were a thousand timeth more exciting in bed than I'd ever been. It wath bloody humiliating, thweetheart. I only meant to shut her up. I just . . . I sthqueezed too hard. And suddenly she wathn't breathing. I tried to bring her round . . . I sthwear I did.'

As a remark designed to cool the situation it wasn't too bright. We all processed the information. And most of us came to the same conclusion. Including Prue. 'You slept with L.S.? Even her?'

Despite the danger, it was hard not to feel sorry for her. She sounded so forlorn.

'It didn't mean anything, thweetheart. Honestly.' The stupid idiot had an ingratiating smile all over his drawn cheeks. He really thought the fact that it had just been one more grope in a lifetime of groping made it okay.

Out of the corner of my eye I could see Winona touching base at the far end. I prayed she wouldn't make too much noise hauling herself out, but just in case . . . I jumped in again, trying to keep their attention on me and away from the water.

'So you buried her in the garden, Rick. And then Tabitha phoned Ibiza and imitated the nanny's voice to give Prue the brush-off. Neat trick. It *was* Tabitha who phoned, wasn't it? "Sorry, baby, it's all off. Your husband's come good", etcetera?'

We all looked down that end of the pool room. Which was the opposite end to where Winona was treading water. Both Tabitha and Melody were sweating heavily and panting for breath. Tabitha was in a worse position because she was still wearing the wool jacket.

The gun wobbled in Prue's grip. The heat, plus whatever she'd popped, was getting to her too. Please, God, it might knock her senseless. Her tone was almost reasonable when she asked, 'Did you phone me, Cat?'

'He told me he'd paid the nanny off. He just wanted to stop you going looking for her. He said it wouldn't do his image any good if it got out his wife dumped him for a woman. I swear to God I didn't know he'd *killed* her. Please believe me, Prue. I wouldn't lie to you. You're my best friend.'

'Am I? That's strange. If I had a best friend who was going to be reduced to living in a miserable staff bedroom, having to be polite to the sort of spoilt rich bitches which – let's be honest here, Cat – we once were, I wouldn't tell her she couldn't come and share my home. Especially if I had a nice . . . *new* . . . *large* . . . *expensive* . . . flat.' With each word, she swayed unsteadily closer to Tabitha.

I risked another check on Winona. She'd flipped on her back and was returning with a leisurely backstroke. Waterloo, his little legs going like the clappers, was gliding beside her. What the hell was she doing?

'Look, darling,' Tabitha cooed. 'I didn't mean you couldn't move in *per se*. Of course you can come stay. I just meant I thought you'd prefer your own space.'

'Oh, I would, Cat. I would.' She tapped Tabitha's chest with the gun. 'But, you see, I can't afford my own space. I don't have any money. I wouldn't have minded not having any money if I could have had someone to love me. And I guess if I couldn't have that . . . I'd have liked a great big divorce settlement. Only, thanks to you, I don't have either. And you have lots and lots of money. Is that fair?'

It seemed to be a rhetorical question. Before Tabitha could respond, Prue had swayed away again, heading back to her prone ex. She prodded his diaphragm with the gun. 'Is that fair, Rick?'

'No. No. Look, thweetheart, if itth cash you want, we can fixth it. Can't we, Stu, mate?'

The idiot had redirected her attention back to the pool. She focused on Winona swimming lengths with the mutt. Amazingly enough she didn't react to the sight at all. Perhaps she hadn't even remembered she'd tied her up in the first place.

Instead she knelt in front of Stuart and put her nose very close to his. 'Will you, Stuart? Are you going to give me lots and lots of Rick's money and make it all go away?'

It was at this point that I discovered something else about Stuart. He was a bloody useless liar! If he *had* killed anyone the fact would have been plastered all over his face at the very first police interview. As it was, I, along with everyone else, could see that there was a problem.

It was Winona who spelled it out. 'He can't. Rick's broke. You didn't really believe any of that rubbish about not redecorating this dump because that seventies retro is *so* chic, did you? None of his old stuff has sold for years. And he doesn't get writer's royalties like Bernie.' She was treading water by the steps with Waterloo bobbing happily beside her. '*And* his new album is bombing. It can't get any play-time. Bernie said it wouldn't. That's why they held the launch party in the office block instead of a club. They've got a publicity budget that's like . . . the pits. Even when they dug a *body* up in his garden, none of the prime-time shows were interested in doing interviews. He's yesterday's news. Bernie says he probably married Christina for *her* money. Isn't that a giggle?'

We all stared at her. Of all the stupid times to break out of the three-syllable sentence. It occurred to me that perhaps Winona hadn't been acting the part of the original dumb blonde record producer's wife. She really *was* a few feathers short of the whole duck. She'd had no plans for a brave escape attempt. She'd simply fancied a bloody swim!

'I don't believe you. Rick can't be broke. He has all this . . .' Prue flung her arms wide. And lost her grip on the gun. Sadly her right hand was towards us, so instead of flying into the pool, it simply slithered over the non-slip floor and beached up against the wall. Muttering to herself, Prue crawled on all fours after it. Rick's snuff box was in her path. Wetting a finger, she dipped it into the spilt powder and rubbed it over her gums. Then she laughed. 'I don't believe it. You total, bloody, shitty *fraud*, Rick.' She jabbed another finger in and shuffled across to me on her knees. 'Taste that.'

I tried to lick delicately. But the minute my lips parted, Prue shoved the entire finger so far inside she nearly gave me a tonsillectomy with her nail. I gagged. And then my taste buds processed the flavour. 'Beecham's powder?'

'Can you believe it?' Prue crowed. 'He snorts cold remedies. Oh, is that pathetic or what? Talk about the oldest swinger in town.'

The revelation had put her in a good mood. Anyone with an ounce of sense would have played along. Sadly Rick had shed any common sense along with his clothes. 'I can't afford pure any more even I wanted to. Why don't you athk Cat for the cash? She'th had all mine.'

'Cat? What did you give Cat money for? I knew you weren't broke.' She giggled. 'Have you been screwing her too? Does Christina know? Naughty, naughty Rick.'

'You've got to be kidding! I wouldn't touch that dried-up hag if she wath the lath shag on earth. Blackmailing bitch.'

Melody started sobbing softly. She'd stopped trying to stand and was hanging by her wrists. Her face was unnaturally pale with a shimmer of sweat on it. Dehydration was probably starting to set in if she'd been trussed up here for hours. 'Don't be horrible to Auntie Cat, Daddy. You're the two people I love most in the world. I hate it when you're horrible to her.'

'Oh, thut up!' Rick snarled. 'Wath the matter with you anyway? Alwayth hanging around me. Following me around. It'th your fault I'm in thith bloody fix. Why can't you go get a life like normal kidth. You're twenty thodding theven.'

'Daddy!' That jerked Melody out of the semi-coma she was sinking into. 'It wasn't me! It's Mummy. What did I do?'

The answer was fairly obvious. I told her. 'You followed your father the day he hid your nanny's body in the garden.'

'No! I didn't! I didn't, Daddy.'

I caught Tabitha's eye. 'Tell her.'

Tabitha's expression slid into her sympo-therapist mode. 'You suppressed the memory, darling. But it was there, lurking like a maggot in beautiful juicy peach, so Auntie Cat took it away for you.'

'And used the tape to blackmail Daddy into handing over the price of a new Docklands flat,' I said.

Tabitha shrugged as far as her taped arms would allow. 'Well, you were right, of course. It was too much of a coincidence – a body turning up in the exact spot where Melody had decided to pretend that Joe had buried Lulu. So I did a little exploratory hypnotism. My poor sweetie, you must have been suffering for years with that nasty secret trying to escape from your subconscious.'

'She'th thuffering,' Rick yelled. 'What about me?'

Prue moved back to his lounger and stared down at him. The slightly dippy expression had been replaced by a hard, cold anger. 'You, Rick? You haven't even *started* suffering yet. But don't worry, my love. Your time has come.'

43

Prue wandered back to her sports bag and disentangled something metal from its clutches. It wasn't – as you might expect in the circumstances – an even larger and sharper means of separating Rick from another part of his anatomy. It was a camcorder.

'It's Raoul's,' she informed the room. 'I borro'd it. Not stole. Borr'.'

Her speech was slurred and her fingers were fumbling with the controls. At one point she had to sit down. She sat on Rick.

My shoulder muscles were screaming their protest at being stuck in a position that's only natural if a girl's making out with a sumo wrestler, and the phone was getting on my nerves. There was an extension somewhere close and the damn thing kept ringing incessantly. It was probably the hospital, trying to contact Rick. Would Christina make them send someone over when they failed to raise him? Or would she decide the useless non-committer had opted out yet again? Was anyone going to come before Prue finally shot something other than the interior decorations – either deliberately or accidentally?

She'd added a radio cassette player to the collection of goodies from the bag. 'Now, lover . . . show time.' Hacking and stabbing with the penknife, she managed to destroy enough tape for Rick to pull himself free. He lurched off the lounger, using his momentum to fall towards the gun she'd left beside the bag. It didn't work. The impending threat sharpened her responses sufficiently for her to snatch it up again.

'Sing.'

'What?'

'Sing, Rick. That's wha' you do, isn't it? So sodding well . . . sing!' With no warning she fired.

The bullet ploughed into the floor between his legs. Rick screamed. Melody burst into noisy hysterical sobs. Waterloo chose that minute to heave himself out of the pool. Padding across, still trailing his lead, he slurped a long-time-no-see down my face.

'Good swim?'

With a large yawn, he shook himself, sending a shower of chlorinated water straight up my nose, and then settled down to lick himself into shape.

Prue depressed the 'play' button and started a tape. The distinctive barbed-wire tones of one of Rick's earlier hits bounced around the pool room, enhanced by the excellent acoustic effects of tiling.

Tentatively Rick started crooning along with himself. 'An' dance.' Prue extended the gun, Rick wiggled his bottom.

'Tha's idea.' Hugging the revolver in the crook of her right arm as if it were a pet, Prue scooped up the camera with her left and trained it on her ex. 'Move around. Strut your stuff, Rick. Like at a concert.

Rick jiggled and wriggled. Despite the danger, it was hard not to laugh. From where I was sitting I got the back view. Without the extensions his scalp was visible through the thinning hair with its central bald patch. The droopy white elephant-jowl buttocks swung merrily over the legs riddled with varicose veins. Judging by the way Tabitha was biting her cheek, the front view was just as entertaining. I got the chance to find out a second later, when Prue ordered him to keep it going.

He swung round. His diddy *creative vibes* kept right on swinging. The crinkly hairs on his concave chest were grey; his face was thin and drawn, the cheeks hollow without the supporting dentures.

'Harder,' Prue yelled. 'Strut it out. Shake it up.'

Panting and gasping, Rick slapped his bare feet to the floor. He looked totally ridiculous. Without his cosmetic camouflage, designer clothes and hyped-up aura of sex, he looked like what he was – a skinny runt within a couple of years of collecting his pension who ought to be chasing grannies down the bingo club, not twenty-year-olds around the dance clubs.

I couldn't help it. I started laughing. Treading water in the centre of the pool, Winona whistled encouragement and clapped. Tabitha was giggling. Behind her the brightly lit swimming pool was reflected in the black window glass. A ghostly Winona *doppelgänger* glided across the courtyard outside. She turned and duck-dived, her legs seeming to slide down through the windows of one of the cars parked out there. Briefly I thought I saw another movement on the far side the vehicle. But it dissolved into the ripples of Winona's aquatic gymnastics.

Prue had stopped recording.

'What are you going to do with that?' Rick lisped.

'Papers, television. Everybody see . . . truth. Fake bastard. Knew you had money. Gave Cat money.'

Ejecting the tape from the camcorder, she pushed it into the bag, returned to a two-handed clutch on the gun and sat down on the lounger. Her eyes were blank, staring at something only she could see. The backing tape came to an end and a wonderful silence filled the pool room. In it the ordinary sounds of lapping water, jerky breathing and soft crying came into focus again. We were all held in a hiatus of the what-happens-next variety.

Gulping for breath, Rick took a tentative step towards his tormentor. 'Prue? Doll?'

She didn't appear to react. He shuffled a little closer. The room became quieter as breaths were stilled and teeth clenched. We willed him on. He was nearly within touching distance and she hadn't moved. His hand was getting nearer . . . and nearer . . . And at that point it occurred to me that since he'd just confessed to murder in front of us, perhaps some of us weren't going to be any safer if Rick did grab that gun. Melody would be okay – she'd do anything for her daddy, and Tabitha had three hundred grand of blackmail money riding on Rick staying uncaught. But what about Stuart and me? Nobody knew we were out here. And there was plenty of room left in the garden.

The only drawback to our disappearance would be Winona. I mean, someone must know she'd come over to babysit – right?

Rick was there. His fingers crept out. And snagged a towel! Very, very slowly he manoeuvred it off the lounger and wrapped it, sarong-style, around his waist. The temptation to scream at him that what the hell else was there left to see was almost overwhelming. It was only stifled by the fact that he was now bending with great caution towards the scissors.

He grasped them and still Prue hadn't moved. Blank-eyed, she stared in my direction. There was no discernible blinking reflex that I could see, but her hands were still curled around the gun on her lap. I could see him weighing up the options. If he tried to get the revolver and she snapped out of it and fought back, it would be difficult for her to miss at such close range.

He decided to quit when he was ahead. Placing one foot carefully behind the other, he backed up with the scissors. I expected him to help Melody first, but he headed for Tabitha.

'Hurry up,' she whispered.

She leant back, putting her weight on her wrists and stretching the tape slightly to give him a better cutting area.

Rick flicked the scissors open one-handed. He held them at the point where the blades crossed rather than on the handle. With a swift downward slash, he slicked open Tabitha's cheek. It was so fast that the pain didn't register for a second. Blood oozed from the cut and dripped in tear-shaped drops on her yellow jacket.

'You laughed at me, you bitch! Nobody laughth at me.'

Bloody hell, no wonder Melody was such a mess. Both her parents had beamed down from the Planet Cuckoo.

Tabitha started to cry noisily. Beside her Melody was whimpering quietly. Rick ignored them. He was heading back this way. Winona and I had laughed too. But Winona was safely treading water in the middle of the pool. I, on the other hand . . . I tightened my grip on the pot, testing its weight.

Stuart said urgently, 'Rick! Get me free. We have to g-get out of here.'

'Moment, mate. Buthineth to attend to.'

He came straight towards me. Stuart lay at a stretch and tried to trip him. Rick stepped away. I rocked the pot. I'd have to try to tip it on him and get my hands free underneath. As soon as it moved I discovered the drawback to this plan. If the palm toppled it would pull me with it. I could end up lying on top of it with my hands trapped underneath and, chances were, a few crushed fingers. I flung my weight back and the plant rocked upright.

Rick had reached me. He sneered. The blade went back. I lashed out with the nearest foot. But I was at such an awkward angle that all I succeeded in landing was a light tap on his shin. I tensed, waiting for the cut.

And then a blur of beige hurtled around the side of the pot. With a snarl, Waterloo launched himself forward. His teeth closed within millimetres of Rick's *creative vibes*. Jumping back meant leaving the towel in the mutt's mouth. 'You little . . .' Rick swished down again. Drops of blood spattered over the towel. Waterloo dropped it to the floor and planted himself squarely in front of me. A deep-throated rumble came from his jaws. Rick jabbed the scissors, cutting the air inches from the muscular body. Waterloo was unimpressed. Barking furiously, he refused to budge. It was Rick who backed down.

He seemed unsure what to do now. Finally he appeared to come to the conclusion that he ought to release Melody and wavered back in her direction.

The shot came next. The sequence is confused when I try to replay it. I think I heard the retort and saw the blood bloom over my T-shirt. Then I noticed Stuart's horrified expression, the gun resting on the floor where it had dropped from Prue's hand and Prue herself oh-so-slowly keeling over.

The doors to the house crashed open and the pool room was suddenly full of officers in flak vests and peaked caps screaming at us to lie on the floor. 'Armed police. Hands on head. Don't move. Keep still. Get on the floor.'

They were rushing and crashing around; securing the gun; securing the blades; securing evidence; untying those who needed it; bawling for the ambulance to be driven up to the premises.

I heard it all through a filter and a long way away. All I could see was the mutt. He was lying motionless, a pool of dark red liquid spreading around him. When they cut me free I tried to crawl to him and an officer shouted and screamed at me to get my hands on my head and move out. When I didn't two of them grabbed me and ran me out.

It was standard procedure. They had no way of knowing who the bad guys were. I could have had a concealed gun and plugged one of them as soon as they moved away. I had to be searched and questioned away from the crime scene. But I didn't care. I yelled and screamed that I had to help him whilst they dragged me out with my arms pinned and my toes scraping over the floor.

44

I had to break bad news to people when I was in the police. Traffic accidents, elderly parents discovered dead in bed by the home help, families whose kids had OD'd. None of those was as gut-wrenchingly awful as having to collect Arlene from the station the next day and seeing her looking eagerly around the forecourt and car park. And then watching her face go still as she looked at me and read the truth.

'He probably saved your life,' Annie said. 'The bullet went straight through his chest and deflected off his shoulder bone. Otherwise, the angle you were sitting, there was a good chance it would have ripped upwards through several vital organs.'

It was two weeks after the pool-room shoot-out. We were perched on the large grey stones that piled against the wooden groynes on Seatoun beach. The sands were deserted apart from a few stray gulls. It was a blowy day that drove the incoming tide in roaring peaks and whipped the softer sands up in clouds that stung exposed flesh. We had to raise our voices to be heard above the wind and waves. Hopefully it wouldn't be too long before it was safe to go back to the office.

Rick was in custody for murder. Tabitha was on bail for withholding evidence, being an accessory after the fact and blackmail. Prue was in intensive care. Christina was back in New York with Emilie Rose and her newest daughter (apparently she'd decided it was a damn sight safer than the tranquil English countryside). And Melody? I'd no idea what had happened to Melody. And frankly – who cared?

Annie put her head close to mine. 'Did you see they're saying that Rick's latest album will be number one by next week?'

'Nothing sells like sex and violence.' Since the news that

the body in Rick's garden involved adultery, lesbianism and murder-by-rock-star, he'd gone from slow-news-day filler to hot media darling. In any way they could get around the rules governing prejudicing the trial, they'd done so. We'd had background interviews with ex-wives, ex-girlfriends, ex-one-night stands and any kids old enough to be outside the press rules about exploiting juveniles.

'His record company have announced they're issuing the entire Alaimo back catalogue,' Annie continued.

'I guess Stuart was right,' I said. 'Murder is the new rock and roll.'

Annie made a noncommittal sound. I glanced at her. She was staring out to sea. This late in the afternoon, dusk was falling over it. It looked cold, steely and bleak. Rather like Annie's face.

I gave her the opening. 'Talking of Stuart . . .' She didn't take it up, so I just took a deep breath and jumped. 'You haven't been seeing much of him, have you?'

'I've been pretty busy. I mean, after the fiasco of Jan's page-three session.'

'Lame excuse.'

'It is *not*. Well, okay, it is. But what's it got to do with you?'

'You are my best mate. I have an obligation to offer well-meant, interfering advice. It's in the job description. What gives? Is it the mental breakdown thing?'

'No. Yes.' She huddled further into her coat, turning the big collar up to shield her neck. 'I feel rotten about it, Grace. I had no idea I *was* that prejudiced. I'd always thought of myself as pretty liberal and non-judgmental. And I truly believed that his medical history didn't make any difference. Then suddenly I hear myself making all these excuses every time he suggests we get together.'

'He's not Pierce Brosnan. Or Harrison Ford,' I bawled over the gusts rattling the boards of the groyne.

'No. He's nice, and ordinary, and the sort of person who could be a friend as well as a lover. I mean, you know, red-hot sex is all very well, but someone to curl up with can be appealing.'

'Providing he's not barking.

'Stuart is *not* crazy!'

'Then why d'you keep giving him the brush-off?'

'Because I'm a shallow, hypocritical bitch. And why the hell are you shouting so loudly? It's not *that* difficult to hear.'

'I was trying to hide the sound of his footsteps.'

I jerked a thumb behind me. Annie twisted round as Stuart scrambled over the salt-encrusted tarry wood. 'You set me up!' Her eyes glared over the top of the collar that she'd clutched at nose level.

'That is also in the job description. I figured I owed him. After all, he could have saved my life too. I don't see how Rick could have let us go after we'd heard his confession like that.'

'I doubt he'd have r-resorted to murder,' Stuart said, skidding down the smooth stones to thump between us.

'Luckily, thanks to you, we'll never know.' It had turned out that during the confusion at the time of Waterloo's dash for the pool, Stuart had managed to punch in Annie's number on his mobile and set it to automatically keep redialling until she answered. Everything we'd said had been transmitted over the open line in his pocket whilst the police had been taking up position outside the oast houses. Hence his need to give a running commentary on the situation inside the pool room.

'We were just discussing Rick's rejuvenated career. He must be glad of the cash if he's really broke. Is he?'

'I can't discuss my client's private affairs.'

'Course you can. You're an accountant, not a priest. Anyway, Winona already told us. God, what a bitch! Is she stupid or totally spaced out?'

'N-neither. She saw me dialling. I think she realised the pool might be the safest place if any shooting started. She's really quite bright.'

'Telling Prue the cash had run out wasn't too clever.'

'Apparently she used to share a flat with Prue and Tabitha and some magazine editor years ago. They all gave her a hard time. She's been waiting for years to rub their f-faces in it.'

'It was a hell of a time to choose,' I remarked. 'She can't be *that* bright.'

'Given the f-fix we were in, she may have thought that could be her last chance.'

Annie still wasn't picking up her share of the conversation. I kept going. 'You've seen *Why*-No-Nah, then, Stu?'

'At the hospital. She had an attack of c-conscience and visited Prue.'

'And you did too?'

'Yes. She seems to have taken everything she c-could get her hands on. Including her brother's prescription drugs. They think she could suffer permanent brain damage. I feel sorry for her.'

'Are you crazy?' Annie snapped.

'Apparently.'

'Sorry.' She pushed herself a little closer to him. 'I didn't mean . . . well, sorry, okay?'

'No problem.'

Now we'd got that out of the way, I steered the conversation back to the interesting gossip with subtle tact. 'So give us the dirt, Stuart. Just how broke is he?'

'Stop hassling him, Grace. He's right. There's such a thing as client confidentiality. You're being a pain.'

'He hired me to be a pain.'

'No. I hired you because I didn't like you.'

'Excuse me.' I squirmed round to stare into Stuart's face, assuming it might be a joke. It was squeezed into deep lines to prevent the sand flying into his eyes, but he didn't look like he was being flippant.

'I didn't like you. That night you came to dinner. I d-didn't like the way you made fun of people who were crazy.

So I didn't care what you found out about me. Your opinion didn't matter.'

'Oh?' Okay, I knew a lot of people hadn't liked me in the past, but it was still something of a facer to have it said straight to my face like that.

Annie saw my expression. And displayed best-mate sympathy in her usual style. 'It serves you right. I told you that sarky tongue of yours gets up people's noses.'

'Yeah. Right.' He'd knocked me off balance. Had I not been described as mouthy but loveable?

Stuart left me to stew for a few more seconds before saying, 'I like you better now, if that helps.'

'I guess.' It seemed a pity to waste the bonding moment. 'So give us the dirt on Rick? Totally skint?'

'Nearly. He's been living off his capital for years now. Ironically enough, about the only asset he had left was the oast house. He never dared sell that in c-case they dug up the body.'

'And then Christina went and did it anyway. Serves the creep right.' I wasn't inclined to waste sympathy on Rick. Not after the way he'd come at me with those scissors.

'Even then I think he thought he c-could get away with it if he kept his head. There was nothing to link him with the body. Even the necklace wasn't proof positive. This Lucy could have thrown it away as she ran off with his twenty grand. Providing Tabitha and Melody kept their mouths shut, there was only circumstantial evidence to connect him to the girl's death.'

'Speaking of the deadly duo – I assume it was money from the sale of Christina's restaurant Rick used for the bribe to keep Tabby quiet?'

'Yes. I didn't know she'd put it in a joint account. If I had, I'd have insisted on being a joint signatory.'

'Do you think Christina will be okay?'

Stuart nodded. 'Sure. She's got her kids. And she's a survivor. I'd b-bet she'll have another successful business up and running in twelve months. Do you know, Rick still doesn't understand why she doesn't w-want to see him!'

'You've been in touch with him?'

'His solicitor. I had to fix up arrangements for legal fees.'

'Are you still handling his money?' Greater love hath no accountant surely?

'I have to for now. It was the arrangements we set up with the banks. They only agreed to keep his credit lines open last year if I c-controlled all the accounts.' Stuart thrust a hand through his hair. It was good to see that the finger splints were finally off.

Annie said, 'You realise he may get off even now? It's only Tabitha's word against his really. Melody was just a kid who had to be hypnotised to remember watching him burying the body. Any half-decent defence counsel will destroy her: implanted memories; psychobabble; jealous of stepmum; doesn't know what she's saying, etcetera. And a screamed confession at gunpoint, heard over a mobile phone, probably won't be allowed as evidence.'

I knew she could well be right. He oughtn't to get away with it. But juries can be strange beasts. And the more so if the defendant is famous. Still, I'd done my bit for truth and justice. It was down to fate and the prosecution now. I asked Stuart if Melody wasn't going to be charged with something.

'What is there to charge her w-with?'

'I was thinking of what she and Auntie Catty did to you. It must be harassment?'

'How could I prove that? I had violent fantasies about murder. So what? I'm c-crazy, remember?'

Without looking at him, Annie reached over and took his hand. He disentangled it. 'I don't want your pity.'

'It wasn't pity,' Annie said, apparently transfixed by the sight of the cream-frilled ripples nudging drifts of olive seaweed before them as the tide rushed in. 'Didn't anyone miss that poor girl at the time? Apart from Prue?'

'She had no family. And back then . . . there were dozens

of so-called nannies and hangers-on going through the place. Who knows what happened to half of them? It's why everybody should have somebody.'

Annie looked haunted. Stuart smiled gently. 'Look, I do understand – honestly. We can take it slowly if you like. Go back to just being friends. You c-can set the pace. Only, well, I wanted you to see this . . .' From his pocket he took out a folded sheet of paper and battled against the wind to unfold it. It was the glossy picture of the George Clooney look-alike with the rich poseur's aspirational lifestyle. With firm, deliberate gestures, Stuart ripped it into two, four, eight and then reduced it to confetti. Holding his palm out, he let the winds swirl the scraps away. 'I think it's long past time to throw out teenage fantasies.'

We watched a curious gull probe a swirling particle of paper, its feathers ripped ragged by the fierce breezes. 'Pity,' Annie said. 'I rather like some parts of the fantasy. The Ferrari especially.'

'Maybe we could reconsider the Ferrari.'

'I'd skip the leather dress,' I said. 'You don't have the tush for it.'

'I think you've exhausted the best-mate interference ration for today, Sherlock.'

I was about to come back with another insult when the sounds of excited barking distracted me. I looked in their direction without thinking. It was just a Labrador chasing a ball along the wet sands. Turning back to Annie and Stuart, I found I was looking at them through a mist. 'Sand. In my eyes.' I rubbed the back of my hand over them and sniffed. 'Gotta go. You two have fun.'

The main street was practically empty, the arcades whistling and flashing in forlorn optimism to attract non-existent customers. It gave me the chance to sort out that damn sand-in-the-eyes problem by the time I reached Pepi's.

'Well?' Jan demanded as I slid into the seat opposite her and Vetch. 'Did it work? Are they hot again?'

'More like tepid. But working towards a slow boil.'

'Think this is going to be, like, *the* one?'

Did I? I'd have liked to say yes. But my gut instinct said no. But then what did I know? I gave a noncommittal shrug.

'Just so long as it stops her watching me. I ain't even allowed to post a flaming letter till she's checked the envelope. I'm not daft, you know.'

'Previous experience would suggest otherwise,' Vetch murmured, scanning down a list of e-mail messages. 'Still, only two dozen this morning. The rush would seem to have passed.'

Jan scowled and rubbed a porthole in the steamed-up window. 'I was using my initiative.'

'Sadly it wasn't your initiative that was on display.'

Jan's appearance in the local paper with Waterloo had been picked up and reprinted by several specialist magazines that circulated nationwide. Since then Vetch's agency had been bombarded with requests for our services. Unfortunately the sort of services that were in demand weren't the sort any of us were prepared to provide. In the end we'd been forced to take down the brass plate outside, ask the phone company to change all the numbers and run the company from Shane's café until the perverts stopped dropping by.

'Dear me.' Vetch looked up from his list. 'Can either of you lay hands on a leather corset and a Shetland pony with a sense of adventure?'

'Yuck. Gross.' Jan shuddered. 'It makes you wanna throw up just thinking about it.'

'That was probably the jam and peanut butter sandwich fritters,' Vetch said.

'I heard that.' Shane jived over whilst Chuck Berry urged Johnnie to be good. 'I ought to be charging you lot rent.'

'Rubbish.' Vetch waved a hand around the otherwise deserted café. 'You should be paying us. We make the place look popular.'

'It *is* popular. I like it. "Go, Johnnie, go." Get yer something, Smithie?'

I passed. There was someone I had to see to lay the final part of Lulu Cazlett's story to rest.

'Are you going past the office?' Vetch asked.

'Nope. I'm going to have a chat with a killer.'

45

Arlene's bungalow was still. At this time on a weekday she ought to be at work, but I guessed she probably wasn't. I'd seen the blokes from the Waste Disposal Site around the town and they'd reported that she'd hardly been in since her return from hospital. I rang the bell. And found myself listening for the storm of barks this activity would have once provoked. But there was no flurry of wet tongue and stupid grin this time. Just Arlene peering bleakly through the gap.

'I thought . . . I mean, how are you?'

'Bloody awful, babes.'

'Yes. Right.' I was no good at this sympathy lark. I half hoped she'd tell me to push off, but in the end she opened wide enough for me to come inside.

The house was spotless, sweet-smelling . . . and lifeless. 'The place is so bloody quiet, I feel like I'm going barmy. Do you want a drink?'

'Not really. I just came to see you were okay.'

'Well, now you know. Here. I been expecting you to pick this up.' She pushed a cheque at me.

'You don't need to.'

'I pay me debts. Take it.'

I wasn't going to refuse twice. I folded it into my jeans pocket. And then we both stood there awkwardly, staring at each other. She was right. The bungalow felt like a morgue. 'What about the arrangements?'

'Next Monday. Ten o'clock.'

'Right. Everything fixed?'

'Yeah. This lot's the best. I picked them special. Transport's real classy. I couldn't have had anything less for my best boy.'

'Right. I'll be seeing you then?'

'Yeah. Okay, babes. Take care.'

It was only a couple of weeks since I'd last seen her, but Edith Halliwell already seemed frailer and less bright-eyed than I remembered.

'The cold seems crueller each winter,' she complained, making her way back to her sitting room. The central heating was on so high that a camel would have been gasping for water in there. 'Sit down, dear. It's good to see you again. I heard what happened to poor Waterloo. Arlene is quite inconsolable. Although I have tried.'

I sat in soft furnishings that smelt indefinably of old person and stared at her. It was hard to think that once she'd been young and full of the same yearnings and desires as Annie and I were now. From where I was sitting I could reach the framed photos that covered the sideboard. I snagged her wedding picture. 'Your husband was a real fox, wasn't he?'

'Fox?'

'Handsome. Dishy.'

'Oh, yes . . . yes . . . he was indeed. I was smitten the first time he came to see Papa for his interview. Love at first sight.'

For both of them?

I asked Edith what her maiden name had been.

'It was Fisher. Why? Are you doing more of your family history research?'

'In a manner of speaking. There were a load of old medical papers in your attic written by a Dr James Cedric Fisher. That would be your dad, wouldn't it?'

'That's right, dear. Papa was *very* well respected. He could have been so much more than a GP. He was asked to speak at all manner of societies. Really distinguished men came to listen. He used to take me sometimes.' Her face lit up as she remembered past glories.

'It was all stuff about mental illnesses. Is that what he specialised in?'

'He was very interested in the treatment of diseases of the mind. His work was considered quite radical in its day. He was quite the rebel.' She gave an almost girlish little giggle, remembering her father's rebellion.

This was getting harder, but I pressed on. 'Lulu Cazlett was mentally ill. Do you think that was what her husband consulted your father about?'

Some of the light faded from her face. 'I don't know. He wouldn't have discussed a patient's treatment with me.'

'She never went to Italy, you know,' I said. 'Her husband put that story about. She was confined to an asylum. Private one. Very discreet. Probably like a posh hotel with bars on the windows, don't you think?'

'Yes. No. Some of those places could be quite . . . unpleasant. Papa took me to one once. They had some rather odd treatments. Quite barbaric by modern standards. But I'm sure they thought they were doing good. One would have to, wouldn't one, to do that sort of thing to another human being?'

'I don't know. Maybe some of them just got a kick out of the power thing. Anyway, Lulu managed to give them the slip. Tried to get home and ended up drowning. The body was washed up in Seatoun. She made the local papers – under her maiden name, Ada Black. Thing is, Mrs Halliwell, there's something that's been bothering me about Lulu's death and I was sort of hoping you could help me out.'

I half expected panic. Or feigned feebleness. Any reaction, in fact, that might put me off my stroke. But she sat up straighter and there was an odd eagerness in her eyes. It was almost as if she was looking forward to the question.

'The thing is,' I repeated, 'I couldn't figure out why she'd come here. The Cazletts seemed to have assumed she was trying to get home. But why come this far? There used to be a railway station in Frognall D'Arcy, did you know? I spoke to Lulu's son about it. In fact, he was the one who'd first put me on to it.'

Greville's remark about buying sweets before the train came to take him back to school had sent me back to Edith's old map. And sure enough, there it was. The thin broken line of dashes that indicated a single-track railway running through that strange gap that divided Frognall into two halves.

'Dug it up years back, Nameless,' he'd barked down the phone. 'Used to be quite a decent little service. Train every hour. Nothing left of it except the old station. Been converted into the pub.'

'It's called Frognall Halt,' I told Edith. 'I suppose I should have realised from the name. Did you ever use the station? When you went to Maudsley?'

'No. We had a car. An Austin.'

'Lulu didn't. She'd have taken a train from Victoria.' She'd have had a choice of two services. The main line split into two south of London – one went inland directly through Canterbury, the other swung north to follow the coast. 'But either way she could have got off at either Canterbury or Winstanton and changed to the local train for Frognall Halt. The Frognall track joined both towns, see?' I held the map out for her inspection. She scarcely looked at it. I pressed on. 'Lulu would have been in walking distance of Maudsley if she was trying to reach her home as they said at the inquest. So why did she buy a ticket for Seatoun?'

Edith said nothing. She still looked expectant. I went on laying out my own brilliance. 'And once she'd reached Seatoun, she was seen on the path to North Bay. Why? Because she wanted a high cliff to throw herself over? Because she was mad and didn't know where she was going? Or because she was coming to see someone who lived up here?' There was an almost imperceptible relaxing of Edith's shoulders. 'Like a distinguished doctor with a reputation in mental cases? Someone who might help her get out of that asylum?'

There was the slightest smile playing around her lips by now.

'She died late on the nineteenth of October 1938, according to the coroner. I looked it up. It was a Wednesday. Cook's afternoon off. The day she and the daily girl went to the pictures and the fish supper. Lulu did come here, didn't she, Edith?'

'Yes. She came.' Her smile grew wider. 'I didn't know she'd escaped from anywhere. I didn't even know she was supposed to be travelling abroad. We hadn't seen anything of the Cazletts for ages. She looked quite distraught. When I asked why, it all came tumbling out about this dreadful place Roderick had sent her to. She asked for Papa. She wanted him to tell everyone she wasn't mad . . .' Edith frowned at the distant memory. 'I think she was, you know. But it didn't matter. I told her Papa was in his study upstairs and I'd fetch him.'

'Was he?'

'No. He and Bertram were both at work. Their surgery was in Seatoun, but I suppose she didn't know that. She must have thought they worked from home. A lot of doctors did combine their living quarters with their working place in those days. I was here alone with the boys; they'd all come down with chickenpox. I'd just managed to get them all off to sleep. The itching was terrible. Little Frank had scratched himself quite raw. I had to tie mittens on his hands . . .'

I stirred, afraid she was about to wander off on some inconsequential reminiscence, but she caught herself back again.

'When I came back downstairs and told her Papa wouldn't see her, she became hysterical. I slapped her face.'

'I'll bet you enjoyed that bit.'

'Yes. I did. I certainly did.'

'The treasure hunt?'

They found all the clues. Some bloke won ... He's married to the gawk, I think. Don't know who they are. Lulu ... said he deserved a prize for winning. Said she'd give him something he really wanted. She's taking him into the hop field. He's laughing, pulling back like he don't want to go, only he does really. You can see he does ...

Nothing seemed to faze Edith. She took the fact that I knew about an event that happened a lifetime ago for granted. 'It was so cruel,' she said softly. 'I always knew the main reason Bertram married me was to get the partnership with Papa. But I could accept that. I could even have accepted an affair, if it had been done discreetly so that I could pretend not to know about it. But she took him into the hop tunnel in front of me. Everyone saw my humiliation. They saw that my husband considered one ... *copulation* with her was worth risking his marriage for. They saw how unimportant I was to him.'

'But you didn't kick him out?'

'I loved him,' Edith said simply. 'And my sons loved their father. But things weren't the same between us. It took many years to erase the poison that woman had dripped into our lives. I hated her. I had no idea it was possible to hate that much. And then one day there she was, begging for my help. Do you know, I don't believe she even realised the damage she'd caused. It was nothing to her what she'd done with Bertram. So I said that Papa was telephoning the police. I told her they were going to take her back to that place.' Her chin came up. She looked defiant. 'She ran out. On to the cliffs. I saw her from the upstairs balcony. I thought she was going to throw herself off.'

'Didn't she?'

'No. She climbed over the wire fence. It wasn't nearly as substantial as it is now. I used to worry myself to death about the boys wandering near that edge. I wanted her to jump. But she was just standing there. So I went across. I kept telling her what they'd do to her in that place. I described all the dreadful treatments I'd read about in Papa's books. Iced water baths. Electric shocks. Really quite awful things. I just kept getting closer and closer. Willing her to go. But she wouldn't. I remember I was anxious about the boys being alone in the house. And she just *wouldn't* jump. So I . . .' She raised her hands to chest level, palms towards me, and pushed against the air. 'And then she wasn't there any more. And do you know what? I wasn't sorry. I was so *happy*. In fact, Bertram and I made love that night. It was the first time for months.'

'Did you guess it was her when "Ada Black" washed up next day?'

'Oh, yes. And I wasn't in the slightest bit surprised when Roderick chose to concoct that story about her dying abroad. He'd hardly want people knowing the truth about having to put her in an insane asylum. She was still very beautiful, you know. That day she came here she looked quite lovely in her fur coat and one of those big hats we used to call picture hats. I could never have looked like that.

'I'm glad you found out, my dear. Do you remember, when you asked me about Lulu I told you I believed there was a sort of divine plan for us, and all our bad deeds are found out eventually? You thought I was talking about Lulu, didn't you?' She sighed softly. 'I wish I could tell you I was sorry now. But that would be dishonest. I never have been. At first I was happy. Then I was scared that someone would find out. And for a long time now I haven't felt anything at all about that day.'

I looked at her and tried to picture her as she'd been. A tall, gawky, plain woman who was frightened of birds.

'*They're having a party . . . Been playing games . . . Silly games . . . They had tea out in the field . . . Cornfield . . . It was real funny . . . Wood pigeons . . . Cornfield's full of 'em after they finished harvesting . . . They were flying all over the place . . . this one woman, she went mad . . . Said they were in her hair . . . Everyone laughed at her . . . Then*

she went to sit back down again and the chair fell over . . .
It was really funny.'

Her whole world had been destroyed that sunny
September afternoon by a casual five-minute act that Lulu
Cazlett had probably forgotten about a week later.

'Will you tell anyone?' Edith asked in the same calm,
unconcerned tone.

'I doubt there's anyone left to care, frankly. About the
only person who remembers Lulu now is her son. And he's
dying.'

Edith sighed again. 'It's sad to be forgotten. But at least I
shall have the comfort of knowing I'll live on in my family's
memories. Don't leave it too long to have yours, my dear.'

She stood with difficulty, pushing down hard on the arms
of her chair. Holding on to the furniture, she steered her
way to the front door and opened it on to an evening that
was already darkening.

I was still relatching her garden gate when Arlene erupted
out of her front door and had a fit in her front garden.

'What the hell's the matter?' I yelled.

'Look, babes . . . look!' She squealed and windmilled her
arms, flying to her own gate and ripping it open. 'They
phoned ten minutes ago.'

A set of headlights was coming up the hill. I waited with
her whilst they drew into the kerb. The driver was wearing
a natty blue overall emblazoned WESTMILL PRIVATE
VETERINARY HOSPITAL. I guessed the passenger was a
vet.

Together they walked to the back of the van. Arlene was
hyper with excitement. I thought she was going to pass out
before they got the double doors open. They fell back to
reveal a large wire travelling cage. Under instructions from
the vet we each took a corner, staggered inside with it and
lowered it to the floor in the second bedroom.

I saw the vet's amused glance at the mini-four-poster
before he issued firm instructions to Arlene regarding diet,

exercise, medication and the necessity for check-ups and physiotherapy twice a week.

'He shouldn't really have been discharged until next Monday, but I think there's more danger of you having a heart attack than him if I hang on to him any longer. The pet ambulance will be back to collect him for his first appointment Friday. See you follow these instructions to the letter or I'll take him back in.' He handed her the written notes. Probably just as well, since I don't think she heard a word.

As soon as we were alone she rushed back and crouched by the cage. 'Oh, look, babes, don't he look *beautiful*?'

Frankly, I thought he'd looked better. He was lying flat on his stomach with his chin between his front paws so you couldn't see the medium-sized scar down the chest where the bullet had entered. He'd been lucky. When Prue's gun had slipped to the floor and fired, the bullet had ricocheted off the wall. Some of its force had been spent before it had plunged into Waterloo. His looks weren't improved by the fact they'd shaved off his fur down his right side, leaving a larger scar over his side and back where they'd sorted out the exit wound and replaced his joint with the finest titanium job that Arlene's money could buy. In addition, Rick's scissors had left a wavy line down one side of his face and hacked off a section of ear. The repair had left it with a sort of lopsided kink.

'Has mumsie's baby missed her? Is he going to give her a big kissy-wissy?'

Waterloo sighed heavily. He raised long-suffering eyes.

'Does mumsie's best boy want to come sleep on her bed?'

'It says in these instructions he has to sleep in the cage, Arlene. You don't want him jumping around and undoing all the repair work, do you?'

'I suppose not. But he looks so miserable in there.'

'It's for his own good. Tell you what. I know how to make him feel at home.' Untying the big pink satin bow from his bed, I tied it on to the front of the cage. 'There.'

'Oh, isn't that nice, baby? Say thank you to Auntie Gracie.'

Waterloo eyeballed me. Curling the corner of his top lip, he displayed a fang. I grinned and left him to it.

Promising to visit soon, I headed home.

It was chilly enough for me to trot briskly down the deserted section of headland where I'd first met Stuart. The autumn mists were already creeping over the scrub, giving the place the feeling of being marooned outside time. There was no pavement and I found myself wishing a car would come by just so I could distinguish between the road and the edge of the rough grass.

I'd walked up. I'd told myself it was because I needed the exercise, but in reality it was because I'd been trying to delay the encounter with Edith. I'd expected her to be weepy and in denial. A calm acceptance of fate hadn't really been in my mental rehearsal of the scene. How was I to know she really believed in some kind of divine plan?

'It wasn't,' I murmured to myself, 'a divine plan. More a sort of diabolical one by Auntie Cat. Although I suppose if I hadn't run into Stuart on this headland that day, I wouldn't have taken the case and asked Edith about Lulu. Not that that was fate exactly. I'd only turned that way because I didn't want to be seen doing my Abba karaoke act by that woman who was slogging her way up here for an afternoon of (possibly illicit) hot fantasy action in her high heels, seamed stockings and (presumably) sexy basque under her phony mink. My thoughts crashed into a wall. What had Edith said about Lulu's big picture hat and fur coat?

It was really very still out here. There wasn't even the far-off drone of an approaching car engine for company. The ocean seemed to have hushed. The lights from the North Bay bungalows and golf course were hidden by the crest of the hill I'd just come over; Seatoun's garish neon illuminations weren't yet visible. And the mist was getting denser. It writhed over the headland like wet, dirty chiffon scarves. Some of the strands had already pushed tendrils across the road in front of me. I increased my pace to a fast trot. Then I thought I heard the sound of other footsteps behind me. Hard, staccato footsteps. As if the walker was wearing high heels. I stopped and so did they. I listened . . . and there was nothing. So why didn't I find that reassuring?

'Get a grip, you silly cow,' I told myself. 'You don't believe in ghosts, remember?'

And then I sprinted all the way out of North Bay and down to the reassuring, neon-lit, tacky, fried-onion-tainted streets of Seatoun before that thing that wasn't there tapped me on the shoulder.